BONDED BY THORNS

BEASTS OF THE BRIAR
BOOK ONE

ELIZABETH HELEN

LUNA FOX
PRESS

Published by Luna Fox Press

First Edition published February 2023

Interior Design © 2023 by Elizabeth Helen

Cover Design and Illustration © 2022 by saintjupit3rgr4phic

Identifiers

ISBN: 978-1-7388279-0-9 (eBook)

ISBN: 978-1-7388279-1-6 (paperback)

ISBN: 978-1-7388279-2-3 (audio)

To everyone who grew up wishing for their own fairytale, featuring far-off places, daring sword fights, magic spells, princes in disguise... and of course, plenty of beasts

TRIGGER WARNINGS

Bonded by Thorns is the first book in the multi-book Beasts of the Briar series. It is a why-choose romance that ends on a cliffhanger. It contains mature themes, explicit sexual content, and is intended for audiences 18+. The following paragraph contains trigger warnings. **Please note these warnings do include a spoiler for the book.**

Trigger Warnings: Fantasy violence and gore; emotional abuse in a past romantic relationship, implied physical abuse in a past romantic relationship, blood and fantasy violence

I

ROSALINA

I have traveled around the world. I've walked the Great Wall of China, eaten dinner at the top of the Eiffel Tower, and ridden the bullet train from Tokyo to Osaka. That's not all. I've led an army into battle on dragonback, seduced a vicious mafia boss, and journeyed back in time to fall in love with everyone from Vikings to the Knights of the Round Table. I've lived a thousand lives.

Too bad the only real one fucking sucks.

I sigh and close the book I've been reading. It's a good one, about a ghost hunter who accidentally falls in love with the spirit she's supposed to track down. Some people call these guilty pleasure reads, but why should I feel guilt for wanting to escape to somewhere else, even for a little while?

The bookstore is dead quiet today, so I've been able to sneak in a few pages... or a hundred. It's typical for autumn. Once tourist season ends, Orca Cove goes into hibernation mode. Only the regulars come around, and they don't need—or want—much from me.

I push a wayward strand of hair behind my ear, not bothering to trap it back into the messy rat's nest I've got piled on my head. Just peering out the big windows at the front of the shop has me reaching for my sweater. Rain, during fall, in the Pacific Northwest is as typical as a bear shitting in the woods, but that doesn't stop the locals from complaining. Careful not to knock over the display of books I've arranged, I press my palm against the moist glass. I like the rain. It makes me feel less guilty for huddling inside, away from everything and everyone else. I'm sure if I said that to someone, they'd think it's weird. But hey, like rain in Orca Cove or bears shitting in the woods, that's to be expected.

The door jingles open and Josie and Tiffany walk in, nattering to one another. They're as typical of locals as you can get; middle-aged, wine-loving, clique-y. Wives of two of the fishing guides.

"Hello," I say, pretending to fix the display instead of staring out at the rain like a weirdo. "How are you ladies today?"

Josie stops and puts her hands on her hips. She's gotten her hair done, short strands curling under her ears. "Rosalina, I walk past this shop every day and you're in the window each time. Doesn't Richard give you a day off?"

Richard is my boss. And I'm sure he'd like to give me days off... permanently. But he'd never find anyone else in town who's willing to open and close nearly every day, with no overtime pay.

"Oh, I ask to work this much." I stand behind the till. "Keeps me busy."

Josie and Tiffany exchange a pitying glance.

"I thought I saw your father driving into town the other day," Tiffany says slowly. "Where was he this time?"

"He just came back from Petra. In Jordan." I turn away, not wanting them to see my face flush. "He's on the road again, though."

"No faeries in Petra, then?" Josie squeaks. She's trying to say it as a genuine question, but there's laughter behind her words. A giddiness in getting more gossip for their little get-togethers at coffee shops and workout classes. I won't give it to her.

"No," I mutter. "He hasn't found what he's looking for yet."

"Come on, let's check the new magazines." Tiffany pulls Josie to the back of the shop.

Leaning against the counter, I put my head in my hands. Maybe this's why Richard keeps me around. When it's not tourist season, the only way to drive business is to be the circus act for regulars to come and taunt.

I shouldn't think like that. Josie and Tiffany are nice enough. And I've had plenty of friends in Orca Cove. Sure, they all moved on after graduation, going to college or making their mark in big cities. I don't hear from them much anymore. And when I do, it's hard to follow up their news about promotions or travel plans or whatever exciting adventure with... I'm still here. Working at the bookstore. Looking after Papa. *Right where you left me.*

I keep myself busy by grabbing a stack of freshly unboxed *Home & Garden* magazines and carrying them to the back of the store, to show Josie and Tiffany. Despite the long hours, I do like my job. I'm literally *surrounded* by books. How could you not love that?

The Seagull's Gullet Book Emporium is long and thin, stuffed full of tall bookcases that turn the place into a labyrinth. Richard took it over from his parents, and I don't think he has a love for the product, but he does have a love for bossing people around and owning a monopoly.

But I'm the one who turned this rundown, leaky, drafty, wooden shack into what it is now. Fairy lights strung along the rafters? Check. Weekly displays of local interests? Check. Never missing the latest James Patterson? Check. Sure, a couple of my ideas have flopped. Like sitting by myself in the middle of the shop, empty chairs dragged in a circle, a steaming pot of tea left unpoured, when no one showed up for the book club I ran. Or the time Richard made me take down my display celebrating local folklore, saying I was giving his business a bad reputation.

But I keep trying. It's all I've got.

That's why I'm happy to show Josie and Tiffany the new magazines.

"It's a pity. She graduated, what, eight years ago? If it weren't for her father, I bet she'd have left with all the rest of the young folk." Josie's voice drifts through the stacks. Stepping behind one of the tallest shelves, I quietly pull out a book and peer at them.

They're huddled together, pretending to look at the magazines, but instead doing what everyone in this small town does best. Gossip.

"Of course, it's her father's fault," Tiffany whispers back. "She's a beauty, there's no denying. Looks like one of them old movie stars, don't you think? No wonder Lucas Poussin was all over her. Remember Lucas?"

"How could I forget?" Josie swoons. "He was the greatest thing that ever happened to her. Shame he didn't take her to the city with him. Saved her life but couldn't save her from her father's madness. Been twenty-five years of Crazy George's ramblings!"

Tiffany covers her mouth with her hand. "It was funny at first. But now it's just sad. He'd rather throw away his money and his daughter's future than accept his wife ran off."

"No, no, she was stolen by faeries! Maybe Santa's got her working in his toyshop." Josie lets out a cackle and Tiffany swats her arm.

My face flushes and tears prick the corners of my eyes. I know the town talks. How could I not? But to hear it so plainly …

I want to storm out and scream that I heard everything they've said. That they have no idea what they're talking about. That Papa isn't mad. That with every trip he takes, every loan he gets to fund an excursion, he's getting closer to what he needs.

But they're not wrong about everything.

Lucas did save my life.

Head down, I slink to the front counter. When I hear them shuffling back, I force a smile on my face and wave them out.

A pang of guilt sits heavy in my stomach that I didn't stand up for myself. For Papa. But what's the point?

Nothing will change the fact that I'm always going to be different.

Maybe they're right about Papa.

Maybe they're right about me.

THE SKY HAS DARKENED to a deep gray, and the streetlights turn on, as I shrug on my coat and prepare to lock up.

Richard came an hour ago to do the monthly inventory. Thankfully, this is one of the only tasks he doesn't trust me with. His dirty plaid jacket hangs over the cardboard boxes as he opens the latest shipments.

"Okay, I'm heading out now," I call. "See you later, Richard."

He grunts as a response, but as I place my hand on the door, his deep voice bellows, "What the fuck are these?"

He holds up a couple of the latest romance paperbacks I ordered. With a delighted squeal, I snatch one from him. "They finally came! Our collection has been stale, so I ordered some things to freshen it up. This one is a fantasy romance about a magical university, and this is a contemporary romance about a girl who pretends to be her brother to play hockey—"

"Romances?" Richard spits. "Rosalina, how many times have I told you? These don't sell." He slaps his forehead with a palm. "How much budget did you waste on this drivel?"

I tug the book against my chest. "It's not drivel… "

Richard digs through the box like an angry mole. "Is this whole damn order romance? What kind of idiot are you?" He stares straight at me, his eyes squinty and dark. "They're going back."

"But… If you'd let me put them on display—"

"Listen, O'Connell," my boss snarls. "You'd think, for living here your whole damned life, you'd know the people in this town don't like change. They want the authors they're familiar with. And they especially don't want mindless, unrealistic garbage like this. The only person in this town foolish enough to eat this shit up is you."

You can't talk to me like that. You wouldn't know literature if it smashed you in the head. You're mean and angry and look like a mole. I quit. These things and more rush through my head, but my throat is so dry, and my heart beats too fast. Then another voice joins the fray: *You need this job. Papa needs the money. You're not capable of anything else.*

Instinctively, I tug down the left sleeve of my sweater. "I–I'll make sure to send the books back. First thing tomorrow."

Richard sighs and rubs the bridge of his nose. "You know, I was friends with George back in the day."

George. My father.

"I want to keep you employed for his sake. Don't make that so hard, okay?"

I nod, taking a deep inhale to suck back my tears. "Okay." Somewhere, I find an ounce of courage to whisper, "Before we send them back, can I buy two?"

Richard waves an idle hand. "Fine. Grab what you want. I'll take it out of your paycheck."

Carefully, I choose two books and tuck them into my purse. "Goodnight."

"Goodnight, Rosalina," he says somberly. As if dealing with me is the worst part of his day. And it probably is.

That's what Lucas used to say.

I step outside into the rain, wishing above all else I could be anywhere but here.

2

ROSALINA

Drizzling rain sprinkles off my jacket as I walk down the street and away from the store. I just want to get home, throw a microwave dinner in, and cuddle up on the couch with my ghost hunter.

Shit. There's a huge mess waiting for me. That's the way it always is. Papa's gone for months, comes home for a few days, makes an absolute wreck of the place with maps and old books and weird artefacts, and then he's gone again.

Petra was a disappointment, he said. Nothing there but dead ends. This time, he's going back into the woods. It always comes back to the woods.

Orca Cove is bordered by the Pacific Ocean on the west and Lake Villeneuve to the south. The sprawling Briarwood Forest covers the northeast. That's where the hunting guides take the tourists in peak season. But Papa says there's something else out there.

I pull my hood over my head and stare at my soggy shoes. He's got a good tent and top-of-the-line gear, but he must be cold. I packed him a bunch of dehydrated food and made sure he's got water purification tablets, but what if he forgets to use them? What if he trips and is out of service?

What if this is the time he doesn't come back?

These thoughts are useless. I've said them to Papa a hundred times. But to him, it doesn't matter. *'She's out there, Rose. I know it. I won't stop until I bring her home.'*

Every small town has their village weirdo. And Orca Cove has Crazy George, my father. The former archeologist who told the whole village his wife got stolen by faeries.

I live close to the bookstore—everything is close in Orca Cove—but I take the long way 'round. Towering pine trees line the streets, and the buildings are all designed to look like log cabins. The hub of our city, Poussin Hunting Lodge, is lit up with golden lights as people head to the pub inside for an after-work pick-me-up. I haven't stepped foot in there in ages. Too many memories.

There's only one thing that'll make me feel better after a day like today.

My feet carry me unconsciously to the street on the very edge of town, away from the houses and the downtown shops. The sky has grown darker, and there are fewer streetlamps, but I know this town like the back of my hand. Puddles splash up around my ankles as I quicken my pace.

And as soon as I see it, a sense of calm fills me. It's a building with a tin roof, a cracked window, a broken door hinge and ugly olive-green paint, peeling off every wall. It's been up for sale for years and has never had any takers.

But one day, it's going to be mine. I walk over to it and place my hand on the wall. I can imagine it now: unlocking the doors first thing in the morning, when the mist still dances around the pines. Walking over to a beautiful long desk with a top-of-the-line computer that never crashes. On one side, there would be rows and rows and rows of books. A huge children's section with a toy box, a section for displays and an entire shelf just for romances.

It would be exactly what our community needs.

A library.

The vision flashes in perfect clarity before me. I'd probably be closer to my goal if I hadn't offered Papa my college fund. But our tiny house was getting foreclosed, and he was in a pit of depression, not being able to follow up on a lead in the highlands of Scotland because he couldn't afford the plane ticket.

Of course, I had to give it to him.

Would I have studied English Literature like I thought? Gotten my master's degree like Lucas? Would I have stayed in a big city like one of my friends?

My reflection peers back at me from the window of my dream building: tall, messy chestnut hair, mascara smudged around brown eyes. If I tilt my head, my image gets shattered in the cracked glass, turning my tired expression into something monstrous.

I may not have my library, but I do have something else. Down the road, a full weeping willow waves her branches in the breeze. She's lost most of her leaves now, but there's still something so elegant about her, like her branches are the skirts of a beautiful ballgown.

Classic village crazy woman. Personifying a tree. Like father, like daughter, I guess. But I like this tree better than most of the residents of Orca Cove. And besides, Papa says this was Mom's favorite tree.

That's why it's the perfect spot to build my own little library. Papa made a tiny house with a glass door and propped it up on a tall wooden stake. It's one of the few things Papa's ever done for me.

I decorated the outside with dried flowers. Roses, specifically. Papa would always ask me what I wanted from his travels. *You, home safely. To stay and not leave me alone again,* I would think. But I never said it out loud. Instead, I would always ask him for a rose, something cheap and easy he could get. And at least that was a promise he always kept, even if sometimes it was little trinkets or jewelry rather than a real flower.

I stocked the little library with all my favorite books. I'd yet to see anyone take or leave a book yet, but—

"Wait, what?" My heart hammers against my chest. The little library … It's destroyed. Books scattered across the damp ground, the pole slants, and the house is smashed onto the road. I sprint over, trying to save the books from the puddles. Then I see one wall has graffiti on it: THE FAERIES DID IT

"No, no, no." I fall to my knees, books slipping from my hands into the mud. I worked so hard on this …

Bright headlights cut through the dark street. I shield my eyes. A noisy, rumbling truck lumbers closer. I can barely see anything with those headlights on full blast. What kind of jackass turns his brights on while going down a residential street?

But the truck … It's coming toward me. Quickly, I leap off of the street and back onto the sidewalk. The truck pulls up along the side of the road, then reverses to be right in front of me.

A protest dies on my lips as the tires crunch over the broken remains of my little library. What does it matter? I couldn't save it, anyway. Dried flowers shed their petals in the mud.

I blink as the truck cuts its engine. Who would stop to talk to me? Now that my eyes clear from the blinding headlights, I can make out the logo on the door of the truck. Poussin Hunting Co. Is it one of the Poussin guides? But why?

A flush of anticipation tingles through my body. *Wait …*

Heavy boots thud on the other side. My heart hammers in my chest as I step around the truck. The drizzle finally breaks into rain and heavy drops pellet the ground, the streetlights gleam harsh shadows off every tree.

"Rosalina O'Connell. It can't be."

It can't be is right. Because standing in front of me is Lucas Poussin. My ex-boyfriend.

My throat seizes. Oh god. He looks … good. I mean, he always looks good. It's been nearly a year since I last saw him. He always graces Orca Cove with his presence at Christmas time, but this is way too early.

Lucas runs a hand through his dark red hair. He's wearing a leather jacket with a black shirt underneath and snug jeans. He looks more 'city' than the usual guys around here, but he still has that edge to him. The edge of a hunter's son.

"Here I was, driving to your house, when I see someone splashing around in the mud. I figured it was some sort of vagabond or other undesirable, so I pulled up to send them packing. And what do I know? It's Rosalina O'Connell herself."

I'm completely drenched in mud, from my jacket to my black leggings. I know there are bags under my eyes, and I'm sure this rain is not doing my mascara any favors. Of course, he looks like he walked off the cover of *Men's Health*.

Lucas narrows his hazel eyes at me, and I realize I haven't said anything. Oh god. It's my turn to say something, isn't it? But as always, I'm completely stuck.

Cause that's what Lucas does to me. Shows up once a year and completely immobilizes me. It's like I regress to being back in high school, hanging onto his every word. The worst part is, I know it's pathetic. You'd think I was sixteen, not twenty-six.

Everyone in Orca Cove thinks Lucas is God's gift to humanity. The only time the residents thought of me as anything other than Crazy George's daughter was after the incident at the frozen lake. Back then, I was Lucas's girl.

My throat clenches as if it's all those years ago, the ice water pouring down at me. I see his hand like a beacon.

Despite myself, I know being Lucas's girl felt better than being the outcast I am now. Being asked about Lucas was so much easier than people asking why my dad was growing fairy circles in the backyard.

But being Lucas's girl didn't feel good when he dumped me right before he left for university. Or the time he came home for Christmas, took me out to dinner, and ordered a salad for me because, *'You've packed on the freshman fifteen and aren't even in college'*. Or last winter when we went for drinks at the Lodge, and I took him home so he could fuck me. I woke up, and he was sexting some girl from his university. I pretended not to see.

He stares down at me, his eyes narrowed. And he smiles. "Babe, you must be so excited to see me."

And despite it all ... I am.

He pulls me into him, and it feels so good to be wrapped up in his warmth. I inhale. He smells like cologne and leather and its so fucking familiar, I can't help myself. "I missed you."

"I know, Pumpkin." He pulls away and gives a shining grin. My chest bursts. He's smiling for *me*.

"I–I'm surprised to see you," I somehow manage. I'm tall at 5'11, and he has one inch on me, but when he stares at me like this, I feel like I'm five years old.

"That's what I wanted." He grins. "I graduated in spring. Did you hear? With honors, of course."

Yeah, I heard. The Poussins are basically royalty to Orca Cove. Everyone was talking about it.

"So, you got a job at some accounting firm in the city?" I ask.

He snorts. "Yeah, I'm done with that. They had a problem with my visionary attitude. I don't need to put myself in a cage, you know?"

"Sure," I say. "How long are you in town for?"

He ignores my question and grips my chin. I suck in a breath, staring up at him like one of his does. "You really are startlingly beautiful," he whispers, but it's not like he's saying it to me. It's like he's saying it to himself. "Such a unique sort of beauty."

My skin itches. I pull down on my left sleeve.

He whips away and heads to the truck. "Dinner at the Lodge tomorrow night, 7 p.m. Bring your dad, if he's not too busy, you know, catching gnomes or whatever."

That's ... That's it? He's going to tell me to meet him for dinner and leave? I should tell him to fuck off. I should tell him if he wants to go to dinner with me, he'll have to pick me up. I should tell him—

But before I get up the nerve to do anything, he's driven away, leaving me alone in the rain with my broken library and wilted roses.

3

ROSALINA

Hundreds of beastly eyes stare at me and only half of them are mounted on the wall.

The Poussin Hunting Lodge is packed. *How many people did Lucas invite?* It's not just dinner with me; he's thrown a party for the whole town.

My oversized scarf, white shirt, and black leggings are underdressed compared to everyone's fancy attire. I awkwardly try to disappear into the crowd. Warmth from the large stone fireplace thaws my cold cheeks. The faint whiff of liquor and tobacco mixes with the tables full of steaming meat and pumpkin pies.

Lucas's family has owned the Hunting Lodge for generations. Part inn, part pub, part guide service. A high-beamed ceiling supports antique chandeliers, each bearing a lantern that casts the room in orangey light. Tables, chairs, benches, and the bar are all carved from dark wood. Autumn leaves and foliage decorate the hearth.

The heads of elk and deer and pelts of bears, mountain lions, and a wolf are mounted on the walls. Lucas killed the wolf nearly ten years ago. Told me he shot it in the back of its head while it was sleeping. Its fur is still soft and dense, almost shimmering in the firelight.

Tension gnaws in my gut, and I force myself to look away. There are so many people. *A welcome home party he forgot to mention?*

The whole town is here, but of course no one tries to start a conversation with me. I spy a lot of Lucas's family, even the ones from nearby towns. Cousins, aunts, uncles, grandparents. *All I've got is Papa, and that's only half the time.*

Lucas's parents have always been kind to me. But even they join in the town gossip about the crazy O'Connells. "At least you'll have lovely grandchildren," had been a condolence I'd heard directed toward Mr. and Mrs. Poussin many times.

They don't have to worry, though. Lucas made it very clear he didn't want a future together when he dumped me before he left for university. I'm just his hometown hook-up now.

Finally, I spot Lucas looking down over the railing from the upper level. I weave through the crowd and rush up the stairs to him.

Lucas pulls me into a hug. An intense wave of relief rushes over my body, and I exhale between his muscular arms before he lets me go. He takes my chin and makes me look up at him. "Saw you come in. You looked positively frazzled."

Well, it would have been nice to know there would be so many people, I think.

Lucas drops his hand. "You would have never made it in the city. It's refreshing to remember how innocent my little Pumpkin is."

"Don't call me that." I hate that nickname.

"I'll get you a job at the front desk here. It'll do you some good to see people from all walks of life."

"I see different people at the bookstore," I remind him.

"What, women and moldy oldies?" Lucas laughs. Then he grips me around the waist and pulls me against his broad chest. "I'm talking about real people. People who have seen the world."

"I've been to many places too," I say. "Well, I've read about them."

"My little Pumpkin." He shakes his head, giving me a pitying look as his hand trails down my arm. His thumb brushes my left wrist.

"Wait—"

He pulls up my sleeve and blinks down at my arm.

"Oh right," he says. "I should have remembered you'd never be able to forget me."

He'd forgotten?

He'd forgotten.

He'd forgotten the tears that streamed down my cheeks eight years ago as I had dry heaved and had barely been able to breathe. He was never there when I needed him. And he was going to leave for university. Pain had clawed inside me like a caged animal. And no matter how many tears I'd cried, not a single one reached him.

I remember that night.

How he'd rolled his eyes, pacing and throwing out his hands. "What the fuck do you want from me?"

I couldn't tell him because I didn't know. Didn't know why it hurt so much when he missed dates or forgot to call, and why it hurt even more when he was there. But somehow, that was more bearable.

There was more pain when he pulled out his hunting knife and ripped off the sleeve of my shirt. "Now you'll remember," he said as he dug the sharp point into my forearm, making the first rough line. "Now you'll remember who saved your life. Now you'll remember you don't need to bother me with your questions."

And I remember the blood that had fallen from my wrist and sunk into the wood of my bedroom floor. How the pathetic splatter of it is still there today.

But he had left.

And he left with his name carved into my arm and my blood on the floor.

Now, he smiles down at me. "You don't have to look so concerned. I'm home now."

"It's just—" He cuts me off with a kiss. His mouth covers mine, and his tongue slips between my lips. As he moves against me, I struggle to pull my sleeve back down over my arm. A rough hand travels down my body, groping at my breast through my T-shirt, then snaking around to cup my bottom.

"I missed this ass," he murmurs into my ear. "The city girls are so skinny. Nothing to grip."

"Lucas." Ice floods my body as I picture him there. How many girls has he slept with?

"Don't be jealous, Gummy Bear." He tilts his head to the side, a half-smile on his face. "You should thank those city girls. How else could I realize what I want?"

I swallow but my throat is dry. "What do you want?"

"Speaking of that, we have to get down to our party."

"Wait." He grasps my arm and pulls me back into the crowd. *"Our* party?"

I'm not sure why, but there's a pit in my stomach, growing and growing. A foreboding, like as soon as Lucas leads me out into the fray, something is going to happen. Something is going to change. Something that can't be undone.

I'm not ready. I'm so not ready.

Lucas drops my arm, then jumps onto the table in the middle of the crowd. He gestures for them to quiet.

"Alright, folks!" his voice booms. "There's good news and there's bad news. What do we want first?"

The crowd vibrates with anticipation, cheering and raising their mugs of ale.

"Alright, alright." Lucas waves his hands to settle them down. "I'll start with the good news. I've officially decided to take over the Hunting Lodge from my parents!"

The surrounding crowd erupts in a cheer, and his dad wipes a tear away with a napkin.

"Expect some modern improvements, though always keeping with long-standing family traditions and values." Lucas flashes a smile. He really is handsome, his hair glowing a burning red in the flickering light of the fire. "Now for the bad news."

An uneasy murmur passes through the crowd. I take a step back.

"With taking on the responsibility of the lodge," Lucas continues, "I've had to consider other responsibilities as well and as of tonight, I'm officially off the market!"

A few laughs burst through the crowd, and I see a group of girls clutch at each other and start whispering. Something dangerous churns within me.

A boom radiates through the lodge as Lucas jumps down from the table to stand in front of me. Then he's not standing anymore. He's kneeling.

There's a small box in his hands, and he opens it. A diamond, square and huge, the light of it is so bright I blink back tears.

"Break the hearts of everyone in town and be my wife, Pumpkin?" Lucas smiles, eyeing the crowd.

Lucas …

Lucas is proposing to me.

I open my mouth, but no words come out.

A part of me can see it: to be his little wife in Orca Cove. Help run the lodge. Maybe feel like I belong.

I can also see the red tail of the letter S peeking out from under my sleeve.

Ice entraps my body and I feel like I'm drowning, heavy clothes pulling me deeper and deeper.

A nervous chuckle sounds through the crowd at my silence. They're staring at me as if they've proposed too. Lucas looks at me, surprise etched on his features. "So, what is it? Yes or yes?"

I thought I'd know my answer. Shouldn't you know the answer when someone is on their knees before you?

The door bursts open. Icy wind and dead leaves blow in, and standing there is the butcher's son, holding something clutched to his chest. He stumbles into the room. "Rosalina, I've been looking for you everywhere."

Lucas stands and pushes me behind him. "Thomas, what is the meaning of this? The lodge is closed for a private event."

Thomas's red hair is wild, his freckled face flushed. "You have to listen. I got turned around hunting in the wood today. Went off the trail mighty bad. Then I saw this. It's Mr. O'Connell's jacket."

"Papa!" I push past Lucas and snatch the jacket from Thomas. It's covered in blood.

"Rosalina," Lucas says, trying to pull me back.

I ignore him and grip Thomas on the shoulder. "Take me to where you found this. I'm going after my father."

4

KELDARION

"Hello? Does anyone live here? I need help!"

The voice echoes through the castle. It isn't possible. It can't be …

"I got lost and was attacked! I mean no harm. I only need a place to rest."

No, no, no.

There is an intruder in the castle.

The unfamiliar voice pricks my ears and I smell this invader's stink even deep within my chambers. It can't be.

Human.

A human has found his way through the Enchanted Vale and into the Briar. My heart thuds as I look up, trying to see past the tangle of thorns overtaking the ceiling. Castletree must be very weak indeed if the Vale is now so thin as to allow humans …

"Is anyone here?" the voice cries again.

A shudder of rage courses through me, and I shake, my heavy white coat flinging off the frost that has settled during the night. Where are the other princes to deal with this insanity?

Ezryn has left to patrol the Spring Realm, provoking goblins for his own sick joy. Dayton is probably passed out in a pile of his own sick. And Farron, of course, is … occupied.

That means it's up to me to deal with this intruder. A snarl sounds deep within my chest. My paws shatter the ice that covers the floor as I stalk toward the door. A human in the castle. It isn't possible.

I fling open the door with my snout and see Astrid sitting there. She hops back, immediately shrinking from the rage in my eyes.

"Master, there's … There's a human in the castle," she peeps.

I ignore her, that icy growl rumbling through my chest again. Humans. Idiotic creatures with mayfly lives. Is the Vale truly so weak now?

The thought—this urgent reminder—of the dying magic makes my muscles stiffen with each step. Maybe the end has finally come. Maybe we will be freed from our misery once and for all.

A strangled howl sounds from the dungeon tower. He's worked up too. This human's scent will stink up the castle for days.

Whispers and gasps echo as I enter the main causeway. The servants flit around, hiding in door frames and scuttling into different rooms. Are they afraid of the human … or of me?

Ice trails from my paws with each step and I look down, stiffening at my reflection. The hideous, horrific beast, stares back at me. With a roar, I scratch the image with my claws. How dare this human force me out of my wing during the night? Why would he brave the Briar and come into my castle? To laugh at the beast?

"Hello?" the voice echoes again and now I'm running through the hallways until I skid to a stop on the ramparts, looking down into the great hall.

There he is.

The invader.

He's a tall man, in his extended years, with brown hair flecked with gray. He carries his weight in his rotund belly, but otherwise looks sturdy enough. Soaked clothing sticks to his skin, and his sack drips water all over my floor.

I always forget how pathetic humans are until I look at them.

I could kill him and be done with it. But Ez wouldn't like that. He's got a soft spot for the pathetic things in life.

Maybe that's why he's got a soft spot for me.

"A wayward traveler, Master," a voice says from behind me. I don't bother turning, knowing it's Marigold. "He's sopping wet. Should I set him up with some tea and a fresh cloak—"

"No," I snarl. "He's not to stay. He's lucky not to die for trespassing."

Marigold sighs. "Yes, Master."

I grit my fangs, inhaling the thick air of the castle, heady and moist. Only a stupid human. I will deal with it, return to my chambers, and it will be nothing more than a disturbing occurrence. ...

"I was chased by goblins," the human cries as he wanders through the great hall. Orange light from the fireplace dances over his skin. "I'm looking for my wife."

"He'll die if you send him back out there, Master," Marigold whispers. "Look at him. Could have been a looker if he weren't so drenched. Sad little mite."

"Goblins are a consequence of trespassing in the Briar," I growl. Sometimes I wish Marigold feared me as the others did. I must deal with this intruder before the servants's soft hearts and softer heads have them throwing him a dance with dinner.

I take a step back toward the shadows. A few harsh words uttered from the dark will have the short-lived being scurrying back out into the fray. I don't need to show myself to assert dominion over my castle.

As I open my mouth to bellow down to the wretched interloper, he walks toward the fireplace and reaches a hand toward the thick, black thorn bushes that lace through the stone wall and creep over the mantle.

"Fascinating," he whispers.

I watch with morbid curiosity, saliva dripping down my fangs, as he traces his hands along the spiny branches. Yes, peasant, not even our castle is safe from the Briar. And you will learn soon this is no sanctuary—

"Roses," he mutters. And he sees it, tucked within the brambles. The final remaining bloom of Castletree. The last symbol of hope that our home may yet withstand a little longer. That there may be hope for the cursed souls who reside here.

"A rose," the human says again and reaches his hands into the brambles. "A rose for my Rose. I promised her, after all."

My pupils dilate as the scene plays out before me: this human daring to take a piece of the last life of our hallowed tree. He plucks the rose from its stem and delicately pulls it back through the brambles. Then he steps into the light of the fire and admires it. A blood-red bloom.

"Oh dear," Marigold whispers.

All the mercy and curiosity drain out of me. He ... He stole it. He took life from Castletree.

I had wanted to offer forgiveness. I had wanted to show humanity. But he lost that right when he stole from the House of the Queen. Now, the man within me lets loose the reins of control and frees the beast.

With a snarl, I leap over the side of the railing, landing with a boom in the shadows of the great hall. The man jumps, the rose falling from his grasp. "Who goes there?"

I prowl to the other side, staying deep within the shadows. He blanches, trying to track my movements in the dark.

"I am the master of this castle," I rumble, "and you are a trespasser and a thief. Do you know the punishment for thieves in the Enchanted Vale?"

The man blinks, and some of the fear dissipates from his expression. "I'm here. I made it. Please help me. I'm looking for my wife—"

"Help you?" My voice bellows like the depths of an icy chasm. "How dare a criminal ask for help? You have wandered into magic beyond your comprehension. Leave now, and be grateful you return with your life, however short it may be."

But the human falls to his knees. "Please, sir. The rose was but a humble gift for my daughter. I've been searching for this realm for twenty-five years. My wife is here somewhere and—"

There is a part of me, deep within, that respects the courage of this pitiful human. But it is clear he has no idea what he has done. He does not understand the true meaning of fear.

And so, with slow, deliberate steps, I walk into the light.

The man falls backwards, eyes wide and glassy, mouth cast in a horrified 'O'. He scrambles away but I descend faster, lurching toward him, pinning him on both sides with my massive paws. Baring my fangs, I am about to roar for him to leave when a light catches my gaze. A crystallized rose, made of moonstone, hangs from a chain around his neck, the intricate metalwork glittering in the firelight.

I pull back and stare at the human.

And, with twenty-five years' worth of wrath and suffering, I straighten to my full height and say, "You want to stay in the Enchanted Vale? Then stay you shall."

I snatch his coat in my jaws and haul him up the stairs. To the dungeon.

5

ROSALINA

All my life, Papa has been called crazy for going on about magic and wicked faeries that steal you from this world and take you far away to enchanted lands. They said he was crazy, that it was his way of coping with the grief of a runaway wife. But here, in the deep dark of the forest, Thomas's pale fingers tremble on the flashlight and I wonder if there's a part of him that's starting to believe my father.

And maybe there's a part of me too.

"This is pointless," Lucas grumbles from behind me. He insisted on coming with us, and neither of us have forgotten that I haven't given him an answer to his proposal. Nor did the shocked crowd, when I ran out after Thomas, all whispering I was mad for not saying yes to Lucas. Maybe I really am as crazy as my father.

None of that bothers me right now. Because I need to find him! Papa's gone out many times before, but he's always come back. My heart races, and not just because of the blood on the jacket. Something is terribly wrong. I can feel it.

Lucas and I creep behind Thomas as he tries his best to remember the path, only the dim gleam of our flashlights guiding our way. I should be grateful for Lucas's presence, his protection, but the way his hunting rifle glints in the moonlight makes my skin prickle.

"Uh," Thomas's voice wavers. "Maybe we're getting close. I'm not sure."

I squint my eyes, but every time I focus on something, the flashlight blinds me. "Turn off the lights."

"You're mad," Lucas says. "We should come back in the morning. I'll get the lodge to organize a search party."

"Just turn off the light," I snap. *"Please."*

Lucas groans but shuts off his flashlight. While my eyes adjust to the dark, the sounds of the forest come alive: the scraping of branches in the wind, the soft hoot of owls, and the scurry of little creatures in the underbrush.

And Thomas's wheezing breath.

A small light flickers, at the edge of my vision, and I cut through the mist toward it.

The wind plays with my hair. *This way, this way,* I swear it says.

An overgrown rosebush stops my advance. The thorny vines twist into the trees, and the roses are heavy in bloom, dark red petals carpeting the forest floor. Strange for roses to bloom in October. Something wet glistens on the petals in the moonlight.

"What the fuck is that?" Lucas turns on his flashlight, and I blink at the sudden brightness.

But there, illuminated by the light, is red blood and torn patches of fabric.

"This is where I found the coat," Thomas stammers.

Lucas leans close. "The blood is fresh. He couldn't have gone far."

There's a broken section of the rosebush near my feet, thorns and flowers torn away. "He went through here."

"Pumpkin, wait," Lucas starts. "Can't we come back in the morning?"

But I'm already on my knees, pushing through the brambles. It's a patchwork of thorns, each as cold and hard as a slab of winter ice. The thorns catch in my clothes and scrape along my cheek. Warm blood drips down my chin. Hastily, I wipe it away and keep moving deeper into the hole. *He must have gone this way.*

Behind me, Lucas mutters a goodbye to Thomas, who has endured enough trauma tonight without crawling through a creepy overgrown rosebush. Branches snap as Lucas shoves through the hole after me.

"I've been in these woods hundreds of times," Lucas says, "and I've never seen wild roses."

"Maybe you weren't paying attention," I murmur. Mud stains my palms, but there's a misty light up ahead, the chill of fresh air. This must lead deep into the forest. Papa could have gotten turned around and been unable to find his way back.

Something akin to hope blossoms in my chest and I keep moving, breaking through the last few thorns into the open air.

And nothing is the same.

The strangest feeling ripples through me and I take a deep breath. The smell is damp and wild, with tinges of moss and wood. A hint of rot and decay, like an old, forgotten grave.

"Where the hell are we?" Lucas straightens, putting a hand on my shoulder.

This is like no place I've seen before. It's like we're still in the rose-bush, but now the vines are thick as tree trunks, with thorns as long as my arm. There are no flowers. Below my feet is loose dark soil and lacing mist. I can barely make out a deep night sky through the tangle of briars.

Behind us, I can still see the rosebush we crawled through, the red flowers, the only spot of color in this whole place.

Slowly, I reach my hand toward a bramble. It's not entirely black, but a deep purple. "Wait—" Lucas shouts.

A current of energy ripples through me as my hand touches the massive branch. I swear the plant shudders beneath my fingers.

Lucas grips my arm and pulls me back. "What the fuck are you doing?"

I turn to him, and I can't stop the smile that breaks over my face. "Don't you see? We're in the land of the fae. Papa finally found it." I pull out my phone. No signal. No surprise there.

Lucas's dark eyes widen as he takes in our surroundings. I can see his mind at war. But somehow, I know this is right. Even the air tastes different. We're far from home.

I run a few paces forward and yell, "Papa! Papa, I found you. It's me!"

Lucas unstraps his rifle, holding it tight in his hands. Bright moonlight illuminates a small trail through the thorns. We begin to walk. Lucas turns every so often, letting out a sigh of relief when he still sees the rosebush behind us. The trail narrows, and one side dips down into a rocky gully, thorns crawling their way across the dark bottom.

I cup my hands around my mouth. "Papa, it's me, Rosalina! I've come after you."

A strange chittering noise sounds from beyond the mist. Then it multiplies, coming from behind and … below. Laughter.

A silhouette emerges from the tangle of fog and vines. Lucas backs up and stumbles into me. I turn and see more shapes closing in on his side too. We're surrounded.

As the moonlight washes over them, disgust and fear flood my body. These are like no human or animal I've ever seen. These creatures look as if they're out of some twisted nightmare. Humanoids with ashen bodies. They wear simple leather armor and dirty rags. Yellow eyes flicker like a dying candle, and sharp teeth poke out from twisted, gruesome faces. Their very skin rots off their bodies, covered in moss and festering yellow wounds. And in their hands, they hold dark black blades, thorns filed and sharpened from the surrounding plants.

Maybe we're not in the land of faeries.

We're in the land of monsters.

6

ROSALINA

Sickening horror courses through my body as the monsters stalk closer. There is nowhere to run.

Sweat drips down Lucas's brow. "Holy shit," he swears, the rifle shaking in his hands.

"Wait," I whisper. "Maybe we can reason with them."

A few misshapen animalistic creatures snarl at the humanoids's heels. Their shape reminds me of a hyena, but they have ashen bodies and festering wounds that drip a strange green sludge. Little forests sprout on their flesh: a small patch of mushrooms along a paw, a cluster of moss around the ear. And they smell of decay and sour death.

Nausea coils in my gut.

Two of the humanoid monsters step toward us. "We have some visitors," one of them croons, voice muddy and wet.

They speak. Lucas's hands tremble on his rifle, and I pray he doesn't do anything rash.

"Looks like they've never seen a goblin before, Launak," one of them chitters.

"No, don't reckin' they have, Aldgog. Peek at their ears, all rounded and short. Lost little humans," Launak hisses.

Goblins. One of the many monstrosities Papa rambled about in his tales. He said they were enemies of the fae. But to see them here, in the flesh ...

There's at least twenty surrounding us, laughing and chanting: "Lost little humans, lost little humans, lost little humans."

"I'm looking for my father," I say.

The chant of the surrounding goblins changes. "Father, father, father. Lost father. Father, father, father."

Launak creaks its head unnaturally to the side. "No fathers around here."

"No, the old man. The old man," Aldgog says, showing a row of yellow teeth.

The goblins move closer as they talk and the ones above us scramble down the brambles. I have no illusions about their intentions, but if they know something about my father, I have to find out as much information as I can before we escape.

"The old man," I say. "Where is he?"

"Don't want to go where the old man went." Something akin to fear crosses Aldgog's face.

"Taken," Launak hisses.

"Who has my father?" I demand.

"Winter." A black tongue snakes out of Launak's lips, and his voice pitches low as he says, "Keldarion and his beasts."

Keldarion ...

Fearful chittering and shrieks sound from the surrounding goblins. "Keldarion. Keldarion. Prince of the beasts."

Fear blossoms in my chest, and I realize the goblins have gotten so close I can smell their putrid breath, like fermenting leaves, old mushrooms, and warm, wet mud. I feel like I'm going to throw up.

"Keldarion and his beasts of the Briar."

"Shut the fuck up, all of you," Lucas roars and cocks his rifle.

"Lucas, wait!"

He fires.

Loud bangs sound around me and light flashes in my eyes. There's the horrible sound of their screeching as bullets fly into the goblins.

His rounds fizzle out, and I stare at the massacre. At least five of the goblins lay dead. The rest stare at us in shock. Black inky blood leaks into the soil.

"Run," I gasp.

We leap over the dead bodies of the goblins, but movement sounds behind us. They're coming.

Lucas falls hard, and his rifle skitters beneath a twisting thicket.

"Shit," he swears. A dark shadow leaps over me—one of the hyena creatures—and throws itself on Lucas. He screams as the creature's sharp claws pierce into his back. Behind, the goblins cheer, voices growing louder at their approach.

"Lucas!" Horror rises within me, and instinct takes over. I snap off a large thorn from the thicket and plunge it into the flesh of the rotten dog's leg. Black tar-like sludge spurts from the wound and it lets out a yelp of pain.

Lucas pushes it off him. The creature rolls, falling off the edge of the gully and into the tangle of thorns below.

With no time to find the rifle, Lucas pushes himself to his feet, and we take off in a sprint, going in the direction we came. Ahead lies the rosebush, the red flowers beckoning. Beyond that bush is safety. There's a deep agony knowing my father is still in this place, but I can't search for him if I'm dead. *I'll come back.*

Something snatches my ankle, and I tumble, clattering over the edge of the cliff, a scream erupting from my throat. I jerk to a stop as my scarf snags on one of the giant thorns. I desperately reach up and grab the fabric, managing to hold myself up. Below me is nothing but the dark gully, a tangled briar of spear-like thorns. Goblins cluster around the edge, snickering and watching to see if I'll fall.

"Lucas!" I scream.

He's almost at the rosebush, far ahead of the goblins now that they've stopped to watch my torment.

"Lucas!" The scarf rips, and I jerk downward. It's holding on by a few fibers.

"Down, down, down she goes," the goblins sing. "All the way to Mother. Down, down, down, she goes."

My feet kick over the open air. I definitely do not want to find out who *Mother* is. "Lucas!"

He stops running and turns to me. His hazel eyes widen.

The end of my scarf rips and I fall, plunging into the briars. My head knocks against the cliffside and my vision goes blurry.

Something firm snakes around my waist, and I jerk to a stop. I'm moving slower, as if drifting through water, as something guides me through the twisted maze of thorns. I feel solid ground beneath me and whatever has me uncoils from my waist.

Everything is hazy, but the briars rustle as the goblins crawl down. Their yellow eyes glow through the darkness. I force myself to roll over and begin to crawl, belly dragging on the ground. A shooting pain radiates through my head.

The world comes to life, spinning, spinning, spinning. But no, not the world. The thorns are moving.

Horrid squelching shrieks pierce through the night. Black liquid drips down around me like rain. My vision fades to the silhouette of goblins impaled on rows of thorns.

Arms wrap around my waist and lift me up. I'm pulled against the broad chest of a man. Did Lucas return to me?

I blink, trying to focus as I look up and am struck by eyes black as shadows and hair the same color.

"Rest, Princess," a smooth voice whispers in my ear. "You're home."

7

ROSALINA

Everything is a blur. I sit up, rubbing my head and trying to make sense of my memories through a fog of confusion. I must have passed out after … after …

What was that? *Who* was that?

What the fuck just happened? My mind reels and my body aches.

This isn't real. Can't be.

And yet the face dances through my mind clearer than any dream. Eyes dark as shadows, hair black as pitch, and the slightest frown on his lush mouth that I wish I could see as a smile …

Okay, what the fuck is wrong with me? I definitely whacked my head because the first thing I'm thinking about cannot be some random guy instead of the actual *monsters* that tried to kill me.

Not just me. They tried to kill Lucas too. Where is he? Last I saw him, he was abandoning me as I dangled off the side of a cliff. I rub my left forearm. Why am I surprised? Because he saved my life once before?

And he'd asked me to marry him …

Okay, I definitely can't think about that right now, or I will seriously lose it. I need to get my bearings and find Papa.

My throat seizes and tears prick my eyes. What if those things found him first and he's—? No. I have to keep faith. He's out there. I'll find him and we'll go home together.

The black brambles are even thicker here, towering way over my head. Some branches are as wide as my arm, but there's a thin path through. One step at a time.

I walk down the path and look up at the cloudy sky. Dusky light shimmers through. Based on the position of the sun, I must have passed out all night and most of today. I need to escape soon, because I don't want to spend another night here. And I can't count on some mysterious and probably not-even-real man to bail me out.

Most likely I had a lucky fall, and the goblins didn't.

I tuck my ripped scarf tighter around me. The path curves through the thicket and suddenly the brambles break, exposing an expanse before me. My heart hitches and I rub my eyes. I must have really hit my head …

Because there's no way there's a castle built into a gargantuan tree. It looks like something out of a storybook or a Studio Ghibli movie. A stone bridge stretches toward the grounds beneath the tree-castle. Maybe it's supposed to be over a moat, but it's hard to tell because there's so many purple thorn bushes tangling below.

Two large statues guard the bridge on either side. I try to make out their shape, but they're so strangled by brambles, I can't tell what they are.

This is what Papa has been searching for all this time. The home of the fae. If they live anywhere, it has to be a castle built into a tree, right?

And if he escaped through the thicket and away from those monsters, he would go here.

I step onto the bridge.

As I get closer, I realize how hard it is to tell what is tree and what is castle. The whole thing is an intricate work of bark and stone, both organic and crafted at the same time. Tall towers reach up to the massive canopy. Some of the highest branches hold autumn leaves, but a lot of the tree is bare. Black lines run the length of the trunk. It looks … sick.

Most notable of all, the thorn bushes stretch up to the top, covering the entire structure, forming a pseudo-skeleton of brambles.

A huge mahogany door awaits me at the end of the bridge. Who lives here? Those goblin things? Something worse?

Maybe if I close my eyes, I'll wake up back in my bed and everything will be normal. Then I can … What? Get married to Lucas?

Isn't that what I want?

The wood is cold beneath my fingers. I sure as hell don't want to know who lives here, so I'm not knocking. I pull it open. An echoing creak sounds through a massive entranceway, and I step through. It's dark and I blink a few times, trying to adjust to the gloom.

"Papa?" I call tentatively. My footsteps reverberate as I walk inside. "It's Rosalina. I'm here to bring you home."

Skittering sounds around me, and I jump, clutching my chest. "Hello?"

Nothing but my echo. I walk further into the castle, my footsteps now softened by the carpet. Plumes of dust follow where I walk. Maybe this place is abandoned.

Even inside, the thorns have invaded. The walls are a mix of stone and wood, but neither was strong enough to stop the thorns from bursting through. They curl over walls, cluster in the corners, and spill over the floor.

A breeze flits through my hair and I swear I hear whispering. I turn in a circle. Nothing. "Hello?"

The door has closed behind me, and there's the oddest object beside it. A beautiful mirror with a gold frame of inlaid roses. The glass has an aged, almost nectar-colored, tone. I want to touch it.

But I can't go around touching creepy items in a weird fae castle. Even I can guess that'll end badly. I need to get out of here as soon as possible. Goosebumps cover my clammy skin. I shake my head, take a deep breath, and try to steady my racing heart.

But my heart doesn't steady. It catches, then quickens, beating powerfully inside my chest. Something twists within me, a great yearning, and my head jerks to the side. A huge staircase, the railing tangled with thorns, leads up into darkness. *There.* I must go there.

I drift like a ghost up the staircase, branches cracking beneath my feet. The stairs lead into a cloistered tower, circling round and round and round as I walk.

My thighs burn and I'm panting by the time I reach a steel door. I heave it open.

Of all the places I've seen so far, this is the most castle-like, the walls and floor all made of stone. Brambles still spread over every inch, and a cold breeze trembles through. A few barred windows let in the dying sunlight. Soon, I won't be able to see at all. I hug myself and pace forward. "Papa?"

I round a corner and gasp. There, in a barred cell, slumped against the stone wall with a massive chain collar around his neck, is a prisoner. Not Papa.

A young man.

8

ROSALINA

At my startled breath, the man in the prison cell looks up at me.

The space between us crackles. His eyes are gold, thickly lashed, and wide. Disheveled brown hair floats in curls over his thick brows, the shorter sides sticking up. His full mouth opens questioningly as he looks at me. He's shirtless, his torso lean and muscled, legs stretched long before him in tattered pants. But what stops me in my tracks and has my heart racing … His ears.

They're pointed.

This man isn't a man at all. He's fae.

And he's also chained to a wall. Fae or not, he needs help.

I rush toward the cell and grab the door. "Hello! Are you okay?"

The man blinks at me, as if he can't believe his eyes. Hey, he's the one with pointed ears and he's looking at me like I'm the weird one?

"Who … Who are you?" he asks. He shoots a look at the window behind me. "You can't be here. You need to get out. Now."

I yank on his door. There's a huge padlock. Do those monsters live here? Did they imprison this fae? "I want to help you. But please tell me. Is there a man here? A human, like me?"

The man licks his lips and sits forward. I notice now his collar is massive. He could easily lift it off. Why does he keep it around his neck like that? "It doesn't matter. You need to leave this place right now. Listen to me, okay?"

"A human," I urge. "Is there a human here? Taller than me, brown hair. His name is George. Please, tell me!"

The fae's throat bobs up and down, and he digs his long fingers into his pants. "Yes. But that doesn't matter. You've got to go. It's not safe."

A flood of relief rushes through me. He's here. He's here! "I have to find him, then I'll come back and free you," I promise. "I won't leave you behind."

"No, no, no!" the man yells. His voice would almost be musical if it wasn't laced with fear. He surges forward, clutching the bars, his face a breath away from mine. He stares into my eyes so intensely; I nearly stumble back. But instead, I shift closer. "Listen to me," he says. "You have to get out now. There's not much time. If you're here when the sun sets—"

His golden eyes flicker with the fading light. He's beautiful, even though his expression is clouded in dread. "I'll figure out a way to get your lock undone," I say. "I just need to find my father."

"No! No!" he screams, shaking the bars.

I turn and run. Papa's here. He's here and I'm going to find him.

Empty cells line the walls, some completely crowded with thorns. "Papa!" I call.

"Rosalina? Rose!"

I rush through an orange sunbeam and skid to a stop in front of a cell. My father.

He's down on his knees and clutches the bars, resting his head against the cold steel. His hair sticks to his forehead with sweat and he's still wearing the same clothes he left in. Except they're soaking wet and covered in mud. His favorite necklace, the one Mom gave him, dangles around his chest. The moonstone rose shimmers in the dim light.

My hands clutch his through the bars. "Papa! Are you alright?"

"Rosalina," he whispers, his voice hoarse. "How did you find me?"

I give a sad smile. "I'll always find you."

"It's real, Rose," he croaks. "All this time. I finally found it."

With a hard yank, I test the door. Locked. "I know, Papa. We can talk about that later. I've got to break you out of here."

"No!" He stands and grabs my arm. "You must leave. Now. Save yourself!"

"Not until you're free," I demand.

"You don't understand. They're monsters, Rose! Beasts!"

Suddenly, the sunlight is ensconced with shadow. My father looks up, up, up, face falling into a mask of horror.

Time stops. There's something behind me. Something terrible and evil. And if I turn around, I'll shatter, the numbness overtaking my body.

A crackle sounds and ice creeps along the floor. It's beautiful, a glimmering white-blue with delicate fractals throughout. It creeps up the bars of the cage and Papa lets go, scrambling back.

Sucking in a breath, I turn around. But there are only shadows. "Who's there?" I call, willing my voice not to break.

Movement shudders in the corner and I turn to face it. Two ice-blue eyes stare back at me from the murk, bright as if lit with blue fire. "I am the master of this castle. You are a trespasser." The voice is deep and gravelly, like the cracking of a glacier into the sea.

Sickening bursts of adrenaline surge up my body, but I straighten my back. "Please, free my father and I will take him far away from here. We won't ever return."

The shadow moves so quickly, I have to spin on my heel to keep him in sight. The one thing I can make out are those ice-fire eyes. "Your father is a thief. He stole from my castle and now he must pay the price. He is my prisoner and shall remain so for all eternity."

"My father is no thief!" I cry. He's a lot of things, but he would never steal.

Papa stands and slams his hands against the bars. "It was only a rose!"

The master of the castle lets out a growl. "Only a rose? You are a robber and a felon. Now you will remain as my prisoner. You wanted to stay with the fae? Then stay you shall, in this dungeon, until your brief life drains away."

Tears spring to my eyes as I stare at my father. So many years I've held resentment for him. Every school achievement he missed because he was researching, all the debt he amassed with his travels, the shame I felt, being daughter to the village weirdo. But he's my dad. And that rose he stole ... That was for me, I know it. For my little library that Lucas ran over.

"Oh, Papa." I grab his hands through the bars and close my eyes.

There's no choice to be made except this one. My whole life, I've sacrificed for him. What's one more? I turn back to the shadows and meet the ice-fire gaze. "I'm the one who asked for the rose. Let me serve the sentence in his stead."

"No, Rosalina!" Papa cries.

The eyes blink and the master seems to still. "You don't know what you're asking for, human."

I lift my chin. "I do. Take me as your prisoner."

Papa screams, "He's a monster, Rose. A monster! Run while you can!"

But I can't hear him. Because the eyes slowly blink, and then the master of the castle steps into the beam of sunlight.

He's taller than any man I've ever seen. His long white hair falls over his shoulders, part of it pulled back to reveal dark brows and those terrifying eyes, like clear pools of moonlight. He wears a black jerkin that clings to his broad shoulders and huge arms. He's beautiful in a sharp and deadly way, like an icicle hanging above your head, about to break.

Like the imprisoned man in the cell, his ears are pointed. He is fae. And I'm in danger.

The fae man steps forward, forcing me to look up at him. I suck in a breath, all thoughts vanishing from my mind.

He tilts his head slightly as if taking me in, his eyes unblinking. Time seems to take a deep inhale.

Finally, he says in that low, gravelly voice, "I am Keldarion, master of this castle and all who inhabit it. If you make the choice to be our prisoner, that means I am now your master. What say you, little human?"

I'm trapped in his gaze. A bursting feeling erupts inside my chest and the words come out in a single breath, "Yes. I choose to stay."

He turns and yanks on the padlock with his bare hand. It rips off in an icy flash.

"No, Rosalina, no!" Papa screams.

The fae heaves Papa up by the scruff of his shirt and throws him out of the cell. I reach for him, but Keldarion grabs me by the back of my shirt. In a single instant, he rips open the door of another cell and tosses me in. The lock clicks.

Father rushes for me but Keldarion blocks him. "I will see to it your father is returned to the human realm unharmed," the master growls. "That is more mercy than he deserves."

"Wait!" I scream, clutching the bars. "Papa!"

"Rose!"

But the master of the castle drags my father through the dungeon and out of sight.

And I am left in the dying light, alone.

9

ROSALINA

The night passes in a fitful half-sleep. I curl myself into a ball in the corner of the cell and will myself not to cry.

None of this should be possible. The realm of the fae can't actually exist. Had all Papa's theories been grounded in reality? What had my mother told him before she left? Something shimmers inside me. All this time, I'd never once asked him why he was so certain Mom had been taken by faeries. Now I wish I had one more moment to speak with him.

Maybe this is all some nightmare I'll wake up from. But every time I open my eyes after squeezing them shut and desperately hoping I'll wake up in my own bed, I'm met with my cold cell. And I can barely see even that, the night being so dark.

With no light, it makes the noises even more horrifying. Somewhere nearby, a creature howls over and over again. I clutch my ears so tight, trying to block out the horrific sound. It isn't like a normal dog's howl, but like a tortured wolf, a being torn between life and death. I am too terrified to even move.

Sometime during the night, I fall asleep and awaken to soft light flitting through the slit of a window in my cell. My body is so sore from sleeping on the hard ground, and I'm covered in goosebumps. I stand up and look out the window.

Wow. I can see for miles up here. And these purple-black thorns ... They cover everything as far as I can see. They intertwine with a rushing river and twist into the dark forest beyond. And above the forest, tucked into the mountain, the brambles seem to be covered in something red.

Roses?

I came from my realm through a rosebush. Could that be my way home?

That mysterious goblin-killer sure carried me a long way ...

My vision swims when I look down. I must be five stories up, at least. Down below, there's the bridge that leads out to the briars. After that, it would be about navigating the thin narrow path to the rosebush.

Did the master of the castle keep his word and return my father safely? There was something hauntingly sorrowful in his gaze, a darkness unlike anything a human could possess. I can only hope that the word of the fae is true and that Keldarion holds up his end of the deal.

It was one of Papa's many rules which he would often mutter: never make a bargain with the fae. But what I'd said to the master wasn't a bargain, but a necessity to keep my father alive.

If Papa is home, I have to make it to him. Whatever vow I made to Keldarion doesn't matter. I will not spend the rest of my life in a cold cell with only a bucket to shit in.

I have to escape.

There's no sense of time in my cell, but I assume several hours pass as I fiddle uselessly with the padlock. I'm pretty good with locks—the one benefit of having a paranoid father who changed the house locks every month and always forgot to give me a key—but this is totally beyond me and my two hair pins. My arms ache from reaching around the cell and pressing my entire body into the bars to get the best angle. I haven't seen or heard any signs of life since waking up. Maybe Keldarion totally forgot he put me in here, and I'll starve to death.

With a growl of frustration, I fling myself back from the bars and stagger to the window. It's not fair. The bridge is right below me and thick, sturdy brambles claw up the side of the tree-castle. If I could crawl out this window, I bet I could climb down, sprint across the bridge, and lose myself in the briar. I'd rather take my chances with the goblins than the monster that calls himself master. I was calling for Papa before. If I could sneak through quietly in the daylight, I may go undetected.

But my window is barely wide enough to fit an arm through. I clutch the sill with my hands and hang my head. Tears creep down my face. How stupid I am to even entertain the idea that I could escape from a fae prison. I'm going to be stuck here until I wither up and die. If this damned window was a little bigger—

"W-what?" I leap back. The border of the window glows a shimmering rose gold. And then the stone shifts, the bricks rearranging upon each other until the window ...

It's wider.

Big enough for me to fit through.

"What the fuck happened?" I turn on my heel, half-expecting to see some fae wizard outside my cell. But there's nothing. Just me, bathed in the brilliant sunlight.

I take a tentative step toward the window. Wind rushes up, blowing my dark hair away from my face. Yep, I can definitely fit through.

Climbing down five stories of bramble bushes isn't an insane idea, is it? I look back to the hallway outside my cell. Further back in the dungeon, the man with the huge iron collar is probably still sitting there, helpless. I wish I could free him, but I can't do anything stuck in my cell. Maybe when I get home, I can think of a way to rescue him.

"Thanks, Castle," I whisper and push myself onto the ledge of the window.

Okay, now that I'm up here, I'm not sure I love this idea. One wrong move and I'll be impaled by a thousand thorns. I stretch my foot out to test one of the thick brambles clinging to the wall of the castle. It seems sturdy enough, but it hasn't had to deal with all of this woman before.

Orca Cove is waiting for me. All my hopes and dreams. My library, Papa … Lucas.

A painful breath surges through my throat. I can't do this. I can't do this. I can't do this.

Suddenly, one bramble extends and hovers right below me. A footrest.

"Great. A sentient thorn." I sigh. "I must not fear."

With the *Dune* mantra playing in my head, I turn around so my knees are on the window and I'm facing into my cell. I brace my hands on either side and lower my foot onto the bramble.

It holds. Okay. My whole body shaking, I lower my other foot onto the bramble. I haven't plummeted to my death Mufasa-style yet, so that's something. Next step: hand grips. I reach over with my right hand and find a sturdy branch, careful to steer clear of the huge thorns. Then I maneuver my body away from the window and grasp tightly to brambles.

Suddenly, the window emits a shimmering glow and shrinks again. Alright, guess I'm all in now.

Look at me. The girl who barely passed gym class scaling the side of a castle like I'm motherfucking Robin Hood. Though I'm sure Robin Hood never had to worry about his scarf getting tangled on outrageously huge thorns or his thick thighs shaking with each step.

Hand, foot. Hand, foot. Hand, foot. Each movement is agonizingly slow as I carefully descend the makeshift ladder. I don't dare look at how close I am to the bridge. All I can concentrate on is one movement at a time. A huge gust of wind blows, and I scream, the brambles pulling away from the castle in a deadly crescendo. I hold on, slamming against the strange mix of stone and bark.

"I can do this," I strangle out and continue descending.

Hand, foot. Hand, foot. Hand, foot. Hand, foo—

"Aah!" I scream as a bramble breaks beneath my weight. I lose grip and fall, my body tearing against the thorns as I slide down, down, down.

I smack hard against stone. Blinking in disbelief, I take in a shaky breath, realizing I've landed on the bridge. It was right below me.

"I'm alive!" I give a maniacal laugh. The window is barely in sight above me. Damn, I climbed far. Take that, Ms. Kimmer, and your "lack of participation in gym" comment on my report card.

I spin around and face the briar. No sign of Keldarion. This is my chance.

Freedom.

My hair and scarf fly behind me as I sprint forward. I run faster than I ever have in my life, careening toward the bramble-covered statues. I'm scraped and bruised from the fall, muscles tight and sore, but I'm alive and I'm free, I'm free, I'm free—

Suddenly, something steps out from behind the statue and slams into me.

IO

ROSALINA

"Oof!" I fall onto my ass, feeling like I collided with a boulder. Before I can register anything, a presence towers over me. My throat constricts, and I'm too terrified to even scream.

The being blocks out the sunlight, covering me in shadow. A man… At least, I think so. I can't really tell because he's dressed in metal armor from his boots to the shimmering gunmetal gray helmet. His helmet is square, intricately etched with petals and vines. A T-shaped visor made of dark glass is the only indication he's able to see out of the thing. The rest of the armor is engraved with delicate scroll-work and elegantly curved floral designs that flow seamlessly across the surface. Each piece sits snugly against the others, as though molded to fit him perfectly.

The knight is so tall, I have to lift my chin to keep sight of him. He steps toward me again, like a cat preparing to devour a mouse. A long black cape drips behind him like a shadow.

"W-who are you?" I manage.

The knight doesn't respond. I take a deep breath. Is it Keldarion? No, the master of the castle was wider in the shoulders. Maybe he's a visitor and doesn't know I'm a prisoner …

I roll over onto all fours and push myself up. "I was just leaving—"

The knight lunges for me. His hand, covered in shiny iron gauntlets, wraps around my throat and slams me into the bridge's stone barricade. Brambles crack behind me.

I gasp for air, but his grip is so tight, I can barely suck in a breath. The knight lifts me until my feet dangle helplessly. I scratch at his hand but it's no use.

"Who are you?" he asks. "What are you doing here?"

His voice shudders through me, and chills ripple up my spine. It's hauntingly calm and smooth despite the reverberation of his helmet.

"Are you a spy for the Prince of Thorns? Another one of his gifts?" His grip tightens, and he slams me harder against the barrier. "Answer me."

I grab hold of his fingers around my neck, trying to pry them away. The edges of my vision go black. With every ounce of strength I have left, I fling out my foot and kick him straight in the gut.

Fucking hell! My foot dings off him like I kicked sheet metal. I think I broke a toe. But it must have taken him by surprise because he drops me, and I collapse to the ground, clutching my neck and coughing.

In a burst of I-just-about-died rage, I glower up at him. "How the fuck am I supposed to answer you when you're choking me out, you overgrown tin can?"

I'm not sure where this courage is coming from. Maybe it's because I almost died. Maybe it's because I've got nothing to lose. Or maybe it's because I'm just so damn sick of being at the whims of everyone else.

He's so still, he looks like a suit of armor standing sentinel in a hallway—a jazzed-up, flowery suit of armor, that is. But I'm not going to give him the opportunity to manhandle me again. I jump up, ready to make a break for the brambles—

He snatches my wrists and holds my hands uselessly before me.

"Let me go!" I scream, desperately trying to tear free of him, spitting and snarling like a wild cat. But it only makes him grip me harder.

Goddammit, he's so fucking still and he's not saying anything. I need to try a different tactic. Taking a huge breath to calm my panting, I stop fighting against his hold and stare into his eyes. Or where I think his eyes are, anyway.

"Look, I'm not supposed to be here. I don't know any Prince of Thorns, or whatever. I'm a human. See my ears? I'm just trying to go home. Let me go. Please."

The knight doesn't reply. It's almost hypnotic, staring into the dark spaces where his eyes might be. My breath catches in my throat. Who is this being? Even though I can't see his face, it feels like he's assessing me, staring *into* me.

"Say something, won't you?" I growl.

"What... is your name?" he says, his strange echoey voice like velvet.

"Rosalina."

"Rosalina," he repeats, and his grip loosens on my wrists.

Suddenly, footsteps pitter-patter on the bridge, and I whip my head around to see a girl running toward us. Like Keldarion and the man in the dungeon, she has pointed ears. Her skin is so pale its nearly translucent, and her short white hair flows behind her. "My Prince! My Prince!"

My Prince? The tin can who tried to choke me out is a *prince*?

The prince turns to the girl and inclines his head. "What is it, Astrid?"

The girl doubles over, panting, her white dress flapping in the breeze. "That human woman! She's not supposed to be out here."

"What?" The prince drops my wrists and turns to fully face her. "What is the meaning of this?"

"She's Keldarion's prisoner," the white-haired girl says. "And she's escaping!"

As soon as Prince Tin Man let me go, I bolted for the bushes. If I make it over the bridge, I can lose them—

"Arghh!" Another sensation tightens around my neck, and I fall backward, landing on the hard stone. The knight has my ripped scarf tight in his grip.

"What are you doing?" I scream as he drops the scarf then yanks me to my feet by my elbows.

"You're Keldarion's prisoner," he says slowly.

"I didn't do anything!" I cry.

The white-haired girl hops beside us. "She found her way through the Briar to the castle and made it all the way up to the dungeon to find her father. She traded places with him by choice."

The armored prince gives a deep sigh. "I'm gone for three days and Keldarion finds a new way to torment me."

He nudges me between my shoulder back toward the castle. Begrudgingly, I start walking. The white-haired girl—Astrid—pulls the doors open and I'm hauled back into the castle.

"Don't bother taking me back to the dungeon. I'll find another way to escape," I say.

The prince doesn't respond. Instead of ascending to the dungeon, we walk up a grand staircase and down a long hallway with walls the color of evergreens and intricate golden designs of flowers and leaves.

"He had her in the dungeon?" He looks at Astrid, and this time, his smooth voice is gone, replaced with a raspy growl.

"Yes, Prince Ezryn," Astrid says, rushing to keep up.

We stop before a door that resembles a tree trunk laced with silver. Prince Ezryn yanks it open, then gestures inside. Slowly, I step inside the room.

The prince turns away, his long black cape snapping. "If Keldarion wants her here, he needs to take responsibility for her. Astrid, you're his servant, so that makes her your charge. Ensure she's fed and watered. And have the others clean this place up. We're not so far gone as to throw a little girl in the dungeon."

"Little girl?" I snarl and storm toward him. "Hey, get back here—"

But he slams the door behind him and is gone.

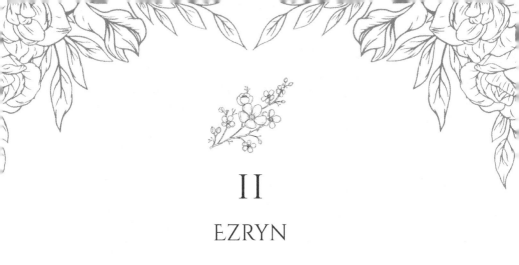

II

EZRYN

I lean against the door frame, ignoring the frost that's slowly creeping over my armor.

Keldarion paces before me, gaze down, a familiar snarl on his face. He hasn't noticed me yet and I'll give him a few more moments before I announce myself. I don't find myself often in the Winter Wing and I need to have a look.

Was it always like this or has it gotten worse? When's the last time I was here? I peer out from the shaded black visor in my helmet. Thorns crystalized in frost scar each surface. The walls shine with ice fractals and the floors are treacherous with black ice. His sword is discarded beneath his bed.

No, it's definitely gotten worse.

I clear my throat, and Kel whips around to face me, his eyes shining like a wounded animal. As soon as he registers me, his body relaxes, and he sighs. "Oh. You're back."

"Arrived an hour ago," I say. "Want to tell me what's going on?"

Kel snorts and continues his pacing. "I don't know what you're talking about."

Dusting the frost off my shoulders, I step into the room. "We're keeping human prisoners now?"

Kel leans against the windowsill, staring out at the Briar. "There was a trespassing thief from the human realm. Would you have preferred it if I killed him?"

I run a finger along the thick layer of snow that's settled over his blankets and pillows. The cold cuts through even my armor. Spring and Winter have a long history and I am no stranger to the clinging remains of a frost, but this cold is unlike any I've ever felt outside of the Winter Realm. "And the girl?"

"The servants talk too much," Kel grumbles.

So, he was going to be a cagey asshole. "We're in the business of imprisoning innocent human girls, then?"

Kel whips around and snarls at me, "If you want a say in how my castle is run, maybe you should actually stay inside it."

I'm perfectly still, not allowing an inch of movement to give away that his words have any effect on me. Times like this, I'm grateful for the helmet. I should have known Keldarion was monitoring my comings and goings.

I take a long, silent breath to steady my emotions and pace away from him. "All these years, not a single soul has been allowed to dwell inside the castle save us, the servants, and Quellos. You've sent away all of Caspian's annoyances. Now, you're willingly keeping a prisoner?"

Kel slams his hands down on the table, sending up a dusting of snow, then sinks his head into his hands. "Her father stole from me. She found him and offered to trade her freedom for his. Who am I to deny her that right?"

I stare at him. I know he feels it even though he can't see my eyes because he sighs, "What is it, Ez?"

What is it? Keldarion has never been one for keeping personal prisoners, not even war criminals. And he certainly has no interest in humans. He's hiding something. A part of me wants to grab him by his shoulders and shake him.

But no one in the fucking four realms would dare try that.

The question turns over in my mind. Why now? Why does he have any interest in this human after having interest in nothing at all?

I think back to earlier when I was coming home and saw the girl hanging precariously off the bramble bushes, climbing down from the dungeon tower.

When she was running toward the Briar like the snakes of Below were on her heels, I swore she was some sort of servant of Sira or Caspian. I was ready to take the life from her right there.

Tin can. That's what she'd called me. It was so ridiculous, I almost could have laughed. Almost.

She'd stared me down with such a fire, I had no idea how to read it. Fear, anger. Something else.

It was a good thing Astrid showed up. I don't know what I would have done. Probably let her go.

But even I dare not disobey the master of Castletree.

Keldarion stares at me with that familiar intensity. He wants an answer to his question.

Maybe I'm a masochist. Maybe I want Kel to feel anything at all, even if it's hatred for me. But I ask, "You can't possibly think the human woman is your—"

Kel flies across the room in a single instant, slamming me into the wall, and holding his forearm against my neck. "Don't say that word to me," he roars. His eyes flash with the power within.

It takes everything in me not to shudder into submission. But I force my muscles to stay still, take a slow breath, and calm my heart. We stay locked together for a moment, two wills facing each other.

Finally, he drops his arm and turns his back to me. "Leave me, Ez."

I turn to the door. "I gave her a room and told Astrid to attend her. We're not beasts."

At least, not yet.

12

ROSALINA

O f all the things I thought might happen when escaping, getting choked out by a giant masked knight was not on my list of possibilities. I rub my neck, flashes of how easily he lifted me burning in my mind. Then he'd dragged me like I was nothing but a sack of flour all the way here.

The masked knight. Prince Ezryn.

I inhale and give myself a moment to take in my surroundings. I'm in a giant room, and … it's beautiful. A mesh of natural bark and stunning architecture. There is a literal *tree* growing out of one wall, blooming with pink cherry blossoms that flutter down and scatter across the carpet.

It's obvious they haven't used this place in a long time. White dusty sheets drape over the furniture, except the bed, which has four posts of gilded gold. A curtain of purple willow flowers drapes around it. The walls are pale pink marble, veined with white and rose gold.

It would all be perfectly delightful if not for the massive thorns breaking out of the wall and cracking up through the floor. The same as the ones outside and in the dungeon. These thorns cover every inch of the castle.

"Do you like it?"

I jump as I see a girl hovering by the door. The masked prince had called her Astrid. She's a slight thing, with short white hair and stunning red eyes. Her pale skin is near translucent, and she wears an ivory dress with a blue apron. Astrid doesn't look much older than me, though that probably doesn't mean much with her pointed ears. If Papa's ramblings had any merit, fae are immortal. She could be twenty or two thousand.

"Oh," she continues, "I'm Astrid, by the way."

"I'm Rosalina." I plop down on the bed and a plume of dust erupts around me. "If that masked demon wants a thank you for moving me from the dungeon to a room, he's not going to get it. A beautiful prison is still a prison."

Astrid's expression falters and a stab of guilt runs through me. Maybe she's as trapped as I am. Who would want to stay in a place that imprisons harmless old men, is ruled by the rudest man in all of existence, and guarded by a terrifying masked prince?

I take a deep breath and pinch the bridge of my nose. "Sorry. I've been through a lot. A day ago, I didn't believe the fae existed."

Papa had been right all this time. Was Mom somewhere in this world? Could she have survived? I suppress a shudder as I think of the ashen goblins.

"You didn't know about us? Really?" Astrid hops toward me. "How did you get here then? Usually, only believers can enter the Enchanted Vale."

"The Enchanted Vale," I whisper. "Is that where we are?"

"Precisely, we're in Castletree." Astrid tugs me toward the window. Outside lie the castle grounds, and beyond that the briars.

"Doesn't seem very enchanted," I mumble.

Astrid's lip wobbles. "Our castle and the land are sick. And it's spreading to the four realms."

"The four realms?"

"Spring, Summer, Autumn, and Winter," Astrid says. "You can't see the realms from here, but we can enter them from the castle."

Before I can ask her what she means, she gestures outside to the briars. "But it's dangerous in this land. I know you don't want to be here, but I wouldn't try to run out there again. It's amazing both you and your father made it here alive."

An image flashes in my mind: the dark-haired man. Had he been real or only my imagination after I hit my head?

"The briars are crawling with goblins and their hounds."

"What do those monsters even want?"

Astrid's nose wiggles, and she bites her bottom lip. "To hunt and kill and cause chaos. They answer only to the Below. Nothing but rabid beasts of the Prince of Thorns. He controls them."

"The Prince of Thorns." I study the dark purple brambles crawling their way up the walls and sprouting up from cracks in the floor.

"These are his work as well," Astrid says.

"Who is he? Another fae?"

Astrid nods. "The most wicked and vile fae of all. He lives in a dark and traitorous realm known as the Below. He is the great betrayer. Someone I pray you never meet."

"The two fae I met here aren't much better. One locked up my father, and the other choked me. Maybe all fae men are assholes." I tug my sleeve down. Or maybe all men are.

"I know it may seem that way, but for those living at Castletree ... There's a great sadness. And the princes are not so bad once you get to know them."

I want to tell her that's called Stockholm Syndrome, but she looks so earnest I attempt to soften my tone. She's the one person here who's shown any kindness toward me. Actually, she's the first person in a long time who's shown me any kindness. I sit down on the bed and give a deep sigh. "So, you work here?"

"Yes, as part of the Winter staff. I'm a lady-in-waiting, though there's been nothing to do lately. I'm sorry I'm jumpy. But how can I contain my excitement? You're here." She sits down next to me and touches my hair. "You certainly are beautiful. I haven't met a human before."

My cheeks burn. "Can you tell me more about this place? What do you mean you're a part of the Winter staff? Who was the blue-eyed fae that locked up my father? And is that terrifying knight a legit prince? Why can't you just weed whack these thorns?"

Astrid's lip trembles. Okay, I guess I came on strong with the questions.

The door swings open and a fae woman bursts in rolling a cart. She appears middle-aged, with blond hair pulled in a knot on top of her head, full lips, and a portly body. Her ears taper into a distinctive point.

She's wearing a simple white dress, but her apron is light pink. Before I can study her further, the smell from the cart hits me, and I let out an embarrassing moan.

"I thought our new guest might be hungry, although I've heard she's already met some of the castle's yummiest offerings," the woman says, giving me a long-lashed wink. "The name's Marigold. I serve the Spring Realm, but I ensure everyone around here is fed and watered. And that includes our new guest."

I want to retort I'm more a prisoner than a guest, but she's brought me food, so I bite my tongue. Plus, my mouth waters from the smell of whatever is covered on her cart.

Marigold notices my gaze, then lifts the lid. A variety of colors fill the tray, from the golden-brown waffles to the deep red of fried tomatoes. The fluffy pancakes glisten with syrup, and slices of juicy oranges and red strawberries shine like jewels.

Marigold wheels the tray in front of me, and I tear into a pancake.

Maybe a smart person would question if the food was poisoned, but I'm pretty sure these fae could kill me if they wanted to. And as soon as the spongy sweetness melts on my tongue, I forget all about that and lose myself to the meal. How long has it been since I last ate? Probably not *that* long but running from goblins and getting kidnapped by fae really builds up an appetite.

After sufficiently devouring the pastries and fruit, I look up to see Astrid and Marigold watching me. I wipe the crumbs from my mouth and awkwardly mumble, "Uh, sorry. I should have asked if you two wanted anything to eat."

"Don't be silly," Marigold says, picking up a teapot from the side of the tray and pouring me a steaming cup. "After all you've been through, you deserve something nice. It was very kind, what you did for your father. All of us staff are talking about it."

At the mention of my father, my hand stills over my fourth pastry. I dump sugar and a nutty-smelling milk into the teacup to delay replying. *Did he make it home?*

"The fae I made a deal with ..." I start, trusting she knows who I'm talking about. "Do you think he actually sent my father home?"

"Of course," Marigold says. "When the master promises something, he follows through with his whole heart. Trustworthy and loyal, that one is. A little on the stern side, though."

I don't understand. Both of them speak so highly of this so-called Master. The white-haired fae with the dark voice and those piercing blue eyes ...

Keldarion.

"Unlike another fae we know," Astrid huffs. "Ca—"

Marigold shoots her a grim look. "Don't speak such a name here. The master forbade it, remember?"

"I don't know how we could forget him. Not with all of this." Astrid gestures to one of the many thorns tearing through the walls. "Or with his constant *presents* to the master."

"I don't know how anyone could forget him once they get a look." Marigold fans herself with a napkin. "Why do the evil ones always have to be so handsome?"

I guess they're talking about the Prince of Thorns. Astrid said he creates the briars, controls the goblins, and is from a place called the Below.

"How's the breakfast?" Astrid blinks her large eyes at me, obviously eager for a change of subject.

"The best food I've eaten in a long time." It's the truth. Fae food sure beats the stale cold Pop-Tarts I usually have as I rush to work. I take a sip of the tea, the taste floral and malty. It's warm and comforting as it slides down my throat. "So, you all live and work here?"

"Yes, we're permanent residents. We wouldn't be welcomed back in our home realms," Astrid says.

"What do you mean?"

Marigold smooths down the folds of her apron. "There is a deep enchantment over this castle, and it's not our place to speak about it. But since this is your home now, you should know some things."

Astrid hops closer, excitement gleaming in her red eyes. "There are four wings in Castletree, each of them representing one of the fae realms: Winter, Spring, Summer, and Autumn. It's customary that the High Prince of each realm resides in the castle with a host of personally selected staff. I'm from the Winter Realm, and Marigold—"

"Is from Spring." The fae woman smirks.

"And we're in the Spring Wing now," I guess, taking in the flowers that drape down the walls.

"Yes," Astrid says, "and there's also the High Tower—"

"And you already met the prince of my realm," Marigold interrupts. I can't help but think it was an intentional disruption.

This castle holds secrets within secrets.

"The Spring Prince?" I snort. "You mean the masked man in the armor? Yeah, I met him. He wrapped his hand around my throat and choked me out."

Marigold sits beside me on the bed, eyes wide. "How hard?"

My eyes widen. "W-what?"

She gives a devious leer. "Well, if any of the princes wanted to wrap their large hands around my throat—"

"Marigold!" Astrid hits her with the side of her apron. "You're so bad."

"What, a woman can fantasize, can't she? Not much else for us to do here."

My face flushes. I think we both have different feelings towards being choked out. Though now I can't stop thinking about how his hand was big enough to wrap around my throat and the strength he possessed to lift me.

I give myself a well-deserved slap on the forehead. What the hell is wrong with me? I turn back to Astrid and Marigold.

"So, the princes and the staff ... Do they ever, uh ..." I trail off, not sure how to word it.

"No!" Astrid says quickly. "They're all very respectful of us."

"Unfortunately." Marigold sighs, then gives a little sniff. "Oh, I almost forgot. I brought you some fresh clothes."

I give a sniff as well. Going through those briars and spending the night in a prison cell has not done me any favors. Marigold ducks down beneath the cart.

She hands me a stack of clothes and I place them on my lap. I can't help but notice how soft the fabric is, and how dirty my hands are on top of it. In fact, I think there's still some dried blood on me. "Thank you."

"You need to stop smelling like a goat who ran through manure." Marigold turns to Astrid. "Take the girl down to Summer and get her washed. I'll have the rest of the staff dust and prep this room."

"You don't have to go to so much trouble," I say. "This is already ten times better than the dungeon."

She waves her hand. "Nonsense. We haven't had a guest in twenty-five years, and that one didn't turn out well at all. I haven't gotten to boss anyone around in ages."

Before I can ask about the unfortunate guest from twenty-five years ago, Astrid loops her arm through mine. "Lady Rosalina, you are going to adore the hot springs. I know it."

Hot springs in a castle? I guess I am a *little* intrigued. Plus, if I'm going to be here until I can figure out a way to get past the goblins, then learning the layout of the castle is a good idea.

I smile back at Astrid. "Lead the way."

13

ROSALINA

"We're entering the Summer Wing," Astrid says.

But I didn't need her to tell me. A warm breeze drifts through my hair, and the air feels thicker. Flowers line the halls of the Spring Wing, with patches of grass and moss sprouting from the floor. Here, sand seeps out between the stone tiles, shifting beneath my boots. The walls gradually change to a light sandy clay, set with different colored shells. Blue nets and glass bobbles hang from the ceiling, and the tang of salt and sunshine wafts into my nose.

A castle with the magic of all four fae realms … I didn't know there was one fae realm yesterday, never mind four of them. I have so many questions about this place.

I can't help touching a wind chime hanging by a window, bark and seashells strung on twine. They ring delicately against the wood, a cheery sound that tingles down my spine. *It's beautiful.*

"Almost there." Astrid wipes a hand across her brow and sweat drips down her face.

"Are you alright?"

"Oh, yes, fine," she grumbles. "I just don't know why *he* has to keep it so bloody hot. But I'm from Winter, so what do I know?"

I give her a weak smile as she pushes on a heavy wooden door that leads to a narrow passage. Water drips from gray stone walls, and it's even hotter than in the hall. Muggy, even. It feels like we're going downward, perhaps beneath the castle itself. After about five minutes, the passage opens into an enormous cavern.

The floor shifts into soft white sand that leads to a turquoise pool. It's a freaking enchanted grotto. Rock walls create a maze of bubbling pools, and beyond the misty haze, I spot a waterfall.

"Wow," I gasp, pretty sure my jaw is on the floor. "How is this possible?"

"Castletree," Astrid says. "The Fae Queen built it. It has the magic of all the fae realms. Within this hallowed castle, she crafted the most beautiful places from each region."

"The Fae Queen," I whisper. "Should I be worried about running into her too?"

"Oh no," Astrid says. "The Fae Queen hasn't been seen in the Enchanted Vale for five hundred years."

"How can you rule a land when you haven't been around for five centuries?"

"Well, she left a Sworn Protector of the Realms and—" Astrid slams her forehead. "I forgot your clean clothes. You get started, and I'll run up and get them."

"Get started?"

"Yes, you can bathe. Wait." She turns to the expanse of the pool and calls out, "Hello! Is anyone there?" Her high-pitched voice echoes off the far rock cavern. "Okay, we're all clear. You can leave your clothes over there and I'll wash them."

Her nose wrinkles and I'm pretty sure she'd rather burn them than wash them. Not my fault I was chased by goblins. But I follow her gaze to shelves built into the stone wall. They're full of fluffy white towels, jars of different colored gels, and bars of soap.

I can't help but let out a girlish squeal. I do want to get this goblin blood off my body.

"Use anything you like, and I'll be back soon with your fresh clothes."

"Are you sure?" I ask. "I can run back with you."

"No, no. Please. Get clean. I insist."

A part of me thinks she's a little grateful she won't have to melt on this beach while she waits for me to bathe.

Astrid hesitates. "You're not going to try to run again or anything, right?"

"I'm just going to wash. Promise." I mean it. No way I'm chancing getting apprehended by the Tin Man on steroids again. And she was right about those goblins. When I make my next escape attempt—which I will—I'm going to be strategic about it.

Astrid gives me a grateful smile as she leaves, and I turn to inspect the stone shelf. There's a small basket, and I fill it with a bar of soap that smells like cherries and a few mysterious vials of goopy cream. Hopefully one of them is shampoo.

I look around a couple times before I strip off my clothes. Astrid promised I was alone. I peel off my ripped scarf and my once-white T-shirt, which is now a more gruesome brown tie-dye. My leggings are torn, and I never want to see these socks again.

I take my basket and pad across the soft sand into the water. It's fucking glorious. The water is velvety soft, and warmth engulfs me as I let out a long sigh. The basket floats in the water and I drag it along, wading deeper.

Sand gives way to smooth rock. Judging by the color of the water, there are probably some parts where my feet won't be able to touch the bottom at all.

I paddle my way to the waterfall in the back where I scrub every crevasse of my body with the cherry soap and dunk under the water. It leaves a salty taste on my lips. I massage the gel into my hair. It smells like a tropical cornucopia: pineapples, mangos, and coconuts.

Then I step under the waterfall, which seems to come from the ceiling itself, and let the water pound over me. When my scalp feels thoroughly rattled, I take the opportunity to paddle around the pool. I could stay here forever.

A splash sounds at the entrance of the hot springs. Astrid must have returned. A soft current of water shifts closer.

"Astrid?" I call out.

There's no reply, and a strange prickle travels down my spine.

"Astrid?"

"I can be Astrid if you want, love," a smooth, cocky male voice responds.

I let out a peep of alarm and push my basket in front of my chest as someone steps out from behind one of the rocks.

A man.

No, a fae.

A fae man is in the hot springs with me.

14

ROSALINA

Holy fuck, he's gorgeous.

He's so tall his entire torso is out of the water, and I can clearly see every inch of his muscular chest. He's totally ripped, and not in the way Lucas was, with his specialized muscles from hours at the gym. This fae's muscles are broad and toned, created from actually moving, and—if the small scars and nicks that line his body are any indication—from fighting.

This water is so freaking clear I could probably see lower if I wanted to. Maybe a small, very small, part of me is curious. But I am no Peeping Tom, so I force my eyes up. Only ogling his eight-pack abs and perfect pecs doesn't seem less creepy at the moment.

"Enjoying the view?" He grins, all white teeth and crooked smile. "I don't blame you."

Only my nose is above the waterline as I dunk in the pool. I need to get out of here. Except there are zero clothes waiting for me until Astrid returns, and even if there were, I can't leave these hot springs without giving him a complete eyeful. My only option is to wait him out.

Of course, he doesn't just have an amazing body. Golden blond hair grazes his shoulders, with small braids threading pieces away from his face. He's got dark brows, and it looks like his nose may have been broken a few times—which is strange because if he's fae, shouldn't he heal quickly? Or is that my imagination talking? His nose doesn't distract from how handsome he is, though. Like his crooked smile, everything about him is captivating to behold.

My core tightens and I flush as, with growing horror, I realize he's studying me the way I'm studying him. I clutch my basket close to my chest and back away, hoping the ripples in the water will stop him from getting too good a look at me, suddenly self-conscious of the soft swell of my stomach and my rubbing thighs. A memory of Lucas slapping my legs to see how they jiggled flashes in my mind.

"What are you doing here?" I ask, sticking my head out of the water enough to sputter the question.

"Bathing," the fae says, finally lowering that distracting muscular chest into the water. "And inspecting Kel's new pet."

Hot rage simmers inside me and I'm surprised the water doesn't boil. "I'm no one's pet."

He raises a dark brow. "We'll see about that."

I swallow and fight to gain control over myself. The need to be angry surges, but his eyes are like a drug. He smiles at me, and it seems so genuine. I stare back at him, breathing hard, waiting for something to happen. My body shivers and the muscles between my legs tighten. I want to touch him more than anything else, and yet I can't move.

Get control of yourself, girl. I wade further away. "Who are you?"

"Who am I?" Another smirk. Is everything a joke to him? "The name's Dayton."

"Dayton," I repeat. I say it so casually, not realizing how it would sound in my mouth. Like sunshine and fire.

He blinks at me. His eyes are blue. Not like Keldarion's, with his ice chip eyes. No, Dayton's are like a sea before a storm ...

Then I realize while I've been staring at his stupid eyes, he's moved closer to me, and I'm naked and he is most certainly naked as well.

I give another peep of fear and walk backwards until I hit a rock wall. Thankfully, that stops his advance.

"And I suppose you work here too?" I ask, if only to distract myself.

His brows shoot up and he laughs, a deep throaty sound that is so joyous it involuntarily brings out a smile of my own.

"Love," Dayton says, "you really don't know me at all. I would rather sift my cock through hot coals than *work*."

A playfulness claws its way out of me, and I smile back. "Well, you're going to have to stop being so lazy. Marigold says she's putting everyone to work now I'm here."

"Now that's unfair," he says. "You can't bring Marigold into this. If you've met her, then you know how positively terrifying she can be."

"You're teasing me."

"Only a little." He gives a white-toothed grin. "What's your name, love?"

"Rosalina." I paddle around carefully as I try to gauge this fae. His kindness seems different from Astrid's and Marigold's. I don't miss the flirtatious tone, and how his eyes haven't left me since he stepped into the pool.

Rationally, I know I should be afraid. I'm literally naked and ten feet away from a male who could overpower me in a second. But nothing in my gut is screaming fear. In fact, it's quite the opposite, like everything in me wants to move *closer* to him.

Maybe it's some fae trick, but if I'm ever to escape this enchanted castle, I need to be brave. I can't make it out of here on my own. I need information, and maybe even allies.

I push across the basket filled with bubble bath, shampoo, and other bottles. "If you're going to bathe, here." My cheeks flush as I quickly avert my eyes, hoping he can't tell how exposed and vulnerable I feel. I cross my arms defensively over my chest beneath the water, though he's probably too far away to see anything.

"Why, thank you." He takes out the bar of soap.

"So," I say, "what can you tell me of the master of this castle?"

"The master? Huh ..." Dayton looks to the rock ceiling as he slides the bar of soap over his body. This might have been a terrible idea because I've totally forgotten what question I've asked as the soap suds slide across his broad shoulders. "The icy prick? More power than brains. Someone you *really* don't want to piss off. But you already knew that, figuring you spent the first night in the dungeon."

"Jeez, word spreads fast around here."

"What can we say? You're the new shiny object that everyone wants to get a glimpse of."

The mysteries keep piling up, but it seems everyone who works in this castle doesn't get out much.

Dayton turns slightly; there's a scar down his spine. A giant one. Three jagged lines ripple down the perfect bronzed skin of his back.

"What happened—" The words are a breath on my lips before I can think better of it.

He quickly turns, flashing another smile as he slides the soap across his muscular chest, then his hand disappears beneath the water. "Can't forget the most important part." His gaze locks with mine as his arm moves up and down.

I'm pretty sure I'd be dripping if I wasn't already in this pool. I lower and blow bubbles in the water, thinking of the first night the master locked me in the dungeon. It wasn't Dayton and the other servants' fault, but I can't fool myself into thinking they're my friends.

Another memory flashes in my mind: the young fae man with the chain around his neck, his golden eyes, the way his hair fell across his brow. I lift my head out of the water a little to stare at the fae across from me. Mercifully, he's thrown the soap back into the basket, though I'm not sure what he's doing now is much better. His torso stretches, muscles elongating as he massages the shampoo gel into his long hair. Something catches my eye. A seashell necklace bobs over his chest, interlaced with pearls and a jagged piece of red sea glass in the middle. It's beautiful.

"Can I ask you something?"

"Anything, love."

"When I first came here, I saw a young man in the dungeon. I was wondering if you knew why he was there."

Dayton ducks under the water, washing the shampoo from his hair. When he rises, dark blond tendrils fall across his face. "A man in the dungeon? Hmm." The water cuts between us as he moves closer. This time I have nowhere to go.

"Yes. He didn't seem dangerous. What was he there for?"

"Well, I have a question for you," Dayton murmurs, and now he's so close I can see all the shades of blue in his eyes, the rippling turquoise and deep sapphire of an ocean. "Was he handsome?"

It's such a ridiculous question. A question that has nothing to do with anything. I should shove him away for asking it. But the face of the man in the dungeon appears before me as if in a waking dream. The depths of his golden eyes, the tremble of his full lips. I can't help but tell the truth. "Yes."

Dayton's brows shoot up, and he laughs again. This time, the sound trembles all the way to my core, and I clamp my legs shut.

The fae moves closer to me and the slick rocks press against my spine. He reaches out to grab a wet strand of my hair. "What do you want with him?"

"To free him," I say, then amend, "At least to a room, like me. It doesn't seem fair he's in the dungeon."

"Why?" Dayton is so close; his warm breath caresses my ear. "Do you want his gratitude? Hope he'll reward you?"

No, of course not. My answer is simple. We're both prisoners, and somehow, I can feel he's as undeserving of that chain as I am. But Dayton's words are a fire within me, and I can't help but be consumed by them. I feel my nipples pebble beneath my fingers, and I drop my hands to fists at my side to quell this ache inside my body.

Dayton's blue eyes burn down at me. His large, callused hand snatches my jaw and forces me to look up at him. "You know, the master isn't the only one to rule this castle. It's also governed by three other princes."

"Three other princes." My voice is nothing but a breath. The connection of his hand on my skin is a current of energy, and I need more of it. My body trembles, and I fight the urge to reach out and touch him.

"Indeed. I'm sure you can figure out who."

I blink, finding words like sifting through sand. Four wings, four realms. "A prince for each of the four seasons."

"Good girl." His thumb skims over my bottom lip. "You might have better luck begging one of them for mercy than our cold master. Do you know how to beg, Rosalina?"

All the breath in me comes out in a single gasp and I am nothing but molten rock, simmering in this water.

"My Prince!" A high, shocked voice echoes across the room. Astrid stands on the shoreline, a bundle of clothes in her arms.

Dayton drops his hand from my jaw.

With the loss of connection, my sanity comes back. How in the blazons had I lost it? And with the return of my mind, the words finally register.

My Prince.

My fucking Prince.

This hot spring fae is a freaking prince. I want to die. Here I've been trying to cajole information out of him like he was one of the servants. I suppose I should be thankful he didn't lock me back in the dungeon.

"Apologies, m'lord," Astrid stammers. "I didn't think you'd be here."

"It's alright, Astrid," Dayton says, making his way to the shore. "I wanted to meet our new guest."

With growing horror, I realize Dayton is getting out of the water. I should look away.

But I don't.

And holy fucking shit. His ass looks sculpted by the gods, and I get the glimpse of something very long and very erect between his legs before he wraps a white towel low on his hips.

"Rosie," he smirks, totally catching my creepy gaze, "why not try charming the Summer Prince for what you want? I've heard he's the most handsome. And best in bed."

Dayton's stupid, perfect laughter echoes in the chamber as he leaves.

15

ROSALINA

The setting sun drips soft pink and red light throughout my room.

Marigold has put the staff to work. Maybe she really is as scary as Dayton implied. When I returned from the hot springs, there were fresh flowers in painted vases, and they had removed the furniture coverings to reveal a white vanity and wardrobe. She'd taken no time at all filling it with beautiful gowns and dresses. The bed has fresh sheets with the faint smell of roses beneath the ever-present aroma of cherry blossoms.

Marigold proceeded to feed me an early dinner. It couldn't have been more than four o'clock, but I'm always happy to eat. The soup was warm and comforting, and I hadn't been able to keep from laughing with my mouth full as Astrid and Marigold drilled me for every detail on my encounter with Dayton.

Dayton, the Prince of Summer.

I'd been naked in the same water as a freaking fae prince. I think my cheeks are still red from it. Especially when Marigold asked me to describe his abs in great detail. She'd probably have self-combusted if I'd mentioned that perfect ass of his.

After I'd finished eating, Astrid and Marigold gathered my dishes but leave a bowl of dried fruit and nuts on the vanity in case I get hungry during the night. They opened the door to the ensuite privy and showed me how to work the latrine—thank goodness the fae have indoor plumbing. Then they bid me goodnight. "Remember, lovey," Marigold had tutted, "don't be leaving your room until sunrise. That's an order straight from the master."

Now they're gone, a surprising pang of loneliness washes over me. It's so weird. I don't get lonely. I'm perfectly content in my little home waiting for Papa. But this place, while beautiful, is different. And they didn't leave me a single thing to do. Tomorrow, I will have to ask if there are any books in the castle.

I grab my phone off the neatly folded remnants of my clothing. Of course, there's no service, and my battery is near dead. But I give myself one moment to look at a picture of Papa, then one of Lucas. Despite the fact he abandoned me, I hope he made it home safely. He'd been so close to the rosebush—he must have escaped. I flip through a couple more photos in my favorite album and linger on an old, scanned photo of Mom and Papa in front of the willow tree. Her long brown hair is curled, and she wears the moonstone rose locket around her neck, the one Papa never takes off. It's one of the few things we have left of her.

Suddenly, I wish he had something of mine as well.

After I give myself a moment of pity, I slam the phone into my bedside drawer, and am instantly overcome with boredom. The sun hasn't set yet, and I'm not tired. My body still feels worked up from my hot springs encounter.

Dayton didn't give me any information about the man in the dungeon. Why can't I get him out of my head? If I knew what he'd done, why they locked him up …

Maybe he's as eager to escape as I am. What if he knows the lands? Perhaps a way to get past the goblins? Something sparkles in my chest, an urgency driving me forward. *I need to find the man in the dungeon.*

I've already changed into the pajamas Marigold gave me, a soft nightdress with pink flowers embroidered at the bottom, so I grab a plain blue cloak from the wardrobe. Then I pull on my old boots and head to the door.

What's so wrong about leaving my room at night? I tug on the handle, and the door jiggles.

Locked.

Of course, it's locked. I take a sweep of the room, looking for anything to pick the lock with. There's a rustle of plants, and I turn to see a briar shifting, growing a little taller. One of its thorns grows long and pointed—pointed like a lock pick.

That's eerily convenient. But I've never been one to look a gift horse in the mouth, so I say a pleasant thank you to the creepy vine and pluck the thorn. The point slides into the latch and I hear the door click open instantly.

I nervously tuck the thorn into my hair and slowly step into the silent halls. *Where is everyone?* I have no plan, only a powerful urge in my gut to speak to this fae. It feels important.

The route Ezryn took as he dragged me by my scarf comes back to me, and I emerge into the main foyer. Down the stairs is the front door and that strange mirror.

This room is empty too. Does everyone turn in early?

From the entrance hall, I follow the same path up the staircase to the dungeon in the tower, carefully weaving around the thorns so as not to poke myself on them.

The damp air sliding over my wet hair sends a shiver down my spine. No torches have been lit, and I make my way by the dying red light of the sun that filters in through the open barred windows.

The circling stairs end, and I come to the cells.

My heart stutters. There he is.

But he's lying down, eyes closed. A surge of dread consumes me until I see the soft rise and fall of his chest. *Just asleep.*

He's still shirtless and wearing nothing but plain brown pants. "Hey," I whisper through the bars. He doesn't stir. There doesn't seem to be anyone else here, but this is where that big icy brute snuck up on me last time, so I don't want to speak too loudly.

Instead, I pull the long thorn from my ponytail and try it in the lock. Within a few moments of fiddling around, it clicks open. Without a sound, I lower it to the ground and push open the barred door.

I crouch beside the man. His hands are free, but the large metal collar is around his neck, attached by a chain to the stone wall.

Something feral sparks inside me, seeing him shackled like this. Immediately, I lift it off his neck, though I'm not sure what good it was doing. It was much too big for him, and he could have easily slipped out of it himself.

Gently, I shake his shoulder. "Hey, wake up."

Slowly, he lifts himself up, floppy strands of auburn hair falling across his brow and revealing the sharp point of his ears. Dayton had asked me if he was handsome, and while that is certainty true, there is something more. An enchanting sort of beauty.

"You," his voice rasps.

"I've come to rescue you," I tell him.

"Rescue me?" he asks sleepily. Then his face shifts into a mask of horror. He clasps wildly at his neck, then looks down at the collar on the floor. "What have you done?"

"I let you go." I gesture at the open cell door.

If taking the collar off had been the worst thing in the entire world, the open cell door is the end of all things.

"Oh no ..." He turns to the cell window as the last of the red dusk dips beyond the horizon, plunging us into complete darkness. His golden eyes pierce mine as he chokes out, "You need to run."

16

ROSALINA

I stare at the fae, trying to understand the fear in his golden eyes.

"Run?" I repeat.

"Run!" he cries, but the command turns into a raw scream, and he doubles over.

"Are you okay?" I reach for him.

His skin ripples, a strange yellow glow emulating around him, and his scream of agony turns into a deep rumble as fur sprouts where his skin once was. His form doubles, then triples in size, changing, mutating. A new creature heaves in a shuddering breath, steam crowding the chilly room as it stands.

A horrifying monster towers above me. It has some resemblance to a wolf, with the long snout, pointed ears, and four paws. But it's like something gruesome and monstrous has happened. From its body protrude black twigs and sharp branches. Rotten, mulchy leaves coat its red-brown fur, and the smell of burning wood steams from its breath.

It reminds me of the goblins and their hounds. Except it's giant, over six feet tall and twice as wide. Terror clenches a fist so tight around my heart I can't even scream.

Suddenly, the giant collar on the ground makes a lot more sense.

The monstrous wolf's gaze is entirely on me. Those golden eyes are the same as the fae man's. But no recognition flashes as he looks at me.

A deep snarl erupts from its maw, and it lunges. Some inch of self-preservation awakens, and I scramble out of the way, reaching for the cell door. My movement accidentally closes it, locking me in here with the monster. A terrified scream erupts out of me. The creature swipes, and pain blossoms on my calf as its massive claws drag across my leg.

Desperately, I try the cell door again, prying it open and slipping through. Pain radiates with every movement as streams of blood trail down my leg. *Holy fucking shit.* I hobble as fast as I can, making for the stairs.

Behind me, the monstrous wolf gives a vicious howl, then lunges through the cell door, its massive body tearing the iron rods from the hinges. I propel myself down the staircase as fast as I can, hoping the narrow space will slow the creature.

I scramble through the thorny branches, using my arms and body to plow a path. Looking back, I see the briars closing in around the monster. The thorns tear at its fur, but the beast is undaunted, and a flurry of broken branches litter the ground in bloodied bits of purple. Stone and bark crumble from the castle ceiling.

A scream tears from me and raw terror floods my body. *Help me. Someone help me.*

The briars snatch at my cloak, tearing and ripping. My hair tangles, ponytail pulling free, and my long hair falls in my eyes. I trip over the last of the thorns, tumbling into the main foyer of the castle. Blood pools beneath me from the wound on my leg.

A rumble sounds from the staircase, falling rock and cracking stone as the thorns are ripped away from the walls.

I try to scramble up, but my hand slips in my blood and I fall back down, smacking my jaw on the hard stone. *Get up, get up, get up.*

My throat feels raw and tears drip down my face as pain slices up my body. I work through the ache, muscle by muscle, until I stand. My ruined leg flares with agony as I force myself to continue hobbling through the entrance hall.

Strange eyes peer at me from the shadows. The eyes … of animals. A raccoon, a bird in the rafters, a rabbit—

My breath leaves me as I'm knocked face first onto the ground. *It caught me.* I scramble, desperately trying to cover my face with my arms. A giant paw digs into my shoulder, pinning me to the ground, and the other cuts across my arms.

A row of sharp teeth shines as it snarls. The smell of burning wood fills the air. It opens its maw wide.

The only thought in my mind is at least death by a monstrous wolf is a bit more awesome than falling off the bookstore stool. And it's certainly better than drowning. A cold chill creeps over me, and I wonder if getting eaten by a wolf will feel like drowning: icy until your whole body burns.

A different rumbling snarl fills the air.

The deafening howl of pain explodes in my ears as a new set of jaws clamp around the neck of the reddish-brown wolf. Another wolf is here, this one twice the size of the first. It slams its jaws shut and lifts the brown wolf away from me with terrifying force. The smaller beast sails through the air in a flurry of fur and blood, yelping until it crashes into the stone wall and lands with a sickening thud.

As the larger wolf advances, paralyzing fear clings to me. Shimmering shards of ice adorn its body and a mesmerizing blue glow embellishes its white fur in a swirling pattern.

The brown wolf heaves itself up from the ground, red blood dripping from the wound on its neck. Its eyes fixate on me, and it snarls. Saliva splatters on the floor.

The white wolf takes one step, then another, until it's covering me with its massive body. It crouches low enough I could touch the soft underbelly of white fur.

A faint hint of wet snow clings to the air, a chill growing in my lungs like the first breath of winter.

The white wolf opens its mouth and howls.

The sound reverberates down to my bones and shudders through the entire castle, quaking the stone. Even the briars shiver away.

If I thought my heart couldn't take anymore, I was wrong. Because two other massive shapes dash into the entrance hall.

Oh my god, it's more fucking wolves. They leap in front of the white wolf and advance toward the brown wolf. These two are slightly bigger than the brown one, but not as big as the white wolf.

One's dark gray, almost black, and he growls low, locking his gaze with the brown one. A show of dominance. The monstrous black wolf has thick fur that is mottled with the bones of small animals: I spot bird skulls and tangled antlers. Pops of brightly colored fungi and moss grow atop its back and legs. The wolf's yellow eyes glow brilliantly in the dark, and it bares its gnarled teeth.

The brown one gives a yip of annoyance but doesn't back down.

All the while, the heavy breath of the white wolf surges over me. It's crouched, ready to spring. I eye the stairs between its massive paws, and it gives a growl, as if it knows I'm thinking about running.

Now, the fourth wolf leaps. Rotten seaweed tangles through its golden fur. Coral and sea stars are stuck along its legs. Shells and sea glass rim its eyes and maw. It clamps down on the back of the brown wolf's neck.

The brown wolf whines, but the golden wolf places a massive paw over its back and forces it down to submission. Finally, the brown wolf gives a final yip and closes its eyes.

A satisfied growl emits from the black wolf, and the golden wolf releases his jaws from the brown one's neck but keeps its paw there. Both of them turn to look at the white wolf.

The super-giant icy white wolf that is still above me.

Oh no, I'm not sure what is happening here, but I really hope it isn't some wolfy battle to see who gets to eat me. I have to get out of here. I scramble out from beneath the white wolf, a terrified scream on my lips. "Keldarion! Help!"

In a smooth movement, the white wolf steps to block my escape route. It's so fucking huge, the head right in front of me. Glowing blue lines swirl around its face—but it's the eyes I'm stuck on. Ice-blue and light as a frozen lake.

"It's you ..." I breathe out.

I turn to the other wolves. If the brown wolf was the boy from the tower, then ...

The golden wolf with coral and seagrass stuck to it ... I know that gold. I've seen it on the head of the fae prince from the hot springs. And the black wolf whose fur shimmers gray in the torchlight, like the masked fae's armor...

Spring, Summer, Autumn, and Winter. The four fae princes.

"You're beasts," I gasp. "You're all beasts."

A rumble sounds from the white wolf and all the remaining heat leeches from the air. Then Keldarion, the fae Prince of Winter, turns his icy gaze on me and opens his massive jaws.

Holy fucking shit, maybe I am here to be a wolfy meal after all. He scoops me up in his mouth. My initial panic fades as no teeth pierce into me. He's carrying me through the castle.

A moment later, I'm tumbling across the floor of my room. The wolf nudges me with his nose until I'm on my stomach. He places a paw on the back of my bloody calf. There's a shock of pain and a tingling numbness. I look down to see a small layer of ice sealing off my wound.

"What's going on?" I gasp, looking up at the wolf, but he's already turned away. "Keldarion?"

But I'm alone again, in a castle of beasts.

17

DAYTON

I hear arguing voices before I even open the door. Ezryn's balls must be as hard as the helmet he always wears. Even though I know Ez will take the lead on whatever is going on in there, I hesitate. The ice crawling up the door frame is not a good sign.

Gritting my teeth, I push open the door. This is my least favorite room in the entire castle. Always too damn cold.

Kel and Ez stand by the window, continuing their argument as I walk in. Like I'm barely of note. It's not unusual.

Farron is curled up on the couch, knees drawn to his chest. My heart pangs. He looks miserable. I plop down on the armrest, and he immediately tucks into my side. His hand clutches the fabric of my pants and I instinctively let my fingers trail through the soft brown waves of his hair.

"What are Daddy and Mommy fighting about now?" I lean down and whisper.

That earns me the briefest flash of a smile before it falters, his golden eyes glassy. "This is all my—"

"Don't," I say sternly and snatch his chin. "Don't go there."

"Ah, Dayton, it seems you've finally managed to get yourself out of bed. You'd be well versed on the events if you'd arrived on time."

Ezryn's deep metallic voice reverberates as he studies me. "I sent Rintoulo an hour ago to retrieve you."

"Did you expect anything less from the drunken Prince of Summer?" Kel snarls, his long white hair framing the hard angles of his jaw.

A broad smile graces my face as an instinctive defense. "Sorry about that. You know, it's a lot of work dragging a giant beast all the way up to the dungeon. A lot of stairs. A lot of *thorns*."

Kel bristles and ice cracks beneath his feet. The man is too fucking easy to rile.

"Enough," Ezryn snaps. "This is serious."

My fingers trail further down Farron's neck, and he flinches. There are still red marks there, but not from me. I'd only gripped the loose skin at the back of his neck. That wound was from where Kel had bitten him. It shows just how hard that bite was that it still lingers on Farron in his fae form.

We've all known for a long time how unhinged Kel is, but last night was something else. And I'll be damned if I let Farron pay the price for it.

"You're right. It is serious." I stand, anger rippling off me like a wave of heat. Water seeps into my boots where the ice melts beneath my feet. "Farron was hurt last night. He could have been killed."

"Farron should learn to control his beast." Keldarion steps toward me. "The pup's had twenty-five years to do it."

Farron's face falls.

"He shouldn't have needed to!" I yell back. "You were ready to snap his neck. For what? To protect some human?"

I'm not easily scared. I've seen Kel tear apart his tower, rip thorns from walls, break stone with his bare hands. I've seen him kill twenty fae with his blade in the time it takes his enemy to draw their sword. But I've never seen him like he'd been when he stepped over the girl and shook the entire castle with his howl. The way he protected her …

Kel growls low in his throat and storms over, pulling me closer to him.

"It wasn't Rosalina's fault!" Farron shouts.

At the mention of her name, Keldarion drops my arm, and we are all still.

"Place blame on me," Farron says sadly. "Kel's right. There's no excuse that I can't control my—the beast. All of you can."

Kel looks at Farron, and if I didn't know for certain that the icy bastard was void of all emotion, I'd swear something akin to guilt flashes in his eyes.

"Why was she out of her room? I told you not to let her out." Kel returns to yelling at Ez. One of his favorite things to do.

"I checked the door before I retired for the night," Ezryn states. "I'm not sure how she left."

As it all comes together, I give a deep sigh. "She wanted to rescue Farron. Damn, in the baths she kept asking about him. Said you were handsome." I ruffle his hair as red darkens his cheeks. "I didn't tell her anything because ... Because, shit, Kel. You never tell us anything."

Keldarion glares at me, and I know he's fixated on my words. Yeah, I'd seen her in the baths, and I can't dwell on it because my cock will harden just thinking of that moment.

The servants had all been whispering about the woman Keldarion had imprisoned. Which was fucking weird. Kel didn't take prisoners. He'd never even taken a second glance at all those gorgeous—usually half-dressed or naked—fae that Caspian insisted on baiting him with at the castle gates. So why would he have imprisoned her? It couldn't be purely because of her loveliness, which is what all the staff had been gossiping about.

But I'd had to see her for myself. I mean, how pretty could a human really be?

Turns out ... fucking beautiful.

Maybe I was biased, but she looked incredible in the Summer Wing's hot springs, those light brown eyes and dark hair against her pale skin. Dripping and naked, the way her cheeks had flushed the most delicious shade of pink, the little peep of surprise she'd uttered ...

Fuck, I'd wanted to throw her on the sand and take her, just to see what other sounds she could make. I hadn't been able to see much of her body. She'd stayed deep in the water, but through the ripples, I'd made out her heavy breasts, the swaying curve of her hips. My cock had turned iron at the first sight of her, and I knew her lips would taste like salt, that her whole body would make me want to lick every inch of her.

Though knowing she was Kel's prisoner, I'd suspected her to be off-limits. I'd be lying if it didn't make me want her more.

"Day," Farron whispers. His golden eyes look me up and down, lightly freckled cheeks flushed. Kel's giving me a death glare. Damn, thinking about that girl got me aroused, and they can smell it.

Let the bastard smell. He's nursing the iciest fucking balls of the century after his last disastrous foray with love, and I have zero sympathy for him. When you trusted who he did, you deserved everything you got. Ez had warned him. So had Farron and I. His whole fucking realm had.

Ezryn gives a dissatisfied sigh and steps between us. "As much as I loath to admit it, Dayton is right. Kel, you need to tell us why she's here."

"I told you," he growls, and those ice chip eyes burrow into me. "Her father is a thief, and she traded her freedom for his."

We must all have the same suspicion. That can't be the reason. There's something more he's not telling us.

The curse of the Enchantress rings as it always does in my mind: *This spell may only be broken by winning the true love of your fated mate; and accepting the mate bond that has long been woven among the stars.*

Absolute bullshit. I've known two, maybe three, people in my entire life who have found their mate. I wouldn't doubt she'd cursed us knowing it can never be broken.

"If you insist on keeping her here," Ezryn says, "then we have to figure out what to do with her. She must have established rules, and we will tell her—"

"We will tell her nothing!" Keldarion snarls. "You want to house her in the Spring Wing? Fine. But she stays in her room permanently. The staff can bring her food and—"

Ezryn doesn't back down. He says in a menacing, low rasp, "You're being as unreasonable with Rosalina as you were with Caspian."

Farron grasps my hand. We've entered the end game. This whole castle is going down.

There's a beat of silence, like a stall in a song. Keldarion rises to his full height and winter explodes around him. Icy shards shatter into the air. I push Farron and myself to the ground and throw my arms over his head.

The beast inside me fights to come out, but I suppress it. The golden wolf would piss Kel off more. Farron trembles beneath my touch, and I bring my lips to his ear. "You're okay. You don't need your wolf. I'll protect you."

He nods, body trembling beneath mine.

Rocks fall from the ceiling as I look up to see Kel slam Ezryn against the wall. He's frozen all the thorns in the room. They're slowly dying, though I know they'll grow back quickly.

"I could rip your tongue out for those words," Kel growls, pushing the Prince of Spring hard against the stones.

Ez tilts his head, ice glinting off the metallic helmet. "No offense, Your Highness, but you'd have to get to my tongue first."

Fuck this guy. One day, he's going to push Kel too far and we're all going to watch his metal guts get strewn across the castle. And the worst part is that his body will be so mutilated, we won't ever know what he looks like, even after his death.

But Kel lets out a long breath and drops Ezryn to the ground. "Do what you think is right, Ezryn. I want nothing to do with the girl."

"Then let her go."

He whips around, white hair falling across his face. "Never."

"If you refuse to keep order in this castle, then I'll have to," Ezryn says. "I will inform Rosalina enough to keep her safe here. Obviously, she'll not be privy to our innermost dealings. But this castle will be her home, as it is to all who dwell here."

Slowly, I stand, drawing Farron up with me. The only sound in the room is the thorns, already growing back, snaking along the walls and ceiling of Kel's room. Damn, that fiend's magic is relentless.

Keldarion's chest rises and falls, breath heavy in his throat. "Tell her what you must. Feed her. Dress her up. Do as you will." Then that piercing ice-like gaze locks into all of us. "But none of you will touch her."

He stalks away into the shadows of his room, and the power of his words radiates through my body. Fuck. Why do I get the feeling that out of all of Kel's crazy rules, this one is going to be the hardest to follow?

18

ROSALINA

Last night, I slept in a prison cell. Tonight, I'm in a beautiful room, with a soft four-poster bed.

It might as well be that cold dungeon.

I tried to help the fae man … but he changed. Papa's raspy warning echoes in my mind: *'They're monsters, Rose! Beasts!'*

Yeah, I figured that when Keldarion shoved me in a cell and Ezryn choked me and accused me of being a spy. I never imagined they're actually *demonic wolves.*

I curl in on myself, wrapped tight in the blankets. That thing … It attacked me. Dried blood coats my leg. The ice Keldarion covered the wound in has long since melted. I know I should have tried to wash it somehow, or at least bandaged it, but I can't do anything but cower in my bed.

What am I going to do?

I'm a prisoner to four fae princes. And I'm powerless against them.

The sky begins to lighten. I think I managed an hour or two between all the tossing and turning. The fear has faded with the night and given way to sadness. I hug my pillow and cry.

My door creaks open and I jolt up. But there's only a little white rabbit. It cocks its head at me, staring with shining red eyes.

"Hi, cutie," I whisper, voice gravelly from crying. "Are you trapped in this castle too?"

The rabbit hops forward, and then in one big leap, jumps upon the bed. I can't help but smile. I always wanted a pet, but with Papa's erratic schedule, it seemed unfair.

The bunny wiggles right up beside my face and I reach out, stroking the soft, downy fur. "Did you need some company too?" I sniff. "It's okay. I'm here."

The bunny is so sweet with her little pink nose, long ears, and shining red eyes that seem so intent on me. Dawn breaks over the horizon, and the first golden rays of sunlight filter through the window. "What's your name?" I ask. "Snowball? Fluffy? Wiggles— AHH!"

Fluffy is ... *growing*. And shedding her fur like some sort of fucking nightmare. I scramble backward, but by the time I blink my eyes, the rabbit is gone and replaced with ... Astrid.

"You can call me Fluffy if you want to." She smiles. She's lying so casually on my bed, her head beside me on the pillow. And she's butt-ass naked.

"W-where are your clothes?" I squeal. "Or your fur?"

She looks down at her thin, pale body. "Oh right. I forgot humans aren't as comfortable with nudity." She giggles and pushes herself up, padding across the room to grab a robe from the wardrobe.

I push myself up onto all fours and gape at her. She turns and stares back, her human eyes the same shade of light red as the bunny's. Wait. Not her human eyes. She's fae, like them.

Astrid crosses her hands in front of her and smiles softly, like she's waiting for me to catch up.

"Why," I ask slowly, "were you a rabbit?"

She laughs and glides across the floor to sit on the edge of the bed. Her straight white hair falls to her chin, and her bangs are cut right above her pale eyebrows. "I'm a hare, actually. They're quite common in the Winter Realm. You should come see them!"

The only thing I know about hares was that one time I was lying in bed with Lucas, and he was stroking my face, staring at me with what could have been love. And he smiled and opened his mouth, and I swore he was going to tell me all the things I so desperately wanted to hear. But he said, 'Have you ever heard the death keel of a hare? Sometimes I like to snipe them with the rifle, but I don't get the sound if it's too clean of a shot. I can get them to make it with my knife, though. It's unlike anything you'll ever hear.' Then he mounted me, placed his hand over my face, and whispered in my ear, 'I want to hear you make a sound like that.'

I don't know if I ever gave him what he wanted.

I squeeze my eyes shut, willing my mind to return to the present. Because I'd much rather be in this room with this fucking werebunny than that moment again.

He's not like that anymore, a part of my mind argues. *He asked me to marry him.*

"Is everything alright?" Astrid scoots up closer to me and runs a tender hand over my hair.

"It's all a bit overwhelming," I say. "A few days ago, I was working in a bookstore. Now, I'm a prisoner in an enchanted castle."

Astrid gives a sad smile. "If it makes it any easier, we're so excited you're here. Nothing exciting has happened in the last twenty-five years."

"Is that how long you've been trapped here?" I ask.

She nods and clasps her hands on her lap. "We could leave, I suppose. But where would we go? There's no home to return to for the cursed."

"Cursed," I whisper. "Everyone in here … is cursed?"

Astrid walks to the window, the dawn light painting her pale body orange. "Fae by day, beasts by night. I suppose us servants should count ourselves lucky. You get used to turning into an animal. I don't think you ever get used to … what happens to the princes."

The hideous, twisted wolves fill my mind, their wild gazes and giant bodies sending my heart skittering in my chest. "What happened here? Why are you all cursed?"

Astrid looks nervously to the door. "Someone's coming."

The door swings open and Marigold comes in with a tray of breakfast. She looks over at me and I can tell she's displeased with my blood messing up the clean sheets. It turns out, I don't have to recount last night. Everyone in the castle already knows what happened. Those eyes I'd felt peering at me had been the staff.

I nibble on my breakfast, opting for plain toast on account of my queasy stomach. Marigold and Astrid tell me the type of animals the staff turn into. Marigold is a raccoon, and there's a bear, and a penguin, and a couple dogs, and the gardener turns into a great owl. When I ask *why* this is all happening, they dodge the question like a freaking border collie in an agility show.

A solid knock sounds from the door. I suck in a breath and straighten. "Come in."

The door slowly creeps open, revealing a towering metal figure.

The masked knight from the bridge. The dark gray wolf who dripped soil and had little bones tangled in his fur.

Ezryn, the Spring Prince.

19

ROSALINA

Astrid gives a deep bow. "My Prince!" she squeaks and darts out the door with Marigold in tow.

My heart sinks. I want to scream at them to stay, to not leave me alone with this … What is he? A monster? A beast? But my throat seizes, and it's all I can do to scramble back against the headboard.

The damn Tin Man does not care to put me out of my misery. He stands there in the doorway, his face completely hidden by that metal helmet.

Breath comes ragged from my throat, and I realize how vulnerable I am, pinned against the headboard as he holds me hostage with an unseeable stare. I'm still wearing the nightgown from last night, and honestly, the thorns shredded most of it. The thin pink fabric clings tightly to my chest and generous hips, the long sleeves billowing but tight at my wrists. My dark hair falls over my shoulders, mussed from my flight through the castle and my restless sleep. I must look like prey to him.

"What?" I finally spit because my pounding heart can't take it anymore. "What do you want?"

The large metal plate of his armor rises and falls with a deep breath. He steps forward.

With each clang of his metal boots against the floor, more fear sputters through me. *Danger, danger, danger,* my logical mind screams. And yet …

There's something in my chest scratching against my ribs, yowling for release. Something that wants me to move closer to him.

He's going to kill me. Why am I okay with it?

In a second that feels like an hour, his shadow falls over me on the bed. I stare up at the unreadable mask, knowing fear marks my face.

"I'm Keldarion's prisoner," I manage. "You can't hurt me. I'm his— Ah!"

The masked prince sits down on the end of the bed, the weight of his body and armor sending me bouncing on the mattress like a trampoline. Then he snags my ankle and yanks my leg up in the air.

"What the fuck are you doing?" I cry, desperately trying to hold my nightgown down to stop from giving him a show.

He doesn't answer, instead twisting my leg up and down as he examines my calf. He gives a breathy sound, something between a sigh and a moan.

"Can you let me go?" I begin, but my cries are shut down when he grabs my hip with his gloved hand and turns me over in one rough movement. Suddenly, I'm lying on my stomach, my face flung into the pillow. His cold, metal hand still grips my ankle roughly.

"What the fuck?" I want my voice to sound outraged, but it comes out a breathy whisper.

He flipped me over like I'm a ragdoll. What is he doing to my leg? Fear bursts through my chest, but there's something else too.

Suddenly, the hand that isn't grasping my ankle pushes down between my shoulder blades, forcing my face harder into the pillow. "Stay still," he commands, his voice cold and calm.

Immediately, I stop wiggling. The pressure of his hand on my back is firm. I'm one-part terrified the Iron Giant is about to murder me, and one fucked-up-part feeling strangely heated as I lie frozen by his command.

The pressure releases on my back, and I hear the pull of fabric and *ting* of metal. Unable to quell my curiosity, I wiggle my shoulders around to see what he's doing.

He's pulled off his gloves, revealing large hands and tan skin. "So, there is flesh and blood in there," I mumble. "I half thought you were an iron skeleton."

He quirks his metal head at me but says nothing. His hands hover on my ankle and the back of my knee, on either side of the nasty gash down my calf.

"Don't move your leg," Ezryn says lowly.

The calm dominance of his voice makes me powerless to resist. I take a breath. His calloused fingers run over my pale skin, and I wince as they touch the wound.

Ezryn reaches into a small pouch attached to his hip and pulls out a handful of bright green leaves. Deftly, he slips them under his mask, revealing a peek of tan neck. Then he pulls them out. They look moist.

"Did you just chew on those?" I ask.

But as he seems to love to do, he ignores me and places the chewed-up leaves right on the wound. "Ew, those have your spit on them—"

He covers the wound and leaves with his hands in a surprisingly tender motion, and a tingle flushes through my leg. The throbbing dissipates, replaced by a warm pulse. He pulls his hand away and brushes off the leaves.

I scramble up and he doesn't stop me. Clutching my calf, my eyes bug out. The wound is completely healed, the only remnant a bright red scar.

"How did you do that?" I whisper.

Again, he ignores me, instead snatching my arms. I yelp, but his grasp is firm, and he doesn't let me go.

He runs a rough thumb over a scratch along my right wrist. Instantly, the warmth spreads through my skin and the scratch disappears.

"These are smaller," he mumbles. "Easier to do."

"Are you some sort of wizard?" I marvel as he pushes up the sleeve of my nightgown and works his way up my right arm.

When he doesn't respond, I duck my head down and glare up into the black eyelets. "Hey, how come you don't answer me when I talk to you?"

For an answer, he yanks me closer, shoving the sleeve all the way to my shoulder. He grips my right bicep and covers a bloody gash where a thorn had snagged me. "Long ago, the Queen blessed the High Ruler of each realm with great magic. I inherited the magic from my mother. All fae have the possibility to be born with an affinity for magic, but the High Rulers receive a great blessing to protect their realm. Such as the Blessing of Spring," he murmurs, his voice so calm, it's almost unnerving. "Rejuvenation."

I suppose that explains all the ice around Keldarion.

Ezryn pulls down my sleeve, covering my arm back up, and reaches for my left wrist. I whip it away. "No," I say, suddenly self-conscious. "This arm is fine."

His mask tilts almost incredulously, but he doesn't push it.

There's something strangely beautiful about his armor; the delicate markings of vines and leaves, the shimmer of the morning sun off the metal. I wonder what it would feel like beneath my fingertips.

It doesn't matter that he healed my wounds. His housemate tried to fucking eat me. And I can't forget that yesterday he had his hands around my throat.

But maybe, just maybe, there was something to the tenderness in which he mended my skin. I have to try.

"Do humans often come to the Enchanted Vale?" I ask tentatively. When he doesn't answer, I continue, "That's why my father came here. He's looking for my mother. He's convinced faeries stole her."

There's a deep rumbling sigh. "It's against our laws to bring humans from your world."

"But could it have happened? Have other humans ever made it through?"

"It's possible, but rare. There are a few humans who have wandered in and made a life in one of the four realms."

"Mother wouldn't have left us," I say, more to myself than him. "My father said their love was brighter than every star in the sky."

Ezryn looks out the window. "You've seen for yourself. There are many dangers here."

Is he suggesting she wandered into the Vale and died? Killed by one of those goblins or something? Fear and anger war inside my chest. "Why are you trapping me here?" I ask. "I don't have anything you want. My father didn't mean to steal from Keldarion. Please, will you let me go?"

"You traded your place for his." Prince Ezryn stands, and his shadow overtakes me again. "You are our prisoner, and you have disobeyed the rules by leaving your room last night. Do not attempt to escape again or you will be punished."

He turns and walks to the doorway. Without turning his back, he says in a low rumble, "You shall meet with the princes in the dining hall."

Rage ripples through me. "You keep me prisoner and nearly kill me last night, and you want me to meet with you? Not a chance. I don't want to see any of your faces—"

"You will meet with us. It is not a request." With a snap of his cape, he turns and storms toward the door. "Astrid," he growls, and the white-haired girl creeps in, having clearly listened to everything, "make her somewhat presentable. If you can."

20

EZRYN

I walk straight-backed down the hall, away from the prisoner's room, then turn a corner. As soon as I'm out of sight from any of the staff, I collapse against the wall, helm knocking against the stone.

My heart pounds, hands trembling. What is this? *Fear?*

From a human woman in a nightgown?

I force in a deep breath and steady myself. I spend weeks out in the wilds hunting goblin packs. I've been ambushed and surrounded, outnumbered and desperate.

But this is the first time in years I've felt … fear?

No.

I feel alive.

I stalk back to my room, only a short trek from hers. *Rosalina.* It's a beautiful name, one that sounds as if it belongs in Spring. Is that why I put her up in my own wing? I should have left her to Kel's devices—

My hands tighten into fists. *No.* She may be a trespasser, but she doesn't deserve to sleep in the dungeon, or even to be condemned to one of the ice-covered rooms in the Winter Wing. Spring is the best place for her.

I give my head a shake as I reach the door to my chambers. I've done what I can. Given her safe lodging. Healed the vicious wound down her calf. Placed her under the watchful eye of Astrid and Marigold. I'll attend our meeting, ensure Keldarion doesn't do anything completely mindless, and then return to the Briar. She will not be my concern for much longer.

I swing open the door. My room is similar to the one I put Rosalina up in, but darker, the walls made of the dark wood of Castletree's structure. The curtains are interwoven ivy that I keep tightly drawn. My room is lit by glowlamps: orbs that bob through the air, filled with little lights that resemble fireflies. The branches of a willow tree jut out from the wooden wall, creating a canopy of catkins around my bed.

The comforting smell of sweet bread and coffee welcomes me. There's a tray on the end of my bed filled with fluffy bread rolls dusted with sugar and a steaming carafe. Marigold must have left this for me.

I always take my meals separately. It's the only way to eat, as no one in the castle can see me without my helm. But I've been spending so much time out in the Briar, I can't remember the last time Marigold brought me food. The taste of stale rations is more familiar than bread.

Perhaps she hopes I'll stay longer this time. I hate to disappoint her, but there's nothing to be done about it. There's no reason for me to stay in this castle.

I give a dismissive huff. Hope. That's what that girl has brought to the castle. Perhaps she's more dangerous than I've given her credit for.

I turn away from my bed and walk to the washbasin, a hollow in the tree that fills with fresh water. A mirror hangs from the wood before me, reflecting the glint of light from my armor. I yank off my gloves and scrub my hands.

The smell of coffee drifts over the carafe, and I take a slow inhale. I truly haven't had one of Marigold's sweet rolls in a long time...

Slowly, I remove my helm and lay it carefully on the side of the hollow. My gaze flicks to the mirror, then down again. I haven't seen my own face in a long time.

When was the last time someone looked into my eyes? It was my mother and father, when I was five years old and first donned my helm. It will remain that way until I meet my fated mated.

I splash water on my face to chase away the idea. *That human and her damned hope.*

I look up, forcing myself to meet my own gaze. What did I think I'd find looking back at me?

Still a man, not a beast. Yet. Though, I am a mess—hair too long, beard unruly. Even though no one knows what's behind the helm, I do not look fit to be the High Prince of Spring.

Pulling a dagger from my belt, I hack off the unruly strands of hair. Then, I run it over my neck and jaw. There. A little more dignified. We have a guest now—even though she'll never know the difference.

I walk over to the tray and grab a sweet roll. It smells like Florendel, the capital of the Spring Realm. It smells like home.

I will return one day to sit upon the throne in the Hall of Vernalion, with no need for my father to rule as steward in my place. One day, Marigold and the rest of the Spring staff will be freed from this curse. I will walk under a crescent moon as a man, not a beast. One day, I will gaze into the eyes of my fated mate and deserve her love.

One day.

For now, I turn my thoughts back to our guest. The stars know Keldarion is no proper host, and the human must be protected. From Farron's beast, Dayton's charm, and her own curiosity.

Hope is not something I ever allow myself to hold on to. But this other feeling, this sense of being *alive* ...

I take a bite of the roll, savoring the sweetness. Perhaps it wouldn't be such a detriment to stay in Castletree. At least for a while.

21

ROSALINA

I must be absolutely mad to attend lunch with these fae princes. One imprisoned me, one threatened me, one tried to eat me, and one, I suspect, wanted to do very indecent things to me. And all of them transform into fucking demon wolves.

It's not like I have a choice. I inhale a shaky breath through my nose and smooth down my skirts. Yes, *skirts*. Astrid has dressed me in a full-on gown. According to her, it's a *day* gown, but to me, anything with multiple layers is fancy. I mean, this thing has a freaking petticoat.

It *is* pretty, though. It's a robin-egg blue with long draping sleeves embroidered with tiny snowflakes and a dark navy corset. The skirt hangs above my ankles, obviously made for a shorter woman. It doesn't bother me. At my height, I'm used to it.

Astrid assured me that the castle's seamstress would make clothes to fit me. What does a prisoner need a seamstress for? I'm going to have to hold my own in this meeting and demand answers about what is really going on.

I'm not usually one to speak my mind, but there's something simmering beneath the surface. A part of me I didn't know was there.

Or a part of me I'd forgotten.

"This way, Lady Rosalina." Astrid opens a double wood door and leads me through.

The dining room looks like something out of a fairytale. Lush velvet drapes frame the windows, and a banquet table of rosewood sits in the middle. The walls are painted a deep crimson hue, with ornate carvings of roses along the top of the archways. This room, like the rest of the castle, isn't free of the resident plant life. Dark thorns twine around every post and window frame, their spines catching the light.

Three fae princes are seated at the table, and all turn to me as I stumble in. One of them stands up, his chair screeching back. "Er, please take a seat."

It's the man from the dungeon. He looks a lot different now. He wears a light-yellow tunic with a golden belt in the shape of leaves and tight brown breeches tucked into shiny black boots. A golden swirling cuff decorates one of his ears, and his fluffy brown hair falls in his face as he inclines his head to me.

I swallow and study the table for a moment as I nervously try to figure out where to sit. There's a chair at either end of the table and three on each side. Sitting beside the man is Dayton from the hot springs; he's wearing a similar tunic in beige, but it's so far unlaced, I can see his belly button.

Across from them is Ezryn. My face reddens thinking of how he'd thrown me around my bed this morning. I wonder if I look presentable enough for him ... Not that I have any idea what that living statue is thinking.

Seems like Keldarion isn't required for this meeting.

"Choose a seat," Astrid whispers. "There's an empty spot beside Prince Farron."

Farron. That's his name. Well, figuring he tried to eat me last night, I'm going to keep my distance.

I could sit next to Ezryn. His gauntleted hands are two mighty fists on the table. He may have healed my leg earlier, but I still haven't forgotten our first meeting. And I'm not putting my throat anywhere near him again. No thank you. Not today.

I would have told him to squeeze tighter, Marigold's cheeky words enter my mind. The damned minx had nearly gushed herself when I told her about Ezryn healing my leg.

An image flashes through my mind, as I picture his hand around my throat as he tosses me onto the table with the same strength he used to toss me on the bed, then his gentle hands unlacing the bodice of my corset and—

Okay, what the actual fuck. Marigold is getting to me because I absolutely do *not* find masked fae princes sexy in any way.

His metallic head turns to me, and I see my flushed face in the reflection. *Shit, this creep isn't some sort of mind reader, is he?*

I take a couple of awkward steps forward; I truly need to find the lesser of two evils.

A door pushes open from the opposite side of the room and for a moment, all I can see is a black silhouette. A sharp icy breeze hits me.

Keldarion is here. He stumbles into the light, and he looks … awful.

Well, as awful as an incredibly handsome fae prince can look. While the rest of the princes have put in a little effort to look regal for the monumental occasion that is having lunch with me (I mean, I can't really say that about Ezryn, but his helmet is especially shiny), Keldarion looks like he crawled out of a sewer.

His white hair hangs limp over his shoulders and is strewn with dirt. Dried blood stains his low-cut black tunic and shadows ring his light eyes. The only delicate thing about him is a crystallized snowflake necklace that lays on his muscular chest.

Keldarion meets my gaze from across the room but looks away with a tight sneer as he heads for the table. Considering the last time I saw him I was lying limp in his massive wolfy jaws, I guess I was expecting a warmer reaction.

I too stomp across the dining room, making considerably more noise in the dainty slippers than should be possible. And before I even know what I'm doing, I'm pulling out the head chair opposite Keldarion and shooting him a glare as I sit down.

Farron also awkwardly falls back in his seat. Dayton leans over and whispers something in his ear, which causes Farron to smile. Someone with fangs that sharp shouldn't be allowed to have that cute of a smile.

The dining room is suddenly alive with staff busying about. Plates of freshly baked pastries, heaps of crisp salad, and colorful vegetables fill the center of the table. Carafes of juice and steaming pots of hot tea are also delivered.

As the staff busy about, I can't help but notice that Dayton greets every one of them by name, stopping to chat and asking about their morning. He really is stupidly charming. One of the female servants lingers a little, a hand on his arm.

Marigold and Astrid told me the princes keep their distance from the staff, but is that true? I clench my hands into fists beneath the table. What am I thinking? He flirted with me once and just made it obvious that's what he does with everyone.

Plus, he's a monstrous wolf.

Dayton is the first one to load his plate, but once it's full, he places it in front of Farron and begins another. "You should try the strawberry jam." Dayton gives me a wink. "Marigold has made it particularly sweet this week."

All I can do is shake my head. I've never been one to refuse food, but my stomach is in knots.

"You need to eat." Kel's sharp voice snaps me out of my anxious thoughts, and I look up to see him staring at me from across the table.

"I'm not hungry," I say back. It's not a total lie.

A muscle feathering in Kel's jaw is the only sign of his annoyance. I'm not sure why getting a rise out of him fills me with such a delicious fire. Maybe it's my way to maintain some sense of control as his prisoner.

"If you don't eat now," Kel snarls, "you'll be hungry later."

"I'll eat food then."

"If you don't eat with us," Keldarion growls low, "then you don't eat at all."

"I'm not hungry!" I push myself up from the table and gesture toward Ezryn. "He's not eating."

Ezryn sits without a plate in front of him. I was wondering if he was finally going to take off his helmet to eat, but it seems a permanent fixture on his face.

"I eat alone," Ezryn says simply. "I do not remove my helmet in front of anyone."

Alright then. I turn back to glare at Kel, but he's already moving, filling his own plate. My stomach growls, betraying all my earlier not hungry propaganda.

Suddenly, Kel drops the plate in front of me so hard I'm surprised the porcelain doesn't shatter. It's filled with all the pastries I'd raved to Marigold about yesterday. That traitor trash panda. Did she tell Kel what I liked? And if so, why the hell would he care?

"Eat," he says. "You're clearly hungry."

Cold air washes over me, fresh snow and pine ensnaring me in its embrace. I try to break the moment by scowling at him, but when my gaze meets the ice-blue of his eyes, my resolve fades. His smoldering stare feels like a burning blaze trailing down my face, my neck, and settling on my chest. Astrid cinched my corset too tight, and I can feel him notice as a growl rumbles from his throat. It sounds different from anger, more … wanting.

I could slap myself. What is wrong with me? Am I that far gone I think I can differentiate between fae growls now?

Keldarion turns away. It feels like this douchey winter prince got the last word, which fills me with an unhinged anger. I stand and grab a hard red apple from the table.

"And here's your lunch," I growl and chuck it at his back.

Keldarion catches it without turning around. He sits back down in his chair and raises a dark brow at me.

I fall back to my seat in a huff.

"Now that we're all present," Ezryn says, giving a deep sigh, "may our meeting begin?"

My meeting with the four fae princes. My stomach roils. This is a meeting of my fate, my future. And I can't mess it up.

22

ROSALINA

All I can do is glare down at the delicious lunch in front of me.

Farron pushes up from his seat. "I want to start by saying … Rosalina. Uh, I mean, I want to apologize for what almost happened last night. I don't have as good of a handle over the curse as the others."

"You have nothing to apologize for," Dayton says softly before I can respond.

"Well, thank you," I say. "I would prefer not to be eaten by a wolf."

"Then you should have followed the rules and stayed in your room," Keldarion growls.

"And you should learn to control your temper!" Does this stupid fae need to have a say in everything? I grab a fluffy white roll and chuck it as hard as I can across the table.

He catches that too.

"You don't have to fill my plate in return," he says as he places the bread roll next to the apple.

"Sit down, Farron," Ezryn says softly, then turns to me. "That rule wasn't created to control you; it was to keep you safe."

"I'd be safer at home," I start. "If you'd only—"

Keldarion stands, palms flat on the table. "In case you've forgotten, you're still a prisoner serving your father's sentence. The others desire to give you liberties and freedom within the castle. If that is not to your satisfaction, then I'd be happy to escort you back to the dungeon."

I sink in my seat and cross my arms. Of course he fucking would.

At my silence, Keldarion keeps his chilly gaze on me. "You will not leave your room at night. Furthermore—"

"I already know what you are! And what happens to the staff. Astrid literally showed me. Why do I have to stay put?"

Keldarion grinds his teeth. "Fine. But don't go back to the dungeon. Farron remains locked up for the protection of everyone. Including himself."

Farron keeps his head down, picking at his food. Dayton notices my attention and catches my gaze with a wide smirk. "And don't stare at the animals, makes them uncomfortable. Also, don't try to eat them. I've had a few close calls before."

"I wouldn't—Wait, close calls?"

"You may go outside to the grounds during the day if escorted by Astrid or another member of the staff, but not beyond the bridge or the wall," Keldarion continues his list of demands. "Also, you may take your breakfast and lunch where you will, but we will *all* dine together every evening."

I open my mouth to complain but someone else beats me to it.

"Kel," Ezryn says. "There may be times—"

"You said you wanted to bring order to this castle, Ezryn," Keldarion says lowly. "Then take it. You can continue your little hunts after dark."

Ezryn doesn't reply, but his hands tighten into fists and I'm glad I positioned my throat far away from him. Ezryn may have cowed to the icy bastard easily, but I refuse to give him the satisfaction of it.

"Why would I want to eat with any of you? You're my jailers."

"Would you rather go back to the dungeon?" Keldarion asks simply.

So, that's going to be his kill card for everything? I take a bite of my blueberry pastry. Fuck, it's so light and crispy. The blueberries taste like the breath of life itself. I devour it in two bites and give a little sigh of satisfaction when it's done.

My enjoyment is short-lived, however, when I glance up and see Kel looking at me from across the table. There's a little satisfied smirk on his face.

Smug fae bastard.

"Another rule." Dayton leans forward, a dimple forming as he grins. "You may bathe in the hot springs with me every day if you wish." He plops a cherry between his lips. "Naked, of course."

My cheeks turn the color of the cherries he's eating as I remember my hot springs encounter with him, the way the soap slid down his muscular chest …

"That is not a requirement," Ezryn interrupts. "Astrid will ensure your complete privacy in those facilities. None of us, nor the staff, will bother you again while you bathe."

I nod, and that should definitely be relief, not disappointment, swirling in my stomach. I'm not turning into Marigold here.

"Unless you beg for it, of course." Dayton winks at me as if he can see right through to my molten core.

I shove my thighs shut and turn back to the table. "What else is there?"

"Astrid and the other staff will show you around the castle," Ezryn says. "You may explore the Spring, Summer, Autumn, and Winter Wings and their facilities with an escort as you see fit. Of course, our personal chambers will be strictly off-limits."

"Unless—" Dayton begins.

"Off-limits," Ezryn finishes.

"And the High Tower." Kel finally moves his icy gaze from Dayton to me. "You are not to go there under any circumstances. It is strictly forbidden."

Something trembles in his words, something powerful, and it's all I can do to nod.

"Okay," I say. "I'll follow your rules if—"

Kel growls at my words. "This is not a negotiation."

"*If* you explain to me what's going on," I finish. My mind flashes back to what Farron said: *The others are better at controlling their curse.* "Tell me about this curse you're under. I can assume no one in this castle wants to turn into demonic wolves and animals at night?"

All of them are silent for a moment, and I don't miss the shift as they look at Keldarion.

"If you insist on her living here," Ezryn says, "then she deserves to know the truth."

Kel gives a dismissive wave of his hand and nods.

"Farron, tell her," Ezryn commands.

Dayton grabs the brown-haired fae's shoulders. "Farron's been researching the curse. He knows the most about it."

"Uh, okay," Farron says. "It's as simple as it is complex. Please do not repeat the curse to anyone. Only the residents of Castletree know the details."

"I literally cannot leave," I say.

"Right." Farron drags a hand through his wavy hair. "This castle is the customary home of the High Princes of each realm and their staff."

It seems strange to me for them all to live in a castle so far away from their realms, but I let him continue.

"Dayton was the last of us crowned. He lived here for about a month before we heard a knock on the door," Farron continues. "Upon answering, we found a beautiful human woman. She asked to look upon each of the princes and we honored her request. But when she requested entry to Castletree, we denied her."

I guess I wouldn't want to let some strange woman into my home either. I take stock of all the princes as Farron tells his story. Dayton's head is cast down, Kel's got the grimace of a century, and Ezryn's still as a mountain.

"That's when everything changed," Farron continues. "I mean, the woman changed. She transformed into an ethereal enchantress. I've never felt magic like that before. Her words tore into us, a spell woven in moonlight as she cursed us."

"And the curse?"

"The residents of Castletree would transform into beasts at night. The four princes would be cursed beyond all," Farron explains. "We are spared on the night of the full moon. Who knows for what mercy."

"No one knows of this," Ezryn says solemnly. "At first, we thought she may have been from the Below, or a powerful fae cursing us in an attempt to seize Castletree's magic. But she never reappeared after that night, and my search has come up empty."

"And there's nothing you can do about it?" I ask. "To break the curse?"

"Not exactly. Fae curses can always be broken," Farron says lowly. "The Enchantress told us we could only break this curse once we find our mates and before—"

"Enough," Keldarion snarls. "You've told her enough."

"Mate? What the heck is a mate?"

"The other half of your soul." Dayton smiles poetically. "Born from the same star. Someone your whole being calls to."

"It's a fae thing." Farron gives me a sympathetic smile.

My mind races. These fae princes are powerful, but they're also desperate. Perhaps desperate enough to give me what I want.

"I'll help you break the curse," I say. They all turn to me like I announced I could magically transform into a fox. Actually, they might not think that's so weird. "I'm serious. If I'm trapped here, I might as well do something useful."

"Why do you care what happens to us?" Dayton blinks his big blue eyes. "We are your jailers after all."

"Because when I break the curse, you'll let me go. That's the deal. Fae like bargains, right?"

My heart hammers in my chest. One of my father's many ramblings: never make a bargain with the fae. But I'm already in so deep, it may be my only way out.

They're silent for a moment before Ezryn murmurs, "It couldn't hurt to have her assist Farron in his research."

"You have nothing to lose by letting me try." I turn my gaze on Keldarion. "And I have everything to gain."

"Come here," Keldarion says, and the command seems to work through my body as I stand immediately.

My throat dries as I pat down my skirts like I planned to do that all along. Then I walk across the dining room, my steps echoing.

Kel pushes up from his chair as I arrive and stares down at me. Damn, I forget how tall he is until I'm quivering beneath him. He sticks out his hand. "Break the curse and you'll be free of this castle."

His words make the back of my neck prickle. There's something not quite right about them. But I have no other choice.

"Deal," I whisper, then lace my fingers with his. His large hand feels too warm for a prince of ice and snow.

"It's a bargain," he murmurs reverently. "Until you break the curse, or I choose to release you, you shall remain a guest of Castletree."

A magical force courses through our joined hands. I feel a tingling sensation and watch in awe as a ribbon of blue light wraps around my wrist and his. An exquisite warmth radiates from our clasped hands and an electric spark ignites within my heart. Wind caresses my hair, and I can't tear my gaze away from his blue fire eyes.

Finally, the spell dissipates, and I look down to see a bracelet around each of our wrists: frosted ice with gleaming rose petals frozen within. A symbol of our vow.

Something else on his wrist catches my interest. Another bracelet above ours in the shape of—

Kel drops my hand, and I let out a gasp. Energy courses through me. "It's a bargain," I whisper.

"And it's all for naught." Kel turns and walks toward the door. "This curse will never be broken."

23

ROSALINA

On the morning of my third day in the castle, Marigold has me in front of the vanity and pins my hair up in a bun with curled pieces framing my face. "Been so long since I've had someone's hair to do," she states when I protest all the fussing. "Let a woman play!"

It's the strangest thing. She and Astrid seem particularly interested in me. After my meeting with the princes, they spent the day following me around, asking me what I needed every two seconds and fighting over what area of the castle to show me next. I have to admit, the company is kind of nice. Between Astrid's optimistic energy and Marigold's constant lusting over the princes, I was laughing and smiling most of the day.

Not something I imagined doing as a prisoner. But the conversation at lunch has given me hope. I can break this curse and earn my freedom. I'll see Papa again and life will return to normal. It's only a matter of time.

I trace my fingers over the frosted bracelet on my wrist, staring at the beautiful red petals within. For a mark of a fae bargain, it sure is beautiful.

My first enforced dinner with the princes had to go down as one of the most awkward family dinners of all time. Keldarion didn't say a single word, Ezryn sat there not eating, Farron seemed too nervous to swallow, and only Dayton and I polished off our plates.

But damn. *The food.* Decadent mushrooms filled with nuts and garlic and a savory red vegetable I'd never seen before. Warm bread that tore apart like clouds. The freshest salad I'd ever eaten, decorated with creamy cashews and pink radishes. And a lovely fizzy orange drink that almost tasted like mango lemonade.

They don't want to talk to me? Fine. I'll eat their food and befriend their servants and find a way to cure their damned curse so I can get out of here.

Now, I admire Marigold's handiwork, bouncing a curl up and down in my palm as the morning light dusts through my window. "Jeez, Marigold, you could have a career in film. You've made me look like an old movie star."

Marigold grabs her chubby cheeks and coos. "Of course I did! You'd fit right in with Vivien Leigh. Now if one of these men could be a bit more like Rhett Butler—"

"What?" I nearly leap out of the vanity chair. "Do not tell me you have your own fae version of *Gone with the Wind.*"

"Of course not, girl." She walks to the wardrobe and rustles through a stack of dresses. "Occasionally, humans wander into the Enchanted Vale and bring tidings of their home. Or some fae go for a visit. The princes used to do it many years ago before the curse. But that hasn't happened in a long time." She gives a little shudder. "Though who knows? You and your father made it through. Maybe the Vale has its own ideas."

I shake my head in disbelief. I can hardly imagine these ancient fae beings shedding a tear over Scarlett O'Hara.

Marigold holds out a beautiful pink gown with a lace overlay of roses and cute cap-sleeves. It's gorgeous. "Here you go, dear."

I scuff a toe against the floor and fiddle with the cuff of my night-gown. "It's beautiful, but is there anything in there with long sleeves? I'm more comfortable with my arms covered."

She raises a thin brow, and for a second I think she's going to fight me on it, but she returns to the wardrobe and pulls out an orange long-sleeve dress, the skirt emblazoned with hundreds of autumn leaves. "You'll fill this one out like a dream. And it's seasonal."

As I finish changing, there's a knock on the door. I glide across the room to answer it, expecting Astrid.

Instead, I'm faced with six-foot-something of pure gorgeousness.

Rein it in, girlie, I tell myself. *He literally tried to eat you two days ago.*

Because Farron—my mysterious fae prisoner who I so desperately wanted to help, aka the rabid wolf monster who sliced open my leg, and Prince of the Autumn Realm—is standing in my doorway.

"Hi," I say.

"Hi," he responds, and his voice cracks. He deepens it and says, "Hi. Hello. Good morning."

I give a little giggle and wait for him to speak. But he just stares down at me, his huge golden eyes taking me in like I'm the answer to the crossword puzzle he's been musing on for the last hour. He wears golden-framed glasses, the round lenses making him look like a sexy professor. His outfit doesn't help dispel that idea: an autumn-brown waistcoat, over a high-necked cream tunic and brown slacks that hug his long legs.

A part of me wants to slam the door in his face for trying to murder me. But there's another part—a totally insane one—that's happy to see him like this. I thought he was a prisoner.

And when I think about what he said, about how he can't control his beast like the others can, I wonder if he's not actually free at all.

"Can I help you?" I ask when it seems like he's totally frozen in place, staring at me.

He jerks, running a hand through his hair and mumbling, "Oh! Oh yes. Sorry. I … You look so beautiful."

I raise an eyebrow.

"The dress, I mean!" he stutters.

Marigold comes up behind me and slaps my ass. "Of course she looks beautiful. And this dress is even prettier on the floor." She cackles to herself and toddles down the hallway.

My cheeks heat and Farron rubs the bridge of his nose, muttering, "Marigold ..."

We both laugh until finally Farron straightens and picks nervously at the cuff of his coat. "Ms. Rosalina, I don't mean to intrude, but I was wondering if you meant what you said yesterday at our meeting." He stares at me, those golden eyes shining beneath dark brows. "Do you actually intend to help us break the curse?"

"Yes," I breathe, then hold up my ice bracelet as if in proof. "Of course I do."

His smile brightens more than the morning sun. "Fabulous. Then come with me."

I follow him through the hallways as servants nod their greetings and give little bows to the prince.

"As I'm sure you've gathered, we've been cursed for twenty-five years," Farron says, speaking quickly. "As with all curses, there is a way to break it. And I've dedicated every single day of the last two and a half decades to trying to do so. When the obvious solutions didn't succeed, I took to research in an attempt to decipher deeper meanings within the curse. So, I spend a lot of time in here." We stop before two huge double doors with opulent handles glazed in gold leaf. He runs a hand over his pointed ear. "I hope this won't bore you."

He pulls open the doors. And I enter the most enchanting library I've ever seen.

24

ROSALINA

With staggering steps, I enter the library and my heart takes flight. I spin in a circle, wanting to absorb everything. "It's magnificent," I breathe.

The castle's library is filled with autumnal wonder. Trees grow inside, ablaze in reds and oranges and yellows, the leaves falling in gentle cascades to the ground. Some trunks merge into high shelves, filled with row upon row of books.

It's the biggest library I've ever seen in my entire life. There are more books than my boss Richard could fucking imagine.

I let out a squeal and rush forward to stand beneath one of the stacks. There's a ladder—a ladder!—needed to get to the very top. And it's even got wheels. I am *so* going to be using that.

"Do you like it?" Farron asks sheepishly.

"I love it." It's not just the mere size of the library, but it's opulence. The leaves rustle in the breeze as light gleams through stained-glass windows, and I can imagine how cozy it would be during a storm, hearing the rain pound against the glass. Murals decorate the walls, depicting each of the four seasons: a flower-strewn meadow filled with does and fawns, a raging ocean hitting a sandy coast, an autumn floor covered in red leaves, and a frozen lake lit by moonlight.

Couches and armchairs surround a huge fireplace, and there are tables and chairs throughout.

And the books themselves … The spines are beautifully colored, from the lightest pastels to the richest royals. The lettering is exquisite, some in gold leaf, others in silver that shimmer like starlight.

The only distraction from the library's beauty are the bundles of purple thorn bushes snaking up the stacks, creeping along the barriers, wrapping around the fall trees, and bursting through the bookshelves.

Farron stands in the middle of it all, a sweet smile upon his handsome face.

I can't make sense of it. The few times I saw him with the other princes, he seemed cowed by their presence. Even now, there's something a bit awkward about him. In an endearing way. How do I reconcile this man with the monster from the other night? And even if I can't … He's still a fae prince.

He's still imprisoning me.

But I'm going to need his help if I have any chance of breaking the curse.

"You do much reading where you're from?" he asks.

"I basically live in books." My finger trails down a gold-lettered spine. "I work in a bookstore, but it's like a fraction of the size of this place." Turning to him, a mischievous grin appears on my face. "Hey, are there any romance books here?"

He laughs and tugs on my hand. My face heats as his warm fingers lace with mine. The floor is covered in a blanket of leaves that crunch beneath our feet as we walk. He pulls me around one of the book stacks then reaches up to grab something above us. His shirt lifts as he does so, revealing a toned stomach and a trickle of warm brown hair dipping below his pant line. A jolt of electricity runs through me.

He pulls the book down, revealing a gorgeous light blue tome. "The fae love legends of romance," he says, and his voice is breathy. "This one is about a princess from the Spring Realm who was betrothed to a prince of Autumn." He leans down, shoulder-to-shoulder with me so I can see the pages as he flips through. Rich notes of aged paper and ink, and a hint of orange and cinnamon linger in the air, along with the faint musk of the old book. The art is breathtaking, like an otherworldly Mucha piece. "But right before her wedding, she left the castle to ride her horse by the riverbank and came upon a carpenter who lived deep in the woods. In that moment, her mate bond awoke in her chest."

"Her mate bond?" I repeat breathlessly.

"I don't believe they occur in the human realm," he says, looking at me through his dark lashes. I shake my head no. His brow creases and he looks upward, as if trying to figure out how to describe breathing. "A mate bond is very rare and sacred. It's said to be the calling out of your soul for another; the melding of hearts; the quintessence of life itself."

Farron stares at me intensely and raises a hand to my mouth. His fingers tremble over my bottom lip, down my chin, and along the curve of my throat. He lays a hand flat on my chest, cresting over the mounds of my breasts, pushed up from the tightly laced dress. I wonder if he can feel the pounding of my heart.

"It's said you feel the mate bond here," he murmurs, his voice husky. "Like a second heart."

"So, she lived happily ever after with her carpenter?" I whisper, if only to distract myself from Farron's hand upon me, his warm palm rising and falling with my rapid breaths.

"Hmm?" Farron quickly pulls back and clears his throat.

"The fae princess?"

"Oh, yes. No. She didn't live happily ever after." He slams the book shut. "When her betrothed discovered she'd been mate-bound, he killed the carpenter in a fit of jealousy. The princess then killed her betrothed and took his throne for herself."

"Not exactly your classic fairytale ending," I say. Goosebumps bloom on my body where his hand had been.

He gives a sheepish smile. "No, certainly not."

"So, Prince Farron, where do we start?"

"Just Farron, please." He pulls me back into the main foyer of the library. "I'm not much of a prince these days. Hard to rule your realm when you turn into a slobbering beast each night."

"You're from the Autumn Realm, right? Isn't there an Autumn King or Queen or someone to rule?"

He grabs a book off a shelf and hands it to me, then leaps up the ladder and throws me down two more. "It's not like that. All four realms—Spring, Summer, Autumn, and Winter—are part of the Enchanted Vale. And the Enchanted Vale was ruled by a queen who lived in this very castle. She anointed four High Rulers for each of her realms. The queen disappeared five hundred years ago, though."

I struggle to keep up with the heavy load of books Farron keeps piling into my arms. "So, you've been ruling the Autumn Realm for five hundred years?"

He laughs. "No. There's been many different rulers throughout the years. My mother was High Princess, but she'd had enough. She passed the title—and the magic that comes with it—down to me as her eldest child."

Ezryn had also said he'd inherited the Blessing of Spring from his mother. Did that mean Dayton and Keldarion received blessings from one of their parents, as well?

With a sigh of relief, I heave the books onto an oak table and collapse in a chair. "Okay, fae politics are crazy. I'm still trying to wrap my head around the fact that there's like this whole alternate dimension literally sitting in the forest outside of my home."

Farron smiles at me, his expression almost boyish. "Trust me, it's better that our world is kept a secret from yours. The magic in our realms ..." He looks down and runs a tongue along his bottom lip. "Let's say it's safer for humans that we keep our distance. As you well know."

"Not that Keldarion cares about humans." I blow a curl away from my face. "I have no idea what he wants from me. Why he won't let me go."

Farron scoots a chair up right beside me and grabs my hands. I straighten, surprised by the intensity on his face. "Listen, Rosalina. When we were first cursed twenty-five years ago, there was some hope at the beginning that we could break it. That we could return to normal. But as the years past, the other princes … They've lost hope. And none so much as Kel. But maybe, just maybe …" His eyes sparkle. "A little human interference is the kick he needs in his stubborn ass."

"Well, if it means being free of him, I'm all for it." I walk over to a thatch of thorns creeping along a windowsill. "These are part of the curse too, I imagine?"

"Actually, no." Farron comes up behind me, his warm breath caressing my neck. "These are a gift from Caspian. The Prince of Thorns."

The Prince of Thorns. Ezryn had accused me of being his spy when we first met. "Everyone seems so afraid of him." Or in Marigold's case … horny and afraid. "Who is this guy anyway?"

Farron shakes his head. "A villain from the Realm Below. The curse not only traps us in beast form every night, but it also weakens our magic. Caspian has used it as an opportunity to spread his dark evil with these thorns." Farron gestures around the library. "They take over everything, sapping Castletree of her magic. Our home is more special than you could possibly imagine. It's her magic that gives strength and vitality to the four realms. Caspian would see our lands become barren with briars and covered in shadow."

Wow. No wonder Ezryn was so upset when he thought I was a spy.

I turn away and march back to the book stack. "Okay, well, we can only deal with what we can control. Once the curse is broken, you guys will have your full magic back and you can kick this Prince of Thorns' thorny ass."

Farron gives a lopsided smirk. "I like your style."

"Give me more details. What have you tried to break the curse?" I pull my hair back, ready to focus.

"What could we do? We are monsters." Farron's eyes stare distantly at the ceiling. "Especially in the first years. Back then, even the others had no mastery of the beast. We stayed in the castle. Ran free in the wilds of the Briar at night. At least then, the only beings we hurt were the goblins."

"Surely you guys have tried to find your mates."

"Dayton, Ez, and I did, in what ways we could. We each assigned our realms vassals to watch over while we're trapped here. No one knows about this curse except for those in the castle. Everyone else thinks we're here trying to stop the thorns." Farron closes his eyes. "My parents are ruling the Autumn Realm right now. As the Blessing of Autumn has already passed to me, it's a grueling job. It's difficult lying to them. But if they knew the truth ..."

I reach out and grab his hand. "We'll figure this out, Farron. I promise."

He tucks a curl behind my ear. "I hope so. For all our sakes."

25

EZRYN

Dawn paints Castletree's bridge with golden light. The doors into the castle beckon me, and for once, I feel eager to get home.

Despite the clear morning, a chill seeps under my clothes, and I suppress a shiver. I spent the night hunting a goblin pack all the way to the western edge of the Briar. In the end, I caught my prey, slaughtering them with tooth and claw, but it took me far off my intended path. When dawn broke, I was far from where I'd stashed my armor. Thankfully, I've planted caches all over the Briar that I always keep stocked with an extra helm, gloves, and a set of warm linens. It feels strange to approach Castletree in only my simple clothing and plain helm.

Though I'm not spending weeks on end in the Briar like I used to, I continue to patrol our perimeter most nights. The thought of a single goblin stepping anywhere near the castle sends a burning rage through my body.

I need to keep our home safe. If that means slaughtering every last monster from the Below, then so be it.

Pulling open the doors, I step into the entrance hall. It's so early, everyone should still be asleep. The creek of the door echoes through the empty room.

Except it's not entirely empty. There's someone standing to the side, examining the fireplace. It hasn't been lit in a long time, the hearth overtaken by briars.

The person turns to me and smiles brightly. A smile that seems too bright for me. "Good morning, Ezryn."

"Rosalina," I breathe. What is she doing up and in the entrance hall? I notice she's still wearing her sleepwear, a simple white chemise, the waist gathered with a bow, the long-sleeved cuffs embroidered with lace. Her long hair is unbrushed, bangs curling over her eyes. Her feet are bare.

There's something wild about the way she looks, like I've caught her in a way I'm not supposed to. I suck in a breath before remembering my manners. "Good morning."

She tucks a strand of hair behind her ear. "Sorry, I hope I didn't surprise you. I woke up early and wanted to see something."

"This is your home as much as mine."

She gives a half-hearted laugh.

"I mean it," I say. Rosalina has been living with us for two weeks now, and she's fit right into castle life. The staff who had long abandoned their jobs have returned to the work that once fulfilled them. The kitchen is always bursting with delicious smells, the furniture is dusted, and every banister that isn't covered in thorns glimmers with polish.

Every time I see her, Rosalina is always talking with someone, or helping them with some odd job or another. Of course, that's when she's not tucked into the library with Farron. He's truly taken a shine to her, and I'm glad for it. The boy deserves a friend.

Admittedly, I've peered in on them working together several times in the last few weeks. I'm familiar now with some of her little habits, like how she always stands and stares down at a text when she's frustrated, or how she has to have at least three books open at all times. Her determination is admirable. It even makes me question myself. *Can she do it? Can you figure this out?*

"Uh, what about you?" She quirks her head. "Couldn't sleep either?"

"I'm not much of a sleeper. The nights are thick with goblins. Someone has to deal with them."

I notice her eyes have drifted from my helm down to my chest. This is the first time she's ever seen me without my armor—I'm wearing only the tight-fitted black shirt and pants from my cache, and simple dark gray helm.

Her gaze is slow, taking in the details of my body as if I were a statue on display. I don't know if she even took in what I said. "I was out in the Briar," I repeat.

"Huh? Oh!" She brings her gaze back to my helm, face flushed. "That's right. Marigold told me you patrol the Briar every night. That's very brave of you."

"It's not bravery. It's duty. I can either sit with the shame of my curse, or I can do something good with it. Like protect my family."

She shrugs. "Seems pretty brave to me."

I raise a brow, though she can't see it. "Brave is trading your freedom for your father's. Brave is allowing yourself to be imprisoned in a world you know nothing about."

She snorts. "That's not bravery at all. That's love. Just love."

Her mouth curves into a strange half-smile, and the words seem to catch in my throat. I flex my fingers, finding my voice. "My mother would say one must be fearless to love, and to let oneself be loved. Love in itself is a leap of faith."

"She sounds like a wise woman." Rosalina swishes the hem of her skirt. "Your duty is a form of love, too, don't you think? You protect Castletree because you love the princes and the staff."

I think of Farron and his excitement whenever he shares new mythos of the Spring Realm with me. Of afternoons spent sparring with Dayton. Of memories of Marigold back in Florendel when she directly served my mother.

And I think of Keldarion. Of how he never did right by me, and I'll never do right by him.

"I suppose you've got a point," I admit to Rosalina. "Still, you've stood up to Kel. If that's not bravery, I don't know what is."

She shrugs again, so dismissive of herself. "That's easy. Kel may act mean, but... He's good. I can feel it."

"You can feel it?"

"When I'm at home in Orca Cove, I don't feel right. It's like... everyone is a triangle, and I'm a circle. Every time I walk through town, they all know I don't belong. I'm a great big spot on their lives." She turns away and looks down at her feet.

Slowly, I walk around until I'm right in front of her. I lift her chin with a gloved finger until she blinks up at me. "We're all spots here."

A beautiful smile crosses her face.

She's smiling like that *for me.*

Quickly, I drop my hand and step back.

"I think that's something I've learned since coming here." Rosalina turns back to the fireplace. "I'm going to keep my bargain with Kel and earn my freedom. And when I return to Orca Cove, I'm going to try to remember it's not so bad to be a spot. Though it's easy to be myself here."

I stand beside her. "How so?"

"Like Kel, Castletree is *good.* Even with all this." She gestures to the briars. "I can feel it."

It's hard to think of Castletree as a place of goodness when I remember what it used to be like before the curse, before the Prince of Thorns stole its magic. Even with the joy that's permeated in the last two weeks, Castletree is a shell of what it once was.

But perhaps some of the Queen's magic lingers deep within the roots. Maybe Rosalina is right—there is some goodness left.

"Trust yourself. You have a strong intuition." I quirk my helm. "You said you woke up this morning wanting to see something."

"Oh right!" She peers at the fireplace. "I wanted to see the roses. My father plucked one from the hearth. It made Kel furious."

"Roses used to bloom all over Castletree before the briars overtook it," I explain. "Over the last twenty-five years, we've watched them die one by one. To us, they represent the loss of our own magic, our ability to protect the Vale." A heavy breath rises in my throat. "They're all gone now."

"No, they're not."

I look at her. "Yes, your father plucked the last—"

She grabs my arm and tugs me toward the hearth. My heart leaps in my chest, surprised by the sudden contact. My face flushes with heat.

Rosalina doesn't let go as she points into the hearth to a tangle of brambles. "Look!"

Roses. Red roses bursting into bloom, nestled safely among light brown branches. These aren't Caspian's briars. These are Castletree's.

"How is it possible?" I breathe.

"I don't know." Rosalina's eyes are bright as she stares at the blooms. "Have you ever seen anything so beautiful?"

I look down at her hand on my arm, then up at her face, her shining eyes, her soft smile. "No," I whisper. "Never before."

26

FARRON

L ife is certainly full of idiosyncrasies.

One day you're High Prince of your realm, living your life as if you have the world at your fingertips. And the next day, you're a blood-seeking monster ready to tear the face off the first living thing you see.

And one day, you're the same blood-seeking monster but a human woman walks into the dungeon determined to free you from yourself. And despite trying to tear her face off … She forgives you.

Like I said. Idiosyncrasies.

It's been almost a full month since Rosalina joined us as our guest. Well, that's not quite right. She's technically a prisoner. She can't go home by Keldarion's orders. Often I wonder to myself if she's planning an escape attempt. But without an escort through the Briars, she'd be fine prey for the goblins.

As I climb the ladder in the library to fetch one of our oldest relics from the top shelf, I cast a glance down at her sitting at the table. She's leaning over some loose papers we found on a back shelf, comparing the information to a different text. Her nose is scrunched up, eyes determined, and dark brow furrowed.

I can't help but wonder if she's enjoying her stay in Castletree.

Every day we meet in the library for research, and every day she brings even more determination and optimism.

After twenty-five years of being surrounded by doom, gloom, nihilism, and total denial, I have to say it's refreshing.

I tuck the small book into my waistband and push my feet on either side of the ladder, sliding all the way down.

"Jeez, don't do that. You'll break an ankle," she says.

I chuckle and hand her the book. She snatches it and immediately starts pouring over the Table of Contents.

It's been so long since I entered the human realm, and I spend so little time outside of Castletree, I don't ever see the few humans who've accidentally wandered through the Enchanted Vale and chosen to stay. Rosalina's nothing like how I remember humans.

Her dark hair tumbles over her shoulders, falling in a wavy cascade down her back. A few leaves have nestled into her tresses. Tracking back and forth across the page, her brown eyes sparkle in the late afternoon light. And the curves of her body are perfectly on display in a tight cream-colored chemise with laces down the front and a flowing brown skirt that sits snugly across her hips. The laces of her blouse have come loose, opening the front to reveal a glimpse of the milky-white mounds of her breasts—

Oh, stars. What am I doing? We're researching. I'm not ogling her like a piece of meat the way Dayton always does.

But though my logical brain agrees with this notion, my body does not. I quickly sit so I can subtly adjust myself under the table. Thank the stars she's so absorbed in her work.

Perhaps I could ignore these pesky inklings of desire if she were merely beautiful. But she had to go and be smart as well, sharp as the many thorns around Castletree. Delight fills me every time we bounce ideas off one another, and she seems to pick up and connect with a concept like no one I've ever seen before. And I've never met anyone who wants to stay in the library for as long as she does. If we didn't have Kel's mandatory dinners—and my beast's arrival every night—I'd suspect we'd stay here until dawn.

Rosalina starts reading out loud, but I can't concentrate, which is entirely abnormal for me. Research is the one thing I can lose myself in. The one thing that gives me hope.

But every part of my mind is concentrating on two things and two things only: the perfect pair of breasts in front of me.

Why did I sit here? I could have sat anywhere else, but I'm front and center now to the entire display. I try to look elsewhere, but I can't help it: my eyes flick back to her, leaning over the table, shirt totally agape. Her breasts hang heavy and soft, the nipples barely covered by the chemise. Damn, if she were to adjust slightly, everything would be visible.

I can't move now. My cock stands at full attention, straining against my pants with urgent need. If I get up, she'll clearly see me pining for her. And that's not an option. This is her home now, and the last thing she needs is to assume one of her captors wants to throw her over this table and fuck her on top of the books we've been pouring over for the last month.

I scrub my face with my hands. No, no, no. What is wrong with me? I'm not like Dayton, a man-whoring rapscallion. Over the last month, Rosalina and I have become ... Dare I say it? Friends?

At least acquaintances in a way she isn't with the other princes. Keldarion seems to loathe her. They spend our forced dinners exchanging snarky comments before Kel usually loses his temper and storms back to his room. Ezryn, despite my urging to get to know her, refuses to engage beyond the most basic exchanges. I can see it in his shoulders: the way he tenses when she tries to talk to him, or even just when she enters the room. And Dayton ... Dayton does as is expected. When he's not too drunk to focus, he stares at her like she's the last drop of water in the Vale and he's dying of thirst.

My face heats, and I have to concentrate to keep my expression neutral.

"—interesting, right?"

I blink, and Rosalina glowers at me. "Farron, are you listening to me at all?"

"Huh?" I straighten, suddenly feeling like I'm a boy again, caught daydreaming in class.

"What I was just reading? It's interesting, isn't it?"

"Y-yes. Very interesting. Good find." I clear my throat. She still hasn't corrected the loose laces of her bodice.

I flick my gaze from her face back down to the spectacular sight of her breasts. It would be so easy to reach out and cup their fullness, to spin her around and push her down onto the table. We've been together nearly every day for the last month. I've seen her look at me when she thinks I'm not aware. Her eyes scanning my body from top to bottom, lingering on my chest, my arms.

What would she do if I tried?

She raises a brow and looks down to where my eyes are trained. Notices the loose laces. "Oh god, I'm a mess," she mumbles and quickly does them up. "Sorry." Her cheeks heat a brilliant pink.

I stand so quickly, my chair clatters to the floor. I snatch her trembling hands away from the laces and they fall loose. "You have nothing to be sorry for. I'm sorry. It's … You make me nervous."

Her eyes widen until the whites show all around. "*I* make *you* nervous? You're an otherworldly prince who lives in a *castle*. And you're smart and nice to me—for some reason—and you're, like, super-hot and oh my god, I've said way too much …" She trails off, eyes down at the floor. With a mumble, she finishes, "I usually wear hoodies."

A beat passes between us and I laugh. She raises a brow at me, then laughs too. "Why are we laughing?"

"I don't know what a hoodie is," I admit. "But it sounds ridiculous."

"You don't know what a hoodie is?" she cries. "Oh my god. I need to get you one. You'll never go back to your waist coats and fancy vests and suspenders—" She slaps my chest softly, before resting her fingers over my collarbone.

"Farron," she whispers and closes her eyes. "If it were up to you, would you set me free?"

Something deep within me snarls in my mind: *No. Mine. Mine forever.* But I shake my head, wavy strands of hair falling in front of my eyes. "Of course I would, Rosalina."

She chews on her bottom lip. "What's it like to know you have a mate out there, someone just for you?"

I let out a deep sigh and lean back in my chair. "I don't know, honestly. As you've learned, mates are quite rare. It's not something most of us grow up thinking about."

"So, fae don't wait around for their mates." She runs a hand along the frozen bracelet on her right wrist. "Do you get married like humans do?"

Grabbing a book from across the table, I flip it open to a page. An image bordered in flowers depicts a fae marriage. "In a fashion, yes. There are ceremonies to dedicate your life to another. Though they don't have the same magic as a mate bond."

"The magic." Rosalina's eyes widen. "The magic we've read about. Is it real? Hearing your mate in your mind, the sparkly feeling, the overpowering sexual urges—" Her face flushes.

"I don't know." My face grows hot as well. "Ezryn's parents were mated. And I believe Kel's grandparents. They may know a bit more about it."

Rosalina rolls her eyes. "Like they'd ever talk to me."

I continue to flip through the pages. "The lack of a mate bond doesn't stop some rather wild fae from trying to mimic the magic with their own chosen partner. It can be quite dangerous." I end on a page with swirling purple and green illustrations.

"Mimic the magic?" Rosalina asks.

I run my finger over the rough paper. "All fae have the magic of bargains, and some fae use them with their lovers to make a love pact. It could be as harmless as remembering to say, 'I love you' every day or else you'll sprout a white hair, or as grave as your own death if you ever strayed to the wayward lips of another."

"Can the magic really do that?"

"Fae magic is powerful," I explain. "The stronger the love, the stronger the bargain. These fae are desperate to recreate the power they glimpse in mates."

Rosalina runs her fingers along the picture, then looks up at me.

"Well, I hope when we find your mate, Farron, she's everything you've ever dreamt of."

How can she know I've been dreading that moment for years? But there's such kindness in her words, I can't help but smile. "Thank you, Rosie."

She flushes. "Rosie?"

"I mean, Rosalina. Sorry, I—"

"No." She grabs my hand, and I wonder if she can feel my racing pulse. "It's cute."

She blinks up at me, her eyes so wide. She's the one that's cute, that's beautiful. I wonder what her lips taste like, the sound she'd make if I were to run my tongue along her neck …

She shifts closer. "You don't deserve this life. You're so good and kind. The Enchantress is truly evil."

At the memory of the Enchantress, anger and shame and utter guilt roar up inside of me. It isn't fair. It isn't fucking fair. I'm not like the rest of them who deserved it. Not like the one who betrayed his realm, or the one who abandoned it. Not like the one who misused his power.

And yet I am trapped here all the same.

"Farron? I'm sorry. I've said too much." Rosalina turns around and rubs her arm.

"No, it's—" As I'm about to decide if I should tell her about the night of the curse, a booming clatter arises from outside the library doors leading from the entrance hall.

Boisterous laughter and the breaking of glass sound. And then … a woman's voice.

"Oh fiddlesticks," I mumble. It can only be one thing.

I sprint out of the library with Rosalina behind me. I have to find out what's going on before Keldarion does.

We run down the Autumn passage, leaves and twigs snapping beneath our feet.

"What's going on?" Rosalina cries. "In case I never mentioned it, I'm not huge on running—"

As we round the corner to the top of the staircase overlooking the entrance hall, I freeze.

Oh, fuck. It's worse than I thought.

He actually brought someone here.

Dayton leans against the rose gold frame of the mirror, a jug of foul-smelling alcohol in one hand, and the ass of a busty blond fae in the other.

It's all I can do to take a snarling breath. The wolf inside me lunges at my chest, clawing at my ribs. He's desperate to break out. And if I let my rage take over, it will be a blood bath in here.

But even that won't be as bad as what would happen if Keldarion sees a stranger inside the castle.

We run down the stairs and into the main foyer. Rosalina doubles over, panting. But her eyes aren't on Dayton or the fae woman. They're on the mirror. Oh right. I suppose we haven't explained that. She probably thought it was a decoration.

The brilliant mirror waves with iridescent light. It's about the size of a door and it lights up the room with fractals of blue and red and green. They flicker across Dayton's bare chest. In fact, he's only wearing the traditional garb of the Summer Realm, a short leather girdle that hugs tight to his muscular ass. His long blond hair falls over his shoulders and he's got that sleepy half-smile he always gets when he's pissed out of his mind.

The blond fae woman is obviously drunk too, grabbing at his chest and laughing between hiccups.

"Dayton," I growl. "What are you doing?"

Dayton flicks his gaze at me, and his eyes sparkle with mirth. "Farron, you've come to welcome me home. Don't worry. It's quite unnecessary." His words slur and he chucks the bottle to the ground. It rolls toward Rosalina. She slams her foot down on it to stop its movement.

"Dayton, this is highly irresponsible, even for you," Rosalina says, and her serious tone almost makes me crack a smile. Almost. "You know what Keldarion did to his last visitor."

"Well, aren't you just Queen of the Castle now?" Dayton laughs.

The fae woman pitches forward, squishing her considerable chest against Dayton's bare body. My heart pounds and I dig my nails into my palms to concentrate on the pain. "Dayton, why are these two nattering at us? I thought we were going to your bedroom." She reaches down and grabs Dayton's cock through the leather.

My face burns, and I hate the way Dayton smiles as her hand massages him. He's putting on a fucking show, tilting his head back and squinting his eyes. "You're right, darling. Look at these two. Like nattering flies." He grabs her by the shoulders and shoves her against the wall, but his eyes are on me. "Maybe they want to join us." He runs his tongue across her jaw and down her neck before burying his face in her tits.

Rosalina stiffens beside me, and her face is beet-red. "J-join you?"

Dayton looks up from the fae woman's breasts. "You interested, Blossom? Come over here, and I'll show you how the fae make love." He licks his lips, gaze intense.

I can't say anything. I can't even move. Rage fills every fiber of my being. How dare Dayton disobey Keldarion's sacred rule? Kel may be a crotchety, paranoid asshole, but this rule protects us. No one comes into Castletree. No one.

And to parade this fae in front of us, this random woman in her sheer gown that barely covers the top of her thighs ... Well, I should have expected that. I'm used to Dayton staring at me when his cock is buried deep in another man or woman. But to ask Rosalina to join ...

I want to rip his throat out. I want to scream at him. I want to storm out of here and let him face Keldarion's wrath.

But I'm rooted to the spot.

Coward.

But ... she's not. Rosalina shakes her head and wrinkles her nose. "Enough. Dayton, you need to grow up. I have no idea how old you are. Probably like four million. But you're acting like a stupid teenager." She storms over and grabs the fae woman's arm. "And you! Do you know how dangerous this is? You don't even know anything about where this idiot has taken you."

"He's the fucking Prince of Summer—" the fae woman begins but Rosalina cuts her off with a tug toward the mirror.

"Yeah, and he's a jerk for taking you here. It's dangerous. But he doesn't care about you." She levels a glower toward Dayton that sends ice down even my spine. "He only cares about himself."

Dayton looks like he wants to respond, but he wavers on his feet before slumping against the wall.

"We need to get you home. How do I work this thing? Farron?" She turns back to me, but my muscles still feel frozen. "Farron, snap out of it. I need you."

I need you.

It's like those three words ignite a fire under me. Rosalina needs me. I surge forward, stumbling over my own feet, before straightening before her. "Y-yes?"

"Work your magic on this enchanted mirror thing," Rosalina says. "We need to send our new friend back home."

"Right." I cough then take the fae woman by the shoulders. She looks like she's going to punch me ... or be sick.

Taking a deep breath, I place a hand upon her forehead and feel for the deep magic within Castletree. Every day, as the curse strengthens, the tree weakens. Even now, I have to strain to bring the slightest bit of magic to my fingertips.

"This is but a dream. When you awaken, you will remember this as a figment of a fitful sleep," I whisper. The wisps of autumn magic—the decay, the falling leaves, the ending that lies within—seep into her mind, muddling this memory.

She blinks, her eyes foggy.

"Now, think of your bed. Can you picture it? Can you see it?"

"Yes," she murmurs.

I point her toward the mirror. "Very good. Keep that picture in your mind and walk through. You'll find yourself exactly where you want to go."

"Such a strange dream," she mumbles as she steps into the mirror. Her body ripples with shimmering light. And then she's gone.

I turn to see Dayton sitting on the floor, his head nodding against his chest.

I know why he does it. The same reason Keldarion won't leave the castle. The same reason Ez prefers to be the beast instead of the man. The same reason I lose myself in research. We're all trying to escape.

But damn if it doesn't break my fucking heart when he does.

"Is he okay?" Rosalina asks, walking over and poking his chest.

He swats her hand. "I'm awake."

"Sorry, Rosie," I say. "I know you were telling me something exciting that you found, but I think I'll have to cut our research session short. I've got to get Dayton to his room."

"Can I help at all?" She looks so genuine, concern painted across her features.

"No, trust me. This isn't the first time," I say.

"And it won't be the last," Dayton slurs before his head falls to the side.

"Okay. I'm going to keep looking at that book you found," she says.

I squeeze her hand, wanting one last piece of contact between us before she leaves. "I'll be in the Summer Wing if you need anything."

She nods and leaves, her wide hips sashaying up the stairs and out of view.

I blow out a huge breath and tell my cock to get on the same page as my head.

And right now, that means dealing with the two-hundred-and-fifty pounds of drunk-ass muscle before me.

"You're an idiot," I snap as I lean down to heave Dayton's arm around my shoulder.

"You like her," he says in a sing-song voice.

I haul him to his feet. Stars, he's heavy. "What?"

"You liiike her," Dayton sings again. "I saw the way you looked at her. You like her—"

I slam Dayton against the stone wall. "I like *you*," I snarl. "And if you pull that shit again, Keldarion will rip your throat out—"

Dayton snags a handful of my hair and pulls, so I'm looking straight up at him. Damn, for being so drunk, his reflexes are still fast. Breath comes ragged out of my throat. Our chests touch, and his pecs glisten with sweat. "You chased away my fuck, Farron."

"You don't need her." My voice is a raspy growl.

"I don't know about that," he says. "My cock is desperate for something tight and warm."

"You're too drunk," I counter.

He grabs my hand and forces it onto his girdle. His bulging hardness is evident even through the thick leather. "Fucking try me, Farron."

27

ROSALINA

I'm the first one in the dining hall when Astrid brings me down after my afternoon walk around the grounds. I'd felt strange after Farron left with Dayton. Something about the whole situation annoyed me. I couldn't stop picturing the fae girl sucking on Dayton's neck like a vampire.

But a few laps around the grounds and tearing leaves into tiny pieces made me feel slightly better. It wasn't like I was jealous. How could I be jealous when I was literally trying to find the princes' mates? But I knew that Dayton's mate wasn't that blond fae.

Thank goodness Farron got rid of her. I'd felt better the moment he'd shoved her through the mirror. It always seemed odd placement for décor, but now I understand what it actually is. An enchanted transportation mirror … The fae woman only had to picture where she wanted to go, and it had carried her there. Unfortunately, it had needed Farron's magic to work, otherwise I could use it to go back home.

The staff spread dinner across the table as I take my seat. Today there's baked squash topped with nuts, a side of roasted vegetables, and more of that fluffy bread.

Where is everyone?

I pull out the book I'd taken from the library to continue my research, more motivated than ever to prove that the fae woman was *not* Dayton's mate.

"It's rude to read at the table." A rough voice jolts me from my book, and I look up to see Keldarion standing at his usual seat across from me.

His pure white hair is wet, dampening the fabric of his shirt. It seems almost a size too small, clinging to all the right places. His scent fills me with a strange thrill, a combination of pine and something more primal—a salty sea musk.

"You were in Dayton's hot springs."

"I do bathe," Keldarion says, loading his plate with food, "occasionally."

I can't help but laugh at that, and when I look up at him, he's stilled, and giving me a bemused expression. Flushing, I look away. The rest of the table is still empty.

"Dayton drank a little too much," I say, careful not to mention the guest he brought in. "Farron went to help him."

"Farron makes a show of trying to untangle the curse." Keldarion utters a sound of displeasure from the back of his throat. "You'll soon find out that he's his own worst enemy."

"Where's Ezryn?" I notice his empty seat.

Keldarion slams a dollop of roasted squash on his plate. "Hunting."

"Hunting? Like for food?"

"Goblins," Keldarion says. "His efforts are a waste, though. For every one he kills, the Below creates two more."

"Why does Ezryn go if it makes no difference?"

Keldarion inclines his head. A water droplet slides down the strong curve of his jaw. "Ezryn has a great hatred for all creatures of the Below. Hunting is how he controls that rage."

I guess it's just going to be me and Keldarion for dinner tonight. Nope, not awkward at all …

Keldarion runs his hand through his hair before returning to serving his dinner, but his scent wafts toward me again.

I can't help but give another deep inhale. There's something so incredibly right about his smell mixing with Dayton's, a fusion of winter and summer.

I shake my head. What is wrong with me? Maybe it's something about being in the fae world, but I never noticed smells this much before.

It gives me an idea. Maybe mates smell the same, and we can use that to help them find theirs. I turn back to my book and thumb through it, looking for any information about scents.

There's a clink in front of me as Keldarion drops a perfectly prepared plate of food. Even with the extra roll, just how I like it.

"I was going to eat," I mumble, turning back to my book, "right after this chapter."

Keldarion grabs my book and yanks it up. "I told you. It's rude to read at dinner."

"It's also rude to steal someone's book." I don't let go. Neither does he, and suddenly I'm dangling as he's holding both me and my book above the ground.

I glower at him and kick my legs. A terrible ripping sounds. I guess this book wasn't built to hold a grown-ass woman, because now I'm falling through the air.

Keldarion drops the book and grabs me around the waist. I let out an unladylike "Oof!" Now he's holding me like we're about to walk into our first house.

This is so embarrassing.

But it's also strange. I'm not worried about being too heavy for him. He doesn't look strained. Just angry.

I'm used to that.

"My book," I whimper as the pages of it flutter around us. I reach out and grab one.

"What was so important anyway?" he grumbles.

"It was for you, idiot. I'm researching mates, remember?"

An annoyed rumble sounds in his chest, which I feel because I'm literally pressed right against it. "It's a waste of your time."

"No, it's not." I can't even look at him. Instead, I read the page in front of me. This is a passage I haven't seen before. My brows shoot up, and I scramble in his arms to get down.

But he doesn't let me go. Instead, we awkwardly tussle until my arms are looped around his neck, my legs around his waist, but I can't concentrate on that because I'm so focused on this page. This could be good. This could be really good.

I finish reading the page. *This is it!* This is the first real lead I've found.

Except I'm still in Kel's arms like some sort of demon spider monkey, and I'm not sure why he hasn't put me down yet. I know he's a powerful force of nature, but he's gentle with me. His hard body presses against my curves and his heat travels through me like wildfire. How can he be a Prince of Winter when I'm melting in his strong embrace? My skin tingles and my heart races. The intoxicating scent of pine merged with salt makes my head spin, and all I want is more.

The touch of our hands during the bargain hadn't been like this. That was nothing compared to now. His muscular arms tighten around me, like he's never going to let me go. His inhale is a delicious shudder.

Wait, what? Is he seriously smelling my hair right now?

Breath catches in my throat. "What do I smell like?"

His body stiffens, then he growls, "Get. Off. Of. Me."

I scramble off him, my heart thumping against my ribs and my throat constricting. His face doesn't show the rage I expected, rather something indefinable, as if he's trying to convey a meaning I can't quite discern. "Your mate ... I—"

"What?" he says through clenched teeth.

"I think I know a way to find her," I say, and his expression softens. I wave the page in my hand. "It says here that sometimes in great trauma, the mating bond can lie dormant for years, even decades. Perhaps all your mating bonds were suppressed during the curse by that wicked enchantress. So, we need to trigger it. Bring it to the surface. It mentions here it can awaken during something big, like a mate being in danger, or during a moment of significance." My fingers dig into the sleeve of his shirt. "If we could figure out how to stage an event like that, maybe you could all find your mates."

"You're rambling," he says, but his voice has lost all menace.

"I have the best idea! Oh my gosh, I have to find Farron."

I duck and scramble to pick up pages of the torn book. "Thanks for the help!" I look back at him as I exit the dining hall, but he's just staring at me, that same unreadable expression on his handsome face.

28

ROSALINA

My mind races with ideas. Of course, it all makes sense now. I have to find Farron and run this theory by him. He said he would be in the Summer Wing, putting Dayton to bed. He should be about done with that drunk idiot by now.

I've heard so many rumors about Dayton and his exploits. I know he's basically the fae version of a man-whore. But to see that girl in his arms, in my home …

My home?

What the hell is wrong with me? This is not my home. My home is Orca Cove. My home is the messy little house I share with Papa. My home is … with Lucas.

But something about that feels so wrong. I've been here a month now and I've found my routine. Being greeted by Astrid every morning. Choosing clothes and hairstyles with Marigold. Spending my days in the library with Farron. Even eating with the princes. As terrifying as they are, I'm learning their little quirks. Like how Dayton and Farron have heated arguments on which realm has the best food. Or how I always catch Ezryn pocketing muffins under the table—I assume he eats them alone, but it's like he doesn't want anyone to know he likes the chocolate ones best. And every once in a while, I catch

Keldarion smirking at something one of the other's has done. It's always gone in an instant, but that one glimpse makes my insides feel lit up like a Christmas tree.

At the thought of Keldarion, my body swells with the feeling of how he'd held me. *Held me?* No, he was only making sure I didn't fall to the floor. I have to get my head on straight. This is not my home.

I have a job to do.

And that means I need to let Farron know what I found right away.

I rush into the Summer Wing, sprinting down the hallway with the walls that shimmer like an underwater grotto. Even the smell here is different: like salt and sand and tropical fruit. The ceiling is painted with a mesmerizing mural of seabirds flitting through the sky, and even the doorhandles are made from shells. As with every other area of the castle, the black thorns cut through stone and glass, strangling the walls and floor.

Where is Farron? He must have put Dayton to bed by now.

I turn a corner and rush toward the biggest door: a turquoise blue wood with a shell-encrusted frame. Dayton's chambers. The door is ajar, and I creep in, peering through the dark to catch sight of Farron.

I've never been in any of the princes' chambers, but as I imagined, it's massive. I bet it's bigger than my entire house. The main room is dark, the dusky light outside mostly blocked by enormous floor-to-ceiling curtains. But a corner of the chamber is lit by tall torches. I creep into the room and peek around the corner.

My mouth dries up and my stomach clenches like a bear trap. I blink, not sure if what I'm seeing is real or some sort of mirage.

I found Farron.

But he's not alone.

He's with Dayton.

Quickly, I pull myself back around the corner, so I'm shielded from view. My heart beats a million miles per hour. I need to leave. This is such an invasion of privacy. I can creep back out the door …

But I can't help myself. It's like every fiber of my being is pulling me back to peer around the corner. Just one more look …

No, it isn't a mirage. Dayton lies on the bed, bathed in the orange torchlight. His long, golden hair falls around his head like a halo, and he's got the cockiest grin I've ever seen on his face.

And he's fucking naked.

His body's strewn out like a goddamn Greek god. His muscular chest glistens, and his hand stretches down to grip the base of his cock.

Fuck. Dayton's hands must be massive to reach all the way around that monster. His cock stands at attention, his hand rhythmically coasting over the hard flesh. The tip shimmers with a pearl of pre-cum, and I swallow, my mouth suddenly salivating.

But it's the sight on top of him that has my heart damn near bursting out of my chest. Farron leans over him, his long, toned body as naked as Dayton's.

I'd seen a glimpse of Dayton's body in the hot springs. But I've never seen Farron like this, without his glasses and his waist coat and his tailed jacket.

I'd be lying to myself if I said I'd never thought about it. How could I not? Every day we'd spent together, I'd gotten to know Farron outside of the rabid wolf who tried to kill me. He is kind and funny and awkwardly charming. And that gorgeous face ... How could I not imagine what he was hiding under all those fancy clothes?

And his body is every bit as scrumptious as Dayton's.

Where Dayton is wide and buff, Farron is lean. His back ripples with muscles, and I trail my gaze down his spine to his perky ass ...

No, no, no. I'm being a creep. I need to leave—

"Fuck, Farron. You're so beautiful," Dayton murmurs and grabs the back of Farron's head, drawing him down for a kiss. "And you're so fucking hot when you're jealous."

"What is there to be jealous about?" Farron murmurs. His hand skirts over Dayton's thick thigh and to the top of his cock. He swirls a finger in the glistening pre-cum, then pops it in his mouth. "You always come back to me."

Dayton growls and grips the side of Farron's face. "Keep being cheeky and I'll come *on* your back, Pup."

"Too scared to keep your promise?" Farron draws his head down between Dayton's legs. "You said you weren't too drunk to fuck. Prove it. I want your cum running down my legs for days."

Holy hell. I grip the side of the wall and clench my thighs together. Heat swirls in my core like a boiling furnace. I knew Dayton and Farron had some sort of ... connection. But they're lovers.

And as much as I need to pull myself away, I physically can't. It's like my whole body is drawn to them, my heart near exploding at the thought of not witnessing this.

Dayton sits up and grabs Farron by the hair, yanking backward to expose his long neck. "You want to be fucked, Pup? Ask me. Beg for my cock."

Dayton's voice trembles through my mind: *Tell me, Rosalina, do you know how to beg?*

Farron lets out a stuttering breath I mimic. More of my weight falls against the wall as my knees buckle. Dayton's storming blue eyes train on Farron.

"I want your cock," Farron rasps, and my own lips move along with his words. "I need it, I *need* you."

"Then get on your knees like a good boy." Dayton sits up as Farron obeys, turning around on all fours, his ass in the air, facing away from Dayton.

Wetness drips down my thighs as I rub them together, desperate for any friction.

Dayton leans over and grabs a vial from his bedside, coating his hand in oil. "Now tell me, Pup, would you like me to go slow? Or would you like me to punish your ass?"

Farron grips the sheets. "Fuck me hard. I want to feel you split me open."

Dayton chuckles and rubs the oil over his dick. "My little sadist." Then he leans back on his heels and admires the view. "Fucking gorgeous."

With a little pat on Farron's ass, Dayton grabs his hips and drives himself in.

Farron cries out, burying his face in the sheets. And I hold on to the wall for dear life, my core electric with heat and need. I can feel myself there, both being fucked by Dayton and fucking Farron. A part of both of them.

In and out, in and out, Dayton ravages Farron's ass. His huge balls bounce with the force of the movement, slapping against Farron's skin. Farron bucks back like a wild animal, jerking his hips as hard as he can against Dayton.

I've never seen anything like it: this desperate need between them. This is what *fucking* means. Not the half-hearted shit Lucas did to me. This is how real men fuck.

And every inch of me screams to get between them. What would it be like? To have Dayton fuck me with the strength in which he's fucking Farron? To watch Farron's face contort the way it is now because of my body?

I dig my nails into the wood wall to keep from touching myself.

"Is my cock hard enough for you, Pup?" Dayton growls, digging a hand into Farron's auburn hair and smashing his face into the sheets. "See what happens when you doubt me?"

Farron moans as an answer.

Dayton snatches Farron up by the hair, pulling him tight against his chest so they're both on their knees. His enormous cock is still in Farron's ass, and now I have a clear view of Farron.

Holy Moses. Farron's cock looks hard as steel, long and pointed up toward his flat stomach. Suddenly, I'm picturing myself on my hands and knees before him, my mouth licking up the dripping pre-cum as Dayton continues to pound into Farron's ass.

But it's more than the intensity of their fucking. Dayton's arms wrap around Farron's body, and Farron looks back into his eyes. It's like electricity between them. They each give a heated smile, a mix of trust and friendship and pure lust.

"I want to see your chest painted with your cum," Dayton says. "Then I'll fill you. Would you like that, Pup?"

"Yes, Day," Farron grits and he grabs his iron length. His hand moves up and down, up and down, up and down. Oh my god. The idea of watching Farron come on himself ... My underwear is soaked through, and I can feel the trickle of cream down my leg. I want

Farron's cum so badly, and Dayton's too. I want it enough to fall to my knees before them and beg for a drop on my tongue.

My insides contort almost to the point of pain, my knees buckle, and I stumble, pitching forward onto the floor.

Their eyes dart to me, looks of shock registering on their faces.

But Dayton doesn't stop. He grits his jaw and fucks harder. Farron stares at me, mouth gaping, and he shouts, "Rosalina!"

His load explodes upward, steaming cum shooting over his chest.

"Fuck!" Dayton yells, and I can tell by the look on his face, he's shooting his hot release into Farron.

Scrambling backward, my cheeks flush with heat. "I-I'm sorry!" I cry. "I didn't mean to interrupt!"

I sprint out of the room, desperate to put some space between us. Because all I can think about is Farron coming with my name on his lips.

AIR. I need cold air right now. I push open the castle door and stumble into the gardens, heaving in the late autumn breeze. Night's chill wafts over me as the sun spends its dying waves, glistening over the thorns that tangle among the hedges. Evenings like this bring out the smells of life, rich with decay and growth alike.

Farron and Dayton are lovers. I press myself against the castle wall, needing to feel something solid. The image of them won't leave my mind. Two perfect sweat-slicked bodies tangled together, the adoration with which they'd stared at each other ...

My fingers delicately press against my chest, lighting me aflame. I'm overwhelmed by the sensations that Dayton had evoked as he drove his huge cock into Farron, looking at me the whole time. The shuddering sighs Farron made as his pleasure exploded like a geyser, erupting across his chest. *Rosalina.* Was that really my name he called out?

A scorching ember ignites within me. My core tightens and my thighs quiver. What would have happened if I stayed? If I surrendered to the temptation? My hands roam beneath my top, undoing the laces and caressing my aching breasts as I replay the image of Dayton and Farron in my mind. My other hand snakes beneath my skirt and grazes lightly at my sopping panties. Waves of pleasure flow through me as my lips part in ecstasy.

An intoxicating sensation spreads like wildfire through my body. I inhale, and an unyielding force wraps around my ankles. Two thorny vines entangle my legs in their grasp. *That's strange.* The sensation is thrilling and foreign, unlike anything I've ever experienced before. My nipples become erect, and I cup my breasts, pushing my head back against the wall, letting out a small sigh of pleasure. I've never realized sex could be like that. The two of them had been on a different plane of existence. Are they in love?

My fingers glide between my legs, exploring the wetness. The vines wrap tightly around my thighs, coaxing me closer to the edge of pleasure. Images of Farron and Dayton flood my mind, the way they moved together with such animalistic passion. Farron's hands gripping Dayton's hair, pulling him closer as their lips fuse together in a fervent kiss that makes me burn with desire. Farron had kissed Dayton like Dayton was the sun and he needed every bit of him to survive. I want to be kissed like that.

Sharp pain cuts my swift moving hand, and my eyes shoot open. I pull my hand from between my legs, a prick of blood on my finger. My skirt falls, and I fully register the thorns wrapped tightly around my legs.

That's not right.

"Get off me," I cry, and the thorns fall away.

"Sorry, you're just so distracting to watch. I got a little carried away," a smooth, enchanting voice says. "But please, don't stop on my account."

I whip my head up and see a dark silhouette on top of the brambles. A male lounges with one leg casually dangling down. I don't need anyone to tell me who this is. I can feel it in my entire being.

The Prince of Thorns has come to Castletree.

29

ROSALINA

Briars shift beneath the Prince of Thorns and carry him down to the ground. He steps from the shadows and into the red twilight.

The person who created this evil briar has no right to such unparalleled beauty. His eyes are like the night sky, dark and deep, with hidden flecks of vibrant purple. Dark waves cascade upon each side of his face, and a thin silver circlet graces his forehead with a single, brilliant blue gem. His lips curl into a roguish smirk as he approaches.

"Well," he says softly, "it looks like my little princess has made herself quite at home in a castle of beasts."

"I'm not yours." I swallow, throat dry. "I don't even know you."

He quirks his head in mock sadness. "But you know who I am."

"You're the Prince of Thorns," I say. *Caspian.* That's what Farron had called him. But I can't make myself say it. Somehow, it seems too intimate.

"That's what they like to call me. Can't imagine why." He gestures around us.

So, I'm finally face-to-face with the monster who is trying to destroy the princes' castle.

He clasps my wrist and tugs me toward him. Eyeing the droplet of blood on the tip of my finger, he frowns. "Sorry about that. But what's a little pleasure without pain?"

"You were watching me," I gasp.

He raises my finger into his mouth and sucks it, long and wet and warm, savoring each and every drop of my essence. His gaze meets mine, and I see a spark of mischief in his eyes. "Delicious," he purrs.

He slowly releases my hand and electricity runs through my veins. His touch has awakened a deep craving in me, and my traitorous body wants more. It wasn't just the blood he was tasting on my finger ...

Angry at my body's reaction, I snarl at him, "I half-expected your tongue to be forked."

"Sorry to disappoint," he murmurs in my ear. His breath is hot against my skin. His lips, stupidly soft, dance along my jawline until his mouth finds its way to my cheek. I gasp as his tongue gently caresses it, leaving a wet trail of heat behind. I squeeze my eyes shut as a strange sparkling pleasure rushes through my body.

"You're so wasted here, with Keldarion and his pups." His voice drops lower, as if sharing a secret. "We know how to appreciate beauty down in the Below. I'd never dream of putting you in a cage."

"Get off—" I don't get to finish. The next thing I know, I'm being tugged back, and all I can see is Caspian flying into the thorns.

Keldarion stands in front of me, his whole body curled around mine.

Oh shit.

Caspian rises from the thorns, picking brambles off his black jerkin and smoothing his pants. Then he looks over at Keldarion, and his expression is anything but fearful. The smile, the bright flash of his eyes ... If I didn't know better, I'd say it was playful.

Meanwhile, the white-haired giant in front of me radiates with all the rage I've become accustomed to.

"What are you doing here?" Keldarion growls.

"Oh, you know, just admiring my landscaping." Caspian gestures to the towering thorns.

I try to step out from behind Keldarion, but he pushes me back. "Leave."

Caspian stalks toward us with all the grace of a slinky black cat. "Aren't you going to introduce me to your ..." He pauses, dark eyes burrowing into me, before flicking to Kel. "New friend?"

Why did it sound like he was about to say something else?

"The four of you have been tight for so long," Caspian continues when Kel doesn't answer him. "And you haven't kept any of my offerings, as delicious as they were. You can't blame me for being curious."

"She's none of your concern," Keldarion says.

Caspian stops in front of us. He's taller than me, but next to Kel, he still has to look up. "Haven't you learned by now, everything regarding you is my concern?"

Keldarion stiffens, his breathing becoming labored. A chill runs through me, and I glance down to watch the ice rapidly expanding from beneath his feet. "You're nothing to me."

Caspian flicks his dark eyes down to the ice, then back up to Kel. "Don't you wish that were true?"

Kel shudders, and I twist my face enough to see his expression. His teeth are gritted, brow furrowed. And I realize he's trying not to explode, trying to keep a rein on his magic.

Caspian walks back toward the briars, but he turns around at the edge. The wind tugs the thick waves of his hair. "The castle's magic is weakening; I can feel it. You're running out of time."

"Leave."

Those starry eyes shift to me. "I'm sure I'll be seeing you soon, Princess. He's made it so obvious already."

A tangle of shadowy briars sprout from the ground, circling around him. There's a spark of magic and he's gone.

I take in a shuddering breath, then the anger I'd been too scared to voice bursts to the surface. "Well, he was freaking rude. I can see now why everyone hates him."

Keldarion grips my shoulders, whirling me around to face him. "Did he hurt you?"

"No. I'm fine." Physically, at least, if you don't count the prick on my finger. But my mind is all kinds of fucked up from his sexually charged evil.

"Everyone here knows you can't trust anyone from the Below," he says, and his voice darkens. "However, you are not from here, so I will tell you this only once. Everything that comes out of his mouth is a lie. He may look charming, and he'll promise you your greatest desires but never bargain with him. Never make a deal with the Prince of Thorns."

There is such desperate urgency in his voice. I nod and try to lighten the mood. "Thank you for coming out. He was super creepy." And beyond beautiful. But I opt not to say that to Kel. I don't think he'd appreciate that fact.

"Are you sure he didn't hurt you?" Kel scans my face, then his gaze works down my body. His hands shake on my shoulders as he comes to my chest, the laces loose.

Loose from when I'd undone them and touched myself thinking about Dayton and Farron. My body heats, and I feel my cheeks redden.

"What were you doing in the garden, Rosalina?"

"I ..."

His hold tightens on my shoulders, and we're moving. He's practically lifting me. My back hits the solid castle wall, his chest presses against mine, and one of his hands clutches the stone above us. "Distract me."

"Distract you?" I gasp. He's so close I can feel his icy breath blowing back the hair from my face. "Distract you from what?"

His grip on my shoulder is as light as his grip on the wall is hard. His fist clenches and a few stones crumble to the ground. "Dammit, Rosalina."

I could duck out of his grasp; I could push him away. But I don't. Something about this encounter with the Prince of Thorns has left him untethered.

Or more untethered than usual.

"Kel." I push some of the messy strands of hair away from his face. His expression crumbles in a strange sort of agony.

A deep growl radiates through his body. "Talk about something. Tell me about one of your boring books."

"Hey!" I shove his chest, but that does absolutely nothing, figuring it's about as hard as the stone behind us. "My books aren't boring."

He takes a shaky breath, then the ghost of a smile flashes on his face. "Farron's research books are. There are more interesting books in the library."

"I'll have to ..." My voice is nothing but a whisper, as my hand drifts back to his face. "I'll have to explore—"

Keldarion lets out a pained groan and spins me around, so he's braced against the wall. "The sun is setting, Rosalina, and I am not in control."

"What?"

"You need to run to your room and lock the door."

"Kel."

"Night is upon us." Keldarion's eyes glow like blue fire. "And I cannot control my beast. Not after ... Go."

And this time, I listen to him. I push away and run to my room.

30

ROSALINA

I spend the rest of the night trying to calm my nerves from everything that transpired. First, discovering something that might actually help the princes find their mates. But I haven't dug into that yet because when I went to find my research partner, he was in the midst of getting the best makeup sex of his life. At least, that's how it appeared.

What kind of relationship do Farron and Dayton have? It's obvious they aren't exclusive, figuring Dayton brought that female back. Maybe I'm thinking of things in human terms. Fae might have different expectations for relationships altogether.

And meeting the Prince of Thorns. *Caspian.* The fury with which Keldarion had addressed him, the possessive way he protected me. Or maybe I'm reading too much into it. All the princes seem to have their own reasons for hating Caspian, and even I can get on board with that. The thorns are really a bad look for the castle.

You're running out of time. What did he mean by that? Is there more to the curse that the princes aren't telling me?

A knock on the door draws me from my thoughts. "Come in," I say.

Marigold pushes in her usual meal cart. Well, Marigold the plump brown racoon wearing an apron. She told me she needs to hold onto some of her humanity, even in this form. I don't know if I'll ever get used to seeing the staff like this.

Despite being allowed to roam the castle at night—as long as I don't unlock rabid Farron—I spend most of my nights curled up in bed, reading books I've borrowed from the library with a warm cup of tea.

"Hi," I say.

"Hello, dearie." She drops her paws from the cart, but still stands on two little legs. "I heard you had quite the encounter this evening. Put the master in a right mood."

That was another thing that took getting used to: the animals can talk. Absently, I wonder if the princes' wolf forms can too. "It seemed like the Prince of Thorns showed up just to taunt him."

Marigold shakes her head. "I wouldn't doubt it. Quite a nasty history those two have."

"What kind of history?" I narrow my gaze. There had been venom when Kel spoke to Caspian.

"Now's not the time. I like to gossip as much as the next, but there are some things even I won't be caught muttering about."

I almost want to prod but a delicious smell hits me, and Marigold reaches her paws up to take the lid off the tray. The roasted squash and fluffy bread from dinner.

"The master was quite adamant you be fed," Marigold explains. "Said you didn't eat any supper."

Of course he noticed that. But my stomach growls staring at the food.

"I'll leave you to it." Marigold exits, her striped tail sashaying behind her.

I look down at my dinner plate. Why am I suddenly feeling guilty for not eating with Kel earlier? Is it because I was the only one to show up? He's my captor. I shouldn't feel bad about anything.

"Arg!" I let out a frustrated growl, then slam the lid back on the tray. I grab a book from my bedside table, put on my fluffiest robe and coziest slippers, then pick up my stupid dinner before I leave my, perfect temperature, room in the Spring Wing.

"Can't miss the Winter Wing," I mutter as I walk. "Just follow the coldest breeze and most hazardous hallway."

One arm flies out to the side as I slip on the ice, while the other clutches my dinner tray against my stomach. I know which door leads to Kel's chambers because when Astrid gave me the tour, she told me to never go there under any circumstances.

I'm not afraid. If Keldarion told Marigold to feed me, then he must have regained control of his beast. What had set him off? Was it Caspian's appearance or something else?

I pause at the door, and before I lose my nerve, give it three hard knocks. "It's me. I came—" Before I can even finish, the door creaks open, as if with a will of its own.

There's no one behind it, and a bitter breeze whips at me through the crack. No worries about my dinner being too hot, at least.

It's freezing inside, and a thin layer of snow carpets the floor. Light snowflakes fall from the ceiling.

"I came to uphold my deal. Dinner with you. Remember?" I lift my tray.

The room is an absolute disaster. The bed barely stands, threadbare blankets drape over the edge and pool on the ground. The ratty couch is covered in snow, its cushions sagging in the middle and its legs crusted with ice. The only light in the room comes from a strip of moonlight filtering through the floor-to-ceiling window, casting eerie shadows on the walls. Menacing thorns protrude from every corner of the room, their long spindly branches reaching out and grasping at the frosty air. *I've never seen so many in one place.*

I swallow in a dry throat. *Is he even here?*

Then, I spot movement in a dark corner, a shuffle of snow, and I'm staring face-to-face with two glowing blue eyes. The rest of the beast is hidden by shadows, but the moonlight shines off those icy spikes that protrude from his massive body.

"You shouldn't be here," the wolf rumbles and I gasp. So, he can speak. His voice is deeper and louder than in his human form, like the cracking of a glacier.

I force my face to remain expressionless, completely nonjudgmental of his messy room and terrifying form. "I'm here because I won't be able to stand you berating me tomorrow for not following through on my end of the deal."

Can he hear the lie in my words? There's a small table beside the couch, and I root through the drawer before I find an old match. I spark it to life against the table and light a half-burned candle stick. A soft, warm glow cascades through the room, and I push a pile of snow from the couch and settle down.

My food is still hot, and we're both silent as I eat. But I can't stand the quiet. "I accidentally walked into a rather awkward situation today with Dayton and Farron." I put down my fork and look across at Keldarion. "Is that what you meant by Farron being his own worst enemy?"

The wolf's grumble is my only answer, so I'm left to fill in my own blanks. Farron seems adamant about breaking the curse, but could there be a part of him that hesitates because of his own feelings for Dayton? I finish the rest of my food, mulling it over. "Honestly, I'm kind of glad humans don't have mates. How awkward would it be if you found your mate and hated them? Or you were already in love with someone else?"

"Mates are incredibly rare," Keldarion rumbles from the corner.

"Probably for good reason. It doesn't seem fair, to have no say who you fall in love with." I wonder if that's what Farron feels. If that's what the engaged fae princess in the book felt after she met her carpenter mate. Or had finding him been the best moment of her life? I realize Keldarion has been silent, and I feel a little guilty. "Don't listen to me. You'll love your mate. She'll break your curse. I'm sure this is me being a naïve human, as usual."

A growl passes through the wolf, and he stands, snow falling off him in heaps. For a moment, I almost think he's going to come to me. But he circles like a cat getting comfortable and lies down again.

Lies down facing away from me.

"Someone's grumpy tonight," I mutter as I put my plate on the floor. Should I leave? I've fulfilled my duty of eating dinner. My gut twists. I know on the days when I'm lost in the darkest parts of my mind, there's always one thing that can pull me out.

From the pocket of my robe, I grab a book. "I'm still a little offended. Earlier, you asked about my *boring* books. Well, my books are anything but boring."

I open the fae book. It's a great story, a romantic adventure Farron recommended about a druidic princess and her ranger best friend trying to reclaim their magic. I'd read through half the book last night. But now I turn to page one and start from the beginning.

"The tree was talking to me again," I say, reading out the first sentence. "It had a faraway voice, delicate as the whisper of wind through the leaves and sharp as the crack of a dry branch."

I lose myself in the words, and Keldarion doesn't interrupt or kick me out. After the first chapter, I notice he's moved slightly, his slitted glowing eyes watching me. And I hope he comes with me into a jungle of adventure, of ancient beasts and old curses, and far from the darkness of his mind.

A SHIVER RUNS through my entire body, and something wet prods my face. I twist, grumbling sleepily. *Why am I so cold?*

"Get on," a commanding, deep voice says.

My eyes flutter open, and I swat out my hands. Softness. Then I'm rolling until I'm surrounded by silky white fur. A soft swaying motion makes my gaze droop. I think we're moving. The next thing I know, I'm falling into a plush bed.

I know these pillows, these blankets. My bed. Some survival instinct takes over and I scramble to get my ice cube body under the sheets. But I miss the softness. The smell of winter.

With a sleepy hand I reach out and grasp a tuft of white fur, muttering something.

The fur slips from my fingers as I drift into oblivion.

Sun washes over me in the morning and I blink awake. When I swing my feet out of bed, they land in a pile of fluffy snow.

Just how long had the Prince of Winter stayed beside me?

31

ROSALINA

I'm halfway through my lemon tart when I spot a naked girl outside my window.

"Girl!" I give a panicked cry of alarm, lemon filling splattering against the floor as I drop my breakfast. "There's a naked girl outside!"

Astrid and Marigold both flutter up beside me. I've been hiding away in my room, taking my sweet-ass time with breakfast, trying to decide whether it was too awkward to head down to the library today to research.

On the one hand, I finally have a real lead I want to investigate. On the other, I don't know how I can face Farron after how much of him I saw yesterday. What if he thinks I'm a creep?

At least my decision is delayed by this interruption.

"Oh dear." Marigold sighs, pressing her nose to the glass. "Not again."

"It's been so long," Astrid says. "I hoped he'd stopped for good."

"Wait, what?" I turn to them. "Having a naked girl at the front door is a regular occurrence?"

"Yes, well, no." Astrid's bottom lip trembles. "It used to happen a lot more when the curse first started."

"No use fretting about it any longer," Marigold says. "Astrid, inform the master."

Astrid visibly trembles. "No way. You know how he is when one of these girls shows up."

"I'll tell him," I say. "Keldarion doesn't scare me."

Marigold and Astrid look at me like I'm well and truly insane, and maybe I am. But it's the truth. I'm not afraid of the master of Castletree. At least, not for the same reasons they are.

"Better you stay in your room. These disturbances always put him in a right fuss. The princes will sort it out," Marigold says. "I'm sure he'll notice she's here eventually; he always knows when someone's in the castle."

From the angle of my room, I have a perfect view of the bridge that leads from the front door. Something is bundled in the girl's arms and she's calling out, but I can't make out the words.

"I'm not going to let her stand out there naked!" I grab an extra cloak from my wardrobe and take off down the stairs to the castle entrance. Marigold and Astrid chase behind me.

Sprinting outside, I skid to a stop in front of the fae woman.

"You look cold." I hold the cloak out in front of me.

She doesn't take the cloak or seem the slightest bit concerned about her nakedness. She quirks her head and says, "Where's Keldarion? I need to see him."

My hackles raise and my fingers tighten on the cloak. Why does this naked fae need to see Kel? Up close, I can see she is beautiful. Shorter and slighter than me, with long curly brown hair and light brown eyes. Her breasts are quite large and firm-looking, barely hidden behind the bundle of clothes in her arms.

This is so weird.

"Do you want to put those on?" I suggest.

She looks down at the clothes in her hands and shrugs, shaking out the slinky black dress and pulling it on. Tentatively, I place the cloak around her shoulders.

She blinks, then steps closer. "Wow, you're really pretty." She runs her hand along the side of my face and stops at my ears. "And a human too."

"Uh, thanks?" I flush. "I'm ... Rosalina."

"I'm Ciara. Sorry, Rosalina," she says, voice low and sultry. "I'm needy. He sent me here before I even finished, you know."

"Who sent you here?"

"The Prince of Thorns," Ciara, Astrid, and Marigold all say at the same time.

I gape at them. "Wait, what? You were mid-bang with Caspian then he used his weird horny-thorny magic to send you here? And this isn't the first time he's done it?"

Ciara runs her hands through her hair. "Why are the most beautiful men the most fucked? Anyway, where is Keldarion?"

Heat flashes across my body. Why does she need to see Kel?

"Rosalina!" I turn to see Farron rushing down the steps, buttons on his vest askew. Ezryn trails behind him.

They both stop and stare at Ciara. "Shit. Not again," Farron swears.

"Could we not have waited until noon for such a loud commotion?" Dayton staggers out. He puts a hand to his head to shield his eyes and wavers with each step. I suppose turning into a wolf overnight did not rid him of his hangover.

But he's only wearing loose sweatpants—or the fae equivalent of sweatpants. They're low enough on his hips I can see the delicious V-shaped muscles. *Fuck.*

My eyes dart between him and Farron. I can't stop it, my face burning with the image of them together.

Dayton probably wouldn't notice if a meteor landed in front of us, but Farron does. His face flushes and he bites his lip, looking so awkward and cute my stomach flutters.

Ezryn marches up to Ciara, and she clutches my arm.

But Ezryn decides she's not in need of choking—despite actually admitting she came right from Caspian. He looks down at her and says, "Follow me. We're getting you home."

She gives me an anxious look before we all trail back toward the castle after Ezryn. I fall behind Farron.

"Everyone keeps saying not again. Does Caspian often send naked people to the castle?"

"It's a strange pattern." Farron gives a long sigh and runs a hand through his wayward hair. "It happened a lot the first few years of the curse. Half-dressed or naked fae would appear at our doorstep, all explaining they'd just engaged in sexual relations with the Prince of Thorns."

"That's messed up." I stop walking and watch the others enter the castle. "Why?"

"Your guess is as good as mine." Farron shrugs. "Probably to torment Kel. If his mating bond awoke to one of these fae, Caspian could forever hold over him that he had Kel's mate first. Or maybe Caspian hates commitment and thinks the front door of the castle is as good a place as any to dump his ... exploits."

"What a creep." I take another look at Farron. "Also, Farron—"

"I'm sorry," he blurts out at the same time as I do.

I let out a sigh of relief and a little laugh as he does. "I didn't mean to be a creeper—"

"Rosie, no." He reaches forward and clasps my hands. "I told you to meet me in the Summer Wing. I wasn't thinking. I should have known that—"

"Dayton is stupidly charming." I smile at him. His hands are so warm in the frosty morning air.

He shakes his head. "That's one way to put it."

"If you don't mind me asking, are you two together? How does that work with finding a mate?"

Color floods his cheeks. "I've known Dayton forever. I spent some time in the Summer Realm and it kind of happened. Then after we were both coronated as High Princes and moved to Castletree, we continued. It's just fun."

Just fun sounds more like Dayton's words than Farron's.

"Looked more than fun," I say before I can stop myself. "I mean—"

I try to pull away, but Farron tugs me closer. "How long were you watching for, Rosie?"

Heat swirls in my core. He'd said my name. Had it been out of surprise or something else? "Not too long."

"Maybe it's a little more than fun for me," Farron says softly, eyes flicking to the front door where the rest of them disappeared. "I'm always looking at tomorrow, the future, a cure. But when I'm with Day, it feels like the only time I'm actually living."

"We all need someone that makes us feel alive."

"We certainly do." His thumb massages my palm. "We're not just with each other. Dayton seeks his pleasures often and sometimes drags me along."

"Like, you get together with someone else?" I can't stop the curiosity from blooming in my voice.

He lets out a heady breath, and I realize I've moved so my whole chest is almost pressed against his, our hands tucked between us.

"Sometimes," he murmurs huskily and his eyes close. Is he imagining something that had once happened … or do his thoughts mirror my own?

Something that *could* happen.

"Rosie, if—"

Loud voices echo from inside the castle, and I give a sympathetic look up at Farron. "We should probably go help."

We run up the stairs and into the entrance hall. Ezryn, Dayton, Astrid, and Marigold all stand around the mirror.

Ciara has her hands on her hips and glares at them all. "I'm not going until I see Keldarion!"

"My magic isn't working on the mirror," Ezryn grumbles. "Dayton's isn't either. It's the same as the last ones. I doubt your magic will work, Farron."

Farron gives a deep sigh. "I suspect Caspian puts some sort of enchantment on them to keep them here. Another way to torment us. Only Kel's magic is still strong enough to break it."

Ezryn turns and heads to the stairs. "I'll get him. But I might require assistance."

Farron gives a pained look before dragging Dayton up the stairs after Ezryn.

I awkwardly go stand beside Marigold, Astrid, and Ciara, who's now as trapped here as me.

"Well, how was it?" Marigold waggles her dark brows. "Sleeping with the dark prince himself?"

"Marigold! You can't ask her that!" Astrid says.

But Ciara has no qualms explaining. "They all say don't go down Below, but honestly, all of my best fucks have been from one of Sira's parties. When I caught Caspian's eye last night, I knew I had to go for it. He's dreamy sure, but it's more than that. We're all curious." She looks Astrid up and down. "You're from Winter, right? Me too. I needed to know: was Caspian's dick really worth the Realm?"

Astrid gives a little quiver and her face scrunches in anger. "The Realm isn't lost—"

"And?" Marigold is practically drooling. "Was it worth it?"

"No." Ciara rolls her eyes. "He was charming until we arrived at his bedroom. He didn't even fully undress. I used all my best moves, but he looked bored the whole time. Crazy, right? I mean, have you seen me?"

She is beautiful from top to bottom, but not only that, she has an allure of confidence I envy.

"After a couple minutes, he rolled off and didn't even come inside me! Sputtered it onto the sheets, shoved my clothes into my hands, and said, 'Tell Kel I say hi'. Such a jerk. I didn't go down there so he could send me to his—"

A frigid blast of air shudders over us and we turn to see Keldarion at the top of the stairs, flanked by the other three princes.

Ciara's eyes grow wide. She moves toward him. When he arrives at the bottom of the stairs, she reaches for him.

My fists clench at my sides. Why is she so intent on—

But Keldarion just grips her wrists and drags her toward the mirror without so much as a second glance. "You are not wanted here."

Ciara lets out a strangled gasp, then looks back and forth. Something clears in her eyes. "I—"

Keldarion stops in front of the mirror and places a palm on it. The glass ripples beneath his touch. "Think of your home. Do not return Below."

Ciara nods. She steps toward the mirror, before turning back. "I almost forgot. This is for you." She reaches into her pocket before pulling out a rolled parchment and handing it to me.

I take it and feel the wisp of magic as she disappears into the mirror.

Kel's breath is heavy above me as he looks down at the paper in my hands. It's a small scroll, closed with a wax seal in the shape of a rose.

"I guess I'll see what it says," I breathe, heart quickening as I unroll the paper. The princes, Marigold, and Astrid all crowd around me.

On it is a single inked line in swirling script.

I was thinking of you the entire time, Princess.

-C

"That fae did look like you." Dayton breaks the silence with a laugh. "Well, you're truly part of the family now, Blossom, to gain the torment of the Prince of Thorns."

32

KELDARION

Sometimes I wonder why I keep Perth Quellos as vizier of the
Winter Realm when listening to his voice is like shoving my
brain through melting snow.

I hold my body rigid, legs crossed, leaning on a pillar in the
entrance hall. It's the only room of Castletree Quellos is allowed in. I
won't bring him into the sitting room or the dining hall. And I
certainly won't bring him into the Winter Wing.

He's lucky he's even allowed in the castle at all.

"Are you listening to me, Keldarion?" the vizier says, enunciating
every syllable. Torchlight shines off his bald head, and his glassy eyes
seem to stare straight through me.

No, I'm not listening. My mind keeps reeling back to a week ago.
Fucking Caspian. He's always delighted in torturing me. But to involve
Rosalina—

"Keldarion?" Quellos snaps.

"Goblins ravaging the cities. Minor rebellions. Knights deserting
from the army. Why do you bother coming when you bring no new
tidings?" I bite out.

Quellos holds me in a cold glare. He's known me since I was a boy.
He advised my father. Gods, the man is ancient. Yet, he still hasn't

figured me out, and it drives him insane. "Keldarion. You are Prince of the Winter Realm. Your people need you to come home."

I touch the snowflake necklace that falls across my chest. My simple white shirt has a wide V, and I wear tight leather pants with dirty boots. I don't want Quellos to get the idea I'll dress up for him. "We've been over this before. If Castletree falls to the thorns, it's not just the Winter Realm that's doomed. It's everything."

Quellos licks his blue lips, stained from consumption of tamen, the seeds of a berry that only grows around Frostfang, the capital of the Winter Realm. Tamen is highly commoditized for its ability to maintain alertness and focus—and for being highly addictive. "I understand the thorns are a threat. But perhaps you need outside assistance. If I were to station here to study this phenomenon—"

"You're needed in the Winter Realm," I growl.

I should never have started bringing Quellos inside the castle at all. But it was better that than return to my realm, the way the others sporadically do to check on the ruling of their homelands. I haven't been back since the curse.

I probably won't ever go back.

He's getting frustrated with me. Every visit it's worse. Every visit he gets more insistent I return.

Goblins pouring into the cities ... Angry citizens seeking an end to my princedom.

What can a beast do about any of it?

With a sigh, I knead the bridge of my nose. "The rule is yours, Quellos. You are both vizier and steward of the Winter Realm. Figure out a solution to these problems."

A tick twitches in Quellos's jaw. "I am not Prince of the Winter Realm. I hold none of the ancient magic. And only you bear the token that allows you to wield the Sword of the Protector."

My hand drifts unconsciously to my snowflake necklace. "And I must stop the thorns—"

"But you're not stopping them!" Quellos roars. He's never spoken to me like that.

And if anyone else did, they would have their throat in my jaws right now.

Breath comes ragged from the vizier's throat, and he gestures to the clumps of purple thorns breaking through the cracks in the stone. "Look around, Keldarion. Every time I visit, it's worse. Castletree's magic is fading. *Your* magic is fading. Either do your job," he takes a deep breath, "or pass the rule onto someone who will."

Shame floods through me. Shame and anger and betrayal. Quellos already knows so many of my evils. If he knew about the curse too …
No, he must never know.

I turn his words against him. Straightening to my full height, I tilt my head to take in the vizier. "So, you've finally gotten the balls to ask for the throne."

Quellos puts both his hands into his wide sleeves. "Some people are meant to rule, my Prince. Others are not." He stands and walks over to the large door that exits the castle. "And every day you spend figuring out which one you are, the more your people suffer."

"I'm the only one who can stop the Prince of Thorns," I growl.

Quellos gives me a half-lidded gaze. "Or is he the only one who can stop you?"

The word comes out a rabid snarl: "Leave."

"I'm on my way out," he says calmly. "Oh, is this a new servant?"

Rosalina stands at the bottom of the stairs, a tray of cookies and tea in her hands. She yelps when she catches my eye and nearly drops the tray. "Sorry! Sorry! I didn't mean to intrude. It's just, I heard voices, and I had too much food to myself, and I thought Kel might want some. Keldarion, I mean. Prince of Winter. Winter Prince. Um, I'm going to go—" She turns on her heel.

"Wait," Quellos says. "A human, are you?"

"Yes," she squeaks. "I'm Rosalina O'Connell."

"Interesting. I never knew you to take humans into your service, Keldarion," Quellos muses.

Ice crackles beneath my boots and I step between them. "You were on your way out."

ELIZABETH HELEN

"Yes. Yes, I was," Quellos says. "Good meeting you, Rosalina. Perhaps we'll see one another in the future." He pulls open the door.

A blast of cold air hits me. Not the cold like my chambers, where *his* briars have affected everything, even my own magic. No, this wind carries the smells of wood smoke and roasted chestnuts. A hint of pine and spruce, from Buttercup Forest, mingles with the earthy smell of the snow-covered ground. The sharp bite of an icy chill lingers in the air after the door slams shut behind him.

It smells like home.

"What the heck? Where did he go?" Rosalina chirps. "That did not look like the Briar out there."

"Did you know that was a private political meeting you were eavesdropping on?"

"I wasn't eavesdropping!" Her face flushes an exquisite pink. "I was trying to be friendly and bring you a cookie."

My boots thud heavy on the ice that forms with each step as I close the distance between us. She holds my gaze. I stop right before her, her tray the only thing between us.

I'm reminded of what she looked like when I pinned her against the castle walls. Small and frightened, a deer mouse to my wolf. Had she known? Known she was safer with me, her captor, than that monster of thorns? The thought of his hands caressing her pale skin—

"Keldarion," she whispers, "why are you looking at me like you want to eat me?"

Slowly, I reach down to her tray, grab a cookie, and bite it. "Thank you, Rosalina."

She releases what seems like a long-held breath. "So ..."

"So?"

"Are you going to explain where that creepy, blue-lipped man went?"

A smile catches at the corner of my mouth. "That blue-lipped man was my royal vizier, and he was going home to the Winter Realm."

"You have to show me how that works," she says.

I suppose it couldn't hurt to explain, figuring I don't want her to accidentally end up somewhere she shouldn't be. "Why don't you tell me what you think?"

She raises a dark brow and sets her tray down on the side table beside a dusty old clock and a candelabra. She hunches over, her fingers running along the door frame. Her chestnut hair cascades down her body like a waterfall, framing the curves of her bosom. Marigold has her in high-waisted pants today, and they cling tightly to her long, full legs. I take in a steadying breath as another image fills my mind.

The nerve of Caspian to send that fae, to compare her even slightly to Rosalina. *He's taunting me.* And there's nothing I can do about it, not without him getting more suspicious.

I turn away. Thoughts of him only cause my heart to rage. This moment is for Rosalina. I'll give her another minute to figure out the door before I show her its secrets.

The nostalgic scent of nutmeg, cinnamon, and ripe apples fill the entrance hall. Golden leaves float around Rosalina. I'm by her side in less than a moment, yanking her hard against my body. I catch the glimpse of a dirt path and overgrown autumn trees before I slam the door.

"How did you open that?" I snarl, whirling her around to face me.

"The door handle," she says, then pushes against my chest to free herself. I let her go.

Rosalina gestures to the door. "I pushed in the handle and this little dial appeared. It had a snowflake on it. Then I moved it. I saw a rose, a tulip, a shell, and I stopped on this leaf. And it opened to ..." She spins to me, eyes wide with excitement. "Was that the Autumn Realm? How is that possible?"

"The Fae Queen built this castle to be accessible from every realm. The castle physically dwells within the Briar, but it magically appears in all four realms," I explain, looking down at the intricate rose-plated dial above the door handle. It's usually hidden. She shouldn't have been able to realize the magic just like that. "The door opens outside of the castle in each realm, but the castle exteriors are mere shells. There is only one interior to Castletree."

"They all lead here, to the Briar," she muses.

"Indeed. Although, each realm has its own royal keep, where the family of the High Ruler typically resides."

"Family," Rosalina echoes, and I hear the pain in her voice. Now she's thinking of her father, the trespasser. "Is your family—"

"My father was a better High Prince than I could ever dream to be, and my mother a gracious and charitable ruler."

"Kel," she whispers. "Where are your parents now?"

"Victims of the Below," I growl.

"I'm so sorry—"

I cut her off and place my palm on the door. A magic current still runs through it. "Before the curse, staff and visitors could freely pass into Castletree. But we've disallowed the use of these entrances. The only one permitted in this manner is Perth Quellos, my vizier."

She studies me for a long moment, then crosses to the mirror that hangs beside the door. "And this?"

"Do you ever stop with the questions?"

She flashes a smile that stutters my heart. "You live in an enchanted castle. There's lots to be curious about."

"The mirror is another relic of the Fae Queen. It can only be used by the princes."

"To go wherever you please," she says.

I raise a brow. "Good guess."

She runs a finger along the elegant gold border. The mirror ripples like waves over water.

"As the thorns continue to suck the life from Castletree, the mirror's magic fades as well," I say lowly.

Rosalina drops her hand and turns to face me.

"And the rose symbol on the dial ..." Her voice holds a strangely whimsical tone. "There was something about that emblem. If I could see it again—"

I yank her arm, pulling her closer to me. She stares up, confused for a moment at my action, waiting for me to speak.

"I don't want to test the magic any more today."

She gives a slow nod of understanding but doesn't back away from me. In fact, she takes a step closer. "Kel, is it true you haven't been back to the Winter Realm since the curse?"

"It is."

Her smile gleams like a first snowfall. "Well, all my snooping has given me a wonderful idea for how to break the curse."

Before I can say anything else, she waltzes away.

I sigh. Let her have hope. The way Farron has hope. The way Dayton and Ezryn cling to their shreds of it.

But I know the truth.

For me, there will never be a way to break this curse.

33

ROSALINA

Our first family breakfast—and by family, I mean me and my four fae captors—is just as awkward as our dinners. Dinners over the last few weeks have followed a certain pattern that usually involves Farron explaining our research, but getting talked over by Keldarion, who is usually yelling at either Dayton or Ezryn, depending on his mood. Sometimes Ez and Kel will team up on Dayton when he's being particularly annoying, and that's always good fun to watch.

Though Ezryn only attends half the time. And Dayton is sometimes so drunk, he passes out before he makes it to the dining hall. And if he does get there, all he can do is sit sleepily while Farron tries to spoon-feed him soup. It's kind of endearing.

Thankfully, I haven't had to endure any more awkward one-on-one dinners with Keldarion.

Besides the dinners, I spend most days with Farron, researching in the library. I'm desperate to learn more about him, the other princes, and the world. But they're all so cagey with information. Even Marigold and Astrid aren't helpful. The former only wants to talk about how incredibly gorgeous the princes are … which is fair. Their future mates better send me lovely thank-you letters. And the latter is too frightened of Keldarion to tell me anything juicy—but that's also fair. His temper is fickler than a cat.

But the scariest thing of all is the more time I spend here, the less I feel like a prisoner and more like another member of the household, desperate to break this curse.

I'm on the right track though. Soon, the princes will have their mates in their loving arms and I'll be home, in Orca Cove getting gossiped about in the bookstore.

I shake my head and shovel half a blueberry muffin into my mouth.

"So," Dayton drawls, swirling his orange juice that smells a little too strong, "what's everyone doing for the full moon?"

The full moon. They're quite excited about it—or at least Dayton is. The one night of the month the curse doesn't take hold. It was a sidebar point in Farron's and my research. We speculate the Enchantress's magic isn't as strong on the full moon, or perhaps their fae magic is at its peak. Whatever the case, for every full moon for the last twenty-five years, the curse has not affected them, nor the castle staff.

I had made a joke about werewolf movies having it wrong, but Farron hadn't gotten it.

"Seriously," Dayton continues, "on the full moon, you're going to—"

"Transform into my wolf and hunt goblins," Ezryn says, sitting there stoically. No food in front of him, of course.

Dayton puts a hand to his heart, flabbergasted. "It's the one night of the month you don't have to change into that mangy mutt."

"The goblins don't take a break from terrorizing our realms," Ezryn says. "I won't either."

"Not me, brother," Dayton says. "I need a break. A chance to be a man."

"A break from what? Day drinking? Sitting in your hot springs?" Farron mutters bitterly.

Come to think of it, he'd been in a bad mood yesterday as well. I would have thought he'd be overjoyed. A chance to not spend the night in that dingy dungeon.

"Getting drunk during the day is nothing compared to tasting a sweet berry wine with the night's sea breeze on your face," Dayton continues. "I, for one, will return to the Summer Realm to bask in her beauty."

"Don't think too highly of him," Keldarion says. "He doesn't intend to check in with any of the political dealings while he's there."

"How can I be bothered by that when all the fruit of Summer's glorious nights will be calling to me? Her sweet wines and even sweeter fae." Dayton grins. "Besides, my sister has all that political stuff under control."

"Your sister is a *child*." Farron shoves his chair back and glowers at him. "You're as delusional about that as you are with everything else."

The smile doesn't break from Dayton's face, but I swear I see something akin to hurt flash in his eyes. "We're all on borrowed time here. You can either have fun while it lasts or spend it huddled up in your dusty old library looking for something you're never going to find. Hey, you never know, maybe my mate will fall on my cock in the Summer Realm, and I'll break this fucking curse myself."

Farron's eyes water, and he storms across the room to the exit.

"Farron, wait," I call out.

"I have to get ready." He pauses at the door, a soft expression on his face. "I'm going back to the Autumn Realm to see my parents. It's good to spend the night there every so often."

With that, he leaves. I'm surprised Dayton's fiery gaze doesn't burn a hole in the wall.

Okay, I have to bring up my plan. But I'm a little nervous now that my right-hand man has left.

"Where are you going for the full moon, Keldarion?" I ask, stalling.

"I'll be here," Keldarion states.

So much for stalling.

"Kel hasn't left the castle in twenty-five years," Dayton says. "Rumor has it that's not the only thing he hasn't—"

"You should watch your tongue when speaking to the Winter Prince," Ezryn snaps. "He was given the Sword of the Protect—"

"Yes, lot of good that did us all," Dayton counters, a fire to his words. Farron must have really affected him. "Kel screwed us all over. For what? To lie with the shadows—"

"Enough," Keldarion snarls, slamming his hands down on the table. A frost springs over the food, making it appear freezer burnt.

Okay, it's now or never.

"I know how to break the curse!" I cry out and stand.

All their eyes burrow into me.

"Well, I have a guess. A hypothesis, really. Something Farron and I think would be worth a try."

In actuality, when I'd told Farron my idea, he'd grimaced and muttered something about how he'd try anything at this point. But he'd abandoned me, so the truth was what I made it.

Kel looks like listening to my idea is far less appealing than beating Dayton to a pulp, which is his current goal. But mercifully, Ezryn turns his metallic-masked head to me and says, "Share your knowledge, Rosalina."

Slowly, Kel sits down, and Dayton turns his attention to me. Nerves flutter in my stomach and a blush burns my cheeks. "Farron and I have been doing lots of research. And I have to say … Dayton's right."

Dayton looks the most shocked of all of them, but Kel's face is equally displeased, and I can imagine the stunned look Ezryn has under that mask of his.

"What I mean is, yes. Maybe his mate will fall right on his, um—"

"If the mere thought of my cock turns you that red," Dayton gleams, "then imagine what you'd look like with it in your—"

"Stop being crude," I snap. "The point is, Dayton is right that he might find his mate in the Summer Realm. You're certainly not going to find your mates sitting in Castletree and never meeting anyone new. It's not like you're going to wake up one day and feel your mating bond burst to life inside of you."

"And why not?" He glares at me.

"Because it doesn't work that way!"

"Doesn't it?" His gaze is a blue fire across the table.

I've read every book on mates in the damned library over the last month, and it seems Keldarion is intent on testing that knowledge. "Okay, technically you could wake up one morning and feel it. But it's doubtful. Something likely has to trigger it."

"And what are these potential triggers, Rosalina?"

I breathe in a steadying breath. "This actually has nothing to do with my—"

"Should we get Farron back here to properly explain?"

"Potential triggers for awakening your bond could involve an incident with you or your mate's near-death. Any intense emotion from either, within a certain proximity, could do it. And proximity is something Farron and I have been researching. From what we can tell, it's not endless. I'm not sure about the magic of this castle, but I don't think your bonds will reach your realms. Possibly into the Briar as that's where the castle is grounded in reality, but unless your mate is a goblin, Keldarion, you're not going to randomly *feel* them."

He matches my glare and plops a grape into his mouth. At least that shut him up for now. I turn back to Ezryn and Dayton.

"I believe the curse has caused your mating bonds to lie dormant. Or it could be the fact that most of you don't leave the castle." Farron told me that at first, he, Dayton, and Ez had tried walking around the realms during the day, but year after year of nothing had eroded their hope. And their mates would have to love them, beasts and all. "Dayton has probably had the most exposure, figuring you do sometimes leave to drink during the day and on full moons. Have you ever felt—"

"Oh, I've felt a lot," Dayton says.

"Listen." I shake my head, running my hands through my hair, trying to remember the passages in my book. "In all the books, they say the bond is indescribable, which is super unhelpful. But from what I gather it's like … starlight igniting your whole body, realizing there was an empty part of your heart and having it filled …"

I trail off and see all of them staring at me with unreadable expressions. Well, except Ezryn. There, I just see my awkward reflection.

"Dayton, have you ever felt anything like that before?"

"No," he says automatically, but his eyes flick to the door before going back to me.

Unhelpful, every single one of them. Every day, I am less and less surprised these idiots have not broken the curse. I swear, I could deliver each of their mates directly onto their laps, and they still wouldn't be able to break this bloody thing.

Alas, I must forge ahead. "Finding your mates is the prominent part of breaking this curse, and we're going to do it with exposure therapy!"

"Uh, what?" Dayton blinks.

"In other words," I throw my arms out for emphasis, "a grand ball!"

"A ball?" Ezryn repeats slowly.

"Yes." I heave in a breath to explain before they can stop me. "It's the perfect opportunity to meet lots of eligible people—and touch them. Sometimes, just being in the same room as your mate can cause the bond to awaken. Farron and I were thinking each of the realms could host one. That way, you can meet fae from all around the Enchanted Vale."

"You know me, love." Dayton smiles. "I'm always down for a party."

"The winter solstice is a few weeks away. If we host our first ball in the Winter Realm, it might also help inspire the people," I suggest tentatively. From what Kel's vizier had been saying, the Winter Realm could use a little pick-me-up.

"The solstice does not fall on a full moon," Ezryn says. "It would have to be during the day."

Hope swells within me. That isn't a no. "Yes, we could market it as a full-day celebration. Spread rumors the princes are looking for partners. That will bring in an eager crowd."

"Dancing with a bunch of fae and drinking during the day?" Dayton laughs. "You have my support."

"I suppose the idea has some merit," Ezryn says. "However, we would have to be most cautious to leave for the castle before nightfall. No one can know about the curse."

"Of course, we can arrange all that! I'm sure your mating bonds will bloom forth in such a romantic setting!" I nearly jump up with excitement. They're totally into it. That is, until I turn to Keldarion.

His expression is stormy, and I'm caught in the torrent as he glares at me. "You can use my realm and invite my people, but I will not be in attendance."

I shoot forward. "Kel, you have to go."

"My answer is final," he snarls.

This plan falls apart if Keldarion doesn't go. Especially because we're starting in *his* bloody realm. Does he think he's just going to wake up one day with his mate bond in place? Or maybe he doesn't care. Doesn't care about this castle. Or the other princes. Or anyone except himself.

"You're a selfish bastard, Kel," I sneer.

I search for the most burnt muffin in the basket, grab it, and chuck it as hard as I can at him. He doesn't catch it, not that I don't think he couldn't. He just didn't think it was worth the effort when it bounces harmlessly off his rock-hard chest.

I reach for another muffin, but he's already crossed the length of the table and snatches my wrist, his hand covering the frozen bargain bracelet. "With that sort of talk, Rosalina, you'll fit right in with the rest of the Winter Realm."

34

ROSALINA

I storm through the halls after breakfast, not watching where I'm going. What is Keldarion's problem? How am I ever going to break this curse if he won't try anything? And if I don't break the curse, I'll never gain my freedom and return home.

"Don't hurt yourself, love." Firm hands grab my shoulders and direct me out of the path of a rather large thorn. I turn to see Dayton behind me. "Everything alright?"

"No," I snarl and keep walking. "I don't understand Keldarion. You'd think he *enjoys* being a beast."

"None of us like it." Dayton trails after me. "But Kel …"

"See! Even you can't think of an excuse for him."

"It's not that. Kel's touchy on the subject of mates."

I pause, something tightening in my chest. "Why is that?"

Dayton's gaze flits back and forth, then he rests his hand on one of the thorns. "Listen, Kel had a great love, and to say it ended poorly would be the fucking understatement of the century."

Keldarion has been in love before? That is surprising. "Was his great love also his mate?"

"I fucking hope not." Dayton laughs. "But no, I don't think so."

"What happened to them?" I ask.

"Enough questions," Dayton hisses, then, "For moon's sake, Blossom, are you crying?"

I wipe my eyes. "No! It's only, how am I supposed to help you all if Kel won't even *try*?"

Dayton sighs and puts his arm around me, pulling me against his body. He's so warm, and I inhale the sweet scent of sea air and sunshine. A sense of calm washes over me.

"If I had a heart, I'd understand why Kel isn't so eager to find his mate," Dayton says. "But since I'm clearly delusional and incapable of feeling, I agree with you. Keldarion is a massive prick and if I have to keep giving my nights up to that asshole golden wolf for the rest of my life, I'll likely kill him one day."

"Yeah, such a prick." I relish in this new sense of peace, feeling Dayton's firm chest on my cheek. But he pushes me away, and my anger comes rushing back in an instant.

"But tonight, that wolfy bastard is staying down." Dayton smirks at me, strands of blond hair falling across his face. "And I've got to get ready."

"Oh."

"Rosalina, love." He must still see the dismay on my face because he reaches forward and knocks me under the chin. "There's three ways to get rid of anger. Fight, drink, or fuck it out. Ask Marigold to whip you up something special tonight. She's surprisingly savvy with cocktails."

He turns, heading down the hall. Something bubbles in my chest, a rebellious longing, like I'm not ready for him to leave yet.

"Take me with you to the Summer Realm," I say.

He pauses for half a second, then snaps, "No," before he keeps walking.

"I want to do what you said." I scramble after him. "Take me with you."

"In case you forgot, you're Kel's prisoner."

I lower my brows. "Technically, I'm a prisoner of this castle and of the fae princes. If I'm with you, I'm not escaping."

Dayton stops walking, and I run into his solid body. "In case you haven't noticed, Kel's not big on technicalities. And I value my head. A lot. Have you seen how handsome it is?"

"Fine." I suck in a breath. "I guess you really are Kel's pup."

I turn away from him, take one step, then two, until I'm whipped around, and my back hits a hard stone wall. Dayton is in front of me, one of his legs pushed between mine.

"Now, who would say such a cruel thing about me?" He brings his face to my ear, soft strands of hair tickling my cheek.

I try to steady my breath. "The Prince of Thorns said it."

"When I found out he'd been here," Dayton lets out a humorless laugh, "found out he'd gotten so close to you ..."

"What?" I tilt my face up, my chest brushing against his torso. Heat skitters along my body.

Dayton squeezes his eyes shut. "Kel should have killed him for coming so close."

So close to me or the castle?

Dayton pushes away from the wall. "Meet me by the mirror at dusk." He glances over his shoulder with a dangerous smile. "And dress for a warm night. We're going to my realm, after all."

35

ROSALINA

"You do not need a stuffed lion." Dayton pulls me away from the vendor's stall, full of sewed plush animals and other fantastical creatures.

"But it's got *wings*, Dayton," I whine.

An hour ago, we'd stepped through the enchanted mirror and into an alley in the Summer Realm. I'd almost asked about switching the door's dial to enter the Summer Realm that way, but Kel had said those paths were shut a long time ago.

Plus, Dayton wanted to arrive close to the Summer Realm's nightlife, and we'd exited the alley into a bustling outdoor marketplace. The bazaar is busy and vibrant, filled with people milling about in colorful clothes, merchants hawking their wares from small carts, and artisans displaying intricate works from jewelry to painting to blown glass. This area is located on the seaside; ships pass through the harbor and the setting sun glimmers off the waves.

Dayton rolls his eyes and pulls out some coins from his pocket. "One stuffed lion."

The vendor widens his wrinkled eyes. "For the Prince, it is a humble gift."

"No, I insist." Dayton places the golden coins down on the counter.

The vendor shifts his eyes left and right. "My Prince, if it is not too bold to ask, when are you returning home for good?"

The playful expression Dayton held a moment ago blanches before he pulls it back into a cocky smile. "Unfortunately, there are still many thorns that surround Castletree. The others can't hold off the dark magic without me."

The vendor looks up and I follow his gaze. The city slopes upward and from here, I can see Castletree in the distance.

But it's an illusion. Dayton had explained to me only the front door is physically here in the Summer Realm. If one were to step through, they would find themselves within the actual castle, tucked within the Briar. Or at least that's how it used to be, before they closed the doors away to help hide the curse.

Below Castletree lies a beautiful palace gracing a cliff overlooking the sea. The Summer Palace, Dayton told me, where his younger sister now resides, the steward left to rule in his absence. The walls are constructed of a mix of ivory and jade stones, with golden turrets that sparkle like the sun itself.

The vendor nods, looking up at Dayton with admiration. "If you ask me, they should have crowned you Sworn Protector of the Realms after what the Winter princeling did."

Dayton gives a weak smile and picks up the lion. He shoves the stuffie into my stomach with more vigor than necessary. What was that about? What did Kel do?

"Thank you," I say.

But Dayton just grunts. Something about the vendor's words have set him off. I turn back to the market. It's so strange to be in a crowd after being bolted up in the castle for over a month.

The wind coming off the ocean caresses my skin, and I wrap my cloak around me. Per Dayton's suggestion, we both have garments of deep black draped around us to help us blend in. Still, it hasn't stopped people from recognizing him.

"I've heard Kel called the Sworn Protector before," I say. "What does it mean?"

Dayton glances down at me, then grabs my hand and pulls me down an alley. We start walking along a stone wall inlaid with carvings. Some are sculpture-like, seeming to jump out of the wall. I desperately try to take it in, but Dayton keeps walking.

"The Enchanted Vale was a prosperous and wonderous place when the Queen left," Dayton explains. "She wanted to leave a protector to preserve that peace in her absence. She took one of the five divine weapons of old and entrusted it to the High Ruler of the Winter Realm."

He stops before the wall, and I take in a carving of five incredible weapons: a sword, a hammer, a trident, a lance, and a stunning bow. Gently, I reach out my hands to caress the etched bow, inlaid with constellations. It's so realistic, I feel like I could pluck it from the wall. "What are the divine weapons?"

"Ancient relics," Dayton says, his fingers fluttering over the trident before dropping to his side. "The Queen and the High Rulers used them during the creation of the Enchanted Vale to defeat the Below. But after the war, she said such power had no place in a world of peace. She stored them in a monastery until the Vale had use of them again."

"Like when she left," I say, letting my hand trail along the wall until it rests on the sword.

"Yes. In her absence, she wanted to leave someone to take care of the Enchanted Vale, so she named the High Ruler of Winter the Protector of the Realms and allowed them to wield the Sword of the Protector at all times. Since then, it has been passed down from each of Winter's High Rulers. Now, it is entrusted to Kel. Though, a sword is no good against a curse."

"So, Kel watches over everyone."

Dayton scoffs. "That's the idea. The icy bastard's supposed to be a guardian of the Vale. He's intended to lead the other High Rulers in times of turmoil. Farron, Ez, and I ... We still look up to him. But he's certainly no great hero to the realms. Not sense the War of Thorns."

I let my hand fall. "Maybe he just needs to find the confidence in himself."

"Yeah, well, he lost the trust of his people a long time ago."

Before I can inquire further, Dayton yanks on my arm and says, "Come on." He guides me back onto the busy main street. "I didn't take you here for dusty stories of the past. I took you here to live."

A huge cheer fills the air, and I look up to see we're passing a massive building: towering arches made of marble and sandstone. The walls are covered in intricate carvings and statues as well, and through the opening I spy seats arranged in tiers. Shouts of the crowd echo through the air. Outside, there are more merchants selling clay disks with engravings of warriors on them.

"What is that place?" I ask as another roar sounds from the crowd.

"The Sun Colosseum, a keystone of the Summer Realm," Dayton says, following my gaze. "It's where all the best heroes are made. Fae test their strength and bravery against each other or against monsters from the Below."

"Wow," I say. "Like ancient gladiators."

He winks. "Where do you think they got their plans from?"

I knew I recognized some of the architecture here. It's like something out of a history book, a merger of ancient Roman and Greek designs. The fae and humans are more intertwined than I ever imagined.

"Though we don't have slaves, of course," Dayton says. "It's a great honor to battle in the arena. In fact, members of the royal house are expected to fight to prove themselves."

"Wait." I grip his arm. "You're telling me you actually fought in there? And lived?"

"Please, it was hardly a challenge." He flashes a dashing smile. "I could take six of those fighters blindfolded."

"Can we watch?"

"Feeling a little bloodthirsty today, Blossom?" Something flickers in his eyes as he looks up at the arena, and I'm not sure if it's sadness, longing, or … fear.

"Dayton?"

He loops an arm around my shoulder. "Maybe another time. The sun is setting, and I have yet to have a drink. Something that must be rectified presently."

WE MAKE our way deeper into the city until Dayton leads us into a bar, though I'm sure the fae call it something else. A beautiful fae woman greets us at the entrance.

"Let me take your cloak," Dayton says.

"I listened to your advice." I unfasten my cloak and hand it to him. "The staff were very excited to help me fit into the Summer Realm."

Marigold and Astrid had made sure I'd blend in. After swearing them to secrecy, they'd been so enthusiastic when I told them I'd be spending the night in one of the realms. Marigold recruited Flavia, a servant from the Summer Realm. She's a former seamstress who spends her nights as a small goat.

The smile on her face when she brought in the assortment of gowns from the Summer Realm had me willing to do just about anything she wanted. Almost. It seems fae in the Summer Realm aren't exactly fans of covering up, and we had to go through quite a few gowns until I found one with sleeves. Or the closest I could get. I settled for light purple fabric wrapped around my forearms and slitted drapes on the upper arms. The dress falls in pleats down the front, pinned on each shoulder with a golden seashell broach. The gauzy fabric gathers at the waist, the pieces not entirely opaque.

Which brought Astrid to her next area of concern. My body, and the lack of self-care I'd been giving myself while here. Well, excuse me. I didn't think things like shaving my legs or doing my nails were important while imprisoned and working on breaking a fae curse.

Clearly, I'd been wrong.

"You want to feel your best when you're on a date with a fae prince," Astrid had said, concerned. To which I had promptly informed her I was in no way going on a date with a fae prince.

All human propriety had been shoved straight out the castle

window as I'd stripped down, and Astrid used a long blade to shave my legs. All the while, Marigold patted oils on my skin and informed us that if I indeed wasn't on a date with a fae prince, then I should try to get some Summer fae dick because they "are the best fuckers and fighters in all the four realms'.realms".

Astrid had simply nodded. And the shaving had not stopped at my legs.

After I'd been scrubbed, washed, and oiled as slick as a baby seal, we'd returned to dress. Flavia had insisted on doing my hair as well. Intricate braids were woven into a crown on the top of my head. She even fastened them to cover the tips of my ears so I would have an easier time blending in. It was the equivalent of sticking a kitten with the lions, but I appreciated the sentiment.

My heart had warmed at these fae women helping me get ready for my non-date with a fae prince. They all made me promise to tell them every detail and my thoughts on the Summer Realm upon my return.

But maybe I don't look as good as I thought I did, because Dayton isn't saying a darn thing. He stares down at me, cloak in hand, blinking stupidly. Okay, I'm sure he's been with fae one hundred times more beautiful than I am, but you'd think he could at least appreciate the effort I put in and fake a compliment.

He turns away and storms into the bar without a single word.

36

ROSALINA

I follow Dayton into the fae bar. It's like nothing I've ever seen before.

Stone tables and elegant marble columns fill a large open-air room. There's a shallow pool with a fountain and lily pads in the middle. Beautiful fae wade through it, holding tall sparkling drinks, chatting and laughing.

The breeze hits my exposed skin, and I suddenly feel like I'm on display as fae eyes fall on me. It's like they're dissecting me. My cheeks flush.

"Come on," Dayton grumbles and grabs my wrist, dragging me through the crowd. "I didn't sign up to babysit you all night."

I sneer up at him, trying to escape the hard pressure on my wrist. "I don't need your help now that we're here."

He brings me to a stunning table right by a railing. I look over the edge to see the ocean splashing up against the side of the building. In the center of our table, there's a candle in the shape of a mermaid's tail.

My breath hitches as I gaze upon the fae prince. His white tunic fits closely to his hard body, and loose brown trousers leave little to the imagination. His only adornment is his seashell necklace that caresses his chest, and a short sword hanging from his belt. Even without the gilded finery of a prince, fae around us swoon in appreciation of Dayton's perfect form. Though his clothing is plain, his beauty radiates from within, igniting an undeniable spark.

"Wait here," he says and stands. "Don't move."

I nod bitterly, but he returns a moment later with a bottle of sparkling pink wine and two glasses.

"Fae wine isn't like your stuff back home. It's powerful, and depending on who bottles it, it can have different effects," he explains as he pours. "Especially on humans. So have a few sips and see how you do."

"I can hold my liquor," I flat out lie to him, remembering the last drink I had being half a bottle of beer alone last New Year's Eve before I passed out at eleven-thirty. "You worry about yourself, and I'll worry about me."

He tilts his head. "Whatever you say, love."

"Do you think anyone noticed I left with you?" I ask, grabbing my glass.

"I doubt it." A strand of light hair falls across his blue eyes. "Does playing the rebel make you nervous?"

Marigold and Astrid had said they would cover for me as best they could. Though I don't think it will be a problem. Farron and Ezryn have both left, and the stupid, pig-headed, stubborn Winter Prince never leaves his freaking room, so no one will know or care I'm not there for a single night.

But all I can do is nod and take the first sip of my wine. I give a little gasp as it slides down my throat. This is like nothing I've ever tasted before. Bubbly and sweet, with a hint of sourness, a delicate flavor with notes of honey and ripe apples.

"Shit, this is delicious." I smile before taking another long swig. "Is this what sparkles taste like?" The finish is refreshing, almost effervescent, making me feel like butterflies are fluttering in my stomach.

Dayton clinks his glass against mine. "Here's to a night of drinking, dancing, and finding a damn good lay."

I blush before drinking deeply.

"That's what you came out for, isn't it?" Dayton asks. "To spite a certain frosty prick?"

"I don't want to think about a single cold thing right now!" I close my eyes and tilt my head back, inhaling the warmth in the air. "We're in the Summer Realm, after all."

"We are," Dayton says, then his voice lowers. "Although, I have to say there is something about you that surprises me."

"Something about me?"

"You talk a lot about wanting to go back to your father." His blue gaze is intense. "But are there no man's arms you're itching to return to?"

I clasp a hand over my left wrist and squirm in my seat, suddenly uncomfortable. "Well, actually ..."

"Who is he?" Dayton asks, and I can't tell if it's curiosity or anger in his words.

"His name is Lucas. We've been on and off since I was fifteen, but I think it's serious now. Super serious." I take a deep breath. "Or at least it could have been, if I hadn't been imprisoned by the fae."

"Super serious, eh?"

"He asked me to marry him right before I came here." I tug on one of my braids. "My mundane human romantic life must seem so boring to you."

The way he's looking at me, he doesn't seem bored. His gaze pierces into mine. But then he laughs, long and loud. "So, should we expect any ill-fated rescue attempts for our stolen Rose?"

"Ill-fated? You're confident." I smile. "Lucas is no fae, but he's a brilliant hunter."

"I've never lost a fight, Rosie, and my first won't be to your human." There's a dark promise in his words, one that causes me to shiver, but not from fear.

"Well, I don't think you have to worry about it." I take another long drink of my wine, trying to drown the sinking feeling in my stomach. "Lucas took one look at those goblins and hightailed it back home. I bet he thinks it was all a bad dream."

"He left you to the goblins?" Fury rages in Dayton's words.

"Look, we'd never seen anything like that before," I say. "I was running too! Unfortunately, I'm way clumsier and fell into the thorns."

Dayton chugs the rest of the bottle of wine, but before he can order another, the server places several more bottles on the table, along with a plate of fruit and nuts and a tankard of foaming ale. "From the patrons. They wanted to pay their respects to you."

Dayton gives a thankful wave to the crowd, and wow, I didn't notice how many eyes were on us. I guess the Prince is a bit of a spectacle. But Dayton's attention is still solely on me.

"What about—" I begin, but Dayton cuts me off.

"Tell me more about this Lucas."

"He's handsome. Red hair. When we were in high school, he basically had his own fan club. I was their number one arch-nemesis." I pour more wine, this one a glittering purple. It tastes like blackberries and the last rays of light on a summer night. "He's big on family. Always talks about getting a house, having kids, y'know the white picket fence dream."

"Are you going to say yes?"

I freeze the cup halfway to my lips. "I honestly haven't had time to think about it."

"There's your answer," Dayton says. "No."

"No?" I slam my cup down. "Why would you say that?"

"If it were a yes, then you'd know. You wouldn't have to think about it."

I roll my eyes. "Look, I'm not a fae with a magical mating bond that sparkles and tells me who is the one. We humans must think with our heads. Like, can we make each other happy long-term? Do we have the same values and goals? Does he—"

"Does he make you come?"

I spit my wine all over the table. Dayton doesn't notice. He leans closer and his voice pitches low. "Is he good to you? Does he leave you satisfied? How many times a night does he pleasure you, Blossom?"

Sex with Lucas was pleasant, and I had enjoyed it most of the time. I liked being close to him, how hard and passionate his kisses were.

But when I think about the mind-blowing orgasms the women in my books have, my mind draws a blank. "I don't," I stammer, "I don't know."

"If you don't know," he gives a rueful smile, "then the answer is never."

"Well, I—"

"Before you say yes to this human, you need to experience someone worshiping your body the way you deserve. You need someone to take you over the edge again and again and again."

Liquid heat pools in my belly as his words rush over me. "Marigold said fae from the Summer Realm were the best lovers."

"Did she now?" Dayton leans so our foreheads are almost touching. He's got one hand braced on the side of the table, and the large muscles in his arms strain.

"Yes." I breathe in and flutter my eyes shut.

"Then I'm sure you can find some fae here desperate enough to give you that." There's a clatter as Dayton falls back to his chair, laughing.

Foolish disappointment swells in my belly. Of course Dayton's not interested in me. He's a freaking fae prince. He could have anyone he wants. Plus, I'm trying to find his mate. I can't think about him like that, no matter how charming and gorgeous he is.

His words settle in my head. What have I got to lose? Would it be so wrong to experience pleasure for a night? I'm a prisoner. When I get back to Orca Cove and say yes to Lucas, I won't feel guilty. We're not really together now ... I didn't say yes.

He's been with so many girls during his stint at university. Why isn't it my turn? Why shouldn't I have fun for one night?

I pour more of the fae wine into my cup and hold it up to cheers Dayton. "Here's to drinking, dancing, and finding a damn good lay."

His eyes widen for a moment before he holds his cup up to mine. "Here's to that, Blossom."

37

ROSALINA

This is the best night of my entire life, and it's not just the fae wine talking. Okay, maybe it's the fae wine talking, but I don't even care. Everything here is amazing!

The food? Delicious. I've eaten two nuts and fruit plates, plus three baskets of bread, and more olives than I can count.

I have no clue how much I've drunk, but it's because wine keeps getting delivered to our table. Dayton and I can barely hold a conversation because so many people keep coming over to talk to him, offering us food and drink.

Right now, he's across the bar, telling some farfetched story to a group of enraptured patrons. I like observing him from afar. Tall and beautiful, he draws people to him like planets around the sun. And he's so charming, giving everyone his full attention. Though a part of me yearns for him to return to the table.

I should focus on Operation Hook-Up, but I'm quite content where I am. There is no shortage of beautiful things to look at, from the marble pillars to the hanging golden lights with dangling colorful gems, to the painted murals. But the most beautiful thing of all are the fae.

I can barely take in their elegant faces, pointed ears, elaborately done hair, and flowing sheer outfits that leave little to the imagination.

"Looking for me?" Dayton falls back down to his seat.

"Checking out my options," I tell him.

He raises a brow, then leans across the table to tuck a turquoise flower behind my ear. "Got you a present."

Warmth blooms in my chest, and I reach for my wine.

"Slow down." Dayton places his palm over the top of my glass. Shit, his hand is huge. How have I never noticed that before? I grab his hand, suddenly wanting to inspect the callouses on his palm.

I giggle and intertwine our fingers. "The wine is fantastic."

"Alright, I-can-hold-my-liquor-Rosalina," he laughs.

I stare at him just so I can take him in. He's more handsome than all the fae here. His sun-kissed skin glows in the dim light.

"Why are you looking at me like I'm a new research book?"

"Your smile right now. It's one of my favorites," I say, my head feeling light and sparkly.

"You have a favorite smile of mine?"

I nod and push the hair away from his face. "You have lots of smiles. Cocky ones, flirty ones, sarcastic ones. Ones where you're really sad, but you don't want anyone to know."

"Alright, alright." He shakes his head, taking a long swig. "You are observant, aren't you? What smile is your favorite?"

I lower my hand to his strong jaw. "I call it your secret smile. You have it when you think no one's watching. I've only ever seen it when you look at Farron. But tonight, you looked at me and ... And it's special."

The beautiful smile is gone from his face in an instant, and he stands, dragging me up with him. "You have a certain smile right now too, Blossom."

"I do?"

"Yes," he growls. "A dopey, drunk smile. You've had too much wine."

"I have had just enough." I giggle. This is better than any human alcohol has ever made me feel. "What's the deal with you and Farron, anyway?"

"Look, twenty-five years is a long time to be stuck with the same people, even for fae," Dayton says. "You can't blame me for having a little fun while I'm there."

That's what Farron had said too. Just fun. But I don't think he meant it. Dayton drags me across the bar while I scowl at him. "I don't think Farron thinks what you two have is a little fun. I think he's in lo—"

"Enough." Dayton swirls, and suddenly there's a cool cup of water in my hands. "Drink."

I do, begrudgingly. Damn, even the water here tastes good, hydrating and smooth down my throat. As I'm silently sipping away at my drink, a few more people come over to Dayton, slapping him on the shoulder, proclaiming how they miss him.

The group buys drinks, but this time Dayton doesn't share with me. He chugs them down as if he wants them out of his sight.

People in the Summer Realm like him. No talks of rebellions here like the vizier warned Keldarion about. *Probably because Dayton's not the icy cretin of the frost world.*

Suddenly, there's a firm arm around my shoulders as Dayton pulls me close. "How are you feeling?"

"More normal." With one cup of water, my head is clearer. "There are a lot of fae here. Which has me thinking we should practice."

"Practice?"

"Finding your mate!"

Dayton groans and tilts his head back. "Have I thwarted myself by sobering you up?"

"Come on, we're in the Summer Realm. Maybe your mate is local."

"Rosalina, my love, this is supposed to be a night for *fun*."

I pull him deep into the throng of dancers, moving dreamily over the lily pond. The closer to all the other fae, the better. "Just try, please."

"Okay, but then you have to do what I want."

"Fine, fine." Dayton twirls me around as we sway to the music. "W-what are you doing?"

"We're dancing," he says, then leans down, his mouth to my ear. "I'm not going to stand in the middle of the room and shout, 'Hey-o! Looking for a mate!' I'll have a hundred fae on me before my next breath."

"Fair." The only reason I'm game for dancing is because I still have all that fae wine sloshing in my system. Everyone on the dance floor looks at us. And while I don't know how many of them can tell I'm human, I'm sure they're all wondering who this girl is dancing with the Summer Prince.

But it's more intimate than dancing. Dayton presses me close to his chest while we sway back and forth. Cold water splashes on my ankles as we move over the lily pond.

"All right, Blossom," Dayton says lowly, "tell me how this works."

"You need to start by being relaxed and open."

"The wine has already done that. Next?"

"You'll want to close your eyes and feel for something unlike anything you've felt before. Like a sparkle. A match being lit inside."

"Where exactly?"

"Most people feel it here." I place my hand over his heart, fingers slipping between the open laces of his shirt. His skin is warm as sunlight.

He stops dancing, and we're still over the water. The other couples sway around us. He closes his eyes and tilts his head back, the muscles in his neck tensing. "Describe what I'm supposed to feel."

"Warmth, like sun-baked sand." I keep my fingers over his heart, feeling it beat faster. "Perhaps an electric shock or the constricting of your heart."

A rumble sounds in his chest, and he groans lowly. "I think I feel something."

My heart sinks and I tremble. "Okay, good. Good. Try to pinpoint where the feeling is coming from." I try to sift through all the information I learned in my research. "Once the feeling begins, some fae describe it like a string tugging them toward their mate."

"Hmm." Dayton scrunches up his brow. "I don't feel it in my chest though."

Could we really have gotten so lucky as to find Dayton's mate here in this bar? "Where do you feel it?"

He shakes his head back and forth, a golden braid falling loose from behind his ear. "Lower."

I move my hand down his chest. "Here?"

"No, lower."

My fingers cascade down his stomach. I suppose there's something to be said about gut feelings. "Here?"

"Lower." His voice is deep and raspy.

I scan the bar. All the beautiful fae here. Which one calls to him? My hand automatically drifts lower, until I realize my fingers are stroking the outline of his steel-hard cock.

"Right there," he says, groaning pleasurably.

"Dayton!" I remove my hand to slap him, but he catches my wrist, then twirls me in front of him before playfully pulling me against his chest.

"Sorry, love." He laughs. "I couldn't help myself. And besides, why shouldn't I feel it there? Shouldn't I want to fuck my mate beyond all sense?"

I scowl. "So, you didn't feel anything?"

"No flowering feelings here. I just really want to fuck someone."

I huff out a breath as we continue dancing. "No wonder. There are so many beautiful people here." And I already know Dayton doesn't discriminate between them. To him, everyone is a potential partner. "And they're hardly wearing any clothes."

"If that interests you, let me take you to another room, one where clothes are optional." He pulls back with a devious gaze. "But we already know you're fond of watching."

I gasp and try to pull away from him. It flashes again in my mind: he and Farron together. "I didn't mean to."

"I know." He grips my jaw with his hand. "Next time, don't leave so quickly. You missed me licking the cum from his chest."

My knees tremble and I think I might faint. I probably couldn't even stand if he weren't holding me.

"And round two, which was even rougher." Dayton's wet mouth moves to my ear. "Between you and me, I think you watching turned him on. I know I liked it."

I flutter my eyes closed. "Round two?"

"You've never had fae cock before, little Blossom." His mouth moves to my neck, his sharp teeth nipping at the sensitive skin. "There's no limit to the number of times I could make you come."

A sultry fantasy rushes through my veins, the impulse to shed my garments and let him ravage my body on this dance floor. I inhale sharply as I imagine what could be, a whimper escaping from my quivering lips.

Dayton pushes me away, and I open my eyes to see him laughing, gazing down at me with a distant, cocky grin. "Or one of these lucky bastards. While I doubt any of them are skilled like me, all fae dick's pretty good. Trust me, I've tried a lot."

I feel dizzy, rejected, and frustrated. Why does he feel the need to tease me? It's clear he doesn't want me. Why do I keep falling for it?

"Right," I say. "Though I doubt any of them would want me."

"You truly must be unobservant," Dayton says. "People have been looking over here all night."

"At you." I gesture to him.

He shakes his head. "At you! I don't know if I want to kiss Astrid for what she did to you or ban her from being in your presence ever again. What's with that grumpy face?"

"Can you not talk about kissing Astrid?"

He gives me a rueful smirk. "Deal, but I think it's the time of night that we go our separate ways. Find a fae and get him to take you to a private room. Do *not* leave this bar. Meet me by this fountain in two hours. Deal?"

"So, you're also …"

"Love, we've done the drinking, the dancing, and there's no mate to be found. It's time for the fucking." He gives me a push on the back. "Spread your petals and bloom, little flower."

I take a glass of wine for good measure and step into the crowd. Sure, no fae males are as gorgeous as Dayton, but that doesn't mean it wouldn't be fun to try something with one of them. And maybe he wasn't lying. Maybe some of them might want me.

"Deal, Dayton," I say. "But let's make it three hours. I think I can outlast you."

He lifts his cup to me as I disappear into the crowd.

38

DAYTON

I can barely see Rosalina; she's buried in a couch surrounded by fae males. The bastards descended the moment I left her side. The scent of their desire is sickening. They're ready to fuck her the moment she gives the go-ahead.

Which she will because that's exactly what I told her to do.

"Uh, are you not into this?" the fae female lounging beside me asks. Her finger runs down my bare chest. I lost my shirt an hour ago.

No idea who took it. I was drunk—but I need to be this drunk to stop myself from doing something incredibly stupid.

"Time to wake up." The fae female squeezes my flaccid cock through my pants. I can't focus on her.

It was a stupid idea to bring Rosalina here. But she'd looked so desperate. I can't give her true freedom without defying Kel, but I could give her freedom for one night.

I just didn't realize how hard it would be. Like when she'd first taken off that cloak and I'd seen what she was wearing. How little she was wearing. I'd wanted to take her straight to a room so no one else could lay eyes on her. Seeing her in the clothes of the Summer Realm, my realm, awoke something primal in me. I wanted to— No. Anything I wanted to do to her is a betrayal to Kel. An even worse one than if I let her go. He'd said none of us was to touch her. And if it was for the reason we all suspected —the only fucking logical reason for any of this—then I couldn't.

It doesn't mean she can't have some fun on her own. I doubt Kel would approve of this, but she deserves to let loose. Especially after the way he treats her.

If I can grant her that, I will.

It's just so fucking hard.

One of the fae males strokes his hand up and down her arm. Another one massages her shoulders. She glances over at me. She keeps doing that. Maybe to see if I've left for my private room yet. Nope. There's no fucking way I'm letting her out of my sight until I have to.

Her arousal is so strong, I can smell it from here. Almost as intense as the time she'd been standing outside my room.

Fuck. When she'd walked in on me and Farron, I'd nearly run after her butt-ass naked and dragged her back between us. Fare and I have shared women before, but he's never been that into it. But he'd be into Rosie. I know he would.

"There we go," the fae female giggles, her pert tits wiggling in my face. "You're hard now."

I look past her to Rosalina. One of the fae males pulls her on his lap, right over his hard cock. My fists tighten and I stand, accidentally throwing the fae woman to the ground.

The male kisses Rosalina.

Anger ignites in my chest. The monstrous golden wolf rages up inside me. I need to get out of here before I turn.

Rosalina pushes him. "Let me go!"

She crosses the room, but the fae male follows her. "I thought you wanted that," he slurs.

"I changed my mind."

Relief floods my chest, and the wolf settles down.

"I haven't," the fae male growls. He pulls Rosalina to him. The braids in her hair fall out, exposing her rounded ears. "A human?"

So we're not fucking done. I push the crowd out of the way to get to her.

"Don't touch me," she cries, her eyes dancing around the room. She's looking for me.

"Worry not, little human," the fae male leers. "I'll try not to break you ... too much."

"I said stop," Rosalina snarls, fury etched on her face, and the fae male hesitates for a moment.

That moment is all I need. I emerge from the crowd and haul him away. "You should have listened to her the first time."

Fear blanches the male's face. "Prince Dayton," he stutters. "I barely touched her—"

"She's the last thing you'll ever fucking touch." A crowd forms around us, but I push them out of the way and slam the male down on the table. His scream only enrages the wolf inside me further. I force his arms out before him.

"W-what are you doing?" he cries, tears falling down his face.

My sword is answer enough. I draw it and arc it down in one swift movement, cutting right at the wrist bones, hard enough for it to embed in the table. His disgusting hands fall to the ground, painting the floor red. Blood sprays from his wrists, drenching my torso, and coating his screaming mouth.

The crowd erupts in a wild frenzy, pushing and shoving each other to escape. I turn to see Rosalina frozen in shock, her face a mix of disbelief and terror. Not wasting a moment, I snatch her arm and drag her from the bar.

Through the chaos, I hear the whispers: "Damocles never would have done this."

"Maybe this is why Dayton's absent. Locked away for his rage."

"Should have left the baby prince in the ring with the wild monsters. Where he belongs."

I need to get out of here. "Send the bill to my sister," I snap at the owner as we leave.

The night air does nothing to cool my burning skin.

"Dayton—" Rosalina grasps my arm. "Dayton, are you hurt?"

I could almost laugh. Of course at a time like this, she would be worried about me. "Didn't you see? It's not my blood."

"Day," she says, "your eyes ... they're glowing."

"Fuck," I mutter. I pull her into a nearby alley. "We need to go back to the castle."

"I'm sorry, this is all my fault," she mumbles. "I thought I wanted to—y'know. But as soon as they touched me, I got this major ick. I assumed it would go away once we kissed, but it got worse—"

I brace my hands on the stone wall. "Rosalina, I really need you to stop talking about kissing that fae." It feels like I'm burning from the inside out. I'm not sure if I'm going to shift into a wolf or explode and take the whole Summer Realm down in flames with me. Shit, it's been decades since I've felt this out of control.

"I was going to say, it was even worse when he kissed me," she continues, because she always has to finish her point. I find it cute as shit when she snaps at Kel this way, but now that she's doing it to me, I want to shut her pretty little mouth.

Forcing my eyes closed, I try to ignore the fire that's burning in my chest. I release the clasp of the largest shell on my necklace and reveal the small mirror inside. I angle the object toward the wall, reflecting the light until it builds a spinning portal on the surface.

"How?" Rosalina gasps. "You have portable mirrors?"

"They connect to the mirror in Castletree, so we can return home at any time." I grab her wrist and pull her through. She needs to be safe inside the castle before I explode.

The magic wraps around us until we stumble into the cool entrance hall, the familiar sight of those bloody thorns welcoming us home.

I take in a deep breath and pinch the bridge of my nose. What the fuck is wrong with me?

Rosalina looks up at me, her eyes wide with concern. "What happened back there, Dayton?"

"I'm sorry if I scared you."

"I wasn't scared. He deserved it." Her face is stern. "Now he can't touch anyone else against their will. At least, not as easily."

"Well, I'm sorry you didn't get your carefree night." One of her sleeves has slipped down and I reach to pull it up.

"I didn't want any of them, anyway." Her hand clasps over mine before I can pull away. And damn if the contact of her skin isn't lighting another sort of fire inside me. "I don't understand what happened to your eyes. You seemed so—"

"No one treats you that way, Rosalina," I snarl. "If I didn't get out of there, I would have torn every one of them apart, then my beast would have shown up to finish the job."

Her fingers curl around mine, breath heavy in her throat. She looks up at me with those big brown eyes, and I'm fucking gone. "Day—"

I pull her toward me and kiss her with everything I have.

39

ROSALINA

Dayton's mouth crashes over mine. My body has a mind of its own, my fingers tugging in his hair, pushing him harder against me as if I'm afraid he'll pull away before I get my fill. And I don't think I ever will.

His stubble scratches against my chin as we move together, his lips exploring with the perfect mix of strength and tenderness. I feel the hunger in him as much as I feel it in myself. There's no sense to the flurry of emotions in my head, but my body knows what it wants, and it wants this. His arms wrap around me and the heat between us is palpable.

I'd thought I needed a fun night with a random fae, but when those males came around, a strange prickling of disgust covered my body. And when one kissed me? Full-on nausea, like I was going to vomit all over the beautiful bar. It had only stopped when Dayton pulled me away.

There's still dried blood splattered across his chest. I run my fingers over it as I break the kiss.

"Fuck, Rosie," he gasps, lips skipping over the sensitive spot beneath my ear.

Don't stop, don't stop, don't stop. I've never felt like this before, as if I'm a tiny shell tossing in a turbulent surf.

Dayton leans down to kiss me again, and my mouth opens against his. He wraps his arms around me, then lifts me like I'm nothing, which is *so* not true. My back gently hits the stone wall, a slim gap between the thorns, and my legs wrap around his waist.

I brace myself on one of the thick stems. It shudders beneath my touch. Hey, at least they're useful for something.

Dayton looks me up and down, pupils blown as they skim over my body. "You're so fucking gorgeous." Then his lips are on my neck, sucking the skin hard.

I cry out, bucking my hips, and feel his solid length beneath his loose pants. A male rumble sounds in his throat as he pushes harder against me.

His lips make their way back up to my mine. He sweeps the hair off my forehead with his large hands as our hips rock, finding a rhythm almost instantly. Like my body was made to move with his.

"Dayton," I whimper his name between kisses.

"Do you like this?"

"Yes. Yes, I do."

He smiles into our kiss. "I'm going to make you feel things you've never felt before. You're going to feel so good, love."

Pure liquid heat pools in my core. Dayton trails one of his rough hands down my front, then slips aside the fabric, exposing my breast to the cool air before his hand covers it.

My back arches into his touch. Dayton squeezes my breast, massaging it gently, before running a thumb over my perked nipple. The sensation travels like a bolt through me, and my muscles tighten.

Dayton gives a satisfied sound, then slides the fabric away from my other breast. But this one he doesn't cover with his hand. He uses his mouth, dipping down, closing his lips around it.

I blink rapidly as my body registers the sensation, and I cry out: "Oh ... Oh!" One of my hands flies down to grip his shoulder, the other tightening on a vine twisting among the thorns.

Dayton licks across the expanse of my chest, leaving a searing heat in its wake. He captures the other aching breast in his mouth and sucks gently, sending electric shocks throughout my body. As he releases it with a soft pop, his trembling fingertips dance across the other. His lips part as he grazes me with his teeth, sending me into a pleasure-filled whirlpool.

He straightens, pushing himself hard into me, and the feeling of my wet breast crushing against his chest is maddening. "Did you like being kissed there, little Blossom?"

"Yes," I mumble against his neck. God, he smells good. Salt and sweat.

One of his hands squeezes into the soft flesh of my thigh and he moves higher. "Anywhere else you'd like it? I doubt that kumquat of an ex-boyfriend was any good but—"

"More like ex-fiancé. Or maybe fiancé?" I gasp.

Dayton rolls his eyes, but his hand moves higher, tickling the top of my thigh and brushing the fabric aside. "Whatever. Ex-fiancé." He smirks. "Did you like his lips here?"

He brushes between my legs, fingers sliding over the slick fabric of my panties. A soft sound escapes my lips and I squeeze my eyes shut.

"So wet, Rosie." Lightly, so lightly, he brushes his hand over the soaking fabric. When he tugs me closer, his steel length pushes against my aching core. "Now, be a good girl and answer the question."

I cry out and struggle to find my words amid my gasping breath. "I-I, uh, I don't know."

Dayton pulls back and stares at me, his expression one of pure frustration. All the touching stops. "Are you fucking serious, Rosalina?"

"What?" I wiggle against him, desperate for any sort of friction.

He pushes me hard against the wall, still keeping one hand braced behind my head. "You're telling me you're considering marrying a fucking deadbeat who never even went down on you?"

"Well ..."

"No." He claps a large hand over my mouth. "Not another word out of your mouth, unless it's a cry of pleasure or my name."

"But Dayton—"

"Perfect." He cuts me off with a kiss. This one is softer than before, languishing.

He grips my hips and lowers himself, guiding my legs over the top of his shoulders. I grab the brambles on either side of me.

"Dayton, what—" My words cut off as he kisses the inside of my thigh. His stubble is rough on the sensitive skin.

He gathers the skirts, and pushes them up around my hips, pressing his mouth between my legs. The sensation of his lips against the wet fabric sends a shockwave through my body. I grab the vines tighter and let out a groan.

He grips the fabric with his teeth, sucking and tugging. Then he leans back and looks up at me with sparkling blue eyes. "Sorry, but this is in my way."

With deft hands, he rips the fabric, letting my panties slide to the ground. A delicious breeze skates over my skin, and I let out a soft mewl.

"Perfect," Dayton growls before moving between my legs, and his mouth drags over my folds. He slips his tongue inside and pleasure ripples through me.

One of his hands cups my ass, helping to keep me up, but the other circles the top of my clit.

"Holy shit," I gasp out, my muscles tightening. Radiating heat pumps through my body.

"You're such a good girl, Rosie," he says. "So wet for me. You taste like the sweetest nectar."

I rock my hips against his mouth. Have I ever felt such pleasure? I'm tempted to tell him he's done too much for me already. The man hasn't even taken off his pants.

But he doesn't make me feel like a burden the way Lucas did. I think he's actually enjoying this. But I can't help it. "You can stop if you don't actually like doing it."

He stills for a moment, his fingers digging into the soft flesh of my ass. "Do you like it, Rosalina?"

"Yes," I say in a breath. "Yes, I've never felt anything like this. I just—"

"Then the fucking gods will have to tear me away from your sweet pussy," the deep voice rumbles against my inner thigh.

I reach a shaking hand down to gently touch his hair, soft and golden. Warmth blooms in my chest, to feel so wanted like this. "Day ..."

"Is that all?" He chuckles before his mouth returns to my aching core. He works me deeper with his tongue, pace increasing. Pressure builds inside of me. "Dayton ..." I sigh out his name, then: "Day. Day!"

He stands, moving my legs from his shoulders back to his waist.

"Wait," I cry out, dropping my hands from the vines and wrapping around his muscular shoulders. Did he change his mind? "Wait, I—"

"And you'll feel it, love." His voice is unhinged, like he's barely keeping it together.

"Are we going to—"

"Not here," he growls.

Disappointment swells in my belly.

He must see my expression because he grips my face. "You're going to come for me, then I'm going to take you back to my room and fuck you the way no one else has before."

He seals the promise with a kiss, and I taste myself on his lips. My soaking pussy rubs against the rough fabric of his pants, grinding against his steel length. "Yes, Dayton."

"I'm going to watch you come apart in my arms." A sharp pain radiates through my neck as he bites down and tugs at my hair. "Then I'm going to fill you with my cock."

My body stills as new awareness floods through me. Dayton cups my entire pussy with his hand and rubs.

"You're soaking, Baby." Dayton increases his movement. "Do you want my cock inside you?"

"Yes, yes, yes," I moan, riding his hand. He circles my entrance, and I feel the liquid heat dripping out of me onto his palm.

"Taste yourself, love." He brings a dripping finger up to my mouth.

I wrap my lips around it like a starved person. I keep my eyes open as I slide his whole finger to the back of my throat. He gives a broken laugh, his eyes rolling back, before he retracts his finger and crashes his lips against mine. "That's it."

He moves his hand back under me and slides a finger inside. I grit my teeth, moaning at the sudden pleasure. He works me in circles before pulling in and out.

I grip his shoulders and roll my hips into the movement. A yummy warmth builds inside my core. He hooks a finger, hitting just the right spot, and I curl over, my lips landing on his shoulder. "More," I gasp.

He adds a second finger and helps guide my hips, up and down now. Our pace increases until I'm completely at his mercy, tossing in the wild storm of his eyes. A wave cresting— "Dayton!" I cry out as I crash upon his shore. My body releases wave after wave of pleasure, muscles contracting around his hand. I'm fracturing, a star exploding in a million pieces.

Finally, I crest down, and he removes his hand, careful to still hold me up against the wall. I can barely breathe.

Dayton clutches his chest with his palm and looks at me with a strange expression: parted lips, the slightest curve on one side of his mouth. A new smile.

One just for me.

His lips are soft as I caress them with my shaking fingers. It feels like parts of me are floating all around, like dust in a sunbeam. Floating with parts of him too. If I were to kiss him now, if we were to make love, I could bring all the pieces together. His eyes close and softly he lowers his face to mine.

"Day?" a stunned voice calls from the top of the stairs.

I whip my head up to see Farron standing there, hair mussed and face flashing with stunned sadness.

Suddenly, a bright light shines over us. The mirror glows, and Ezryn runs through. Black blood splatters his helmet and armor. He stalks forward and growls, "What have you done?"

40

ROSALINA

Dayton's grip tightens on me as Farron and Ezryn both walk toward us. Well, Farron walks and Ezryn storms, his metal armor clinking in the open hall. He pauses before us, and oh my god, I forgot Dayton messed up my dress, and everything is on display. But Ezryn just yanks Dayton away, and I fall straight on my ass.

Ezryn draws back his fist and punches Dayton in the face. "You disobeyed your prince."

Blood gushes from Dayton's nose, but he tilts his head and laughs. "Worth it."

"What did you do, Day?" Farron cries.

All I can do is fix my dress as guilt simmers in my gut. Shit, I guess I should have figured out more specifics about their relationship. But it felt like I'd been possessed, a fire scorching in my belly, and the only thing that could put it out was Dayton's touch.

Dayton holds up his hands in a peaceful gesture, still a little wobbly on his feet from the massive hit Ezryn gave him. "It was just a bit of fun. Besides, you don't even like going out to drink."

"Dayton, you're an idiot." Farron tears at his hair, a look of horror crossing his features. "You took her out of the castle? Kel is going to *kill* you."

"He won't get the chance." Ezryn grabs Dayton by the back of the neck before slugging him in the gut.

"It was my fault!" I stand and scream at them. But not a single one of these muscled idiots pays attention to me. "I *asked* to go. Stop fighting!"

Farron lunges toward Ezryn but gets pushed aside as Ezryn lands another hard blow to Dayton's ribs. Farron falls hard to the floor, and a thin line of blood drips from his skull. Dayton looks at him, then back up to Ezryn, and snarls, "Alright, so you want to dance, Ez?"

Ezryn looks like he just really wants to hit Dayton again, but this time when he tries, Dayton tears out of his grip and leaps behind him. He hits Ezryn where there must be a gap in his armor because Ezryn pitches forward.

"Stop it!" Farron screams, jumping between them, but it only causes Dayton to accidentally clip him on the shoulder.

Farron falls back, slamming into Ezryn, and the two of them clatter to the ground.

"Can you all please—" My words cut off as a chilly breeze blows down the hall.

"Oh fuck," Dayton says.

"No," Farron gasps, then leans over, clutching his stomach.

"Shit. Don't turn now, Fare—" Dayton rushes beside him.

Farron shrugs him off, growling, "Get away! You're the problem, Dayton."

Dayton flinches back as if Farron landed a physical blow.

Ice shivers across the floor until it covers the entire entrance hall. And emerging from an icy cloud is the Prince of Winter. Keldarion wears a tight black shirt and pants, his long white hair cascading over his shoulders. Fury rages in his frost-ridden eyes.

He swipes out a hand, and Dayton flies back in a chute of winter air, crashing against the wall before being encased in ice up to his waist.

Ezryn scrambles up and kneels before Keldarion. Farron is still rolling on the ground, the pain in his gaze intense.

And I'm standing in the middle of it all, unsure what to do.

"Fuck you, Kel," Dayton snarls, and it's like I can feel the sparkle of magic emanating from him, white hot fire. The ice encasing him melts, and he storms toward us, blond hair wild.

Ezryn and Kel exchange a look.

"This is your fucking fault, Kel," Dayton says. "You can't lock her here and pretend—"

Farron lets out a horrible sound, half beast, half man. His fingers claw at the ice. I'm torn between wanting to run to him and wanting to run away. Dayton stops his advance, concern flashing in his eyes.

Kel nods at Ezryn, who stands and walks over to Farron. His eyes glow.

Ezryn kneels before Farron, then takes off his gloves, revealing his elegant, tanned hands. He takes Farron's face between his palms and mutters something too low for me to hear.

Small, iridescent roots break out from the floor and slither their way over Farron's body. Forehead to helmet, the magic slows Farron's breath.

Dayton watches with wide eyes from across the room, unmoving.

Kel increases his pace toward … me. Okay, maybe I should have taken my opportunity to run.

It takes everything in me not to shrink back as the Winter Prince looms above me. I have a million things I can say to defend myself, but before I get a single one out, he scoops me up and throws me over his shoulder.

"What the!" I gasp and try to kick my legs. Which is as effective as hitting a brick wall. He doesn't answer me as he walks up the stairs.

I lift my head and meet Dayton's gaze, who gives me a sympathetic shrug. At least whatever plant magic Ezryn did has stopped Farron from shifting. He's bracing himself against Ezryn's chest.

"Kel! Where are you taking me?" I demand again.

The answer comes to me as the stone floor of the castle turns to solid ice.

Keldarion is taking me to the Winter Wing.

41

FARRON

"Breathe with me, Farron. Breathe."

Blood hammers through my head as Ezryn's soft voice drifts through me; the tight embrace of his roots hold me still, keeping me safe in their cocoon.

Back, I think to my wolf. *You're not needed here. Stay back.*

"That's it, Farron. Listen to my voice. Stay with me."

Inhaling deeply, I flutter my eyes open to see the shine of Ez's helmet, his bare hands holding my shoulders. "H-hey."

The roots release and I fall against Ezryn's chest. "Good to have you back, brother," he says, a firm hand around my back. His armor is cold against my cheek and stinks of goblin blood, but I don't care. I need a moment of connection.

I hate losing myself to the wolf. Hate that after all these years, it still has such a hold on me. And unlike the others, when the wolf comes out, I have no control. Whatever base instinct the snarling demon inside of me wants, it gets.

I've accepted that every night, the wolf is going to win. But during the day or the full moon, I've never had an issue losing myself to my anger and to the beast like the others have. I always keep it under wraps. But tonight—

Dayton.

I push away from Ezryn and stagger up to where Dayton leans against the wall, gingerly touching his bruised cheek from where Ez slugged him.

"Stop it," he growls.

"Stop what?"

"Stop looking at me like a sad puppy." He turns away. "If you two hadn't lost your fucking shit, Keldarion would never have been the wiser."

"So, you were going to hide the fact you have a relationship with Keldarion's prisoner?" I grit out.

Dayton rolls his eyes. "I don't have a relationship with her. We were going to fuck."

Ezryn stands, his armor clattering, and walks stiffly to the mirror.

"And what's your problem, huh?" Dayton calls after him. "What do you even care what I do with her?"

The glowing light from the mirror paints Ezryn's armor like a swirling aurora borealis. His voice is too calm as he says, "She's not one of your playthings, Dayton. You have a responsibility to protect her. As Keldarion's prisoner—"

"I'm fucking sick of hearing she's Keldarion's prisoner," Dayton roars and I stumble back. "She's not his fucking property. And she wanted me. So Keldarion can stuff that up his frosty asshole."

Ezryn gives a deep sigh. "I'm going back out on patrol."

"Why did you even come, anyway?" Dayton grumbles.

A blanket of silence settles in the room, a heavy breath held within armor and stone. Ezryn says lowly, "I felt a … disturbance. I needed to be here."

Before anyone can reply, he shimmers through the mirror and disappears.

How strange. After returning from the Autumn Realm, I'd been in the library browsing the top racks of a bookshelf when I'd nearly fallen off my ladder. It was like a heady scent had wafted in front of me, a pull from the deepest recesses of my chest. It hadn't been unpleasant … until I'd seen Rosalina and Dayton.

Together.

"I'm going to bed." Dayton shoves past me, heavy steps echoing out of the room and into the hallway.

I stay still. My head feels like a flood of every emotion, all rushing too fast. I can't make sense of them.

"Well?" Dayton calls. "Are you coming?"

And then one emotion shines out the clearest: anger.

I storm after him. He's giving me the most satisfied little smirk anyone could conjure. I draw my fist back and smash it into his face.

"What the fuck?" Dayton cries, grabbing his cheek. "What is your problem?"

My hand throbs with pain and I give it a shake, trying not to make it obvious. "You couldn't finish your fuck with Rosalina, so you'll find the next available body, is that right? That's always what I am to you, Dayton. Something to be fucked, filled, and discarded."

Dayton leers down and grabs my chin. "When you put it so romantically, how could I not?"

I slap his hand away.

"Okay, okay." Dayton steps back. "You're jealous. But over me or Rosalina?"

"No, I—" I stop and turn around, my face on fire. Am I jealous? Is that what this feeling is? Or is it something else?

It wasn't that it killed me to see Dayton and Rosalina together. In fact, the image of him holding her in his arms, the look of ecstasy on her face—it was the most beautiful sight I could imagine.

But I'd held myself back every single day since she'd been here. There were so many moments when I'd been leaning over her to look at her work, and she'd cast her glance up—what if I had moved before Dayton had? What if I had kissed her first?

But I hadn't. Because I followed Keldarion's rules. Because, though none of us said it out loud, we all suspected it.

There could only be one reason Keldarion was keeping her here.

Even if that reason made no sense at all.

And maybe ... maybe a small part of me is jealous. Because I understand Dayton well enough to know he lied to Ez when he said Rosalina was just another fuck.

He's only ever looked at one other person the way he looked at her.

We may never find our mates, but I thought we'd always have something special.

"You know I don't care who you fuck," I force out. "If you hurt Rosie, I'll show you what real pain feels like. It will be an agony you won't forget."

In a swift movement, Dayton has me pinned against the wall, his forearm against my throat. "I will *never* hurt her," he says, his voice a raspy growl.

My breath surges through my throat. His face is so close to mine, the smell of sea salt and fruity wine mixing between us. Stars, even with his expression coarse and rigid, he's so damned beautiful. Dark lashes over storm-blue eyes, his wide jaw appearing as if chiseled from marble. His long blond hair flows in a messy mane over his thick neck and collarbone.

Suddenly, his expression softens, and he drops his forearm. "And I'd never hurt you, Fare. Not on purpose. I'm just an idiot."

"No arguments here," I mumble, massaging my neck.

Dayton backs up and stares at the ceiling, as if this confession is for the sky and not me: "Here's the problem. Even though I know it's going to hurt so much more, even though I know my whole fucking self is going to get destroyed," he finally meets my gaze, voice cracking, "I can't stop myself from wanting you."

I close the distance between us, pulling his neck down toward me, and kissing him as if this were the first time, the last time, a kiss for infinity. He wraps his arms around me and twists until his back is against the wall, and he's holding me as tight as possible. And I want this so badly, want to be closer to him, want to feel the distance that has always been between us fade away. I would crawl into his skin if I could.

He breaks the kiss and snatches my jaw. "You fucking hit me."

"You fucking deserved it."

Dayton barks a laugh and grabs roughly for my ass. "Come with me, Pup. Let us fuck until our worries disappear and we are but on a cloud of bliss."

"Everything is so easy for you. Drink or fuck the problems away."

His lips catch my earlobe. "If only I was as good at that as I pretend to be."

The words send my heart surging because I always knew they were true; knew the more reckless Dayton is, the worse his heart feels.

"Let me in," I whisper against his mouth. "Let me help you."

A blankness crosses his expression before being replaced by a wild grin. It's a mask. I know it, but I don't press.

"No more talking," he says. "I'm going to make you scream until your throat is too raw for words."

I give a small smile back. It's alright. I'm used to this.

And I won't give up. Because maybe one day, he'll realize he's safe with me. He can let down the walls he's built so high. One day, he'll let me protect him.

WE STAGGER through the hallways back to Dayton's chambers in the Summer Wing. He throws me on the bed and stands between my legs, peering down at me like some sort of sea king from legend: his chest naked and shiny with perspiration, hair wild and mussed from my hands; the seashell necklace dangling between his pecs.

The blood on his chest only makes him look hotter.

"Do you see this?" He grabs his thick cock through his pants.

How could I not see it? It's the cock of a god: huge and straining, and I know it so well I can practically taste the salty pre-cum I know trickles down its girth.

"Answer me." He yanks my shirt collar and pulls me up so I'm eye-level with his cock.

"I see it." My voice comes out a wavering tremble.

He grabs the back of my head and smashes it against his groin. The hard length rolls over my face, the damned fabric of his pants an evil barrier between me and the silky skin beneath.

"Do you feel it?" he growls.

"Yes," I mumble against the hardness.

"Tonight, this is your cock. All yours, Farron. I'm going to make you feel so good."

His words make my shaft throb and pulse, begging to be touched. Unable to resist, my tongue falls out, desperately trying to lick his length through the fabric.

Before I can get far, Dayton pulls me up by my jaw until I'm staring into his intense gaze. I probably look a trembling mess before him. "I'm going to claim you like it's the first time. You belong to me."

Of the four princes, I'm the youngest. The weakest. But when Dayton owns me like this, I don't feel weak. I feel like a fucking god, my body creating feelings for him so intense, he can't control his roars of pleasure. My body can make his cock come like a waterfall. My body can drain the Summer Prince.

Dayton smashes his lips against mine. Each tug of my hair is ecstasy. The feel of his rough hands along my neck, ripping open my shirt, pinching my nipples … It's utter pleasure. When our cocks slam together, I groan, feeling ripe with need.

With an urgency I know he feels too, I pull his pants down and cup his heavy balls. I let out an unconscious sigh of relief to have him in my hands.

"Yes, Pup." He throws his head back. "Fuck yes, love."

I tug delicately, first on one then the other. I could listen to his moans of pleasure forever. Why can't it be like this? Why do we have to obsess over mates and curses? Why can't it be me and him in this bedroom for the rest of our near-immortal lives?

Rosalina.

The thought shakes me, and my cock pulses in response. No, it wouldn't be right to be just here with Dayton. *I need her too.*

Her brown eyes and dark hair flood my mind and suddenly, I launch myself at Dayton's cock, gobbling it up like a starved man. He chokes out in shock, then practically purrs as he pushes deeper into my throat.

I imagine she's watching us right now, the way she had earlier.

That I'm staring at her as I force Dayton's enormous length deeper and deeper. What if she shared our bed? What if while I sucked Dayton, she sucked me?

I have to shove my pants off and pump my cock from the thought. Imagining her perfect lips around my shaft, her sweet gaze as she swallows my seed.

Pre-cum pearls at my tip and I slick my fingers through it. Dayton sees and grabs my hand, popping my fingers into his mouth. He sucks me in the same rhythm I'm sucking him, and it's like I'm a man crazed. I can't get enough of his cock: I want it deeper, harder, more, more, more.

"Easy now." Dayton pushes gently on my forehead. "Greedy pup. My cum is for your ass, not your mouth."

He slaps my cheek in a patronizing manner, but I don't care. Right now, I'd eat out of his hand or turn in a circle if he asked.

He looks down at my cock and bites his lower lip. "Fucking gorgeous." Then his eyes drift up to my face. "You, Farron, are fucking gorgeous."

The world could be on fire, and I wouldn't care as long as Dayton keeps looking at me like that. He pushes on my chest and lies me down upon his bed. "Legs up."

I do as he says, the position extremely vulnerable. My whole self, laid bare for him. I've had sex with my fair share of fae throughout the years, but I've never been comfortable being so open with any of them like I am with Dayton. The history of our friendship—the laughter, the talks in the dark, the shared experience of being cursed—makes me safe with him, no matter how exposed my body is.

Dayton runs a lazy hand down my chest, then firmly grabs my length. "This, Pup, is a great cock. Did you know? I quite like this cock." He leans down, keeping his eyes trained on mine the entire time. "In fact, I love this cock."

My heart dances in my chest. I know he only means we have amazing sex. But when he says that word, I feel like I could leap off the top of the castle and fly over the briars.

He buries his nose into my balls and inhales deeply. "Your scent drives me wild, Farron."

And when he says my name, I nearly come all over his face.

"If you like my cock so much," I manage, "why don't you give it a kiss?"

Dayton chuckles darkly. "Oh, I'll do more than that."

Stars explode across my vision as Dayton's warm tongue laps up my length. But he doesn't stop there. He pops my balls into his mouth one at a time, eyes dark and hungry.

"Your lips feel so fucking good," I groan.

My balls rush out of his mouth with a wet splat. "I know." With no mercy, he grabs them in one of his hands, lifts them up, and strokes his tongue down to my hole.

"Fuck, you are delicious." His fingers leave red marks on my thighs.

I want to reply but I'm only capable of guttural cries and moans as his tongue swirls around and around.

"I need to make sure you're nice and loose for my cock," he says. "You know, Farron, I won't hurt you." He looks up and gives a wink. "Unless you want me to."

I think I grunt a response but he's grabbing the oil vial from his bedside table and slicking his fingers. An oiled knuckle slathers the warm liquid over me, and I shiver in delight.

That shiver turns into a toe-curling spasm as he pushes his thick finger into me.

"Does that feel good, Pup? That's just one finger. I know you can take more."

"Y-yes," I say. "But right now, I want your cock so bad—"

"Want?" Dayton growls. "Tell me you need it. Tell me you'd fucking die without this cock. Tell me you live for this cock."

"I need your cock," I tell him as he pulls his finger out. "I'd die without your cock. I live for your cock."

"Good boy." He draws himself up between my legs, gives his shaft one smack against mine, then sheathes himself inside me.

Both of us cry out from the sensation: I feel stuffed full, and I push against him, easily relaxing to take his entire length and girth. It's like my body is made for his; the pain gives way to pure rapture as he draws himself back then smashes into me.

"Tell me you need me," he growls.

"I need you," I say.

"Tell me you won't leave me."

"Never," I swear, an oath sworn with our bodies.

Dayton gives a mighty roar, pumping me with an intensity I've never felt. My cock smacks against my stomach with the force of our movement.

My vision swirls with color, and I swear my tongue hangs out of my mouth as he uses my body to purge whatever darkness is inside him. And I don't care. I'll wait forever if I have to. Wait for the day Dayton realizes it's been me all along.

He's not my mate.

But he's the closest thing I've got.

"Farron," he groans.

"Do it," I respond. "Come in me. Fill me."

The mere thought of his thick load exploding inside of me, filling me so deeply, stuffing me full of *him*, sends me over the edge.

"Dayton!" I cry and grab my cock. It explodes over my chest, pulsating with spurts of heat.

"Fuck," he grunts, and I nearly lose myself from the pure pleasure as his cock throbs, spilling his hot seed deep inside my body.

The stars spark out before me, and I stare blankly at the ceiling. I think a trail of spit drips down my chin, but I don't care. Dayton pulls out and rolls off the bed, grabbing a cloth from the attached washroom. With an easy grin, he lies down beside me and starts mopping up my chest and backside.

Finally, he tugs me close and kisses the top of my head. As my hands wrap around him and graze down his back, I feel the puckered skin of the large scars there.

I shiver.

My beast almost came out tonight.

Rosie had been there. What if I'd hurt her? Or hurt Dayton again? Why does it feel like the wolf is getting stronger?

We're running out of time.

"Hey, hey." Dayton grabs my face and makes me look at him. "You're shaking."

I take a deep breath. "I'm fine. I'm fine." My hands trail through his hair. "Your braids came out. I'll redo them."

"Tomorrow, Pup." Dayton gives a long yawn. Then his eyes narrow. "What does it feel like to you?"

"Hmm?"

"When we make love?"

I close my eyes and relive the experience in my head. How does one put euphoria into words? "It feels like starlight igniting my whole body. Like an empty place in my heart is being filled."

"Is that so?" Dayton whispers.

I twist my head to look at him. "And for you?"

Storm clouds swirl in his eyes and for once, I think it's happening. The walls are torn down. The moment is now.

But he just laughs and slaps my cheek playfully. "Feels like a fucking good lay." Then he rolls over and plops his head on the pillow. "You should go back to your wing now."

I lay there for one moment more. One moment to pretend.

Coward.

That's what the Enchantress had called me.

As I change into my clothes, body sore and raw, I know in my heart she was right.

42

ROSALINA

Keldarion heaves me off his shoulder and onto his soft bed. I kick, tangling my legs in the sheets.

"How do you get the balls to—" I pause and bring the sheet to my nose. There's the fresh smell of soap. "You actually had your sheets washed?"

Keldarion leans on the bedpost, ice chip eyes looking over me. "I have one night a month as a fae. I want to make the most of it."

Frowning, I push myself off the bed. "Well, I'll leave you to it."

A few steps in and my legs feel like jelly, though I'm not sure if it's from all the fae wine, from being heaved around like a sack of grain over Keldarion's shoulder, or the mind-shattering orgasm Dayton ignited within me.

My body heats thinking of it, and I stumble. Kel leans down and scoops me up.

"I can walk myself!"

"Apparently not." He sets me back on the edge of the bed, then kneels on the floor, making us eye level.

"Why did you bring me here, Kel?"

He keeps staring at me. I must look like such a mess, my hair splayed every which way, makeup smudged. My dress is thankfully put back together, though I can't help but notice my lack of panties with the silken sheets rubbing against my legs.

"I asked Dayton to take me to the Summer Realm. I wasn't trying to escape. And he didn't force me to do anything," I say, not able to bear his silence anymore.

"I know. Dayton's a scoundrel, but he'd never push himself on anyone." Keldarion crosses to the other side of the room. I can't help but notice he didn't answer my question. Kel opens the armoire and pulls out a pale beige tunic before returning to me.

"What's that for?"

"You can't wear *that* to bed." He gestures vaguely at me.

I cross my arms protectively over my beautiful lavender dress. "No. I love this dress."

Kel's eyes flash. "I can't imagine who wouldn't."

My cheeks heat under the intensity of his gaze before reason crosses my mind. "I'm not staying here. I have plenty of nightgowns in my room."

Kel keeps his arm outstretched.

Giving a grumble, I sigh, "Do you have anything with long sleeves? It's freezing in here."

Kel rolls his eyes, but then steps over the thorns toward the armoire. There are more thorns in the Winter Wing than anywhere else in the castle. *Why is that?*

Before Kel returns to me, he kneels to light a fire in the hearth. Kel strikes his flint and steel together, and sparks of orange and red leap through the air as he coaxes the crackling embers to life. A small flame rises steadily, washing the room in a warm, glowing light.

The warmth makes my eyes droop. "Do you think Farron is okay?"

"Ez will take care of him." Keldarion tosses a long-sleeved black shirt at me. "Spring's magic is soothing."

"Will you go check?" I ask him. "Make sure he didn't turn into his … beast?"

"He's fine."

"Well, at least step outside the room while I change." I glower at him.

He gives me a look that says I could walk around the castle naked, and he couldn't care less, but finally gives a dissatisfied grunt and leaves the room.

Why did Kel bring me here? He could have as easily locked me in the dungeon tower again if he was mad at me for leaving. Or brought me back to my room. I'd thought maybe he was going to lay into me for going to the Summer Realm ... but he's being surprisingly soft. Well, as soft as a man who's all icy edges can be. But the more important question is: why aren't I fighting to leave? I know the way to my room. If I left, he wouldn't come after me.

I let my lavender dress slip to the floor and pull the black tunic over my head. Oh, yep. No underwear. *Stupid Summer Prince.* The tunic is long enough to cover my ass, barely. I need to find some pants before Kel comes back. I skip over the thorns to the armoire.

Something beside the table catches my eye: clear tumblers and dusty square bottles with different colored liquids. Keldarion has some fancy drinks.

Hey, he forced me here. I'm going to help myself. I pour a little into a glass and give it a sniff. Yikes, that's strong, all right. I already tried fae wine tonight—why not a little of their liquor? I need all the liquid courage I can muster if I'm going to spend the night in the Winter Prince's room.

Tipping back my head, the liquor shoots down my throat. It's cool and crisp, a little like peppermint. A faint warmth spreads through my chest. I have to be careful, or I might drink too much. I'd hate to end up passed out on the icy floor.

But a part of me knows that won't happen. My eyes drift back to the bed: four elegant silver posts draped with a white canopy. Thick fur blankets lay atop freshly pressed sheets. It's too big for one person, and I flush.

I turn with the glass in my hand to find Keldarion standing in the doorway watching me. I quickly put the glass down and try to look like I was doing something other than drinking.

"What did you have?" Keldarion crosses the room in two steps.

"Just a shot." I smirk. "Chill out. Or I guess, you're already chill. Like all the time."

He snatches the bottle off the table. "Rosalina, this is *fyrana*."

"Relax, Kel." I smile, suddenly not feeling even a little bit afraid of him. "I already tried fae wine, but that's out of my system. Dayton was a bore with all the water he made me drink."

"One shot of *this*," Kel squishes my cheeks with one hand, "is equal to you drinking two bottles of fae wine. In an hour."

"That seems much more efficient," I mumble against his hold. "You have really pretty eyes."

He drops his hand and steps back as if even the thought of me looking at his eyes is insulting.

"What's that in your hand?" I quirk my head.

"The others are fine, by the way," Keldarion says lowly. "I found something you left behind."

My vision is a little sparkly, but I still manage to focus on what Keldarion holds out. Light blue lace. My broken panties.

I snatch them from him. "Don't touch those!"

"Would you rather Marigold find them in the morning?" He gives the slight hint of a smile.

"She would *never* let me live that down." I scowl at him, then cross to the fire before tossing them in. They're certainly not salvageable.

"If you must know, I brought you here to make sure you didn't have a bad reaction to the fae wine," Keldarion says. "But now you've had that liquor, I'll have no choice but to stay up all night to make sure you don't choke on your vomit."

"You're lying." I turn to him. "You just thought of that now. It's an excuse."

"An excuse?" He balks. "Look, there is one night—"

"You're a man, I know. How do you usually spend it? Moping alone?" I spread out my arms. "I don't know why you brought me here. Maybe you're lonely."

I'm not sure if we're talking about tonight or forever.

Kel crosses his arms and leans against the wall. "Trust me, it's better to be alone than—"

Kel had a great love. Dayton told me that. Someone has hurt Keldarion, and I'm not sure if there's any connection to the curse, but it's still affecting him.

"I'll stay," I say.

And I'm not sure if I'm talking about tonight or forever.

"But I'm not, you know, *doing* anything with you. So don't get any ideas," I say. Though I wish my body would get on board with my head. Because Keldarion looks way too good cast in the firelight, arms crossed over his broad chest, that stern expression on his handsome face. I would have thought I'd be satisfied from Dayton, but I'm left wanting more.

Liquid heat pools in my core as I squeeze my thighs shut.

"I'll be sleeping on the couch, obviously."

It's startling how fast that man can sap the heat from everything. Including me. *Icy prick.* "Right then."

Something catches my gaze, flickering beneath his bed. I bend down to it because anything is better than withering under his cold stare.

At first, I think it's a long icicle, but then I spy the hilt. I grasp it before straightening, and a cold breeze blows over my bare ass.

Oh no.

I look across at Keldarion, who is giving me another one of those looks of absolute horror. "Oh shit, sorry. I totally didn't mean to do that." My whole body is probably the color of a tomato. "You see, all shirts are pretty short on me—"

"Drop that right now, Rosalina," Keldarion says.

Okay, so good to know a little accidental mooning means nothing to him. I hold up the object in front of me. It's a sword. It looks like it's been crafted from ice, the blade as clear and cold as glass. But it's been smoothed to be more reflective, like a mirror. At its base, the blade flares out and is wider than the slender hilt, which has been wound with gilded vines and a jeweled rose where the cross-guard meets the blade. The sword itself is a story …

A story I know. Dayton's words drift back to me. *The Queen entrusted the High Ruler of Winter with a divine weapon to protect the Vale in her absence.*

"This?"

"Yes, that." He reaches for it.

The sword glows, glittering gold at the base and a sapphire blue at the blade. Magic radiates through me, pulsing in my ears. Maybe it's all the fae alcohol, but this is the coolest thing I've ever seen.

"Whoa." I stagger away from Kel. "This is so neat."

"It's not a toy, Rosalina," Kel growls.

"It's beautiful."

"Put it down."

"It doesn't seem like you're taking very good care of it." I examine the sword. I didn't realize you can feel magic, like the waves of heat on a desert horizon or the taste of clouds swooped too low.

"Rosalina, you need to put that down now, before you hurt yourself." Kel grabs for the hilt, but I spin out of his way.

"You're always so grumpy, Kel. And why not? Surrounded by these things all day and night?" I gesture to the thorns. "That guy was a total creep. A hot creep. But a creep all the same."

If looks could kill, the one Keldarion gives me would send me straight to the grave. But thankfully they can't, so I turn back to the thorns. "Why don't you prune them?"

With all the stupid confidence a shot of *fyrana* gives one, I swing the beautiful sword right across the brambles. At the same moment, Keldarion screams, "Rosalina! No!"

The thorn turns black then breezes away in a cloud of ash. "Hey." I blink. "That actually worked."

A rumble shudders through the castle, and a great crack forms along the wall. There's the shifting of rock and suddenly a whole section of the ceiling crashes down.

Keldarion grabs me around the waist and throws me to the side. We roll together on the hard floor.

My vision blackens then spins, and I blink, trying to get my bearings. Keldarion is braced above me, breathing like a wild animal. A new purple vine slithers up, right where the last one was.

"We can't remove the thorns," he says roughly, then reaches down and grabs the sword from my trembling fingers and sends it skittering across the icy floor.

His hand returns to mine, lightly tracing his fingers over my palm. "Are you hurt?"

"No."

His gaze travels to the tunic raised high on my waist, exposing the soft swell of my stomach and the aching mound between my legs.

Keldarion braces himself on either side of me, his white hair a wild halo around his face as he gazes down with raw hunger.

The air between us is heavy, and the moment stretches until I can't take it anymore.

"You saved me," I whisper, and his gaze intensifies.

"Of course I did," he says gruffly, and his eyes fall to my mouth. He leans closer. His breath is like a promise on my lips.

I close my eyes, and in that moment, I feel like I'm flying, like I'm completely free, like I'm exactly where I belong. Then, in a flash, he pushes himself up and away from me. The moment is gone, leaving me breathless and dizzy.

"The thorns appeared a few days after the curse began," Keldarion says, grabbing his sword and stuffing it into a leather sheath. "I tore every one of them from the castle. But twice as many appeared the next day and removing them increased the decay of Castletree. Somehow, he's tied his foul magic to our home."

"Cunning bastard," I say, pushing myself up and pulling my top back over my thighs.

"Don't you mean hot bastard?" A pair of pants hits me straight in the face.

"I mean ..." My words trail off as I slip the pants on.

Keldarion grips me under the armpits and lifts me to my feet. "You need to go to bed."

I don't complain this time as he carries me across the room. Instead, I bask in the feeling of his closeness, letting my head drop to his shoulder. "I'm sorry I ruined more of your wall."

"I appreciate the sentiment."

"My shoulders are sunburnt," I mumble, my cheek resting against the exposed skin of his neck. "I was only in Summer for a little bit before sunset too."

He plops me down in the bed and returns a moment later to place a glass of water in my hand. "Drink."

I take a couple sips before putting it on the bedside table. He collapses onto the couch, so tall his feet hang off the end.

"Are you going to be okay there?"

"I sleep on the floor every other night."

"But you're a wolf then."

"Go to sleep, Rosalina."

I stretch my arms above my head, relishing the silken sheets against my fevered body. My mind feels sparkly and light. I'm not ready to sleep yet. "I had such an amazing night. The Summer Realm is so warm."

Keldarion gives a grunt of acknowledgment.

"Dayton was so nice too. He cut off a man's hands for touching me. That's why there was blood on his chest."

"He did what?"

"I've never felt like that before." I can't help but feather my hands over my body, down between my legs. Thinking of Dayton's mouth there, and Kel a few feet away … It makes me even wetter. "Will you bring him here?"

"I will absolutely not bring him here," Keldarion says, cool and fast.

"It's okay," I say dreamily. "He's with Farron."

"How do you know?"

"I …" My words trail off, and I'm having trouble finding them in my blurry mind. "I can feel it. They're together. They love each other a lot, but they're bad at saying it."

Maybe it's a hunch, but it's almost like I can feel them, passion radiating through me. Or maybe I'm only imagining how great their makeup sex would be. But I know Kel needs me more.

I slip my hands beneath the band of my pants, feeling my aching heat, and a little sigh escapes my lips. Shit, why does my body feel like this?

There's a flurry of movement and Keldarion is above me. He yanks my hands up and locks both my wrists above my head. Holy crap, he's fast.

"You need to go to sleep, Rosalina." His voice is raspy, untethered.

A mixture of fear and something else swirls in my body. "Is it true you haven't had sex in twenty-five years?"

He takes in a long, shuddering breath. "Dayton says a lot of things, as you well know."

"Well, is it true?" I drag my eyes down his body. Through the thin fabric of his night pants, I see a long outline. "It's obviously not from—"

"I'm a beast, Rosalina." The grip on my wrists tightens. "The others might be willing to forget that fact, but I cannot."

He's so handsome: the long nose and dark brows, his eyes so full of pain. I should agree with him. He's the one who imprisoned me here, who's keeping me from my home. But a swell of different emotions rise when I look at him.

"He also said you were in love before," I whisper.

A calamity flickers over his face, and he lifts off me to sit at the end of the bed.

"You shouldn't be ashamed to have loved, Kel," I say softly. "Love isn't a bad thing. You know what's bad? Hating someone, judging someone. Loving someone is actually quite nice in comparison. Love is good."

His breath shudders in his throat and he runs a hand through his hair. "Not when it comes to me."

As muddled as my mind feels right now, I know he's never going to find his mate with that kind of attitude. "I don't believe that."

He glances over at me, then my bedside table. "Drink your water."

I grab the glass and slide closer to him, close enough my thigh brushes his. "I'll make you another deal. Fae like bargains, right?"

"Only the evil ones." He brushes a stray piece of hair away from my face.

"I'll drink this water if you go to the ball."

He laughs, a low, soft rumble in his chest. "Even for a human, that is terrible. You want me to return to the realm I have not visited in twenty-five years for an event I will loathe, for you to what? Drink a glass of water before bed?"

"Exactly." I smile up at him. "I want you to come to the ball. You want me to drink this. See? We both win."

He stares at me for a long moment before he whispers, "Drink."

Cool liquid pours down my throat. I'm not sure this will stop me from suffering the hangover of a century tomorrow morning, but it can't hurt.

I place the empty cup on the bedside table and stare at him expectantly. He brings his hands to my lips and wipes away the excess droplets with a brush of his thumb.

Clasping his hand with my own, I hold it against my cheek. "Come to the ball, Kel."

"No one wants me there."

"I do." I stare into his eyes, willing him to believe it. "Isn't that enough?"

"It is enough." He drops his head against mine in a sort of surrender. His lips brush my ear as he whispers, "I will go to your ball, Rose. But I will not find my mate there."

43

ROSALINA

A feeling of contentment washes over me. I can't remember a more pleasant sleep. I savor the warmth of the sheets, the aroma of pine and winter hanging in the air. Have I ever been this relaxed?

My eyes flutter open. The red morning sun flickers over the ice coating the room. I sit straight up.

Oh shit.

Oh shit. Oh shit. Oh shit.

Did I really spend the night in the room of the Winter Prince?

"Keldarion?" I call tentatively.

There's no movement. The room is empty and my head pounds.

Pinching the bridge of my nose, I drink some water and try to recall the events of last night. The stuff with Dayton and bugging Keldarion is all pretty clear, but when did I fall asleep?

My whole body cringes as I recollect sleepily leaning on him. Did I put my head in his lap? Or was that a bad dream?

I'm never drinking alcohol again.

I scramble around the room and retrieve my beautiful purple dress from the ground. My mind flashes with the image of Dayton pushing aside the fabric, his lips sucking on my breast …

The door creaks open, and Keldarion steps into the room. He's got a breakfast tray in his hands.

As soon as I see him, another memory flickers before me. His hands in my hair as I leaned over the bed and vomited into a bucket.

A literal fae prince had to stay up all night with a stupid human because she couldn't hold her liquor. And now I'm ruining his morning too.

"Good morning," I peep, my voice raspy. Probably from all the upchucking I did last night.

"Rosalina, you shouldn't be out of—"

"Thank you for the water and the shirt. I'll wash it for you and, uh, the pants. I'll stop bugging you now."

I scurry into the hall before he can mention the humiliation of last night. My tummy does not appreciate the sudden movement.

Every step I take sends a shudder of nausea through my body. Fae hangovers are no joke. I need to go back to my room and sleep.

But something trembles in my chest, and I pause. I've stopped at the junction of all four wings. There's a door right at the top of the staircase, one I've never gone through.

The door leads to the High Tower. They forbade me from entering. *But why?*

The door is a beautiful, light oaken wood with ornate carvings of the four seasons. There are fluffy clouds near the top, and a tangle of rosebushes at the bottom. Silver scrollwork decorates the edges and its handle is crafted from gleaming gold.

The longer I stare, the more it's like I can see magic emanating from the seams, a bright and crackling aura. I can't help but place my hand on the wood before grabbing the handle. Warmth radiates into my fingers, and a slight hum pulses that sends little tingles throughout my body. I turn the doorknob.

Locked, of course. But if I—

"Whoa there, Rosie!" Firm hands grasp me around the waist and pull me away from the door.

"Hey!" I whirl to see Dayton.

"I'm all for breaking rules, sweetheart, but there's some even I won't cross. And neither should you."

I stare back at the handsome prince, still in shock he could sneak up on me like that.

"What's in the High Tower?"

"It's a secret," he says with a wink.

"What kind of secret?"

"Ah." Dayton grins, mischief dancing in his eyes. "A hundred gnomes. Kel keeps them up there to make his cookies."

"You're teasing me," I say.

"Only a little." Dayton's gaze trails over me. "I see the beautiful dress has finally met its demise. Cute look, a little big on you."

"It wasn't like that. Keldarion—"

"Is a frigid bastard, I know. If a beautiful woman like you can't get him to break his celibate streak, stars, nothing will."

My cheeks heat. I had accidentally flashed him twice, and he hadn't cared at all. Maybe the man is nothing but a giant ice cube.

"Listen, Rosie." Dayton takes a deep breath and runs his hands through his hair. "What happened last night ..."

A knot of anxiety forms in my chest, and I know whatever he's about to tell me won't be something I want to hear.

Dayton blows out another breath. He almost looks awkward. And Dayton doesn't get awkward. "I won't let it happen again. It was a mistake to kiss you and ..."

Of course, he thinks it was a mistake. He probably realized I'm not one of his regular hookups, and he actually has to see me again.

"Right. Of course. I mean, we're looking for your mate, after all." Traitorous tears threaten to spill from my eyes. Stupid, stupid, stupid Rosalina. *You knew he was like this before you went out. Why are you surprised?*

"Great." He turns then mumbles, "Good talk. And never open that door, okay?"

He heads toward the dining hall. I'm left trembling and frozen before I storm toward my room. It's fine. Nothing unexpected happened.

I swing my bedroom door open, and Astrid is already laying out a dress for the day. The second she notices me, her nose twitches and she asks, "What's the matter, Rosalina?" All my thoughts and emotions come spilling out of me in a sob.

FOR OVER AN HOUR, Astrid sits with me, stroking my hair while I recount every detail of last night. Shit, why does this feel like I got played? I know who Dayton is. And I don't want anything from him. He has to find his mate.

I nearly lose it when Marigold comes in carrying a breakfast tray. A breakfast tray that looks suspiciously like the one Keldarion had been carrying into his room this morning. Had he been trying to serve me breakfast in his bed?

I understand my feelings for Dayton: the attraction, lust, and regret all make sense. But I don't dare dive into the part of my mind where I stashed my feelings for Kel. That is way more confusing. My captor, who always brings me my favorite food. The vicious beast who also holds my hair while I vomit.

Astrid recounts the events to Marigold while I eat my stupidly excellent breakfast. I bitterly wash down some buttery toast with orange juice, thinking how Kel chose all the best foods to help a hangover.

"I bet Dayton doesn't mean it," Astrid says. "The way he looks at you makes me think you're something special to him, Rosalina."

A part of me thinks she has a point; I mean, the guy cut off someone's hands right in front of me. But he was so dismissive this morning. "I need to stop worrying about the princes and get back to trying to break this curse. Not just for them, but for you two as well."

Marigold puts her hand on her hip. "Well, that would be nice. It's not easy to have a good time when you're a racoon every night."

"But you always find a way," Astrid chuckles and motions for me to change.

I feel an odd sense of loss as Keldarion's clothes fall to the ground. "I can't imagine. What was life like for you before the curse?"

Astrid helps me into my day dress, fastening the corset. "Honestly, not that much different for me. There were more visitors in the castle. And the staff made more trips into Winter with the master. It was a happier place in Castletree, many parties and balls. There were always things to do."

"I miss those parties." Marigold sighs.

"What about your family?" I ask. "Do you miss them?"

"I'm an orphan," Astrid says. "Work in Castletree was highly prestigious, coming with fine lodging, all the food you could eat, and respectable pay. Prince Keldarion made sure the jobs were accessible to anyone who needed one. Working here is the best thing that's ever happened to me. Well, except for the hare part. But, hey, nothing's perfect."

"Astrid is selling herself short." Marigold taps her on the nose. "She's a quick study and a harder worker than anyone I know."

"So, you all lived here before the curse?" I ask, sitting down at the vanity as Astrid tugs the knots out of my hair.

"Yes. It's customary for the princes and their staff to live in the castle," Marigold says. "Back home, we'd stare at Castletree and dream of being chosen to serve in its hallowed halls."

I stand and look out the window over the vast horizon, beyond the castle grounds to the sprawling thorns. Somewhere out there is the rosebush that brought me here. Out there is my home.

"Oh my moon!" Astrid squeals behind me. "It's snowing!"

Snowflakes sail past the window. Marigold gives an annoyed sigh behind us. "I'm going to have to dig out the woollies now."

"Oh!" Astrid vibrates with excitement. "Snowball fights, snow angels, decorating for solstice, hot cocoa with whipped cream! The garden pond freezes, and we went ice skating last year. Doesn't that sound fun, Rosalina?"

It's nice to see her so excited about something. "Yes to everything except the ice skating."

"What? You don't know how?" Astrid furrows her brow. "I could teach you."

"No, that's not it," I say softy, gripping my wrist. "I ... I had a bad experience with ice skating before."

Astrid opens her mouth to say something when Mr. Rintoulo, the butler who shifts into a giant brown bear at night, knocks on the door and delivers a parchment scroll.

Marigold unwraps it before looking up at me. "Here's the proposed guest list for the ball. Astrid and I can get on sending invitations today."

"Good," I say, determined to stay focused on my goal. "Because I have more news."

Astrid and Marigold both turn to me with wide eyes.

"Keldarion has agreed to come," I say, my heart in my throat. "We're going to find his mate. We're going to find all their mates. Break the curse. And we'll finally get our freedom."

44

KELDARION

"I didn't think I'd find you up here." Ezryn's voice echoes through the empty chamber. I don't turn to him, my gaze completely focused. Briars crunch beneath his heavy footsteps as he walks toward me. "Kel?"

"Do you know how many times," I murmur, "I've come up here and hovered my hand over the petals? Pictured crushing it in my fist? Ending it all by my choosing."

I trail my finger over the stem of a sapphire blue rose. It's planted in a row of dirt that falls loosely in the center of the room. The Enchantress's magic lingers everywhere. Three other roses grow along the same plot: one with pink petals, the other with turquoise, and the last with orange.

Ezryn walks over to the pink rose and stares at it. "You speak of the temptation to destroy your flower and become a beast forever."

"Is that not better than to live in this in-between world? Pretending we still have a hope at humanity?"

Sparkling magic radiates from the petals. How easy it would be to put useless dreams aside forever. With a single crush of my hand, I could destroy this object of derision and free myself of the pain of hope.

"It's madness really," Ez says, "that we should suffer so much from such a fragile thing."

"Or that something so beautiful creates such monsters." I tear my gaze away from the flower and pace to the middle of the chamber. "What do you want from me, Ez?"

Ezryn tilts his helmet to look around the room, the dying sunlight reflecting off the polished metal. As is the honored custom for all Spring Realm royalty, no one outside of blood family or mate-bonded may see their face. Despite being friends since childhood, I have no idea what the color of his hair is, or what his smile looks like. Yet, I know him so well, I can practically see the searching gaze he gives me beneath the mask.

"Do you remember what this place used to look like?" Ezryn asks. "The golden leaf along the moon-white walls? There was a chandelier right above us. Perhaps it's still there. Hard to tell what's beneath the thorns. And if I recall, there was a mural on that wall of the Queen's creation of the Enchanted Vale. I remember thinking it was the most beautiful thing I'd ever seen."

I narrow my eyes at Ez. He's stalling. A strange sensation of melancholy shifts between us. When was the last time we were in the High Tower together? The Queen's Tower?

Though it had been left vacant for the last five hundred years since the Queen left the Enchanted Vale, it has always been maintained. A space of history. Of immense beauty. Of an ancient and visceral magic.

No wonder it was here the Enchantress cursed us and planted the four objects that sealed our doom.

I ignore Ezryn's comments, knowing he is delaying what he is truly here for. But no matter. If he wants to reminisce, then I shall indulge him. "Tell me the truth, brother," I rasp. "Did we deserve it?"

Ezryn stills. "Of course we did, Kel."

Did I think he would offer me amnesty for the evils I brought? No. Ezryn would never forgive himself; I could not ask him to forgive me.

"We never found out who she was," Ezryn muses. "The Enchantress."

I can see it as clearly as I did twenty-five years ago. It was impossible. She was a stranger, a mortal. We had all but chased her from the castle when she …

She transformed. Into something beautiful and terrible: a vision of light so brilliant, it turned everything else to shadow. I knew in that moment that this being saw me to my very bones and understood what lingered in my heart, and she would not stand for it.

We were wicked beings. All of us had taken the mantle of High Prince with the responsibility to lead our people and wield our magic in a way that upheld the honor of the Queen.

Instead, Dayton fell to drink. Farron hid in his keep. Ezryn gave way to sorrow and rage. And I …

I rub the aching bargain that wraps around my wrist. I betrayed the Vale and everyone in it.

"Some things are better left unknown." With a sigh, I turn to my brother. "Ezryn, why are you here?"

The small shift in his gait alerts me he's uncomfortable. "Kel, we need to talk about Rosalina."

I walk toward the door. "What is there to speak of? You can't find her presence displeasing. You're barely around."

"Why did you take her to your chambers last night?"

My voice comes out a husky growl. "To keep her safe." My fists curl. I had smelled it, even deep within the Winter Wing: her arousal. It was like a tether, drawing me toward her in a fevered trance.

And to see it was *Dayton* causing such a reaction …

I had wanted to rip his throat out with my teeth. I needed to shelter her away.

Protect what was *mine*.

"Kel," Ez's voice is so soft, "you know you are more than the Protector to me. I have stood by you, and will continue to do so, through whatever darkness arises. You can tell me anything and I will not run from you."

I want him to stop talking. I whip open the door.

"Is there a reason you are keeping Rosalina a prisoner?" he says, and I can't block out his voice, no matter how much I want to. "Do you know something about her?"

I know she changed everything the moment she entered Castle-tree. I hadn't wanted to feel anything for her, hadn't wanted to get to know her. It would have been so much easier if she wasn't ... wasn't ...

Wasn't Rosalina.

The stubborn, beautiful, frustrating creature that makes everyone fall in love with her with a single smile.

I always thought I would do anything for my realm, for my people. But when I look at Rosalina—Ez asked if I know something about her. Yes. I know she doesn't deserve the fate she's been forced into. For that, I will suffer so she doesn't have to. Even if that means despite her want, despite her endless research, Rosalina will never break the curse. Because I won't let her. I know now I'd let every single person in my realm succumb to goblins and thorns before I let her. "Ez, leave it be."

"I let it be the last time you brought someone into our fold," Ezryn says. "We both know how that turned out for your realm. For you."

And for us, brother, I think. Ezryn has stood beside me these last twenty-five years, but it has never been the same since he betrayed me. I hold my wrist, covering the bracelet. "If only you knew how deeply I am still tangled in his thorns."

He walks right behind me. His heavy breathing reverberates through the helmet. "Did you make a bargain with Caspian?"

"Ez," I say, but my voice does not come out as a command. It comes out broken. As I turn to face my friend, the sun shifts beneath the horizon and the beast shivers out of my flesh. Ezryn's monstrous form faces me, a black wolf of bone and fungus and churned earth.

There's still hope for him to find his mate. Maybe that will break his curse. But as I lay upon the cold earth, his snout touching mine, his paw across my own as if he could protect me from myself, I know there is nothing left for me.

Not since the Prince of Thorns took it all.

45

ROSALINA

I force my eyes to stay open as the pages of the book blur before me. The last few weeks have been endless late nights of research, ball planning, and outfit fittings. Well, mostly me nagging the princes to go back to their realms during the day for their fittings. They've hired the best tailors in each realm to do the outfits. It is the first time in twenty-five years all four of them will be in the same place, so they have to look their best.

The only prince that wouldn't go was, unsurprisingly, Keldarion. So, Marigold took his measurements—something she thoroughly enjoyed—while I giggled in the corner at how uncomfortable he looked. Kel had rebutted by telling her to take my measurements, saying of course I would need something decent to wear as well.

I insisted it be nothing fancy. This was about them, not me.

I sit in the library reading a book on etiquette and formal dining manners, something far less interesting than fae mates. But I'm determined to make this ball a success and not look like a fool while doing so.

Since I can't travel to the Winter Realm, we've been planning the whole thing via letters the Winter staff deliver during the day. By some miracle, Keldarion and Perth Quellos have agreed to open the Winter

Realm's door to a select few staff for travel back and forth while performing preparation duties.

A week to the solstice now. As much as I'd love to go to the Winter Realm before the ball, Keldarion wouldn't allow it. I'm just happy he's going to the ball at all.

I turn the page of my book and it lands on the proper steps of the waltz. I've been practicing with Astrid and Marigold, but mostly for fun. It's not like I'll be dancing there. The princes will dance with potential mates, and I doubt any fae will want to dance with the human.

I sneak a glance up from my page and spot Farron across the table, his chair tilted back on two legs, a pen dangling between his teeth, glasses perched low on the bridge of his nose. Butterflies stir in my stomach as I take in the sight of him. His wavy locks fall across his forehead and into his eyes. He is breathtaking.

Farron looks up and our eyes meet. He gives me a soft half-smile, and it makes me want to run across the room to him and—

A cold burst of air rushes around me. Keldarion? Is he here? I straighten. A window has opened behind us, blowing in a cloud of snow.

"Stars!" Farron leaps up and runs over to it, latching it closed, but not before it leaves a dusting of snowflakes over his brown hair. I laugh and jump up, relieved at any break from studying.

"I hate winter," he grumbles.

I stand on my tiptoes to brush the snow from his hair before looking outside. The briars have transformed into a winter wonderland, and even the river has frozen over. Down below, Astrid and some of the other staff are skating over the frozen pond on the castle grounds, laughing and having fun. Even amongst the curse, there is joy here.

But as my gaze fixes on the frozen lake, I can't help but remember that shock of cold, the endless shivering, the hero.

"It's cold and wet, and everyone keeps tracking snow into the library," Farron continues, brushing the last of the flakes from his jacket.

"I like winter," I say, trying to forget the icy shiver in my body.

"Everything's so bland, all white," Farron says. "The bright red and orange leaves are what I miss the most."

I poke him in the cheek. "I think you're being a little biased, Mr. Autumn Prince."

He flushes, then crosses his arms. "Alright, what season is your favorite? The one you liked most as a child? Don't let any of us cloud your judgment."

"You're going to think I'm lying, but I'm not. I love them all. I was literally the kid who wrote down all four on my school assignments." The snow falls in huge, graceful flakes. "Take winter, for example. You say it's bland, but have you ever noticed the pink shade of snow during a sunrise? Or how berries never look as red as when they're surrounded by white? The pleasure of a warm fire on cold, wet feet? And it's plenty cozy to read by."

Which is what the two of us had been doing: bringing our books to the gigantic library fireplace and staying right until sunset when Farron had to return to the dungeon. I only fell asleep in front of that fire twice, both times I was embarrassingly dragged back to my room by a certain, annoying, icy wolf.

"Then comes spring with the flowers and the rain, and it's like you remember how beautiful life can be. Clear, blue skies and bright green trees and flowers, and the way your heart lifts when you walk around. It's a time for new beginnings," I say. "There's summer, with sand between your toes and bright mornings and days so long you think it'll never be night. Summer, when the sun on your face feels like the warmest kiss in the world ..." I flutter open my eyes to see Farron looking at me with a soft expression.

"Yeah, I like summer too."

"Then we get to autumn." I walk around him. "It's okay, I guess."

"Hey now." He grips me by my sleeve and spins me around. "You can't gush about the others and leave out fall."

He doesn't let go of my arm, and I'm left staring up into the particular gold of his eyes. "You've already mentioned the color of the leaves, but there's the way they crunch under your boots. The smell of the forest; mushrooms popping up, and fields filled with pumpkins. Gray foggy mornings, and clear nights with moons as bright as the sun."

"Some people say autumn is the death of life," Farron whispers.

"That's not true," I whisper, placing my hand on the side of his face, "and you know it. Autumn reminds us that everything is temporary, that moments must be savored. Autumn is beautiful."

"Your eyes," Farron says.

"What?"

"Your eyes are like a sunrise over the golden hills in the Autumn Realm."

"Do you miss your home?"

Farron swallows and his eyes drift far away, then he says softly, like it's a secret, "Perhaps not as much as I should."

Something tightens in my heart, and I don't need him to explain. I step away. "When I first arrived, I wanted to return home more than anything."

I feel Farron trail behind me like a shadow. "And now?"

"Now ..." I breathe. "I'm always so worried about my father. But I trust Keldarion when he says he got Papa home safely."

"Kel wouldn't hurt him," Farron assures.

"Though I can't help but wonder if he's looking for me right now. What if he tries to come back through the rosebush—"

Farron slides an arm around my back, pulling me against him. "The Vale is mysterious, and the paths through are always changing. I'm sure your father is safe in Orca Cove."

His words fill me with relief; the last thing I'd want is for Papa to rush back here and find the goblins first. "Everything is so complicated."

Farron gives me a sad smile. "I understand more than you know. For twenty-five years, all I've concerned myself with is breaking the curse. I don't have to wonder if I'm strong enough to rule a whole realm or think about how my decisions affect an entire nation. It's my parents' problem again. But I guess that thinking is the cowardice that got me here to begin with."

"Farron, don't say that! It wasn't your fault."

The door to the library bursts open, and I break away from Farron. Mandaria and Paavak waltz in carrying their stack of lists. Both staff from the Winter Realm, they have been my principal assets in planning this ball. Marigold informed me they had been the event coordinators before the curse. Mandaria brought the brain and Paavak, self-proclaimed, brought the sparkle.

I leave Farron and walk over to them for a detailed update on the ball's progress. It's been gathering quite the interest and excitement from fae in the Winter Realm.

"Honestly, they've had little to celebrate in a long while," Mandaria says, tucking her long blonde hair behind a pointed ear. "It may even help calm the riots. It'll be good for them to have something to look forward to."

"I agree," I say.

Mandaria casts a longing look out the window at the snow. At night, she transforms into a penguin, so I can only imagine she's loving this cold weather.

"By the way," Paavak lowers his voice, giving me a serious look, "do you have any more of the goods?"

"It's not a secret! Books are meant to be shared." I can't help but laugh, then quickly run to the table and grab the books I set aside for them.

The three of us have been on a romantic book trend, even verging on the scandalous kind. Hey, if I could get Astrid and Marigold in on this, I might have more luck with a book club here than in Orca Cove.

It started by finding books that would help us plan the ball, but as I got talking with each member of the staff, discovering their likes and dislikes, I slipped other books in too. Most were guesses based on the synopsis, because I hadn't had time to get that much fae reading done. But there were quite a few human books in the library. None from the last twenty-five years, of course, but some classics I recognized.

Once word got around I was handing out books, staff started coming to me, asking for recommendations. I even had to start a little tally sheet with books out, so I didn't misplace any. Fae librarian Rosalina at your service!

I hand Paavak the book and he gives a little yip of excitement that sounds awfully like the small dog he turns into at night.

"I haven't read these two yet, so you'll have to let me know how they are," I tell them.

Mandaria looks at the back of her book, reading out loud: "Far-off places, daring sword fights, magic spells, and a prince in disguise? Sounds like a perfect read."

"Only one prince?" I give a little wink at Farron. "Sounds dull."

I wave goodbye to both event coordinators and feel Farron approach from behind. "You've made quite the impression on the staff, Rosalina."

I turn to face him, but he doesn't back up, leaving us chest to chest. "I'm just trying to help."

He tilts his head. "You're doing more than that. In the last few months, it's like a light has returned to Castletree. You've brought hope and purpose again. And it's not only the staff; it's us as well."

"I've hardly—" I try to back up, but he cages me with his arms.

"Don't be so modest. Before you came, it was different," Farron says. "Ez eating meals with us? That's new. Keldarion comes out of his room. I swear there were some months I didn't see him at all. And you may not believe this, but Dayton has been drinking less. Well, a bit."

A sudden awkwardness fills me at the mention of Dayton's name. It's a topic I've been avoiding with Farron the last few weeks. Guilt simmers in me.

"About Dayton," I whisper. "I've been meaning to say this for a while, but every time, I've chickened out. I'm sorry I kissed him. You two have something and—"

Farron cups the back of my head. "You have nothing to be sorry for, Rosalina. It's not like that between Dayton and I."

"But you were jealous when he brought that fae woman to Castletree. I saw it, and when I kissed him—"

"Not just kissed him." Farron's voice drops a pitch, but not in anger. Another emotion swells. "You were in his arms, moving with him."

"I'm sorry—" I blurt out and try to push away from him, but he doesn't let me. Instead, he presses me back against the bookshelf. It wobbles, volumes flying down around us.

"I already told you, Rosalina." Command ripples in his voice, stern and urgent. A darkness I forget he possesses behind that sweet smile. "You have nothing to be sorry for."

My hair slides out of my bun and falls around my face.

"Watching you come apart in Dayton's arms was the fucking most beautiful thing I've ever seen in my entire life."

My breath comes out in heady gasps, my chest brushing against his.

"In fact, if Ez hadn't been there, I would have watched you more." He dips his lips to my ear. "So now we're even, huh?"

A startled gasp escapes my mouth. *When I watched him.* Heat tightens in my core. "Actually," I say, "to truly be even, Dayton would have to walk in on us—"

My words cut off as my brain catches up to what I'm saying.

But Farron's whole body stiffens. He grips the bookshelf hard on the side of my head, veins in his arms standing out. "Dayton wouldn't act like us if he walked in. The man has no self-control. He'd—"

"Join," I whisper, remembering what he'd said in the Summer Realm.

Farron's hand slides from the back of my head to brush the top of my chest. "Rosie, you can't say these things."

My fingers clutch the soft fabric of his vest, drawing him closer. What would the Prince of Autumn do if I stood on my toes, bringing my lips to his?

I duck under his arms. "I can't mean it, though. I don't," I say without turning around. "The ball is soon, and you and Dayton and Ezryn and Kel ... ...You'll all find your mates, hopefully. And that's the end of the story." A deep, hollow echo fills my chest. "The end of my story."

46

EZRYN

I t's like a dream.

I sit on a throne in the grand ballroom of the Winter Realm, a place I haven't been in over twenty-five years. We're surrounded by people dancing, eating, flirting, merrymaking. Sunlight gleams off huge ice sculptures of swans and polar bears. Every time I turn my head, some courtier vies for my attention.

Yes, it's like a dream. A fucking nightmare.

"Gods, Ezryn, do you have a metal rod up your ass too? Relax," Dayton croons, leaning forward to look at me from his throne. Easy for him to say. Relaxing is all he does. "I know you're more comfortable with goblins and beasts than fae, but at least put some effort in. Our girl pulled this off."

Our girl.

She's not *my* anything. She's not even my prisoner. She's a passing houseguest who has beguiled Farron, charmed Dayton, and … done something to Keldarion. I'm the only one with enough wits to know I should keep my distance.

Admittedly, I'm impressed by what Rosalina has accomplished in the few months she's been at the castle. Not only unearthing new understanding of the mating bond through her research, but also initiating an event in the Winter Realm—a place that badly needs some joy. It's beyond impressive. And even more than those combined ... She convinced Keldarion to attend.

I hadn't been able to convince Keldarion to take a damn bath in twenty-five years.

But she's not *mine*.

"She's quite stubborn once she sets her mind to something," I say begrudgingly to Dayton.

"You've got that right." He adjusts the collar of the long, turquoise tunic he wears. It goes over one shoulder, revealing half of his bare chest, in the traditional style of the Summer Realm. He looks more put together than I've seen him in decades.

I suppose the same could be said for me. As is the way for royalty in the Spring Realm, I keep my face hidden behind my helmet. But I've exchanged my usual armor—scratched and filthy as it is—for something lighter and more ceremonial. Metal plates of darkest green line a black tunic of fine fabric; I wear pants of the same, with only metal tassets for protection. It's still far more practical than anything the other three are wearing, but I feel exposed. On display.

I can't believe I'm at a party. Something I never thought I would see again. Not that I was in any hurry to be surrounded by these people: they hover around us like flies above a carcass. The princes rarely make an appearance anymore; we're a commodity for gossip and speculation. And being in the Winter Realm, Keldarion bears the brunt of it.

Thankfully, the Winter Realm's vizier, Perth Quellos, has staved off the hungry horde for now by positioning us on four thrones on a dais at the front of the ballroom, bordered by guards. Keldarion's throne is the grandest, of course, not only because we're in his realm, but because Winter was chosen as the Sworn Protector by the Queen hundreds of years ago.

Does anyone else notice Keldarion isn't wielding the sword?

Even through the tinted visor of my helmet, the glint of ice is everywhere. Icicles hang from tables full of snow yams and roasted chestnuts; Kel's royal ass rests on a frozen throne; and ice frosts the windows letting in the brilliant sunlight. Although I'm sure many of the guests wonder why a grand ball is being held in the middle of the day, none of them question us. That's one surprise they're not prepared for.

A grand staircase with a brilliant sapphire carpet lays at the end of the ballroom, where guests are introduced. All the most lovely and eligible fae of the Winter Realm are here. There's an excited fever in the air, but something else as well. I can see it in the eyes of the courtiers, of the guards, of the merchants in attendance. They're looking at Keldarion not with hope in their eyes, but accusation: *Why have you left us? When are you coming back? Don't you know we're struggling?*

Though his face is as stoic as ever, I know Keldarion's one well-intentioned comment away from ripping off his fae flesh and running out of here, teeth and fangs bared.

Thank the stars this madcap idea of Rosalina's is beginning in another realm. I can't imagine being surrounded by my own citizens. Having them stare at me with that same questioning gaze. Having my brother's eyes on my every movement. Seeing Father barely able to lift himself from the throne to give it back to me.

Perhaps it will all be worth it. Perhaps one of these lovely diamonds, twirling before me with their long looks and hungry expressions, will be my mate. We will seal the mating bond and the nightmare I've been trapped in for twenty-five years will be over.

I nearly bark a laugh. There are no fairytale endings for monsters.

"Introducing Lady Ingrid Whitley of Westfrost!" the herald cries as yet another fae woman strides down the stairs. I barely glance at her.

"Introducing Sir Kristoff Dederic of Silverwick!"

"Introducing Lady Gretchen Foxglove of Annestron!"

Farron, sitting on the throne between Kel and Dayton, sits forward and looks at each of us. "Anyone feel anything yet?"

"Nothing but the ache for a strong drink," Dayton says, barely glancing at the fae making their way down the staircase. They're some of the most beautiful and stately in the entire Winter Realm.

I feel nothing.

My locket sits heavy on my chest, hidden by my tunic, and I unconsciously place a hand over it. It's usually safely beneath my armor. It's a small wooden square engraved with Spring's ancient runes, a token from the Queen passed from High Ruler to High Ruler. Opening it would allow me freedom from this place, my way home through the mirror.

"We have to keep trying," Farron says. "For Rosie."

Keldarion stays as statuesque as ever.

A strange, melancholy feeling falls over me as I stare at the three princes. I was mere acquaintances with Dayton and Farron before the curse, but after twenty-five years sharing the same suffering, we now have a brotherhood unlike any that could be borne by blood.

Keldarion's parents had been dear to my own, and so I'd grown up with him. I'd thought our friendship transcended brotherhood. We were comrades-in-arms, confidants. Even after the War of Thorns, when he'd been betrayed for the one he loved the most and everyone abandoned him, I stayed.

Then the Enchantress cursed us.

And no amount of friendship could stop the ice from covering Keldarion's heart.

"Introducing Lady Aurelia Mastiff of the Balsam Wood!"

"How many more introductions must we suffer through?" Dayton sighs. I notice, like myself, my brothers have taken no interest in the parade of fae men and women.

My legs bounce up and down. I'm not used to sitting for so long, let alone being stared at like a piece of meat for the carving. Despite the Winter Realm's rebellions, the growing number of goblin attacks in all realms, or the fading Castletree, there's obviously one thing that's more important: the fact that all four fae princes are sitting right here, and they're all eligible.

"I need a break," I say and stand. "There's no point to even being here—"

"Introducing Lady Rosalina O'Connell of Orca Cove!"

A vision shimmers down the stairs: a long navy dress of rich velvet adorned with sparkling gems. The long sleeves are trimmed with blue lace, and the bodice cuts low over her full chest. An incredible tangle of diamonds, collar collars her neck, and I can't imagine what sins Marigold pulled to apprehend this outfit. Her dark hair falls in gentle waves over one shoulder, and her face is done up with paint: dark lips and sparkling blue shadow around her light brown eyes.

A strange flutter shudders through my chest, and I feel the urge to shelter behind my throne. She's heading toward us, a bright smile on her face. Her eyes dart from one side of the thrones to the other, from Kel in his royal blue regalia, a crown of ice and bone upon his head; to Farron with gold dust shimmering on his cheeks; to Dayton with his legs spread wide and hands on his knees; to …

Is she looking at me?

Is that soft smile for me?

I need to sit. The rest of them are sitting. I step back, but stumble over my own boots, catching my armored heel on the edge of the throne. I fall, reaching for nothing, and land with a clatter on my ass.

"Ezryn!" she cries.

As quick as I fell, I right myself, straightening my helmet and trying to lean against the throne as if I'd meant to do that all along.

"Are you alright?" Rosalina asks, picking up her skirts and surging toward us. Immediately, two guards step into her path.

"Let her through," Keldarion's voice booms.

The guards hesitate for a moment, then step out of her way. Rosalina gives them a little satisfied smirk and the most pathetic curtsey I've ever seen before walking up to us. The others stand to greet her.

"Wow," she says. "You four look amazing."

We look at each other and it's as if we're thinking the same thing: *It's you who looks amazing.*

Of course, Dayton is the one who steps forward, grabbing her by the elbow and pulling her toward him. "And you look positively ravishing. A Winter queen in the flesh. Don't you think, Kel?"

Kel hasn't blinked since Rosalina first appeared at the top of the steps. His ice-blue eyes are wide, and his nostrils flare as he inhales deeply.

"You're beautiful, Rosalina," Farron says, and she smiles warmly at him. Her warmest smiles are always saved for Farron. And why not? His wolf may be the most monstrous of us four, but there's no doubt his heart is the purest. If only one of us could break this damned curse, he's the one I'd hope for above all else. The one who most deserves a second chance.

"Your realm is absolutely stunning," she says to Keldarion. "I feel like I'm in some sort of winter wonderland. Like Kris Kringle's going to come around the corner at any second."

Kel surges forward and snatches her forearm. "Who is this *Kris Kringle* you speak of?"

Farron clears his throat. "It's a legend from the human realm, Kel. A mysterious entity who watches children while they sleep and breaks into people's homes at night."

"Oh. A legend." Kel steps back. "Do not fret, Rosalina. There are no evil beings here."

Rosalina looks between Farron and Kel and then doubles over laughing. "Oh my god. You guys can never visit the human realm in December. You'd beat up the mall Santa!"

Again, the four of us exchange confused looks. Rosalina catches her breath and wipes a tear from her eye. She puts a hand on Kel's shoulder. "You are too funny."

I swear I see Kel's soul shoot out of his body. And now it's our turn to laugh.

"What?" she cries.

"I think that's the first time anyone has ever referred to Kel as funny," Dayton wheezes.

"Unless you count his hair," I say dryly.

And now we're all laughing again. Even Kel can't help but smile.

But out of the corner of my visor, I catch the crowd. Young fae gather together, whispering behind their hands. They're all staring at … Rosalina.

But of course, they are. A human woman dressed as a fae. Allowed entry to the royal dais to greet the four most powerful males in the Enchanted Vale. They see us talking with her, laughing with her, touching her …

I could train my senses to listen to them, but I don't want to know what they're saying. Our business with Rosalina is none of theirs.

As I'm turning my attention from the crowd, one gaze gives me pause. Perth Quellos, the vizier, stands in a sunbeam beneath a window, a white-knuckle grip on his glass. The way he's looking between Keldarion and Rosalina sends the wolf inside me snarling. There's always been something about Quellos that makes me uneasy … But Keldarion trusts him.

But I trust myself more.

"Sooo, how's the plan going?" Rosalina gives an exaggerated wink and tears me from my thoughts. "Any stirring of special feelings?"

"Just a little indigestion." Dayton shrugs.

Rosalina furrows her brow and taps her foot on the floor. "I've been watching you from outside the doors most of the party. You four have been sheltered up here like a gaggle of old maids. You have to get out there and *touch* people." She clears her throat. "In a totally consensual, non-creepy way. Find someone and dance!"

Dayton gives a roguish grin and shrugs. "Aye aye, boss." He drifts over to the nearest cluster of women and immediately has them in a giggling fit. In a smooth movement, he grabs one's hand and twirls her onto the dance floor.

Rosalina claps her hands. "Okay, you're next!" She grabs Farron's shoulder.

"I think I need another drink first. Or actually, I need to use the little fae's room—" he squeaks, but he's no match for her. She shoves him into the fray, and he's immediately swept up by a chesty older woman.

"Ezryn?" She smiles up at me.

"I'm going, I'm going," I murmur, my voice reverberating through the helmet. Another reason to thank the stars for this damned metal thing: I'd rather fight a thousand goblins than face this dance floor.

Mercifully, the crowd picks up that the princes are dancing, and a fae woman immediately pushes herself into my vicinity, saving me the embarrassment of having to find my own partner. I barely register her before I take her hand.

No sparks. No starlight.

Just the incessant pull toward the dais. I look back to see Kel and Rosalina doing as they always do—arguing. Of course, he's refusing to even try.

I swirl my dance partner around.

"It's a wonder to see you here, Prince Ezryn," she mumbles. She might be beautiful. Or perhaps she's hideous. I barely comprehend her. "Word has it you haven't been spotted in the Spring Realm in quite some time."

I grunt a response and turn her, so I have a clear view of the dais.

I blink and run a hand over my visor in case my vision deceives me. No.

Kel has chosen a dance partner.

He walks past me, arm held aloft, clutching Rosalina's hand.

It's as if the entire ballroom takes a collective breath.

"What in the realms is Prince Keldarion doing with that human?" my partner sneers.

Kel sweeps Rosalina in his arms and the music slows, a passionate lilt filling the air. A small smile creeps over my lips. Inside, my chest eases for the first time all night.

"He's dancing," I murmur, "with our girl."

47

ROSALINA

There were many things in my life I knew I'd never do. And most of them were for very practical reasons.

I'd never go to university because there wasn't enough money. I'd never move away from Papa because he needed my help. I'd never refuse Lucas because he'd ripped a part of me out and kept it ransom in his back pocket.

And I would never dance with a fae prince because my life was not magical. There were no such things as fairytales, and I was not the main character.

And yet, after I chide Prince Keldarion of the Winter Realm for not taking a dance partner, he stares at me with that icy blue gaze, puts his rough hand on my cheek, and says, "The only person in this room I want to dance with is you."

I take a sharp breath. That cruel voice in the back of my head, the one that sounds like a chorus of Lucas and my boss and all the towns-folk back home, screams at me, *'You know Keldarion. He'd rather debase himself and dance with you than bother to find someone better.'*

But there's a different voice, one that's louder and stronger, and this one comes from deep within my core. And this one says, *'Yes to this dance. Yes to all the others. Yes to dancing through the stars, throughout the* ages, throughout the realms, throughout every universe. Yes to him forever and ever and ever and ever.'

"You need to find your mate, Kel," I finally manage. "Dance with someone who you feel a spark—"

"It's not a spark. It's an eternal fire that burns from deep within my heart and reaches out to you." Ferocity flickers in Kel's gaze. "And every moment I am not touching you, it eats my soul inside out, tearing me apart, until merely looking at you is an anguish I would only wish upon my worst enemy."

I stare stupidly at him before I burst out laughing. "Just because I called you funny one time doesn't mean you can make jokes like that now."

Kel's fingers dive into my hair, and his other hand lands on my waist. He pulls me close. "Dance with me, Rose."

Okay, so there's really going to be no arguing with him. When I manage a nod, his eyes crinkle and he gives me a smile, one so sweet I yearn for all the times I've missed it before.

He holds my hand aloft and leads me down the dais and onto the dance floor. I swear, every person in the ballroom turns to stare. It must be quite a sight: the Winter Prince's first dance in over two decades.

"Everyone's looking at you," I whisper.

Keldarion chuckles. "It's not me they're looking at."

My face heats and I stiffen, realizing how much attention I've drawn to myself. I must look so ridiculous in this grandiose gown and jewelry.

"Relax," he murmurs. "You look beautiful."

As we make our way to the middle of the dance floor, we pass by Farron and his aged companion. His eyes twinkle and his smile jump-starts my heart.

Nearby, Dayton has an arm around a busty blonde fae, but he's staring at me. He winks and warmth spreads through my body.

And before us, Ezryn stands with his hands limp on a fae woman. He nods, and a sense of peace and comfort ripples over me like sunshine.

Keldarion stops and spins me, before resting one hand on my waist and taking the other in his. "I hope you know how to dance," he whispers, "because I'm terrible at it."

The music picks up into a waltz dreamier than any I could imagine from the human world. It's like the music descends upon me in a breeze that lifts my feet and turns everything else to clouds.

And Keldarion is a liar. He's not a terrible dancer, not by any stretch of the imagination. He's extraordinary, leading me through the motions effortlessly.

And I'm lost in the labyrinth of the moment: his long white hair falling over his shoulders, a few strands pulled away from his perfectly carved jawline and cheekbones; the finery of his clothing, so soft I can imagine how it would feel against my bare skin.

His hand fits perfectly around mine, and for this one song, this one dance, there is nothing else.

"You've helped me come to an important decision, Rosalina," Keldarion says. "Having decided, it makes me feel … lighter."

I tilt my head. Now that he says it, there has been something different about him today. Like a weight has been lifted off his shoulders. "What is it?"

"After the ball, when we're all together, I'll tell you," he says lowly. "How do you like the Winter Realm?"

"It's the most beautiful place I've ever seen," I say. "It suits you."

"And you." His eyes drip over my body. "Do you like the dress?"

"Of course. And this necklace! I have no idea where Marigold got it, but—"

Keldarion gives a small smile. "I sent for it. It belonged to my mother."

"Oh! Oh." My jaw drops open. "I promise I'll give it back right after the ball! Right after this dance. And I definitely wasn't eating truffles and then touching it. Okay, I was, but only a little—"

He laughs richly. "The necklace is yours to keep, Rose. Think of it as a gift."

"For making you attend a ball?" I snort.

"For waking us up."

Our bodies press together, closer than the dance requires. Boldness swells in my chest, and I ask, "Am I still your prisoner?"

"Oh, Rosalina, you're reading my mind now," he murmurs. "On the contrary. You were never my prisoner, and I was always yours."

My words are a breath: "What do you mean?"

The music rises and I spin under Kel's arm. He pulls me close, then dips me low. "You are the cove in which our storm-struck ships moor. The beacon of light in the darkest night leading us home. A candle whose flame flickers against the coldest wind. You've given them hope."

He draws me up and I follow his gaze around the room. Ezryn, Farron, and Dayton. Staring at them, one wish burns brightest against all else.

"I want to break the curse," I say, falling back into the dance. "I want you all to be able to protect your realms again. Get your true magic back and save Castletree from the briars. To have the freedom to be who you truly are."

"I want that for them too," Keldarion says.

I stop dancing and put my hands on either side of Kel's face. His eyes shimmer as he stares down at me. "But Kel ... What about you?"

He places his hand over top of mine and leans into the touch. "Time is running out, Rosalina. I've lost so much of it to the cold and the dark. For what time I have remaining before the beast takes over ... I want to spend it doing all the things I wish I could have more time to do. Finally doing what is right." He swishes me into the dance again. "And that means I will take no other dance partner but you, my Rose."

No other dance partner but me ...

No. No. No, no, no, no, no.

Kel can't do that. He *needs* to find his mate. He *needs* to break the curse. As much as it kills me inside to think of him with someone else ... I can't lose him to the spell. I won't.

I pull away. "Kel, what are you saying? Stop. You have to *try* to break the curse. Why won't you try?"

"Breaking the curse will not bring you the freedom you seek," he hisses. "Only I can give you that, and I will."

"No. I help you break the curse and we'll both be free."

"Rosalina," he mumbles, "lower your voice."

"Kel, *try*."

His gaze is intense as he snarls, "I would rather die than have this curse broken."

"No." Tears spill down my cheeks and the couples dancing around us have all turned to stare. "You can't do this, Kel. You're selfish. You know that? What about your friends? What about the people who ... the people who love you?"

"Rosalina." He reaches for me, but I pull away.

"You're a selfish bastard!" I cry. "And you always have been. That's why you're cursed."

Before he can stop me, I turn and flee through the ballroom, my tears turning to ice.

48

ROSALINA

I sprint out of the ballroom and down the hallway. I need to get out of here. It's like the walls are closing in on me.

It's all too much. The life I've created over the last few months … It's so fragile. Keldarion was right. I never was a prisoner. I was an escape artist, running away from my real life.

I want the princes to find their mates more than anything. And I'm terrified to lose them at the same time.

But more than that, I can't watch Kel wither away. Now I truly know he'll never believe in me. Never trust me.

I throw open the doors until I'm bathed in afternoon light. A snow-crested garden lies before me, hedges and topiaries caked in snow. In the middle lies a huge stone fountain with a frozen water arrangement, shimmering like frozen fireworks.

I fling myself down upon the fountain and cry. At least out here, my tears freeze instantly, and my sobs are stolen by the wind.

"Now, now, my child. Whatever could cause such distress in a daughter of the earthly realm?"

I blink up and see a blue shape hovering above me. It takes me a second to place him. The Winter Realm's royal vizier, Perth Quellos.

"Oh, I'm sorry, is this place off-limits? I'll leave." I sit up and dust snow off my dress.

The vizier sits beside me and offers a kindly smile. He's bald, and his skin is pale, almost blue-tinged. His lips are stained like he's just eaten a bucket full of blueberries. "Do not trouble yourself. The Winter Realm is open to all children of the earth."

I wipe under my eyes, sure I've destroyed the beautiful makeup Marigold spent an hour on. "Thanks."

Perth licks his violet lips. "His Royal Highness has often been known for his … temper. May I ask what he said to distress you so, Lady Rosalina?"

"It's my own fault," I mumble. "My own expectations. I wanted to be helpful."

"I hear you were quite instrumental in the organization of this event." Perth strokes his chin. "I was surprised that His Majesty agreed to it."

"He only allowed it to happen because he never intended to make an effort anyway," I grumble. "If he'd *try* to find his mate …" I take a deep breath and quiet myself. I know even the vizier isn't privy to the princes' curse.

Perth stands and puts his hands behind his back. He's unsettling to watch … Like all fae, he has an ageless elegance about him, yet his face looks both youthful and withered. Like a young man forced to watch the world on repeat. "A very interesting idea. Mate bonds have been known to increase magic within the fae. If Keldarion was to find himself mated, he may have the power to finally free Castletree from the Prince of Thorns." A darkness casts over his ice-white eyes. "You truly have been busy, haven't you, little human?"

Something shifts in the air between us; my instincts go on high alert, and I stand. "Thank you for checking on me. I'm going back to the party now."

"But we've only just gotten a chance to speak. And there's so much we have to talk about, don't we?" He smiles and I notice even his teeth are stained.

"Perhaps another time. I should go—" I turn my back to him.

"How long have you been in love with Keldarion?"

The blood in my veins freezes. I feel like one of the statues adorning the tables: stiff, see-through. "I-I'm not in love—"

Then Perth Quellos circles me, voice biting. "Was it when he took you in like a stray cat? When he had his little servants dress you up so you could play make-believe as a fae? Or was it when he danced with you and made a mockery of our realm? What about the other princes, hmm? I see how you stare at them. Think you'll spread your legs for the Prince of Summer, and he'll crown you his princess? Oh, yes, human, I hear everything. And it's almost painful to watch how pathetic you are."

I can't speak, paralyzed by fear and shame. "W-why are you saying these things to me?"

Perth stops circling and stands right in front of me leering down. "Because you have one thing right. Keldarion is a weak and useless ruler, and unless he rids himself of the Prince of Thorns' clutches for good, the Winter Realm will suffer. If that means he must find his mate to increase his magic, then so be it. And to that cause, you are a sorry distraction."

"I'm helping them." Why is my voice so weak? I haven't heard my voice this way since ... since I was with Lucas. Being in Castletree, surrounded by my new friends, made me forget just how much I don't belong. But Perth's gaze has brought me right back to reality.

Even here, I am a spot. "Are you helping them?" He sweeps one of my tears away with a long fingernail. "Or do you hope for more? Come now, dear one. Has it never occurred to you that one of them could want you? Love you?"

"No," I whisper, and I mean it. Because no one has ever loved me in the way mates are described in the books, in the starlight way. No one ever could. Keldarion joking about feeling that for me was the cruelest thing he could have done.

Because in my deepest, most hidden fantasies during my time in the Vale ... I have wished for that.

"How did you picture this ending, little human?" His voice slithers across my mind. "One of them would mate you? Imagine. You are but a maggot to an oak. One is enduring. The other is a disgusting, crawling creature who is barely alive from dawn to dusk."

He steps closer, and I pull away from him, tripping and falling onto the fountain. He leans down to me, hands on either side of my body. "The Winter Realm is on a knife's edge of all-out rebellion. Your presence is disturbing the order of things. You know what I'm saying is true." He puts his stained mouth next to my ear. "There is no future for you in the Enchanted Vale."

Every ounce of energy saps from me. There's no escaping this. I'm right back to Lucas's bedroom, crying as he carves up my wrist. I'm under the water, sinking into the depths. The dance I'd shared with Keldarion is a distant fantasy. *This is how the story goes for people like me.*

I close my eyes and wait for it to be over.

Perth's breath smells like meat and bitter alcohol as it drifts over my face. "Now that we're clear, I will arrange your departure back to the human realm. Don't worry. I will make sure you are fairly compensated for your time here." He laughs darkly. "I always make sure to pay the whores."

Just as a flood of tears pours down my face, a breeze whispers over my skin. I fling my eyes open and see Perth Quellos being ripped away from me and thrown to the ground.

And standing before me, body rigid and breath heavy, is the Spring Prince.

49

ROSALINA

"Ezryn!" I cry.

But he stalks over to where he's thrown Perth Quellos on the frosty ground. He grabs the vizier by the collar and heaves him up.

"I don't care who you are, Quellos," Ezryn's voice sounds like how steel feels, "but if you speak to her like that again, I will rip your forked tongue from your mouth."

"Ah, Spring Prince," Perth says in a high-pitched voice. His feet fight for purchase, but Ezryn holds him aloft like he's nothing but the white robes he wears. "I didn't hear you approach."

"Nor will you the next time you speak down to the Lady of Castletree," Ezryn growls. "Because your head will be gone before you know I'm there."

Perth's face scrunches up. "When Keldarion hears how you've threatened the royal vizier—"

"If Keldarion heard you," Ezryn snarls, "you'd be dead."

With a heave, Ezryn chucks the fae man to the ground. The vizier scrambles up and backs away. "Run to your guards and your courtiers," the Spring Prince says and steps in front of me. "Be sure to keep yourself from our sight."

With a glower, the vizier straightens his robes and marches back into the castle.

It's like I can breathe for the first time since going outside. "Ezryn …"

There's a great clatter, and Ezryn's armored body sits beside mine on the edge of the fountain. "Are you alright?"

Tears sting my eyes. "Y-yes—"

Ezryn grabs my trembling hand. "You can say no."

I stare into his dark helmet. Although his face is hidden, the black glass of the visor too dark for me to see his eyes, it's like I can feel the compassion of his expression. A sense of safety rushes through me. "N-no, I'm not." I give a half-sob, half-laugh. "He was really mean!"

Ezryn reaches for my face, almost as if to wipe my tears away, but pulls back. "Trust me, I understand. I've been on the other side of one of Quellos's tirades before. He takes issue with anyone close to Keldarion besides himself."

A small smile perks my lips. "I can hardly see you letting him lecture you."

Ezryn shifts in his seat. "When I first inherited the rule—and the magic that accompanies it—from my mother, I had no control over it. Keldarion never saw me as evil for my transgressions. But Quellos made sure to let me know what a danger I was to Kel. To my realm. To my family."

"That's terrible." Before I can think, I reach out and take Ezryn's hands. He stiffens for a moment, then relaxes. His hands are huge, the gloves thick and finely crafted. "I can only imagine how scary it is to suddenly have a bunch of magic powers you're not sure what to do with. Was your mother able to help you?"

A moment of silence passes between us. His voice echoes softly, "My mother passed shortly after I inherited the throne."

There goes foot-in-her-mouth Rosalina again. "I'm so sorry, Ezryn." My chest beats hard against my breast, and slowly, I reach for the edge of the glove and pull it off. He doesn't stop me. I place the glove on my lap and hold his bare hand. Snowflakes fall upon his tanned skin, and I trace a finger along his calloused palm and fingertips. "But your magic is good. I know it is. Like how you healed me when I first came to the castle. Or how you used it to calm Farron down. Your magic is good, Ezryn. And so are you."

Ezryn releases a breath, a warm, tinny sound from beneath his helmet. He moves swiftly, twisting his hand now to clutch mine. "How I wish you were right."

The air feels full between us, and I can tell he's staring down at where our skin touches. My heart pounds, and I feel a nervous twist in my belly. It's so simple, just my hand in his, and yet it feels like I'm naked and laid bare. Maybe it's because this small glimpse of his skin is so rare, so vulnerable.

"Ezryn," I whisper. "How come you can't show your face to anyone?"

"It is the way of the Spring Realm. Every member of the royal family shields their face. It is an ancient tradition. The act of remaining faceless shows our dedication to our people. We are servants to the realm above all else, warriors of the earth. If a member of the royal family were to reveal their face ..." His voice pitches lower. "It is the greatest dishonor one could ever imagine, punishable by banishment from the Spring Realm forever."

"Wow," I whisper. "That's ... intense. So, no one has ever seen your face?"

"The old laws state that one's face may be shared among blood, but my family is very strict. Once I reached five years, I donned my helmet and have not been without it since."

My eyes bug out and I shoot toward him, hands on his knees. "Wait! Do you *ever* take it off? Like do *you* even know what you look like?"

He chuckles. "Yes, I can remove it when I am alone. I do eat and bathe, you know."

"Oh, yeah." I laugh.

"And," he looks up at the sky, "I will remove it in the presence of my mate."

I lose myself in the way the snowflakes dance over the shine of his armor, across his visor. I wonder what they would look like on his eyelashes. "That's kind of romantic."

He huffs. Slowly, almost as if he doesn't want to, he reaches for his glove and puts it back on. "I think you've been out in the cold long enough. Shall we go back to the party?"

I look toward the castle doors. Perth's voice rings in my head: *Human. Maggot. Whore.* "Everyone's going to be looking at me. Judging how ridiculous it is for a human to be here. Thinking I'm some hideous monster."

Ezryn stands and reaches his hand down. "You are the Lady of Castletree now. We monsters have to stick together."

He'd called me that to Perth. *The Lady of Castletree.* Tears prick my eyes again and I take in a shaky breath.

Ezryn stumbles back. "You're crying ..."

"No, no, this time I'm happy," I say quickly. "I've never belonged anywhere before."

I'm getting used to it: the stillness of his body as he takes information in, and then the quick movement after. Ezryn holds out his arm for me to take. It's kind of hilarious, this huge, armored body doing such a gentlemanly gesture. I can't help my smile as I take his arm.

We walk back to the ballroom. A lighthearted waltz has arisen, and I laugh as I see Dayton swept up in a dance with a burly fae man, and Farron has a trail of elderly fae women following him. Keldarion, on the other hand, sits on his throne, head in his hands.

"No one sulks quite like Kel," Ezryn whispers.

I giggle before a thought hits me. *You're a distraction.* "I should let you go."

"Ridiculous human," he mumbles and pulls me onto the dance floor, sweeping me into his arms.

Warmth flows through my body despite his cold armor. This dance is faster paced, and he twirls me around until the room spins.

"Ez!" I cry, laughing, and collapse against his chest. It's like an electric shock passes between us as we touch, and I gasp. I can hear his breathing despite the music and din of the crowd.

He tilts his helmet down at me.

"Ezryn," I whisper, "what color are your eyes?"

"Brown," he whispers. "My eyes are brown."

I reach a hand up to his helmet, fingers gliding against the cool metal. It's like the whole rest of the world has disappeared into a haze around me. "Brown ..."

Suddenly, doors *whoosh* open and an icy gust of wind blusters over the entire ballroom. The crowd gasps and the music careens to a stop.

"Well done, Keldarion," a rich voice booms from the doorway. "You've always known how to throw a party."

And standing at the top of the staircase, leaning nonchalantly on the railing, is Caspian, the Prince of Thorns.

50

ROSALINA

The Prince of Thorns is here. In the Winter Realm. At the ball *I* organized.

The room is so silent, every one of Caspian's steps down the stairs echoes like a grave toll. Ezryn grabs my shoulders and pulls me flush against him, positioning his body in front of mine. I twist around to catch sight of the other princes. Dayton and Farron sprint across the ballroom. But not to Caspian.

To Keldarion.

They each grab one of Kel's arms, keeping him tethered to the throne. And the look on Kel's face …

My heart feels like it's splintering.

Pure rage and anguish ripple over his features.

Caspian, on the other hand, offers the crowd a smile, so beautiful for one so evil. "I've come to pay my respects to the organizer of this fine ball," he says, voice reverberating throughout the room. "It seems my invitation got lost in the mail." His midnight eyes land on me.

Caspian … has come to see me? What game is he playing?

Caspian stops when he gets to the bottom of the stairs. He's finely dressed, in a dark jacket with silver lining along the cuffs and a cape of dark purple. His long black hair descends in waves over his shoulders, adorned with a circlet bearing a magnificent a sapphire gem. Those starry eyes ... He's so beautiful, I feel myself holding my breath just to take him in.

"Not a very warm welcome," he says. "I'm not here to cause trouble. I simply want to dance like all you lovely fae."

"Get out of my realm," Keldarion snarls from his throne.

Caspian chuckles and starts walking again. The fae part before him. "I truly am not here to see you, my dear Kel. I'm here for ..."

His lips say 'her'. But in my head, I hear, *You.*

Breath seizes in my throat. I hold on to the back of Ezryn's armor like it's the only thing that will keep me tethered to the earth.

"His Majesty, Prince of the Winter Realm and Sworn Protector of the Vale, has told you to leave," Ezryn says, voice all dominance.

Caspian raises a brow and stops right before Ezryn. He's so close. If I were to poke my head around from behind Ez's giant metal back, I could touch him.

"Ah, Ez, darling. It's been a long time. I see you're still Keldarion's metal dog."

"And you're as unwelcome here as ever," Ezryn growls in return. "Don't do this, Caspian. You want to fight? Fine. But leave her out of this."

Caspian examines his fingernails. "Unlike you, Ez, I don't follow Keldarion's every whim. I know you'd cut off your own hand if it guaranteed a belly rub from His Frostiness, but I have other business to attend to. And today, I'd like to dance with the prestigious guest of Castletree."

Ezryn emits what can only be described as a feral growl, made all the more terrifying by the reverberation of his mask.

The tension in the room is palpable. I swear if I breathe too loudly, it could pop the whole thing, and the ballroom would implode.

"Hey, Caspian, you weren't wanted at parties twenty-five years ago. You're not wanted now," Dayton booms from the dais. He's still got a firm hand on Keldarion's shoulder. "Why don't you be a good boy and see yourself out?"

Caspian gives a dark chuckle. "Sure is easy to be the tough man when you're standing beside Kel, isn't it, Dayton? Remind me again, who is ruling the Summer Realm right now?"

Dayton stiffens.

"Oh, right," Caspian drawls. "You left your child sister in charge. But I think your realm got off lucky. Better than the drunkard who let his brothers go off to battle alone. That ended well for you, didn't it, Prince of the Summer Realm?"

Farron looks from Dayton's ashen face to Caspian and snarls, "Shut up. You're the villain here, Caspian. You're sucking the life from Castletree—"

"Ah, if it isn't our little researcher. Life is behind a book, isn't it? You must love my thorns. You spend every day hiding away, trying to find a cure for them. But what would you do if they were gone, and you had to go back to actually ruling? Don't try to fool me. You should be on your knees thanking me for the gift I've given you." Caspian's voice has lost its mischievous banter. He's all darkness now.

Farron looks like he's been struck by arrows. He staggers back, hand to his breast.

"Enough." Ezryn steps forward to Caspian. "Guards, bring me a sword—"

"Of course you need a weapon. What is the Prince of Spring without blood on his hands?" Caspian paces before him, a scowl thrashing his angelic face. "The goblins love to talk, you know. You're the favorite ghost story down Below. The Black Beast of the Briar."

"Silence," Ezryn rasps.

"I know how you delight in killing them," Caspian says. "How sometimes, you do it slowly. You torture them, letting their screams fill your ears like their blood fills your mouth. It's alright. I can appreciate the art of torture."

Ezryn storms up to him until they're eye to eye. "I'll take your tongue."

But Caspian doesn't back down. Instead, he smiles. "They fear you. And you love that. I know you well, Ezryn of Spring. Is it true the only time you've ever been at peace is when you're a monster, covered in blood? That you kill my goblins slowly so their screams will drown out the cries of all those you failed?" He flashes a white grin. "Like your mother?"

Now, Ezryn is silent. A tear falls from my face to the floor, and it sounds like a sonic boom. I turn to Keldarion on his throne. *Do something. Help them.*

But Keldarion stays pinned as if by invisible shackles, his features twisted in sorrow.

"All of you," Caspian spits. "Pathetic."

Rage floods my body.

Who does this guy think he is, crashing *my* party, belittling *my* princes? Perth Quellos made me feel like an ant under his boot, a feeling that was all too familiar. I'd been made to feel that way my entire life by the people in my town, by Lucas. And I took every hit, every jab, because it was easier to be knocked down than to stand up.

But now, a fire burns within my flesh. And I will not lie down on these coals. Not anymore.

I step in front of Ezryn and shove the Prince of Thorns in his perfectly pressed chest.

He stumbles back, and a gasp erupts from the crowd.

Caspian looks down at his feet, then up at me, a single eyebrow raised. He opens his mouth—but I don't let him speak a word.

"We get it, Prince of Thorns. You're jealous." My voice is a breathy growl. Now I'm the one pacing in front of him. "The four princes have each other. And what do you have? Your goblins and your briars. No wonder you pass your time stalking the princes and obsessing over them." I walk right under his nose and glower up. "You wish you could be them."

Caspian smiles down at me. "Oh, my sweet Rose, you have no idea what I wish."

"Shut up. I'm not done talking." My heart roars in my ears, but I don't care. I'm so fucking sick and tired of these insecure men. "Are the princes perfect? No. Have they made mistakes? Yes. But they're still here. Showing up because they care about the Vale and everyone in it."

I poke his hard chest. "And what do you care about? Spreading your ugly-ass garden? Making a fool of yourself at parties?" I shake my head. "You're the pathetic one, Caspian. And you know it."

Caspian is silent, and I take in a breath, awaiting his thorns to rip out of the crowd and envelope me. But when they don't, I turn my back to him and stare at my princes. Ezryn, Dayton, Farron, and Keldarion. Each of them, so broken. And yet, the shards of them glitter like stardust. "The princes have more courage and heart than you could ever imagine, Caspian," I whisper. "I can tell your life has been very sad. I'm sorry you've suffered." My eyes shimmer with angry tears as I face him. "But you don't get to tear them down because of it."

Caspian runs a tongue over his plush lips. His dark eyes narrow, and a traitorous smile tugs at the corner of his mouth. "What do you know? My rose has thorns."

I pull my shoulders back and march right beneath his nose. I stare up at this prince of darkness and I do not flinch. "You said you came to the party to see me and to dance. Well, here I am. Let's dance."

"Rosalina, don't," Ezryn says, but I wave him away.

"Caspian?" I press.

Caspian runs a hand through the dark waves of my hair. "It would be an honor to dance with you."

I nod at the musicians, and they look up at Keldarion. His hands dig furrows in his icy throne, but I urge him with my eyes: *I know what I'm doing.*

In a pained gesture, he signals the musicians onward.

The waltz begins.

No one else is dancing. The Prince of Thorns and I move as if we are two petals drifting through the breeze, like we're a singular ripple on a moonlit lake. If I thought Kel was a good dancer, Caspian puts him to shame. His every movement is fluid and sensual.

I can't look away from his face; he holds that sardonic expression, barely blinking. His eyes are black holes, and I'm caught in their gravity.

"So, tell me, how do you like being the Princess of Castletree?" Caspian asks bitingly.

"It's wonderful," I snark back. "The food is marvelous. You should come for dinner sometime."

"Oh, Princess, you don't need to invite me." He dips me low. "I always show up."

My breast surges with rapid breath, and his eyes flick to my bodice. He gives a wicked smile.

Needing to focus, I say, "Why are your thorns all over the castle? Why won't you remove them?"

He twirls me and pulls me flush against his chest. "You wouldn't like it if I did that."

"What do you want?" I urge. "To steal the magic of Castletree? Why?"

"I'll let you in on a secret." He smirks. "I do believe we want the same thing."

"I doubt that, Caspian."

His thumb rubs small circles on my waist. "Listen carefully, Princess. Trust your own instincts above all else. The world will tell you that you don't belong. That you are a mere human. That you have no dominion over the sway of destiny." He leans forward, warm breath caressing my jaw. "They are wrong."

"Why should I trust anything you have to say?" I breathe.

A crackle of energy erupts between us as he throws his head back, long dark hair falling away from his face. "Because I happen to be an expert on things below the surface."

The music rises, and our movements sway faster, faster, faster. I have the distinct feeling I'm losing myself in a current and there's nothing I can do to gain purchase again.

"Our dance is almost at a close," he says. "And so, I'll tell you the real reason I'm here. Your precious princes are hiding something from you."

I don't reply. Can't reply.

"The High Tower you're forbidden from entering?" His voice is soft, and for a moment, it's almost as if he's speaking *inside* me. "Time is running out. See for yourself."

"There's no way into the High Tower."

"You'll find the way easier now. Trust only yourself." The music rises into a rushing crescendo, and we spin and spin and spin until Caspian dips me so low, my hair brushes the dance floor.

"Our time together has come to an end, Princess," he whispers. "Thank you for a memorable night."

Then his tongue licks from the dip of my breasts, up my neck, and to my lips—

A clatter sounds and I turn to the dais. Keldarion shoves Dayton and Farron away from him and surges.

Straight toward us.

51

ROSALINA

Keldarion is upon Caspian before he even has a chance to draw me up. He tackles him to the ground, and I smack hard against the floor. Keldarion lifts Caspian up by the front of his tunic.

Caspian stares down at him with a bemused expression on his handsome face, mouth quirking into a mocking smile. "Oh, Kel, you had me worried. You nearly let me get an entire dance in before your jealousy got the better of you. And here I was, thinking I wasn't special to you anymore."

"Leave." Keldarion's eyes flash with dark promise.

I stand at the same moment Caspian pushes out of his grip. He lands gracefully and snatches Kel's wrist. "I had to come. I was getting impatient."

His gaze flicks to me, and something crawls around my head. Slowly, I stare at my reflection in the icy wall. A crown of thorns weaves across my brow.

"It looks better on her," Caspian says, as he adjusts his own sapphire circlet.

Kel freezes, and I feel like I'm trapped in a strange little bubble with them. Caspian stands on his toes, bringing his lips to

Kel's ear. "Just how long before you break, and she belongs to me?"

It's the movement of Caspian's hand that catches my gaze: his thumb brushing over Kel's wrist in a strangely intimate gesture. Brushing over a dark shape right above the frozen bargain bracelet I created with Kel. *What is that?*

"Never," Keldarion snarls. With a roar, he throws Caspian across the ballroom.

Keldarion stands before me, hunched and panting. Frost crackles beneath his feet, and the tips of his fingers shimmer blue with ice magic. If his rage gets the better of him, it will reveal his secret to all the nobles of the Winter Realm.

Caspian picks himself up from the floor and dusts off his jacket, looking positively unbothered. A rush of wind blows my dress and hair as Dayton, Farron, and Ez all sprint to Keldarion's side.

"Even now, you can't bear to hurt me, can you?" A cruel smile carves up Caspian's handsome face.

"You. Are. Not. Welcome!" Keldarion howls, and a series of huge icicles, tips sharpened to deadly points, erupt out of the floor, surging toward the Prince of Thorns.

Caspian raises his hands, and the floor splits with enormous purple briars, wrapping around his legs and lifting him out of the way of the ice daggers. "When will you get it through your head?" Caspian yells. "You are *not* in control."

More thorns explode out of the walls, the ground, even the dais. Guests scream and stampede from the ballroom. The briars shove over the tables of food. Ice sculptures smash to the ground, splintering into millions of pieces. Kel's throne is wrapped in a thornbush until only a glimmer of blue is visible beneath.

The thorns rise Caspian higher into the air. "Ah, I do love a little chaos." His black eyes settle on me, and he winks. "Goodbye, Princess." The briars wrap tighter and tighter around him and then—

He's gone.

A sigh of relief is nearly out of my throat ... But a murmur shivers through the panicked crowd.

"He brought the Prince of Thorns here."

"Once a traitor, always a traitor."

"Keldarion allies again with the Below! He's brought the thorns back to Winter!"

"It's Keldarion's fault for trusting him at all."

I stand on shaky legs. The princes have formed a circle, all staring outward.

Something is wrong.

A nobleman steps forward from his hiding place behind a table crowded with briars. "Look at this! Prince Keldarion returns after years of abandonment, only to have the Prince of Thorns ambush us! He is still in alliance with the Below—here is the proof!"

"No," Kel growls. "My allegiance is to the Queen."

A fae woman screams from the crowd, "Then why do you not carry the Sword of the Protector? Why didn't you kill Caspian while he was here?"

"I didn't ..." Kel stutters.

Oh no. The rebellions Perth Quellos kept mentioning. Is this the making of one? I turn in a circle and catch sight of the vizier skulking in a doorway. Why isn't he doing anything?

Something sails through the air and lands upon Kel's fine tunic. A pomegranate. Purple juice slides down his chest.

"Down with the Prince!" A young noble shouts. "Let us take back our realm from the traitor!"

"I'm not a traitor," Kel roars. "Stop this—"

But a fever has overcome the crowd. Panic rushes through my veins, but there's nothing I can do. Guests rip up the thorns and brandish knives and forks from the tables. A group rushes the dais and begins overturning the thrones. Ezryn and Dayton step before Keldarion, and the spark of magic erupts around them. A swirling water barrier forms as Dayton moves his hands like a conductor. Ez touches the floor and the ground beneath shifts, turning into churned earth and a tangle of roots so thick, the nobles surging toward them trip and fall. Kel stands stricken between them.

Where is Farron? Is he okay? I turn in a circle, locking eyes with a fae woman, her expression one of wild fervor. "You were dancing with the Prince of Thorns. Are you one of his succubae from Below?"

She holds the carved decapitated head of a swan: the remains of a fallen ice sculpture. "I'll pound your fucking round ears into your skull," she cries.

A scream on my lips, I fall back. But a breeze ripe with red and gold leaves blusters from Farron's hands as he leaps in front of me. The fae woman sails across the room, the swan's head shattering on the floor.

Farron turns to me, an auburn curl falling between his eyes. "Hurry. I have to get you out of here."

He grabs my hand and I let myself be tugged across the ballroom. Total anarchy has fallen. Guards have formed a perimeter around the other three princes, protecting them from the rioting nobles, and others try to subdue them. But I see some guards on the other side, trashing the ballroom with their spears.

"What's going on?" I cry.

"The Winter Realm has been burned by the Prince of Thorns before," Farron pants, shoving me beneath a table as we attempt to pass through a heated tussle. "This is the culmination of fear and rage from that last betrayal."

"But they're taking it out on Kel." My beautiful dress rips as Farron tugs me to the other side of the table.

"Well, Kel hasn't exactly been a model ruler," Farron mutters. "Come on."

"But he's trying to make it better!" I cry, panting to keep up. Where is Perth Quellos? He's been the one ruling in Kel's stead. But I don't see him anywhere.

Farron shoves me out of a door and into an empty hallway. We sprint until we're out in the garden. I blink up, trying to find the sun through the dark clouds.

Farron grabs his shimmering leaf locket and holds it out. The iridescent mirror beams with light. "Hurry, Rosalina. This will take you back to Castletree."

"Not without you." I grab Farron's arm.

He shakes his head. "I have to stay and help allay this in any way I can."

"What about Kel? He's in danger. They could kill him."

"Ez and Dayton will never let that happen. I'll never let that happen." Farron touches my cheek. "Trust me."

Doors clatter open and out streams a group of nobles holding carving knives and sharp thorns ripped from the briars. "You'll be safe at home, Rosalina," Farron breathes. "Go."

You'll be safe at home. Those are words I never understood before. Home used to be a dark cottage, sitting in my loneliness, waiting for Papa to arrive. It used to be walking through the damp streets, both desperate and terrified to see Lucas.

Now, I think of my warm bed in the castle, of sitting in front of the vanity with Astrid and Marigold. Of the murals of crawling ivy and lush meadows that remind me of sunshine and the smell of fresh earth.

I think of the cherry blossoms that float down to my bed, of the warm embrace of salty water, of endless books, of the gleam of ice.

For the first time in my life, I know the words to be true: I will be safe at home. At Castletree.

With one last look back at Farron, I leap through the light and the calamity behind me disappears.

52

ROSALINA

I watch helplessly as the sun dips lower. Where are they? Why haven't they returned yet?

I don't know how long it's been since I arrived back at Castletree through the mirror. Every minute feels like a year as my stomach twists and my mind races through all the horrible possibilities.

Even the servants who went to the Winter Realm haven't returned. Could they be hurt? In danger? If they don't get back soon, night will fall, and their secret will be revealed to everyone.

My ruined gown floats like an icefall over the blanket as I flop on the bed. I shouldn't have left … But what could I do? I'd only have been a liability to the princes.

Maybe Perth Quellos was right all along.

I thought dancing with the Prince of Thorns was the peaceful resolution. How stupid I was. He really is a trickster.

Your precious princes are hiding something from you.

My hand drifts to the thorn crown upon my head and I look up at the ceiling. Everyone has been so secretive about the High Tower. What is it? The one time I'd tried the door, it was locked. Kel told me that place was strictly forbidden.

I stand and pace the length of my room. What are they hiding that could be any worse than the curse itself? After all we've been through these last few months, they trust me.

I know it.

But ... Caspian's words linger in my mind, a ghost shivering through my skin.

What is in the High Tower?

I go to the windowsill and take another look at the sun. They're still not back. And I can't do anything here waiting for them.

Time to take my destiny into my own hands.

I close my eyes, and feel a deep knowing, a visceral thing I've sensed since living in Castletree. There's something more to this castle, to these thorns. They can *hear* me.

"Show me the way to the High Tower," I whisper. "Show me the path."

A groan shudders behind me, and I turn to the cherry blossom tree in the corner of my room. The trunk, overgrown with briars and purple thorns, cracks open. The thorns retreat, the bark lifts, and the pink petals shiver to the ground.

Where once my cherry blossom tree had been is now a narrow staircase. A path up into the chasms of Castletree.

"Trust yourself," I whisper. And like a tether is tied to my heart, I glide up into the dark.

The staircase is pitch black and winds around and around and around. I'm heading straight through the heart of the tree, and up to the tallest branches. It's like I can feel the pulse of magic from within.

A sense of something very sacred and very ancient.

Each step is deliberate, and I swear my heart beats with the same thrumming magic. There are briars in the stairway, but not so encompassing as elsewhere. Instead, a single branch of thorns winds around the walls on either side, almost serving as a railing as I ascend through the dark.

Finally, I reach a wooden door. I turn the handle and step into the top of the High Tower.

Blinking, I take in the large chamber. Huge stained-glass windows let in the fading light and paint the room in brilliant red and blue and orange and green. And the briars ...

No other area of the castle, not even the Winter Wing, is so infested with them. They lay like a carpet over the floor, tugging at my dress. Up, up, up the walls they stretch, tangling at the precipice of the ceiling. It's as if they are the skeleton of Castletree itself.

My breath catches. In the very middle of the chamber lies a crescent shape where no briars dare touch. The floor is tiled in a vibrant mural of a starfall: shimmering lights descending from the heavens. And four roses grow from a small patch of rich earth.

One has pink petals and is shrouded in emerald light from the stained-glass window. Beside it grows one of turquoise petals, bathed in yellow light. Next to that is one of brilliant orange, the glass dusting it in dark red. And finally, there is a startlingly blue rose, a color so potent I feel like I may freeze if I touch it.

And the roses are wilting.

I fall to my hands and knees, the magic radiating from the roses washing over me like a tidal wave.

The roses look as if they're barely hanging onto life. The petals are wrinkled, leaves drooping. A precious blue petal falls from the one on the end and withers to ash upon the ground.

"What does this mean?" I say. "What are you trying to show me?"

And as if Castletree hears my plea, light from the stained-glass windows sparkles and *moves*. It twists together, swirling and arcing, a rainbow of luminous color, until it forms an image.

I gasp. Standing before me are ... my princes.

I know it's them, even though they're bare images made of light. Ezryn standing behind his flower, his hand clasped on a sword. Dayton, his hair shorter but his smile the same. Farron, shrunken and timid. And Keldarion, his hair a white tangle upon his head, a feral grimace on his face.

They're looking at me.

No, not me. Something behind me. Someone.

I turn to see the silhouette of a woman made of dusky gray light. Her shape shimmers forward through my body and she stands before the princes. She holds out four roses. Each one glimmers as if made of its own prism.

I realize now.

"Castletree," I whisper. "You're showing me a memory."

The princes look down upon the woman, their prismatic doppelgängers moving in ways so familiar. Ezryn turns his back to the woman, Dayton laughs, Farron shrinks away, and Keldarion ... Keldarion points an accusing finger.

A deep sense of dread fills me. Because I know how this story ends. I've seen the nightmare in person. This is no lost traveler asking for shelter against the bitter wind.

This is the Enchantress.

And suddenly, a brilliant white light erupts from around me and the woman turns inward on herself, robes cocooning around her. She is a gleaming entity of starlight made whole, features hidden by a celestial glow.

Tears flood down my face and I don't know why. I step forward, grasping for her hand, but she's out of my reach.

The princes fall back in her wake, their own light dimming. The roses she once held now float above their heads.

"The universe is cyclical," the woman's voice says, and it's like the shimmer of stars through the atmosphere. "Day gives way to night and back again. Spring to summer, summer to autumn, autumn to winter, and winter to spring. Those who die go back into the cosmos, their spirits remade into the grass and the animals and the fae reborn."

This voice ... It sparks something inside of me, like a dream I woke up from but can't remember. I collapse to my knees, stretching my arm up to the memory.

"And as the universe is cyclical, so is the rule and magic of the realms," the Enchantress says to the princes. "Destiny has passed this rule to the four of you." Her voice darkens. "And you have squandered the responsibility."

The four princes collapse to their knees, heads bowed. The fae enchantress grows even larger. "In your current states, you are all undeserving of the great destiny that awaits you. This providence shall not be disregarded in the way you have all failed your realms and your people."

"Please, offer us forgiveness," they say in unison.

Her voice is the ocean breeze and the cracking of ice during the first thaw. "You must earn your repentance."

Then she turns to Ezryn. "Here stands the vigilante, who seeks vengeance instead of redemption. Who drowns his sorrows in blood and bone instead of facing what lies beneath. Here stands a beast who will let his realm go to rot as long as his sword is wet with blood."

Ezryn collapses, clawing at his skin.

Leave him alone! I want to scream, but my voice is trapped inside of me.

She turns to Dayton. "Here stands the fool, who escapes within the flesh for fear of his fate. Who languishes his time and talent. Here stands a beast who will let his realm go to rot as long as his mind is muddled enough not to comprehend."

Dayton falls to his knees, back arching, face twisted in anguish.

But the Enchantress is not finished. She looms above Farron. "And here stands the coward, who pretends passiveness is pacifism. Who hides behind investigation instead of admitting indecisiveness. Here stands a beast who will let his realm go to rot as long as his curtains are drawn so he need not see it."

Now Farron falls to the ground, his shape curling inward.

And finally, the Enchantress turns to face Keldarion. He falls to his knees, groveling. But I know it's not for himself. It's for the others.

I scream into the void, begging her not to do what I know happens next. But it's no use. This is a memory. And the course of time has been ravaged by destiny.

"Here stands the Sworn Protector of the Realm, the traitor who betrayed his people for love." The Enchantress's voice booms like the felling of a forest. "The one who sought glory and passion. Here stands a beast who will let the entire Vale go to rot for the sake of his own selfish heart."

"No!" I scream.

But there's nothing I can do to stop the past.

With a triumphant rise of the Enchantress's hands, the princes contort, their bodies metamorphosing into something monstrous and horrible. Their backs break, their faces change to snouts, and claws replace what once were the hands that have since held me.

And now before me are the wolves.

The roses hover above their heads and the Enchantress reaches up to touch each one. "I lay a curse upon this castle, upon all those within it, and upon each High Prince of the Vale. Every night, you shall take the hideous form of a beast. This spell may only be broken by winning the true love of your fated mate; and accepting the mate bond that has long been woven among the stars." A shining tear runs down her starlight face. "For only then will you have proven you are worthy of your destiny."

The wolves lie low before her, the looks of torment clear even on their light-born faces.

The Enchantress rises higher in the air. "These roses will remain in Castletree. When they have wilted and returned to the ash," the Enchantress closes her eyes, "the curse will be sealed forever, and you will be beasts for all time."

The wolves howl, and it sounds like a thousand storms raging at once. Amongst the calamity of light and wails, the Enchantress spins, and the image vanishes before me.

53

ROSALINA

Suddenly, it's so very dark.

I gasp, falling to my knees and clutching the briars, tearing my hands. That's what they hadn't told me … That's what Caspian knew.

What misdeeds have each of my princes committed in the past? ?

But a more pressing urgency clutches at my heart.

Time is running out.

I scramble across the floor, not caring as the thorns bite into my hands, until I reach the roses. Each one is bowed, the petals drooping toward the dirt. Twenty-five years they've been cursed … How much longer do they have?

I must save them. They can't be cursed forever. Not just the princes lost to the beasts within, but the staff too. Astrid, Marigold … trapped as animals for the rest of their lives. And without the princes' magic to stop the thorns, Castletree will fall to Caspian.

"No, no, no," I cry. I dig my fingers into the dirt. There has to be something I can do to buy us more time. If I could give the roses some magic, keep them alive longer …

A soft sound swishes, and a few brambles wriggle toward me. "Help me," I whisper. "Keep the flowers alive."

The brambles slowly creep up my body, lacing around my arms. But I'm not afraid. It's like a shiver of energy passes through me. We can do this together. Tears fall from my face, and idly, I notice they shimmer purple. A strange violet glow illuminates beneath my skin.

"I can break the curse, I promise. I just need you to bloom for a little longer."

My fingers, laced with thorns, drift over the flowers. First, the rose of Spring. It trembles. I think of Ezryn, of his hands on mine as he healed my wound. Of the strength holding all his broken pieces together. He's a mystery, one I desperately want to solve.

Then, I carefully run my hands up the rose of Summer. I think of Dayton's secret smile, the rarest treasure. The heat of his kiss, the warmth I felt in his arms. He has so much to give; I will see he has the chance.

My heart thrums as I caress the rose of Autumn. My darling Farron. The first person in my whole life who I would consider a true friend, one who truly knows me. I want more days in the library with him, and I want the chance at a night too.

The flowers I've touched ... Their stems straighten. The petals bloom. They're not whole, but there's life there.

But I'm not done. Last, I touch the rose of Winter. My Winter Prince. My Keldarion. My captor and my savior. I need to tell him that. Tell him he saved me in so many ways. Tell him he can save himself. I *know* he can.

His rose blooms beneath my touch. More, I can give more to them—

A roar sounds in my ears, and suddenly I'm yanked to my feet. Keldarion's got a vice grip on my arms, a look of pure fury on his face.

"You are forbidden here." His voice is a beast made sound. He lets me go, quickly checking the flowers. "You don't know what you could have done!"

Fear races through my chest. Even when Keldarion first captured me, I never saw this rage within him.

"You never told me you were running out of time," I breathe.

"What are these?" He grabs the brambles wrapped around my arms and tears.

I scream as the briars rip from me, and I feel helpless before him.

"You have no idea what you could have done!" he roars again and rushes back to the flowers, ripping the nearby briars from them. It's like a darkness has cast inside him, a place where light goes to die.

Sounds clatter in the doorway, and there stands Ez, Dayton, and Farron.

"Rosie," Farron's voice shakes, "what are you doing here?"

But I'm tired of being blamed for things that aren't my fault. "You lied to me. You all did. Made me believe the Enchantress was evil. But what have you all done?" Fear ensnares my heart. "She called you beasts. All of you!"

"Caspian is the monster!" Kel cries. With a roar, he snatches a cluster of briars from the ground and rips them. The castle shudders.

The other princes stand stricken in the doorway, but I clamber up. Keldarion runs to a wall and pulls more thorns from their hold. A great *crack!* sounds as part of the roof collapses. A massive branch lands and I scream, cowering against the wall.

But Keldarion doesn't stop. More and more, he rips the briars from the walls and ceiling. The castle moans, almost a cry of agony.

"Kel, stop!" I scream. "You're making it worse!"

"Everything is ruined," he snarls. Blood drips between his fingers as the thorns cut into his flesh. "It's all over!"

My plan failed; I've only made this worse for him. Forced him to face the people he's hidden from. And now I've discovered his greatest secret.

With a massive heave, Kel rips up two fistfuls of briar. Stones shake loose from the walls, and I scream as a huge branch breaks through the windows, showering us in colored glass.

"The castle is coming undone!" Ezryn cries. "Hurry, it needs more magic!"

The princes rush forward toward the roses, falling on their hands and knees in a circle.

"Channel your energy into the tree," Farron instructs. "We have to hold this place together."

Dayton looks up, panic across his face. "Kel, we need your help."

But Kel is deep in blood and briars. He looks up through his sweat-damp hair, eyes burning with blue flame. His gaze locks on me. "You don't belong here. Leave."

"Kel," I whisper.

"*Leave*," he growls again.

And with Castletree, my home, crumbling around me, I run.

54

ROSALINA

ce and snow spray against my bare legs. My feet are completely
numb, my thin silver slippers already soaked through.

I don't care, the outside of my body might as well match my
heart. Nothing. I feel nothing. All I know is I have to get away, get
back home. My real home.

No one follows as I dash across the bridge and run into the deep
thorn bushes covered in snow.

Ice clatters from the giant briars as I weave through them. The
rising moon provides an ivory pathway. I need to get back to the rosebush, back to Orca Cove, back to Papa and Lucas and everything else I
left behind.

I was a fool for ever thinking I belonged here. Tears crystalize on
my cheeks, and my clumsy steps push me against thorns that rip my
beautiful gown and scratch red lines down my arms and legs.

It's not like I can feel them, anyway.

I tumble, skin shredding on the thorns, before I land in a pile of
muddy snow. I lay there for a moment, breath falling out of me in
heavy gasps.

A familiar chittering laugh sounds through the air. My blood turns
to ice. *No …*

Several yellow glowing eyes peer out from the gloom.

The goblins are here.

Trembling, I grip a vine and pull myself up. *Run! Rosalina, run,* a smooth voice screams in my ear, so loud it blocks out everything else. *Run! I'm in a bit of a predicament at the moment. I can't get to you, I can't—* The voice cuts off in an anguished cry, but the sheer desperation in the words shoots my body with adrenaline. I spring into action, throwing myself into the tangle of thorns and off the haphazard path. Who was that? It sounded so distant, but familiar at the same time.

I can't worry about anything except escaping the goblins. Last time, they surrounded Lucas and me. I won't be caught the same way again. A chitter of excitement sounds as they realize I'm running. The thorn bushes shake, and snow and ice spray down as the goblins crawl after me.

"It's late for the little princess to be out of her castle," a goblin cackles.

"Where are your wolves? Where are your wolves?" They chant.

I push myself deeper into a tangle of branches. There's a small gap of light ahead, and I make for it, wondering if it can at least give me some bearing on where I am. Maybe I can see a place to hide or escape.

A wretched shriek pierces the night air as a hideous goblin appears before me, having descended from the branches above. Its enormous bug-like eyes shine like embers in the moonlight, its pallid skin covered in a slimy layer of moss and toadstools. This one wears ragged leather armor and clutches a deadly scythe fashioned from thorns.

A blood-curdling scream tears from my throat as it advances toward me.

"What a pretty little human." The goblin licks its lips. "What a shiny little dress."

Fear curls in my belly. Behind me, the thorns move as more goblins close in. *No. No.* I am not ending the worst night of my life by being eaten by a freaking goblin!

"Sorry, I don't think this dress would suit you," I snarl. "Blue clashes with your mold."

Then I do the only stupid thing I can think of. I run toward it with all my might, shoving it back against the brambles.

A giant thorn pierces right through the goblin's gut, splattering black blood on me. It drops its thorn sword, and a shrieking cry escapes its lips.

The thorns twist and enclose around it. The briar patch is moving. *Shit.* There's a chittering and wail of other goblins still hidden among the thorns.

I need to escape. I don't want to get tangled and speared like my goblin friend. It's too easy for them to surround me here.

I make for the light and push out into a sloping snowy hill mostly clear of thorns. Down below is a frozen river and a forest of trees beyond. And there, on the crest of an opposite hill in a gap of trees, is the rosebush. The red flowers show in stark contrast against the moonlight. I have to make it across the river and through the forest before the goblins eat me.

Easy-peasy for a girl in a ballgown who hates running.

I have no choice but to try.

Behind me, the briars continue to swirl, as if a little offering of goblin blood was all they needed to come alive.

Stay in the briars, Rosalina, a voice demands in my head. I recognize it now. It's the Prince of Thorns. Caspian.

"What, so your little friends can eat me?" I snarl and push myself out into the snow. Fat chance. That's right where he wants me. I'm not giving him another way to torment Kel. "And get out of my head!"

The snow is deep here, up to my knees as I trudge through it. A wild call sounds from behind me, and I risk a glance over my shoulder. More goblins emerge from the thorns.

The movement of the briar has stopped, probably because that idiot prince realized I wasn't dumb enough to fall for his trap. But it must have seriously freaked the goblins out, because it's not just a couple of them pouring out of the briars. Ten, twenty, fifty. Fear courses through my body as hundreds of them flee the giant thorn bushes. And they're all heading toward me.

I cry out and throw myself down the snowy hill. Momentum takes over and I'm tumbling head over heels. I try to shield my face but soon lose all control of my body. Smashing through the snow, I careen to a stop at the bottom of the hill. Above me, the world spins and spins.

I force myself to my feet. Everything in my body aches. My vision is blurry. Dark shapes race down the hill, getting closer and closer. Shit, those things are fast.

The only way to the rosebush is over the frozen river, but without a bridge, I don't know if I can cross. I stop at the lip of the shore, but hesitate for what feels like an eternity, my foot hovering above the ice.

My hesitation is the opportunity the goblins need.

A wild chant rises as the mass of goblins surrounds me. They're clustered so close together, I can't even count them anymore. In a panic, I throw myself onto the ice, sliding as I try to escape. A deep groan shudders beneath me. How thick is this?

A few goblins follow onto the frozen river, causing it to moan further. This damn river is so wide, but I don't dare stop.

But they are faster. A goblin snags my dress and I fall. My body stings as my blood spreads across the ice from a gash on my knee.

Black shadows whirl over the frozen surface as the goblins catch up and surround me. A swarm of them covers the shore. Their hounds crouch low, snarling, foam dripping from their putrid mouths.

"Leave me alone," I cry, struggling to my feet. They've circled me, and there's nowhere to run. "What do you want?"

They cast knowing glances at each other and laugh, some of them mockingly calling out:

"Dances with the prince, she does."

"Break the curse. Break the curse. Thinks she will break the curse."

I swirl, desperately trying to find an opening.

"Mother and brother would not like that."

"Not like that. No, no, no."

The creatures' breath smells of spoiled milk and sulfur, a cloying odor that fills the air as their circle tightens.

"Your prince can burn in hell," I spit.

A blinding pain shoots through me as one of them lunges, cutting its thorn sword across my thigh. I cry out, doubling over.

"Thy shall not mock our prince," the goblin snarls, then licks her lips at the sight of my blood. "Red as a rose."

"Red as a rose!" Another goblin attacks, swiping for my face.

"No!" I shriek, bringing up my arms desperately to defend myself. The sharp glint of the blade slams into my skin, slicing the flesh of my upper arm.

"Red as a rose. Red as a rose. Red as a rose." A sickening ring of malicious laughter encircles me, each chuckle rippling in the icy air like a deadly wave.

"Down, down, down to Mother you will go." Their chant changes, and they stomp their feet. Two of them grab me.

"No!" I scream and tear myself out of their grip. "No, I won't."

One of them quirks its head at an awkward angle. "Her head will look pretty on a pike."

Raw terror floods my veins. Two of them grab my arms, another wraps its moldy fingers on my dress, ripping into the fabric. And the one with the long thorn blade stalks before me. "Your shiny eyes will be earrings. Your hair bronze rope. Head on a pike."

I thrash wildly, screaming. Pure rage lights me from within. And a voice that doesn't sound entirely my own snarls with a dark promise, "I will see your guts splattered across the ice."

They look at each other and snicker. The goblin in front of me raises its thorn sword.

A deafening roar cuts through the air, and the goblins go silent, right before a massive white paw tears through a cluster of them. The goblin in front of me turns just in time to see a nine-foot white wolf leap into view. It engulfs the goblin's head in one bite.

He tosses the remains to the side before his wild blue eyes meet mine.

Keldarion has come for me.

55

KELDARION

A fire beyond any I have ever known fuels my body. And this is one time I am grateful for the wildness of my beast. Rosalina's blood stains this ice.

So every single one of these despicable monsters will die.

"Get down," I growl.

Rosalina obeys, and I stand over her, surveying the surrounding goblins. Something wild has affected them, and they're not backing down. *Why have you sent so many? For her or for me? Another one of your vicious schemes?*

A cluster of goblins raise their swords and charge. I swipe them, claws shredding their flesh. Guts paint the ice black. Whirling, I snatch another two, feeling bones break beneath my powerful teeth.

"Look out!" Rosalina cries.

Pain stings my front leg as a goblin slashes it with his thorn. I swipe the goblin away and bite the last few surrounding us. Still more goblins pour in from the edge of the river.

"To the forest," I growl.

Rosalina nods, then pushes herself up from beneath me. She runs, but I notice her awkward gait. The gash on her leg sends another flurry of anger coursing through me. I don't dare pick her up. If the goblins catch us, I will need to fight them. And I don't want her near for that.

The forest on the far side of the river draws close as we make it halfway.

"Wait!" Rosalina clutches my fur. "It's too thin!"

Below us, the ice spiderwebs.

"I'm too heavy," I say.

She looks around desperately, searching for another way.

"I'll hold them off," I say. "The ice is thick enough for you."

Rosalina looks up at me with glassy eyes. "What?"

"Go," I say again. And I hope she knows exactly what I mean. Go to the forest. Go to the rosebush. Go home.

I always thought the choice would be difficult. *My realm or her.* But in the end, there is no choice at all. Let my realm fall, let me become a beast forever. She is worth everything.

Rosalina is everything to me.

Without waiting for another word, I run back toward the goblins. A wild elation fills me, and I let the beast consume my mind until I know nothing but the taste of rotten blood, the sound of snapping bones and horrified cries, the putrid smell of decay.

Minutes drift by, or perhaps hours; I no longer comprehend time.

Thorns dig into my flesh and their claws rip my fur. Every bite of pain is nothing more than I deserve. To have sent her away in the manner I did ... My body should lay broken in repentance.

And maybe it will.

Another set of goblins crawl onto my back, and I no longer have the strength to push them off.

"Do not back down now!" one of them cries. "He is weakening! We will take him to our prince. A most mighty gift!"

A wild roar fills my throat and I thrash. Death would be sweeter than returning to the Below. A claw digs into my forearm, then a rope.

But that's a choice these monsters won't give me.

It doesn't matter. The pain fuels my fury at myself. My broken body will be trivial reparation for such an unforgivable sin.

"Hey! Stinkfaces!" a voice calls.

No.

Rosalina is still here. Right where I left her, in the middle of the ice.

Why didn't she run?

"I thought you wanted my head on a pike too?" she yells. "Unless *Mother* doesn't actually care."

The goblins chatter excitedly. "Two prizes for Below. Down they go. Down they go."

Some move toward her. Rosalina lifts her beautiful crown off her head and plucks a long, straight thorn out. Then plunges it into the ice.

No ...

She's trying to draw them to her. Draw them to where the ice is thinnest. Where it will break under the weight.

Rosalina is trying to save me.

But doesn't she understand? It can never be that way. No matter what she does, no matter how hard she tries, my doom is already set.

And there is one last thing I can do for her.

I draw myself up on my hind legs, and with a mighty blow, crash down onto the ice. It cracks and splinters. And I hear the furious roar of the river still rushing underneath, great chunks of ice rising around us.

Goblins cry out in panicked fear as they try to run from the collapsing ice, but they can't escape. Their scrambling bodies fall and are swept beneath the surging river.

The last I hear before the icy water takes me are Rosalina's desperate screams.

Cold engulfs me. Cold even a beast of Winter will not survive. And I wonder if I will sink all the way to the Below.

56

ROSALINA

One moment the giant wolf and a hoard of goblins are standing across from me and the next, there is nothing but the winter wind and the rush of the river.

That stupid icy bastard. *I* was going to save *him*.

I would have sunk to any depth if it meant giving him a chance. It was so strange. In the space of a single breath, sinking beneath the ice went from my biggest fear to nothing. Because I realized my actual biggest fear was happening right before me. With every strike the goblins made against Keldarion, with every drop of his blood that spilled upon the ice, I knew no other fear could compare.

Cursing his stupid name, I put my thorn crown back on and hobble to the broken ice. I slow as I approach. It's still coming apart in great chunks. But this isn't a lake. It's a river; anything that fell in is being carried downstream where the ice is too thick to break out from.

I don't have much time.

The moon is bright, and shadows sweep fast beneath the ice. The goblins. Kel.

Taking off in a run, I ignore the blinding pain in my leg. I need to get to him. Nothing else matters. The river narrows ahead, and more briars close in around the edge.

Something slams up beneath my feet, a hand flat against the ice—an ashen-faced goblin, eyes wide, bubbles rising out of its nose as it drowns. It sinks as another drifts pastpast, then another. A swirl of goblin bodies dances below the frozen depths.

Up ahead, the river is dammed with a thick cluster of briars. The bodies have piled up beneath the ice or slammed against the brambles frozen within the water. A kaleidoscope of goblins swirl beneath my feet, desperately pounding at the solid surface.

"Kel!" I scream. "Kel!"

Running from one end to the other, I see nothing but dark, rotten shapes. I slam down to my knees, trying to see deeper. Nothing.

He has to be here.

He *has* to be.

I fall against the ice, feeling nothing but cold beneath my skin. Why would he do that? Why would he throw himself in?

The river is dammed. He should be here. Tears of rage and sorrow drip from my eyes, yet I can't accept he's gone.

He's *not* gone.

Something sparks inside me. *He is here.* I raise my head, feeling my heart stutter. Something tugs in my chest, my whole body shaking like I've been electrocuted.

As if I'm being pulled, I jump to my feet. It feels like there's an arrow exploding from my heart, guiding me. I rush to the edge of the river and crawl beneath a cluster of a low-hanging briars.

Quickly, I swipe away the top layer of frost and see white fur pressed against the ice.

"Kel!" I grab the crown of thorns off my head. It twists in my hands and smoke rises from beneath my palms. The crown changes, lengthening into an enchanting purple sword.

"Creepy but great," I say and plunge the thorn into the frozen river. The ice cracks, a hideous groaning sound. I spring up, taking my sword with me. The hole widens, ice chips floating away. The white wolf's body rises to the surface, along with a couple bobbing goblins. All dead.

But he's not. I *know* he's not.

I fall to my belly and crawl close to the edge, then I reach out and grip his fur. Fuck, he's heavy. "Kel," I cry.

My arm brushes against the biting cold water and I hook my fingers around a tuft. With a grunt, he crashes against the edge. I need to get his face out of the water.

Carefully, I position myself on the rim and sit up. I grip his fur with both hands and *pull*. He doesn't even budge. I lose my hold and fall back, cold water splashing over me.

"No, no, no," I say, crawling back and grabbing his fur. I can do this. I have to. I scream, the muscles in my arms straining, but he doesn't move any more than before. My grasp loosens on his silky fur and he splashes back down.

I try again, soaking my whole front body in the water, trying to hook around a paw or his middle. He's not moving. And I'm running out of time.

Desperate feral cries escape me, and I try again only to fall back with momentum, smacking my head hard on the ice. I roll over and, with a hopeless cry, curl into a ball.

I can't lift him out. He's too big. I'm just a weak human who doesn't belong here.

And he'll die for me.

He'll die for nothing.

I shake with sobs and the cold feels like it's slithered into every part of me.

Something soft lands on me, more velvety than snow, and I reach up to brush it off. I blink as it comes into focus. A gold rose petal. Another one lands on my arm. The briars above me have bloomed a single beautiful golden rose.

The briar patch is a rosebush.

Slowly, I stand up and reach for the rose, and the thorny stems curve toward me.

Just like when they wrapped around my body when I'd fallen off the cliff the first time the goblins attacked.

How they created the ladder down from the dungeon.

And helped me save the enchanted roses in the High Tower.

The cage they created for the goblins when I was trying to run away.

What if Caspian isn't the only one who can control them?

As the briar with the gold rose lowers, I reach out and grasp it, feeling a connection shock through me. My consciousness springs out into the web of surrounding briars.

Into the web, I pour my anger, my frustration, my desperation, and my love. I will save him.

The branches begin to move. They reach down into the water, carefully wrapping around the giant wolf and lifting him ...

My heart stutters in my chest, and I grip the stem tighter, feeling my connection loosen. *Not yet.*

The briars lower the white wolf to the side of the river. I gasp out, dropping my hold on the gold rosebush. My legs shake. I feel like I've been running for a thousand years ...

I collapse, vision blurring. But I can't stop now. Just a little more strength. Slowly, I crawl over the ice. My fingers sift through fresh soft snow on the riverbank.

Almost there ...

I touch cold, wet fur. Keldarion shudders beneath me. He *shudders.*

He's alive. With great effort, he raises to his paws and coughs up water. His blue eyes peer down at me.

I throw my arms around his neck, finally feeling that insistent tug slacken, having brought me right where I belong.

57

ROSALINA

Fae must recover quickly because something wet nudges my back, and through blurry eyes, I see the giant white wolf standing. He inclines his head and understanding dawns. With great effort, I pull myself onto his back.

The tips of his fur are frozen with frost. But there's no other way. I don't think I could take a single step.

I have no idea where we're going, only that soft snowfall covers me, and all the cold of winter has seeped into my bones.

Distantly, I register the biting wind has lessened, and I blink my eyes open to reveal the solid stone walls of a cave.

The wolf gives a great heave and collapses. I tumble off him, hitting the rocky ground. Keldarion's eyes flutter closed, and I take in the extent of the wounds along his body. A trail of blood has followed us into the cavern.

And I realize, maybe fae don't recover that quickly. Even if they're beasts. Maybe he gave everything he had to get me here.

"Where are we?" I ask, pushing myself up and looking around the cave. It's a small inlet with smooth walls, lit only by the bright moonlight.

"One of Ezryn's caches," Keldarion grits out, pain lacing each word.

Okay, Rosalina, time to get your act together. Keldarion is wounded. We're too far away from the castle to make it there. I'm at high risk for hypothermia.

One of Ezryn's caches. He must use these when he spends the long days out in the Briar hunting goblins. Which means there must be supplies here. A shiny wooden container sits tucked near the back wall, obstructed by shadows. I crawl to it, trying to ignore the pain in my leg and arm, and the fact I can't feel my fingers and toes right now.

There's a small lock in the shape of a cherry blossom, but it clicks open at my touch. *Pretty shoddy security, Ez.* But then again, I can already tell that while vicious, these goblins aren't exactly geniuses.

As soon as I lift the lid, I let out a prayer to the Spring Prince. This thing is chock-full of resources. Blankets, extra clothes, what looks to be dried packets of food, canteens of water, a plain metal helmet, matches, and ... I open a woven pouch to reveal long strips of bandages and several tins of strong-smelling ointment. Hopefully, that's enough medicine to help a giant wolf.

"Make a fire first," Keldarion barks. "Get warm then treat your wounds."

"It's only a scrape." I roll my eyes. "I'm not the one bleeding a puddle onto the ground."

The blood pooling around his back leg makes my heart seize with worry. But I take his advice on the fire. I'll be no good to anyone if my fingers are too frozen to work.

There's a pile of wood in the corner and matches at the bottom of the crate. With my limited, embarrassing camping skills and Keldarion's growls of everything I'm doing wrong, I get a decent fire going.

A few choice curse words escape my lips as my fingers prickle, then defrost.

"Now, I have to see how hurt you are." I turn to Keldarion. "Can you turn back into a man? It will be easier."

He points his snout to the cave entrance. Stars flicker in the navy sky.

"Right. It's still night." I knot my fingers behind my neck, then smirk at him. "Well, I did want to be a veterinarian when I was a kid."

It's hard to tell on the maw of a wolf, but I think I earn a smile ... or a pained grimace. The ice on my dress is melting and cold water drips down my legs. But none of that matters until Kel is better, or at least not bleeding. I grab the first aid pouch and sit before him, grateful for the warmth of the fire on my back.

Spreading the contents of the pouch before me, I let out a little sigh of delight. "God, I love Ez."

Kel raises a wolfy brow.

I pick up the first tin and hold it before his snout. "He labeled the containers with numbers and pictographs. Very helpful. I mean, I'm still not sure what they all do, but he healed me before, so I trust he knows what he's doing."

"Healing is a magic many rulers of the Spring Realm have possessed," Keldarion says. "Ezryn is talented. He could be masterful if he saw the same virtue in it as he does his other gifts."

I continue organizing the supplies. If I had to guess, there seems to be a mixture of an acidic smelling disinfectant, a smooth white balm, and a clear gel sealant.

I know the disinfectant stings because Kel lets out a snarl and bares his large fangs when I apply it. He doesn't scare me anymore; I flick him on the nose and tell him to stop being such a baby.

I work from the largest cuts to the smallest. Thankfully, the sealing gel stops the bleeding, but I can't do much about the blood tangled in his fur. I have to work carefully around the jutting ice spikes on his body, though it seems most of the frost is melting. Will the wounds still be there when he turns back into a fae? Will it be better or worse?

As I pack away the supplies, Kel nudges my leg with his wet snout. "Don't forget."

I apply the balms to myself, then bite out another curse. "Shit, that really does sting."

"Stop being a baby." The healing gels must be working because there's humor in his voice.

"I take back every nice thing I said about Ez," I mutter, applying the rest of the ointment.

"You need to get out of those wet clothes," Keldarion rumbles.

"Who are you, Dayton?" I snark at him, but head over to the supply crate.

"You'll make yourself sick."

"I'm kidding." I pull out one of the cloth blankets and a soft long-sleeve black shirt and pants. Is this what Ez wears underneath his armor? "Close your eyes."

The wolf's snort is my only reply. But I don't even turn around to check. I trust him. I strip out of my now tattered dress, placing the diamond necklace carefully on top, then use some of the fresh bandages to wrap around the scars on my wrist. Closing the large blanket around my shoulders, I waddle to the fire, spreading out both the ruined dress and the black shirt and pants. My body is still damp, and I don't want to get my only dry clothes wet again.

"Okay, you can open your eyes now," I say, sitting across the fire. "I'm going to wait in this until I dry off."

But Keldarion narrows his glassy eyes at me. "Come here."

I immediately obey, closing the blanket tighter around myself and sit against his chest. The white fur is warm from being so close to the fire.

"Are you cold?" I ask. "There's only one blanket, but you can have this—"

He curves in a C shape around me, resting his massive head on his paws. "I am perfect, my Rose."

My Rose. He called me that at the ball, and again just now. And I can't help but remember the feeling that called me to him, like a star bursting to life beneath my breast.

"I am sorry for it all," he says, the words rumbling through me. "All you've ever done is try to help but—"

"Don't worry about it," I say. "I'm just glad you're okay. Are the others—"

"They're using their magic to keep Castletree standing." Pain etches his words. "But when we realized you left the castle, I knew I had to find you."

"Well, you did say '*go away*'."

"I thought you'd return to your room. I would never send you into the wild alone," Keldarion says. "Rosalina, I am so sorry. For making you a prisoner, for every rude remark, for sending you away. I know what I need to do now."

"You need to rest. Are you sure you're not cold?" I burrow into his neck, fingers running through his soft white fur. "After I fell in freezing water, I was cold for a whole week."

His ears perk straight up, and he growls, "When was this?"

"A long time ago."

"Tell me." His ears slowly lower, and he shifts closer. "And no, I'm not cold. The cold rarely bothers me. Though being trapped in a frozen river pushes even me to my limits."

Distantly, I run my hand over the scar on my left wrist. "I was fourteen, and the lake in Orca Cove had frozen over," I begin. "Papa was away as usual. The Rockies, maybe, or Nunavut. I can't remember, but the kids in my class talked about going ice skating on the weekend. I used all my stashed savings to buy skates, and I felt so guilty about it, because I knew Papa could use the money. But I wanted to go so badly, even though no one invited me."

"Why wouldn't anyone invite you?"

"I don't know." I sigh. "I didn't fit in with the rest of the school. The few times people tried to talk to me, I always ended up saying something awkward, like going on about the latest book I was reading, or a TV show I was into. I think I once spent thirty minutes explaining how you could swallow falling stars to get magic."

"Well, I for one think that sounds very interesting," Keldarion's deep voice rumbles.

"There are a lot of books I'd like to read you," I whisper. "But anyway, I showed up hoping everyone would think someone else invited me. I wasn't a great skater. I hovered on the edge of the group.

"Then I heard a long crack, and beneath my feet, the ice splintered like glass. And the next moment there was nothing but cold. I felt a weight on my ankles. All my winter clothes were so heavy. My first reaction was to scream, but the cold water gushed down my throat."

Kel's heartbeat increases. Maybe he's remembering his own experience earlier.

"I was sinking and sinking. Then there were arms around me, and we were moving. Suddenly, freezing wind bit my face, and a voice yelled in my ear, 'Kick, kick!' And I did. I coughed, water sputtering out. And I realized someone had jumped in after me."

My whole body has gone still remembering the feel of his arms around me. My body is not my own, lost to the cold and wet, and lost to him.

"He pushed himself onto the ice, never once letting go of my jacket, or letting me sink back down. Then he pulled me out of the water, all by himself. I collapsed on top of him, coughing, and when I opened my eyes, all I could see was a boy with hair bright as the sunset.

"He said, 'Who are you? How have I never seen you before?' The other kids covered us in their jackets and tried to keep us warm until the paramedics showed up. We were whisked away in an ambulance, and I was shivering so bad. But he sat beside me, threw his arm around me, and told me I was safe now, that he'd look after me. His name was Lucas."

I turn to Kel, wondering if he's even interested. He's just watching me. His eyes narrow. "Go on, Rosalina. I want to know about your life, as hard as it is for me to hear about you in pain."

"I don't think I've ever told anyone this story," I mumble. "I don't know why. It's something everyone in the town already knew."

"But they never heard it from you," Keldarion says.

I nod, tugging the blanket tighter around my shoulders. "My father was too far away to get me from the hospital. Actually, they couldn't even get in contact with him for three days. But Lucas's family insisted I come home with them. They lived in the inn, and they gave me an entire room of my own. At the time, I don't think I'd had a better week in my life. It was nothing but hot soup and warm fires. Lucas and I spent everyday binging reality TV. It didn't feel weird at all. He kept going on about how he couldn't believe we'd never met before. I knew who he was, of course. Everyone in town knew Lucas. Orca Cove's golden boy, perfect and handsome—"

A low grumble echoes from Keldarion, and I can't help but give a little laugh.

"When we went back to school, everyone treated him like a hero who had slayed a dragon, and I was the princess he rescued. The school even had a whole assembly on ice safety and the police came to give him a medal. If Lucas had been popular before, he was revered now."

The firelight plays over my pale skin and Keldarion's white fur.

"After that, it was like everyone *saw* me. Girls would tell me they liked my scrunchie, or how beautiful I looked."

"You are beautiful, Rosalina," Keldarion says.

"Maybe that was all they could think to say to me. It felt like the more they saw me ... the less of me there was left. I didn't talk about the things I liked, and I did fewer things I enjoyed. Lucas was the sun, and I was his shadow. And I was so good at it, he forgot he had his own. But I was terrified of being alone. And being a shadow next to someone ... Well, wasn't that better than being by myself?"

An angry rumble sounds through Keldarion, and he curls closer. I bring the blanket up, disappearing into his warmth.

"What about here? Do you pretend?"

"No." I laugh. "I mean, why would I? I have nothing to lose. A prisoner—"

"I told you. You're not a prisoner."

I nod, remembering his words at the ball. "After the ice skating, it was fate, I suppose. I owed Lucas my life and—"

"Saving someone's life does not grant them ownership of it."

His words settle in me before I continue, "He was my hero, and I was his ..."

"Do you love him?"

My fingers tighten around my wrist until it hurts. "I always thought so. I mean, yes. In a way. I wonder sometimes ... is all love good?"

Kel's breath is heavy, and his whole-body shifts before he says, "No."

Tears fall from my eyes, and I wipe them with the back of my hand. "Don't be thinking about yourself now, okay? This is my pity party. Your mate is going to be very lucky when you find her." The last words are a struggle, feeling all wrong in my mouth.

"I told you before, Rosalina. I will never have a mate."

I could tell him off like I did at the ball, but my strength has waned. "You'll fall in love again, Kel," I whisper. "It's not hard, actually."

My eyes flutter closed, and I let the warmth of the fire settle over me as I drift into a deep sleep. It's not hard to fall in love again, because somehow, it happened to me.

The frost and darkness do not enter my dreams. There's only warmth. The star that led me to him blooms in my chest, sending a cascade of contentment through me. Images float by; softly falling snow, a boy roasting chestnuts and stringing orange slices above a mantel. I see Kel, younger, with a sweet smile. An older fae runs her hands through his hair, kissing his cheek. Now, there's a field of flowers and he's sticking them between the metal plates of another small boy's armor, laughing. A young Ezryn, I know it.

My dreams feel like memories not of my own, but the best kind, the kind that stays locked within the heart. Dark satin sheets strain beneath Kel's large, veined hands. A desperate kiss sends heat coiling to my core, and his raspy voice fills my head: "There is nothing in this world I would not give up for you, no sacrifice I would not make." Passion and lust fill every part of my body, and distantly I feel the coarse blanket against my bare skin. "Then prove it, Kel. Prove it to me."

The bracelet around my wrist burns my skin, and I descend further into this dream. Into this memory. A rain-splattered night. The face of a beautiful human woman, four roses in her hands. Then, a light, a light so bright I can't see. The Enchantress flashes before my eyes, her face glowing with the light of the stars.

Here stands a beast who will let the entire Vale go to rot for the sake of his own selfish heart.

My eyes shoot open, a gasp upon my lips. The fire has simmered to embers, and moonlight still dances on the mouth of the cave. Stars flicker in the night sky.

Cold shivers over my body, my blanket partly fallen away, but a hand grips tightly around my waist. Consciousness returns as I feel the contour of a shape against my back. A shape not of a wolf.

But of a man.

58

ROSALINA

There are at least four things fighting in my brain, causing me to go into an absolute panic. It's taking everything in me to stay still.

One, Keldarion is very clearly a man. Like super fucking clearly a man, even though it's still night out. It's not the full moon. This shouldn't be possible. *How is this happening?*

Two, I'm naked. Stupid idiot that I am for falling asleep in only the blanket before I could change into Ezryn's spare clothes. This wouldn't be such a big deal except—

Three, the fae prince is also butt-ass naked, as he's holding me so tight, it's hard to breathe. I fell asleep next to a wolf! A wolf! This is very, very different.

I mentally catalog every place his body touches mine. His arm is snaked around my waist, holding me tight against his muscular chest. His other arm has created a pillow for my head, his hand dangling near my breast. He's not exactly groping me, but if I moved a little, he definitely could be.

Again, all of this is comprehendible. But what's sending me into an absolute tizzy right now is how our legs are tangled together. My hips seem to mold perfectly into his, and his erect cock presses against my ass.

And four, the absolute worst thing is how I don't want to breathe. I don't want to move. His head is bent, curling into my hair, and I can feel the soft steadiness of his breath, the beat of his heart. I don't want to wake him, because I have never felt this good in my entire life. I want to be pressed this close to him forever. No, that's not true. I want to be closer ...

Delicious heat flutters through me and my muscles tighten. Wetness pools between my legs. Fuck, I bet he could slip right in, no problem. Well, maybe. It feels monstrous.

The idea sends a skittering of sensation through my body. My hips involuntarily rock back against him. A low rumble sounds from his chest, and he shifts.

I was wrong that he couldn't hold me any tighter. His upper arm glides across my breast, and the other tugs me in a steel embrace. His hips pitch up to meet mine, cock sliding across my ass.

"Kel." His name slips out of my mouth, part moan, part plea.

And I know the precise moment he wakes up. His hold on me slackens, and there's the sharp intake of air.

Then he's moving, and the shock of his body away from mine is painful. He braces his arms on either side of my head, looking from the sparkling night sky to his bare chest to me sprawled on the ground below him.

We're staring at each other. I am becoming his. I feel no embarrassment in my nudity, just a powerful connection between us that transcends any physical sensation. A spread of light blossoms over me with each stroke of his eyes, like every part of me was made to be seen by him.

As he's looking at me, I'm looking at him. The wide breadth of his shoulders, the hair sprinkled across his chest, the perfect straight line of his nose, and the dark brows that shield those ice chip eyes. Wounds still mar his flesh, as they did the wolf, but they don't seem dire. There's a softness in his expression I've never seen before, like his frost has ... melted away.

"Kel," I whisper because it's the only word in existence. The only word my being is capable of comprehending. As I trace the contours of his face with the tips of my fingers, a surprised sound rumbles in the back of his throat. He clasps my arm, holding me there. His lips tilt to kiss my palm.

The world seems to fade in and out with the beat of our hearts, and I see on my right wrist the bracelet of ice and roses, the bargain tying me to him. To this place. There's a mirror of it on his arm. But there's something above it, another bracelet on his wrist. It bleeds to life in stark focus before my eyes, a frosted purple shape with sharp thorns ...

Another bargain?

"Rosalina." His voice is low and deep and sends a thrill through my body. I shudder and writhe against the mounds of soft blankets beneath me. I need more than his mouth on my hand.

"How are you like this?" I trace my fingertips over his chest, feeling the delicate strands of hair and taut muscles beneath.

"Because," he says softly, "I've seen more magic in your eyes since you've arrived at Castletree than I've seen in the last twenty-five years."

Slowly, almost tentatively, his rough hand trails up my arms, delicately touching my collarbone. Then, his knuckles brush the side of my breast as he drags his hand lower. I could not say what is more magical—his touch or how his features have melted into the softest expression, lips parted, eyes curious.

Soft wispy breaths escape me as his palm flattens over my stomach, fingers spreading, thumb brushing just below my belly button. A pulsing need courses through me, and a desperate murmur escapes my lips.

"That sound." He traces a line over my lips. A desperate movement, as if he could capture the sound in the palm of his hand.

My tongue scrapes against his fingers as he pulls away. I'm not sure if it's me who raises my hips, or it's his body that falls, but suddenly we're pressing against each other. My breasts push on his chest, his steel need rubbing my stomach.

"This is tearing me apart." His lips flutter against my neck. "I can't save them and you. I'm supposed to be the one to protect the Vale, but I can't. Rose, you will hate me most of all."

"Keldarion." I take his face in my hands. "You have no idea all the ways you have saved me."

A tear runs down his cheek, and I press my lips to it, tasting the salt. He makes a desperate groan, and roughly grips my waist, pulling me flush against him. I cry out. His cock rubs against my entrance. Fluttering heat courses through me.

"If only I was strong enough to have you," he growls.

"Then have me," I whimper. "Have me."

He glides his hand up to the dip of my waist, lightly touching my breast. His touch is all I've ever wanted, all I'll ever need. "Rose," he growls my name like a warning.

But I'm done with warnings. I'm done with being afraid. I pull back, staring into his ice blue eyes. "Kel, I'm yours."

His long lashes flutter, and he fixes me with a gaze full of desire. "And mine you will stay."

Suddenly, he pushes himself up and stumbles away from me. A look of pained agony flashes across his face before the harsh crackle of magic fills the cave and he doubles over. Frost covers his body as the fur and spikes of the white wolf appear.

I gasp, cold swirling around the cavern. I pull the blanket back around me. "Kel!"

But the white wolf stalks to the cavern entrance, then growls, "Restart the fire and go back to sleep. I will patrol and ensure the goblins haven't regrouped."

"Kel, wait." I scramble up, but by the time I make it to the entrance, he's long gone. And I'm here alone, staring out over the snowy horizon, eyes roaming the forest, the river, the rosebush, and the Briar. And beyond all that, Castletree.

Farron, Dayton, and Ez are there. Have they brought enough magic back? Is everyone okay? I tremor with the brand of his touch, the echo of his words. Keldarion may be gone now, but tomorrow, he'll take me home. And we'll keep working until we break this curse.

I won't give up on him. I won't give up on any of them.

59

ROSALINA

A roaring fire snaps and crackles, and the smell of sweet spices fills my nose. I roll over, curling deeper into the blankets, before slowly blinking my eyes open.

Dawn's soft light fills the cavern, and Keldarion sits across from me. He's a fae male again and dressed in what appears to be Ez's extra clothes: a simple black tunic and pants. I also put on an extra set of clothes from last night after Kel left.

"Good morning, Rosalina." Kel's deep rasp breaks the silence.

"Good morning," I answer, pushing myself up and trying to pat down my wayward hair.

Kel bends over the fire, stirring something in a metal pan, before taking it off the heat and dumping the contents onto a tin plate. Jeez, Ez really thought of everything here.

Kel sets the plate down before me. "This isn't as good as what our chef makes, but it'll give you the strength you need for the journey."

"Thanks," I mutter. It kind of looks like couscous with some vegetables and spices mixed in. I take a couple bites and let the rich flavors and warmth fill me.

I can't help but awkwardly glance over at Keldarion, methodically packing up the camp. *Are we going to talk about it?* Are we going to talk about how I woke up naked in his arms and he looked at me like ... I don't even know how to describe that look because no one has ever looked at me that way before. Except maybe for Farron when he sent me through the portal, or Dayton when I was trembling in his arms. Or maybe the look is a feeling, because I swear Ezryn gazed at me that way when we were by the fountain.

"How are your wounds? Can you walk?" Keldarion plops a pair of boots down in front of me. "I stuffed the toes with socks. They should be adequate."

I put down my empty plate and roll up my pants to see the gash on my leg. It's shrunken down to nothing but a thin red line. "It won't be a problem. What about you?"

"I'm fine." With an almost somber smile, he says, "Maybe you should have become a veterinarian."

I stick my feet into the boots. They won't be the comfiest things, but at least they'll do the job. Kel must notice my grimace because he says, "It's not far."

Maybe not far when you're a beast or a fae prince. I know I ran a long time to get away from those goblins. "We'll have to find a safe spot to cross the ice. Unless you know of a bridge."

Kel stays silent, packing the supplies back into the crate. He's in a strange mood. It could be many things: the disaster of last night's ball, almost freezing on the ice, or how we'd awoken. I'm not sure he's ready to talk about any of those things.

I'm not sure I am.

"Do you think the others will be impressed when I tell them I rescued you?" I smirk.

"They already worship you like a queen," he says. "You'll be a goddess to them."

A warmth settles in my core as I hear him speak fondly of the other princes. "As it should be," I say jokingly.

Kel's face softens as he looks at me. "You deserve nothing less, my Rose."

"I actually didn't do it all on my own."

With the last of the camp packed up, Kel smothers the fire with his boot. "What do you mean?"

I swallow in a dry throat. "The thorns helped. It was like I could move them. They picked you up and lifted you out of the water. I mean, you're a giant wolf, and even heavier all wet and—"

I trail off immediately, knowing I've said the wrong thing. Keldarion is still, except for the rapid rise and fall of his chest, the storm breaking across his gaze.

Slowly, I stand, determined not to cower under his anger. If I can hold my own against the Prince of Thorns, then I can with this icy bastard. "Look, I know the thorns are attacking Castletree. But what if they aren't all evil?" I try to flesh out the reasoning that has been racing through my mind. "They listen to me when I need help. That's how I got out of the dungeon my first day. They made a ladder to help me escape. And in the Briar, the thorns protected me from the goblins. I think they wanted to help the roses in the High Tower too."

Keldarion is still as the frozen world beyond us. Only the tightening of his fists lets me know he heard my words.

"Kel." I move toward him.

He steps out of my way, snarling. "The Prince of Thorns is the only one that can control the thorns. Not even his mother can do that. The briars are his twisted torment alone."

"Okay, but what if—"

"No, Rosalina." He grips me by the shoulders, forcing me to look at him. "It means he's been watching you all this time. It might have seemed like help, but it's all a cruel game."

My heart shudders in my throat. My first night here, the dark figure that had brought me to the castle ... Had it been him?

"If that's true, then he saved your life." *And mine.*

Keldarion growls and runs his hands through his matted white hair. "He doesn't want me dead. He wants me to watch as he takes the castle, takes our realms. Takes everything I hold dear."

"I know you feel that way," I say, not sure why I'm pushing it. "But I *felt* the briars, and they were—"

ELIZABETH HELEN

"Rosalina, listen carefully," Kel says. "Every single part of the Briar is evil. Every single part of him is evil."

I break away from Kel, anger rising. "Then why did you align with him? I heard the people in your realm. What happened with Caspian?"

It's like I can see the fractures break apart in Kel's face when I utter the Prince of Thorns' name.

"It is none of your concern," he says.

I storm over to him and pull up his sleeve. "What bargain did you make with the Below, Keldarion?"

There it is, wrapped around his wrist. A bracelet of frosted briars.

He looks at me with sorrowful eyes. "One that has doomed all the Enchanted Vale."

A silent gasp escapes my throat, and I try to back away, but Keldarion grips my face and pulls me toward him. What could he mean? All the Vale? Is it tied to the curse?

"Don't you see, Rosalina?" Wild panic flares in his eyes. "I won't let him take you."

"He won't," I stutter. "You're here. And Ez and Dayton and Farron. They'll protect me."

"Soon, they won't even be able to protect themselves. You saw it yourself. Castletree is dying."

Tears stream down my face, and I shake my head. "No, because we're going to break the curse, and everything will be all right and—"

"He's following you. He *wants* you." Kel's palms tremble. "I will not let him have you. Don't you see, Rose? This is why you must go home."

"But there are thorns at home," I start to say before it feels like ice has been poured down my veins. I've fallen back into the river. "Kel, no—"

"The decision is made. You've done more than enough for us." He straightens. "You are free."

Keldarion doesn't mean to take me back to Castletree. He means to take me to the rosebush.

To take me back to my old life.

60

ROSALINA

As the Prince of Winter walks me through the frozen forest, my body feels numb and tingly, and a chill runs down my spine. I barely register the beauty of the snow-covered trees. A part of me is still frozen.

Keldarion keeps a brisk pace, and I follow in his footsteps, feet stumbling in my ill-fitting boots. I always knew this day would come, the day I returned home to my old life. I never belonged at Castletree, among the fae princes and beasts and thorns.

Caspian was wrong. I am just a mere human.

Kel stops so suddenly I nearly slam into his back. Before us are the twisting brambles of the blood-red rosebush.

I've thought about this place so many times since I came here, but to see it again …

"I sent your father home well beyond his means." Kel hooks a sack over my shoulders. "But since he doesn't sound like the most responsible person, please sell whatever you need within this bag to allow yourself a comfortable life."

Distantly, I open the flaps of the bag. Glittering inside is the jeweled necklace. "Your mother's necklace … I can't sell it."

"You will do what you need to. As must we all." Keldarion steps aside, and it's like the rosebush has changed since I've been here, now framing a dark tunnel for me to walk through.

I don't even look up at Keldarion as I step toward it. Back to Orca Cove. Back home.

But that word no longer feels right in my mind. I have never felt at home there.

"No." I plant my feet before the roses.

"What?"

"I haven't upheld my bargain. Prisoner or not, I made a promise to you, Keldarion. To all of you."

His brows lower deeply, and he grabs my wrist, hand closing around the whole width. "Our bargain would never benefit you, Rose. Fulfill it and you would leave Castletree, but you would not have freedom. Only I can give you that now."

Something dangerous simmers beneath his words. "Tell me what you mean."

"Your duty is fulfilled," he snarls. "The bargain is complete."

Magic crackles around us; golden sparks fly, illuminating the pale morning. A brilliant sparkle flames around my wrist as the bracelet of the Winter Prince shatters. My hand locks around his forearm, and I feel with an intuition beyond understanding that something between us can never be broken.

"No!" I cry, a roar of my own. "You don't get to do that. I'm *not* going back."

"What about your father?" He doesn't let go of my arm.

"He was never there for me!" I say, and an anger I've been building for twenty-five years rages out of me. "Let me go tell him I'm safe. Come with me while I tell him I finally found somewhere I belong. And then take me home. Kel. Take me home."

"Your home is through there." His voice wavers, hand shaking over mine.

"No, it's not. My home is through the Briar and across the river. My home is at Castletree." I clutch him. "Listen to me, Kel. I know this more than I've ever known anything."

A deep growl echoes in his chest, and he picks me up. For one moment, I'm at peace, feeling the hard planes of his body against mine. Then I realize he's moving closer to the rosebush.

I try to scramble out of his arms, but his hold is a vice grip.

"This isn't a negotiation."

"No!" I scream so loud I swear I shake the briars and the trees. Loud enough, the princes of Castletree can hear me.

And it must shock him, for his hold loosens enough that I fall to the ground. "You haven't even let me say goodbye. Farron ... He can't do all the research on his own. There's still so much more I have to learn about Dayton. I think Ez is finally starting to like me. Some of the staff have library books I haven't checked back in. And I haven't gotten to tell Astrid and Marigold what their friendship means, and Kel—"

My voice breaks off in a sob, and I stare up at Kel through blurry tears. "I couldn't find you," I choke out. "I couldn't find you when you'd fallen under the ice. But a light bloomed in my chest. A light that led me straight to you."

His eyes widen as he stares down at me, the breath heavy in his throat. I tangle my hands in his shirt, pushing myself closer. "I can still feel it, even now. Kel, you can send me away, but I will always find my way back to you."

"Rosalina." His voice is as much a warning as it is an invitation as his hand reaches up to brush the side of my face.

My heart opens, as vulnerable and fragile as a snowdrop. "Am I your mate?"

His lips crash against mine. I lose myself, pushing everything I have back into him. His name dances upon my lips as I part them ever so slightly, savoring the sweetness of his kiss. A spark flares within me as he holds me tightly against his heart.

I lose myself in his storm. The world around us dissolves into a misty haze. Our lips move in a dance I suddenly know all the steps to. *Kel is kissing me.*

For someone so strong, he's gentle, delicate. I push back into him with all the force, all the bravery, I've learned in the Vale. Our mouths open and I devour his taste, like the first breath of fresh air on a snow-crested morning.

When I must breathe, I glide my lips along his jaw, gasping. Then, I throw myself back into his tempest. A growl rumbles in his throat as he takes my bottom lips between his teeth, devouring me whole. His hands tangle in my hair, and his large hands clutch my body like it's the only thing tethering him to this world.Kel whispers my name in reverent devotion. "Rosalina, my Rose." Coarse stubble scrapes against my cheek as his lips move to my ear. "This way is closed to you forevermore."

Then I'm falling, crashing through vines and brambles and red roses. I see Kel's face distantly through the tangle of thorns.

He let me go.

I crash to the hard ground and let out a desperate cry of rage and sorrow. "Keldarion!" Without wasting a moment, I push myself to my feet, surging back to the brambles. Stinging cold pricks my finger: a frost spreading over the vines, the roses. They crystalize and die.

Kel's killing the rosebush. The one way to the Enchanted Vale. Wild panic fills me, and I rush back as the frost spreads faster and faster. I trip over a root and roll until my face lands in a pile of mulchy leaves.

I brace my hands on the muddy ground and look up. The last of the rosebush freezes over before disappearing into a mist of ice and snow. Around me is the familiar wood, suddenly void of all the color I had learned how to see.

I am back in Orca Cove.

But I'm not home.

61

THE PRINCE OF THORNS

Pathetic. That's the only word I can think of as I stare down at the miserable creature slumped in the corner.

He barely even raises his head as I enter through the window.

Either I'm losing my touch, or he's even worse than I realized.

"What?" I smirk. "Not even a hello for an old friend?"

A deep rumble echoes through the large white wolf, and it shakes its body, chips of ice and snow falling to the ground like twinkling chimes. But there are other parts still attached to him: jagged spikes of ice jutting out from the back of his legs and fluorescent blue scars etching around his face. All reminders that this is no mere wolf, but signs of the Enchantress's curse. The only thing the spell left untouched were his eyes, blue as the winter sky.

Well, his eyes and his temper. That's always been a problem.

I force myself to look away and onto the utter destruction of the room. Torn curtains, broken furniture, and winter creeping its icy claws across every inch of this place. Frost covers even the dark thorns crawling along the chamber's walls. It's utterly covered in my handiwork. *It has to be.* Keldarion's uncontrollable winter keeps destroying them.

It's beyond irritating to upkeep.

I give an exaggerated shake and look down at the wolf. "I know you prefer the cold, but this is getting ridiculous."

"Get out," the beast snarls, pawing forward. Even in this form, he's taller than me, the giant maw in line with my face.

"You can't expect me to miss *this*, could you now?" The black ends of my cape drag in the ice as I walk in a circle around him. "How far you've fallen, Prince."

He doesn't answer and I continue to pace, trailing a hand over the soft white fur of his back. "What a pathetic creature you've become. The sun is up, yet you're still a beast." I gesture to the window. "Not to mention your realm is on the brink of open rebellion. What are you going to do if they storm the door? The castle doesn't have enough magic to keep it shut for much longer."

"Leave now."

"I always thought I was going to have the honor of doing you in," I say. "But it looks like your own people will do that for you."

Nothing. His body shudders, more chips of ice falling off his massive frame, and his eyes cast downward.

"She's been gone, what, a month?" I shake my head and run my hand through my hair. "She has broken you, hasn't she?"

He roars loud enough to shake the castle. Daggers of ice fall from the ceiling, and jagged spikes jut from the floor. *Here we go.*

"Rosalina." I speak her name like a poem, and I can see the reaction of his body like a physical blow. "Your—"

"Don't."

"Of course you would send her away. You always were dramatic when it came to ... *love*," I say, unable to keep the anger out of my voice. "You'd rather damn everyone in the Enchanted Vale than break the curse."

Kel lunges, knocking me to the ground with his massive paws. His snarl reveals teeth long as my hand.

"It's been a long time since you had me on my back like this, Kel."

I tug his ear and tilt the wolf's face closer to me. My thorns push through the frozen ground with great effort, cracking the surrounding ice. They twine around his legs and over his massive paws so he can remember who is in charge and who is the cursed sullen beast wallowing in his sorrow.

"Though," I continue, "I don't recall your breath being quite so bad."

He pulls his head back, growling, and the thorns snap off him with a quick shake of his body. *So annoying.*

"I'll rip you to shreds." His claws curl on my chest, just hard enough to leave a thin red line along the skin.

"Oh, Kel, we both know if you were capable of doing that, you'd have done it when I first betrayed you."

The wolf jolts, hackles rising. Ice and snow tremble in the air before they shower over me. I blink through the cold to see a man. His white hair falls long and loose, and his muscular chest heaves in breath like a drowning man finally come up for air. Though I cannot say his expression is any less beast-like. Something feral has permanently etched its way in: brows lowered and teeth gnashed. Why, I'm surprised he's not foaming at the mouth.

His large hand still presses down on my chest. Slowly, he moves, fist tightening in the fabric of my shirt, before moving to clasp my wrist. "Break it," he practically begs. "Please, Cas—"

I cannot and will not let him speak my name to me, so I cause thorns and shadows to surge through the ice. But not before I raise myself, bringing my lips to his cheek as I whisper a promise for all eternity. "Never."

My thorns wrap around me and drag me back to the Below, leaving the Winter Prince alone.

I clutch my wrist, fingers stroking the frosted thorns that bind me to Keldarion. No, our covenant will never break. Because one day, the Prince of Winter will give into Rosalina, and when he does, I can't wait for the magic of our bargain to drop his mate right at my doorstep.

Thank you so much for reading Bonded by Thorns! We hope you enjoyed your adventure in the Enchanted Vale.

Reviews help others find our book. They are vital to indie authors like us. If you could take a moment to leave a review on Amazon and Goodreads, it would mean the world to us!

You can leave a review on Amazon here:

You can leave a review on Goodreads here:

THE ENCHANTMENT CONTINUES IN...

Woven by Gold

Beasts of the Briar 2

I've been rejected by my mate and banished from the fae realm. But nothing will keep me from my princes.... And nothing will keep them from me.

Read Now

ACKNOWLEDGMENTS

This book has been an absolute joy to write. It has been such a pleasure to relive one of our favorite childhood stories and reimagine it in a totally new way.

Thank you to the wonderful community we've met online, and to anyone who has championed our strange story in any fashion. We are forever grateful to you for helping us realize our dreams.

Thank you endlessly to our family and friends for your unwavering support. We love you so much.

Here's to more books and definitely more beasts!

Elizabeth & Helen

ALSO BY ELIZABETH HELEN

Beasts of the Briar

Bonded by Thorns

Woven by Gold

Forged by Malice

Broken by Daylight

Novella

Prince of the Arena

ABOUT THE AUTHORS

Elizabeth Helen is the combined pen-name of sister writing duo, Elizabeth and Helen. Elizabeth and Helen write fantasy romance and love creating enchanting adventures for their characters. When they're not writing, you can find them snuggling their cats, exploring their rainforest home, or rolling the dice for a game of Dungeons & Dragons. You can connect with them on TikTok, Instagram, or Facebook.

Facebook Readers' Group

Join our Facebook Readers' Group to interact with like-minded bookish people, get behind-the-scenes info on the creation of our books, receive sneak peeks for Book 4, and chat all about the Enchanted Vale and the fae princes!
facebook.com/groups/elizabethhelen

AuthorEizabethHelen.com

f facebook.com/elizabethhelenauthor
instagram.com/author.elizabeth.helen
tiktok.com/@authorelizabethhelen
amazon.com/author/elizabethhelen
goodreads.com/elizabeth_helen

BONUS STORY

PRINCE OF THE ARENA

Before the curse, Farron travels to the Summer Realm to watch Dayton compete in the Solstice Games.

Read this Dayton and Farron spicy and sweet bonus chapter exclusive to newsletter subscribers.

ElizabethHelen.SubStack.com

PLAYLIST

Spoilers ahead!
Scan the code with the Spotify app.

Overture | Alan Menken *(To get into the vibe!)*
right where you left me | Taylor Swift *(All about Lucas)*
Sauron | Bear McCreary *(When you get saved by a hot but creepy fae)*
The Song of the White Wolf | Sonya Belousova *(Meeting the Master)*
Hey Mando! | Ludwig Goransson *(Ez's Theme)*
Lucy Meets Mr. Tumnus | Harry Gregson-Williams *(Meeting Astrid)*
Gannicus | Joseph Loduca *(Dayton's Theme)*
Nori Brandyfoot | Bear McCreary *(Farron's Theme)*
August | Taylor Swift *(Farron x Dayton love <3)*
Wintersong | Marcus Warner, Fatma Fadel *(Kel's Theme)*
Stories | Belle *(Trying to read an icy prick your fav book)*
Bejeweled | Taylor Swift *(If your ex could see you now at a fae ball!)*
Who Is She | Patrick Doyle *(Rosalina enters the ball)*
Beauty and the Beast | Angela Landsbury *(Kel and Rosalina dance)*
The Christening | James Newton Howard *(Caspian's dramatic entrance)*
Blinded By The Light | Neal Acree *(Rosalina rescuing Kel)*
Labyrinth | Taylor Swift *(When they wake up together)*
Evermore | Dan Stevens *(Kel in his feels)*
The Great War | Taylor Swift *(Kel and [redacted])*